What Do I Want?

"What do you want me to do for you?"
"Lord," he said, "I want to see!"
Luke 18:41

A Novel By

Diane C. Shore

DCShore Publishing
dcshorepublishing.com

Scripture quoted by permission. Quotations designated (NET)
are from the NET Bible® copyright ©1996-2016 by Biblical Studies Press, L.L.C.
http://netbible.com All rights reserved.

Scripture quotations marked (NLT) are taken from the Holy Bible, New Living
Translation, copyright ©1996, 2004, 2015 by Tyndale House Foundation. Used by
permission of Tyndale House Publishers, Inc., Carol Stream, Illinois 60188. All
rights reserved.

Scripture taken from the New King James Version®. Copyright © 1982 by
Thomas Nelson. Used by permission. All rights reserved.

Scriptures taken from the Holy Bible, New International Version®, NIV®.
Copyright © 1973, 1978, 1984, 2011 by Biblica, Inc.™ Used by permission of
Zondervan. All rights reserved worldwide. www.zondervan.com The "NIV" and
"New International Version" are trademarks registered in the United States Patent
and Trademark Office by Biblica, Inc.™

1.10

ISBN-13: **978-1-7326785-3-8**

DEDICATION

This book is dedicated to our Source of Life, our Source of Hope, and our
Source of Strength! All praise and honor and glory go Heavenward!

Father, thank You for sending Your One
and only Son into this world to save us and set us free!

Jesus, Your bright light shines into the darkest places!
There is healing and deliverance in Your mighty Name!

Holy Spirit, without Your guidance,
we would all be wandering around in a smoky haze!

PROLOGUE

Sometimes, Truth can be stranger than Fiction. This may be one of those times! This book will challenge you, and stretch you, but your life and the lives of those you know may never be the same after reading it.

Take a moment and look at the two pictures on the front cover again. Go ahead, I'll wait… Okay, you're back. What you were looking at is the exact same photo taken just four days apart. With fires burning nearby, the skies became full of smoke. The once beautiful landscape could no longer be seen. The fall colors on the trees became dull. The air was dense, and breathing became difficult. Check it out again… Yes, that's the same roofline, the same trees, and the same foothills. But it all looks so different. And this smoke was many miles away from where homes were being destroyed by fires, and lives were being changed forever.

But God, in all His amazing ways, gives us a way to see something astounding in these two pictures—the realization that His children, true believers in His Son, Jesus Christ, may be living in this haze every single day…unknowingly. It doesn't feel like smoke, smell like smoke, or burn our lungs like smoke—but what it does is weigh heavy on our souls, cloud our minds, depress our spirits, and hurt our hearts. It's not called **Smoke**, it's called **Life**. Can you relate?

That's the *astounding* smoky part…now comes the *astounding* beautiful part. There's **Hope**!

Jesus came over 2,000 years ago to rescue us from the dominion of darkness…from this heavy, toxic, smoky haze. That's right! There's a CURE for what ails us. It's in the strong wind of the Holy Spirit! But this powerful Good News is not being shared nearly enough. And even when it is, it may seem more like it's something from the past, or perhaps it's for someone else, and not you. But it's here, it's now, and it's for YOU!

In this fictional tale filled with the Truth of God's Word, join Randy and his wife, Linda, behind their *closed doors*, so to speak. Watch as they find out just how *smoky* their lives really are. Read about how they react when the *smoke alarm* goes off. And then follow them to where the *fire escape* is, should they choose to accept the freedom being offered.

This story has been described as a combination of, "True fiction and real life." There are Biblical Truths revealed in here that the enemy never wants you to know! Dive in, and be set free! Clear blue skies are yours to be had, in the power of Jesus' name! Amen!

1

LINDA

I put down the phone feeling confused and totally out of emotional energy. With such a busy day ahead, I don't really have time to be thinking about what's happening to my marriage. At this point, I'm out of answers—I don't know what to do. As if this trip to Chicago isn't hard enough—I've got deadlines to meet. With Randy berating me about laundry, and hanging up on me, he's got my emotions on a roller coaster again. I can't stand this! How long am I supposed to put up with his rudeness? He blames all this on a dirty shirt. I blame it on... Well, I don't know what. But I know me not getting his shirt washed before I left is far from the problem.

Returning to my hotel room after another long day of work, I'm finding it so hard to relax. This morning's phone call still echoes in my head. Our marriage is so dysfunctional. I miss the days when the kids were home. Oh, there were hassles then, especially through the teen years, but at least there was more activity that hid the misery in our marriage. It was good to talk with Hannah earlier. She's tired of being tired. But she will probably get over some of that once she gets into her fourth month. I remember I did. Rob and Hannah didn't waste any time in moving away from home when opportunities arose. They probably had enough of our home life. And now with Hannah pregnant, I don't know how often we will see her. Her husband, Blake, doesn't get along all that well with Randy. Maybe they're too much alike? They say a daughter will often marry someone just like her dad. I feel bad for Hannah sometimes. But what can I do? I can't even handle my own marriage. It's probably best that they live near Boston. And with Rob being in Florida, maybe he is finding some peace? Hannah and Rob have turned into decent adults. I'm proud of them. But I hope with all they've experienced through the years with Randy and me, we haven't wrecked their own search for happiness in this life.

I need to turn out the light and see if I can get some sleep. I have another busy day tomorrow. There is no way I am going to call Randy tonight. I know it would just upset me more. With the time difference, I'm sure he's just in front of the TV watching a game. That's fine. I'll leave him to it.

Turning over and seeing the clock through the blur of morning eyes, it's 6:23. The last time I looked it was after 1:00 a.m. I couldn't get my mind to stop spinning. This is not near enough sleep for me, and now I have a full workday ahead. Pulling back the drapes I see the sun is trying to come out this morning. There're some clouds, and maybe some rain expected. I have a good view of the city from this room. I like Chicago, with all the bridges over the river that runs through the city. I wish I had time to take a tour, so I could really appreciate the architecture. I've seen the people getting on and off the boats, having a great time doing that. I don't have time on a business trip. I wish I had a husband that I liked to travel with. Randy is just no fun. We've tried it, and it's better that we keep to our routine at home. Too much time in a car or plane together never turns out good.

After getting to work, I wait a bit before calling Randy. I don't know why I even do it after him hanging up on me. But I guess I feel obligated. With him being two hours behind me, I'm more fully awake than he will be. He does answer though:

"Good morning."

"Hi, Randy. How did you sleep?"

"Okay. Woke up a couple of times."

"I slept okay, too." I don't want to tell him I was still upset, and I lost sleep over it. I divert to another subject, which I'm good at doing. It's easier than confronting him. This isn't the first time he's done that, and it probably won't be the last. "I talked to Hannah last night. She's feeling good now that she's almost to the three-month mark, although still tired. They will find out the sex of their child soon. They're hoping for a boy. It doesn't matter to me."

"Mmm-hum," Randy mumbles back.

"Randy?" I can tell he's really not listening.

"Yeah?" he answers—I know he's not even really connecting that there might be a problem.

"Randy…I think we have some things to talk about when I get home." I don't know if he detects the frustration, or even the sadness in my tone.

"Sure. Um…yeah," he says.

"Okay, well, I can hear that you're involved in other things, so I'll let you go."

"Okay. Yeah. I need to get to work," he responds.

"Bye, Randy."

"Bye, Linda."

Hanging up, I know that conversation wasn't worth much. He's involved in whatever, and neither one of us cared all that much.

I have meetings in the afternoon, and lunch with a new employee first, so I better get to it. I've worked at this job in finance for over 20 years, and I like it most days. The good thing is, if Randy and I do call it quits, I have an income. I won't have to worry about money. I wonder where I would go if I left? I know he's not going anywhere. Maybe I could move in with my sister, Venyce, for a bit? Since her husband died three years ago, she's been pretty lonely. I don't know where Venyce's name came from. Mom and Dad never said. She's always had to spell it for people through the years. They want to spell it V-e-n-i-s-e because it sounds like Denise—we've laughed about that so many times. At least Linda is easy to spell.

Maybe I'll call her tonight when I get back to my room. She won't be surprised. She's been very aware that things aren't good with Randy. She even tried to talk with him a couple of times. That usually ended in a disaster. He wasn't about to listen to Venyce, even though she really was kind to him. Venyce loves God, and she is very involved in her church. It seems like a good church. I have been there a couple of times, although Randy and I mostly go to the church in the next town over for the holidays. Maybe we should try to go more often? Maybe that would help? We need something, and from what Venyce has told me these past few years, God has been her strength through her grief. She joined a grief group, and it's really helped, too. There are a couple other women in her group who are widows, and they spend time together.

Back at my desk after lunch, I hear my name called:

"Linda?"

"Uh, yes?" I answer, looking up from the desk where I have my head buried in my computer, but have my mind on so many other things.

"We'll be meeting down the hall in conference room three in ten minutes." It's my co-worker, Evelyn. She's been around a long time and likes to be in charge around here. When she says *jump*, most people do;

5

me included. But today I don't seem to care about pleasing her all that much.

"Okay. I'll be there," I respond with little enthusiasm. She did pull me out of my thoughts and back into the job at hand. I better finish up these last stats here, and head on down there. Evelyn doesn't like it when we stroll in late. Even though she's not the boss, she takes it personally.

The meeting is long and arduous throughout the afternoon. I'm glad to get out of the office at the end of the work day. Stopping at a pizza stand on the walk back to my hotel, I take a look around the city. With so many people walking from work, it's a mad rush down the sidewalk. Many are headed to the "L." In the Bay Area, I'm used to calling our transit system BART. But in Chicago, I found out it's called the "L," which is short for "Elevated." Some of the tracks do run above the city, but I've seen those that don't. Thankfully, I can get to my hotel walking. It makes it nice at the end of the day to get some fresh air.

I give Randy a call about 8:00, but he doesn't answer. I'm not surprised. Then a text quickly arrives:

"Linda, exhausting day. Let's talk tomorrow."

"Okay. Sleep well," I text back, glad to not have to talk.

It's definitely time to give Venyce a call with it becoming more and more obvious that things are not going well with Randy. I scroll to find her name, so wishing this wasn't necessary. But it is...

She answers cheerfully, "Hi, Lin. How's it going?"

"Hi, Venyce. Okay. How are you tonight? I'm in Chicago, so a couple hours ahead of you."

"Oh, really? Another business trip? I'd like to go with you sometime," Venyce says.

"Yeah. It's business. That would be fun to travel out here together. I was just thinking today how I'd like to visit this city sometime for pleasure and take a look at the sights. If you joined me on a business trip, we wouldn't get much free time together."

"Well, we should plan a fun trip again soon then—to there, or somewhere else. I'm feeling okay to do a bit more traveling now. You know, we've done a little, and I'm grateful for that. But my heart was so sad after losing Earl. It was hard."

"Yes, I know. It's not been easy for you. But you have stayed strong, Sis. I'm proud of you for that."

"Thank you. I don't know how I would do this without God. Earl loved Jesus, and he was more than ready to see Him face to face. I didn't want him to go. But Earl always reminded me how Jesus said to His disciples in John 14:28, *'If you really loved me, you would be happy that I am going to the Father, who is greater than I am.'* Earl wanted me to be happy for him. After all, he fought that cancer long and hard. He was tired."

"I know he was. I'm so glad I came by the day before he passed. I will never forget the sparkle in his eyes when he told me he would be leaving soon. I thought he should be so sad. But he wasn't. He told me he hated to leave you and the family, but he knew it was his time. And he knew that God would provide for all of you. And He has, hasn't He, Venyce?"

"Yes. It's not easy, but it is possible with God. I cling to God's promises like never before. And you know what? It makes me a better mom and grandma. There are many things I should have done with my children when they were little, but I was so busy. I thought I didn't have as much time for Jesus then either, even though we took the kids to church. Isn't that crazy? I thought sitting in church once a week would do it, and then we could go on our way."

"Well, Sis, you did better than me. Randy and I are still mostly Christmas and Easter people. And I know I need more than that…which sadly, brings me to this phone call. Things are not good with Randy. I don't know what it's going to be like this time when I get home. It seems worse than ever. We can barely talk on the phone these days. He hung up on me. It's just getting impossible to live with him. I was wondering if it's really not good when I return if I could stay with you for a while? Maybe take some time to think it through. I don't want a divorce. I really don't. But I'm so unhappy with the way things are."

"Let me think and pray on that, okay? I'm in no way telling you that you can't come and stay with me. You know I welcome you any day, any night. But this is a big step for you both, and I want to be sure that what I'm doing to help you is in line with God's will. I hope you understand what I mean."

"I do, Sis. I know that divorce is not God's plan for any of us. But you and Earl had an exceptional marriage. I always envied how you were able to talk with one another, and even laugh so much together. Randy and I just don't have that. So far from it…"

"I know. It's been difficult for you, Linda. But God has ways to help us even when things seem impossible from our perspective. And sometimes, a little break can help. I just have to make sure that opening my door to you isn't closing the door on what God might want to do in your marriage. So, let me pray on it some, and we can talk tomorrow night, okay?"

"Okay. Please do pray. I'm not so good at praying, and I know I have leaned on you through the years to sort of carry my faith. I'm thinking it's time I start to grow into this on my own. Maybe getting some time away from Randy will allow me to do that? And then who knows what God might have planned for my marriage? I really have no idea at this point."

"I'm so glad you called, Linda. Let's talk tomorrow. I love you, Sis. Good night."

"Love you, too, Venyce. You're a good sister, and example of a godly woman. I want to learn from you. Nite."

2

LINDA

Randy is avoiding my call again.

"….leave me a message and I'll get back to you."

I don't really want you to get back to me, I think to myself, as I wonder what to say.

"Randy, I'm at work, and have a full day ahead. Just wanted to touch base with you this morning. Talk to you later."

Turning back to my computer, I know I didn't sound nice. I didn't say that I loved him. Just cut it short, and not so sweet. I don't even know if he'll notice. And I don't even know if I care all that much. Even the phone calls are getting so difficult.

Evelyn suddenly appears at my desk. I look up when I hear her say, "Linda, the files you gave me yesterday don't make sense. Can you come into the conference room with me in about 15 minutes? I want to look them over before handing them off to Daniel." Evelyn's back at it today. Her voice has an edge to it, and I'm not looking forward to this little meeting at all. She reminds me of Randy. Always sounding intimidating, and she's not even in a place in this company to be like that. She's pretty much my equal. We have to merge our work at times. I don't complain about how she does hers—not sure why she has to give me a hard time about mine. Oh well, I only see her a couple times a year here in Chicago. Other than that. I'm left to myself. I feel bad for the people who have to work with her all the time.

Coming out of the conference room, I'm glad that's over. My mind then wanders more to my conversation with Venyce last night. She is so wise. Even though I wanted her to gladly tell me to come on over, I know she's doing what's best. She's always been like that. She doesn't just jump on things. She thinks and prays about it. I need to take a lesson from her. Probably many lessons from her, and whomever else, if I really do leave Randy. That will be a huge step, and a scary one. He's been my life for the past 40 plus years. He's the father of my children. I can't just cut him out and pretend he never existed. I don't think divorce is ever that easy, no matter how unhappy people are. I do care about Randy. I do think I still love him. I just can't live with him and have any peace in my life. I need to find peace again, with or without him. I think that should be my goal. Peace. Maybe I'm starting to know the *what*. I just need to figure out the *how*.

I find myself sighing a lot during the day, and I feel so tired. Maybe it's because I know things are coming to a head and I don't want to really face them. I've learned through the years how to walk on eggshells around Randy. And it's worked, for the most part. I let him have his way, and he makes sure I know what that is. This is out of character for me…to think of leaving him on my terms, and not on his. I wonder how he will take it? Maybe he'll be glad I'm out of his hair? Honestly, I don't know at this point.

The walk back to the hotel feels welcoming again. There's always a certain sense of freedom when leaving a work building. My time is mine then. I don't have to worry that I'm not focusing on the job at hand, which is extremely hard to do this week. Before, I just ignored the hard stuff at home when I got here. This time, not so much. This time it seems like a game changer, to put it in Randy's terms. He loves his baseball. And I don't mind it. Really. I like to watch some of the games with him. What I don't like is that he loves baseball more than me…that's what it seems like. That doesn't feel good. And with a grandchild on the way, won't we want to be an example to future generations how a loving family should function? It seems like the ante is being upped as we move into this next season of life. Our kids know we're far from perfect. They've seen so many of our marital and parental flaws. But I don't want this new little one to experience what the kids have through the years. I don't want grandchildren to hear the harsh words between us. If we aren't together, will it spare them that? This may be why I'm just not willing to live the status quo any more. Change is needed here.

As I walk along, I start to pray. It's almost like I can't help it, and yet it feels strange at the same time. Prayer hasn't been a huge part of my life like it has for Venyce. But she was desperate. She was so broken when Earl was sick, and now gone. I saw it on her face. I wondered if she would ever smile again? It wasn't like a depression. Grief appears in a different form. It was more like something in her had died and she had to let God mold and shape her life in a new way now. Things for her would never be normal again, as she knew them. But lately, just this last year, I'm starting to see more smiles. I'm starting to believe she will learn how to live what she calls a "New Normal." I wasn't sure what she meant when she would talk about that. But I'm seeing it lived out in her life. She knows she still has a ways to go, but I'm so proud of her for not giving up.

As the prayer comes from inside me, I feel a lift. Some of the heaviness is gone, and I'm thankful. That may be a touch of what Venyce experiences. I should do this more often. The mad rush of walking commuters isn't even a distraction. It's like talking to God is taking me to a place above it all, and I feel some peace in the process. I want to talk to Venyce about this later when I call her. She will be a good one to bounce it off of. Randy would just think I'm nuts. I know he believes in Jesus. He did go forward that one Easter. He said he felt that he should. When he prayed with the person up front, they took him through a prayer that to him meant receiving Jesus as his Savior. He was changed for a few days…a bit nicer. But then once he got back to work and it piled up, it seemed to quickly disappear. I gave my life to Jesus a few years before that, and even though I understood what it meant, it didn't really change me all that much either. I still feel the same insecurities, the same fears, the same anxieties. I don't really get it. But I want to. I hope to.

I bought Randy a sign for his office soon after that Easter. He hung it up. I saw it when I dropped in one day. I remember looking at it and reading, "When you find a Bible that's falling apart, you'll find a person who's not." Neither one of us have a Bible that's falling apart…maybe that's why our marriage is? We probably should have put a little more effort in before getting to our own place of desperation. But maybe it takes that. I once heard a pastor talking…what was it he said? "Deliverance is for the desperate. If you're not desperate, come back when you are." I don't even know quite what he meant. I know the Lord's prayer says something at the end about "Deliver me from evil." I memorized that as a child in Sunday school. My parents would send me with my brothers to learn about God, I guess. They never went, and it was never talked about at home. It's amazing how the memory works when we are young. I wish I could memorize things that easily now.

Ahhh, this hotel room feels welcoming. Throwing my stuff on the desk, I flop onto the bed. It feels good to be out of the hectic office, and the commuters on the streets. Ordering some room service, I kick off my shoes and change into some comfies. I'll be home in two days…I better relax here while I can.

After dinner and a hot bath, I give Venyce a call. She is always quick to answer.

"There you are, Lin! I've been waiting to hear from you."

"Hi, Sis. How are you today?"

"I'm doing just fine. It's been a good day. There are some that are tougher. This was not one of them."

"That's good to hear. I'm always happy for you when you are not feeling the pain and missing so much. I know it's a daily ebb and flow."

"It is. It keeps me close to Jesus and the Hope He gave to us through His death and resurrection. It brings it to life when you have someone who's not here in this life with us anymore. I never had to think about Heaven as much as I do now with Earl being there. The Bible says *'Blessed are those who mourn, for they will be comforted.'* I'm understanding that verse a whole lot more now. I do feel God's comfort as I draw near to Him each day."

"Speaking of drawing near, I was walking back to the hotel here, and I started praying. Now, I know you pray all the time. But I don't. I do have to tell you, though, it felt good. It's like all the commotion down there on the street…you should see the people heading to the 'L' at the end of the day…it's like all the commotion faded away for a few moments and I was lifted above the chaos. It felt so good. Is that something you normally experience when praying, Venyce?"

"Not always, but it surely can happen. When we pray, we are escorted right into the Throne Room of our Father in Heaven. We are welcome there. It's interesting how the other day I saw my granddaughter walk into her parents' bedroom without a thought of interrupting them. Their door was open. When it is closed, the grandkids are very good about knocking. But when I saw the ease that she had about entering, it made me think about how welcome we are into the Father's Room in Heaven. He loves it when we join Him there. He wants an intimate relationship with us, and through His Son, Jesus, we can have that now."

"Well, I felt close to Him walking on the busy street. Honestly, I really enjoyed it and I want more of that. Do you think when I get back, even if I don't stay with you a while, we can work on this together? I really need some up close and personal help. Just going to church doesn't seem to do it, although going more often would help also." I laid it out there and waited for Venyce's reply.

"Linda, that would be wonderful, to spend time together like that. And, if you are willing, I have a friend, Trisha, who is very good at helping people grow in their faith. Would you like me to introduce you to her? I could even send her your number if you're ready for that."

"Well, if you think that's what I should do, I'll trust you. Yes. Let's do that when I get back—and go ahead and give her my number. Why waste time? I've wasted enough already."

"Okay. Don't feel any pressure when you hear from her. She is very patient to wait on God's timing for when you would want to meet her. But knowing her, she won't take long to reach out. Also, I have given you staying with me for a while some prayerful thought. It seems if that is what you need to find some healing in your relationship with Randy, you should do it. I don't know how Randy will take it, but it may be what wakes him up also. I once heard that if we keep doing what we've always done, we'll keep getting what we always got. So maybe you should change things up a bit. God keeps us moving forward in our relationship with Him. That is what we will be focusing on together."

"Thank you, Venyce. I need your encouragement and help right now. I'm sorry to put this on you, after all you've been through, but…"

"But nothing. God's Word says we are to comfort others with the comfort we have been given. I think that's in 2 Corinthians. I have received a lot of comfort in so many ways these last few years. It's starting to be the time when I am able to give some back. And I know with Trisha in the picture, too, you will find a new way of living this life through her encouragement and prayers. She's been so helpful to me."

"I love it. Thank you. I need to go now. It's been a long day. But we'll be in touch soon."

"Sounds good. Love you, Sis. Bye."

"Bye for now."

Hanging up, I feel encouraged already. I'm glad Trisha will be in the picture. I don't want to lean too heavily on Venyce. Although I know she wouldn't mind, I really want to be respectful of where she's at with her grief. Earl was a great loss to her.

3

LINDA

Coming out of a meeting, I glance at my phone. Randy has called me. With the time difference, and me being at work long before him, he probably thinks I avoided his call. That's not good. Not that I really feel like talking to him, but I know I should. Oh, there he is again.

"Hi," I say, sounding out of breath.

"Hi. Sorry. Been busy," Randy responds.

I really don't know what to say after that. I could say I've been busy, too, and that's why our phone calls are short and infrequent. But busy wouldn't keep me from talking to a man I felt something for. I just don't feel much at this point.

"How's work?" Randy asks. It seems he's at least trying to make some sort of connection now.

"It's okay. I'm looking forward to being done with this week," I answer with barely any emotion.

"What time do you land?"

"6:45. Don't pick me up. I'll get a ride." Wow, that was curt of me...

"You sure?" Randy asks.

"Yeah. I'll see you between 7:30 and 8:00. Don't wait dinner." Sadly, I'd rather get a ride than ask Randy to pick me up. The ride home would just be uncomfortable with him. The company pays for it anyway.

"Okay. I'll see you tomorrow then," Randy says.

"Okay. Bye." I can tell I'm not trying to make him feel better at all, and wonder if he even cares whether I do.

Randy simply finishes with, "Bye."

Letting out a long sigh, my heart aches. I don't want it to be like this.

Far from it. But it's been going downhill for so long, I don't know if my marriage can be salvaged…even with help from Venyce and her friend, Trisha. Maybe I'm just hoping I can find a new life by myself, with some sort of peace and happiness in it.

"Linda?" Oh, now it's Evelyn again. I really can't wait until this week is over.

"Yes?" I say, turning to face her.

"That last report you gave me isn't making sense. I would like it if when you present it to Daniel, you let him know that I didn't have anything to do with it. It's not the way I like it done."

"Uh. Okay, Evelyn. I'll make sure he knows," while thinking I can't believe her rudeness. Like she knows the job so much better than I do? Where does she think she gets the right to be like that? I can't wait to get out of here at the end of the week.

"Good," she says, almost huffing off.

I find a corner office that's empty and set up my things in there for the rest of the day. I can't work in the main area with her wandering around. It's good some of the employees are off at that work faire. It makes it quieter in here, and I can hide a bit. Isn't that what I do best? Hide? Hide from Evelyn. Hide from Randy. I feel like hiding from the world…

Eventually meeting with Daniel, he seems perfectly happy with the report. I neglect to mention what Evelyn said, on purpose. Why should I point out that she's unhappy with it if he's not? Daniel is a great boss. He is always encouraging and happy to help. I wonder if he notices Evelyn and her peculiar ways? Should I ask him? Probably not. It's best that I just finish my work here in Chicago and get out of town silently.

Arriving back in my room after work, I settle in to eat a sandwich I picked up on the way. It feels lonely tonight. Although there's a form of peace here, I really would like to be with someone. I wonder after meeting with Trisha if it will be possible to get my marriage working? The kids won't be happy if we split. That's never good for them at any age. Rob doesn't even have a girlfriend yet. I don't want him to think if he meets someone that it can't be happy. I'm afraid at this point it may be too late. He's seen and heard too much. I should give him a call…

"Hi, Mom. How ya doin'?" Rob answers.

"Oh. Pretty good. How are things with you?" I ask trying to sound upbeat.

"Not bad. I really like this new place I found. Great view of the ocean, and not too expensive. You won't believe how cheap apartments are here in Florida compared to California! It's fun to go looking when you see what you can get for the money!"

"I've heard that. When did you get fully moved in?" I ask.

"I did a lot this last weekend. Just a few more things still left in the old place. But I have two weeks to get it out and cleaned, so no pressure."

"Oh, that's nice. Good planning on your part. I talked to Hannah."

"How's she doing? Am I going to have a niece or a nephew?" I can hear the excitement in Rob's voice to be an uncle.

"She doesn't know yet. They will find out soon. But she's feeling good, just tired."

"It's so strange to think of my sis as being a mom. I know I'm not ready to be a dad, even if I did have someone I was seriously dating," Rob says.

"It's a big responsibility. That's for sure."

"Where you at, Mom? I know you were going away on business this week."

"I'm in Chicago again. I'm looking forward to getting home…well…I…" I stop there. I don't know quite what to say to Rob at this point. I don't want to lie to him.

"What's up, Mom? Is Dad okay?" he asks.

"He's fine, Rob. I have to be honest with you. You're not a kid anymore. I don't know how much longer we will be together."

"You guys are divorcing? SERIOUSLY?"

"I don't know, hon. Not yet. But I can't lie to you. You know things are rough between your dad and me. Have been for years. And I'm sorry for the things you have seen and heard. I know it's been pretty ugly at times. Kids shouldn't have to hear those things growing up."

"Yeah…"

"Are you okay?" I ask, feeling guilty, and rightfully so.

"Yeah. I'm okay. I don't want you guys to be miserable together. It's just never easy, I guess, to hear that my parents might be getting a divorce. It honestly scares me to think about marriage."

"See, that's what I'm worried about, too. That you won't think marriage can be a good thing. I want you to know that there are plenty of good marriages out there. Please don't think they are all like ours. They aren't."

"I know. But many are. Sadly," Rob says.

"There has to be a better way, Rob. And I hope to find it one day."

"If you do, let me know! There's a gal at work that I've been a bit friendlier with lately. And I want to maybe take her out soon. I've really tried to keep my relationships light and easy. But Jane seems different— not like anyone I've met before. I do know I'm not ready to step into what Hannah's got going—husband, baby, and all. I give it to her…she's brave!"

"I understand. Take it one step at a time. I hope things go well with Jane. I need to get some rest now, Rob. Good talking with you. I'm sorry…" I stop there.

"Sorry?"

"Yeah. Sorry to have not set a better example in marriage, in life. I've made a lot of mistakes. I hope to get some of this figured out one day. I know you think your parents are all grown-up. But really, we are just kids in older looking bodies. I don't want to just grow older now, I want to grow wiser."

Robs laughs. "Okay, Mom. Well, I love you, and you're a good mom. Don't worry about it."

"I love you, too, Rob. Glad you like your new place. Hope to come out there soon for a visit."

"That would be great. Bye," Rob says.

"Bye. Sleep well."

Hanging up, I feel sad. It's just as I suspected. Rob stays away from serious relationships because of what he's seen. That breaks my heart. Something has to be different. I need to talk with Trisha and get some of this figured out. Where did we get so off track?

Turning out the light, I lie there in the dark thinking how life might have been different. I also wonder if God can really change what is, and mend what's been so broken. I surely hope so.

4

LINDA

By the next morning, Trisha has sent me a text. Venyce was right, she doesn't waste time. She sounds nice, just from her message. I won't answer it right away. I want to think about it a bit.

It's my last day here in Chicago. I'll leave the office early to get to the airport on time. I've heard Evelyn is out sick today. I was wondering why I hadn't seen her...not that I miss her.

Giving Randy a call, more out of habit than want to, there's no answer. I wonder if he's avoiding me?

"Linda?" I swivel my chair around and see Daniel standing in the doorway.

"Hey there," I say to him, hoping there's not a problem.

"I just want to thank you for all your hard work this week. It's always good to have you here in Chicago with us. I know it's a lot of work when you get here. But it's done now. And very well, I might add."

"Thank you, Daniel. I'm glad you're pleased. And if anything comes up, let me know. I know we covered a lot."

"We did. I'm going to be leaving for a meeting across town, so I wanted to say 'Bye' and have a good flight home."

"Will do! Great seeing you again. Enjoy your weekend," I say with a silent sigh of relief.

"You, too," Daniel says with a wave of his hand as he walks off.

Wow. That helps my morning. Daniel is so easy compared to Evelyn. Maybe God was being nice to me today by keeping her home sick...just not too sick, I hope.

There's Randy, calling me back...I better answer.

"Hi."

"Hi. How did you sleep?" Randy asks.

"Okay. Ready to get home," I tell him.

"Yeah."

"Are you glad it's Friday?" I need to try a bit harder to be interested.

"Always. It's been a different sort of weird week," Randy says with a strange tone.

"Oh, really?" I respond

"Yeah. Just stuff. I'm…well, we can talk when you get home. You wanted to anyway," he says.

"Yes. I do," I say, wondering what's on his mind now. "Okay, well I gotta go finish up here so I can catch my flight. See you tonight." I'm trying to sound a bit happier.

"Yeah. See you later. Have a good flight. Bye."

"Bye." Sadly, I'm glad to have that conversation over. What's going to happen when I get home? I'm almost afraid to even think about it.

Being a Friday, the airport is busy. But my flight is on time. Seated next to the window, I try to get some rest. It's not easy. There's too much on my mind from the week in Chicago, and what's to come at home. I must have eventually dozed off because I suddenly hear the announcement to prepare for landing. After stopping at the gate, I take a deep breath while unbuckling my seatbelt, whispering, "This is it. Time to 'face the music.'"

I sit in silence during the ride home. The driver is a young man, and I can tell he's not much for conversation. That is fine with me tonight. He stops in front of the house, helping me get my bags out. That was nice of him. Randy's watching the game when I come through the front door. He gets up to give me a stiff hug, and I don't return much more. Why pretend?

"Hey," Randy says while glancing at the TV.

"Hey. I'm tired. I'm going upstairs to unpack." I can tell he's focused on the game as he immediately goes back to his chair with no offer to help with my suitcase. I don't really care. I'd rather be by myself and leave him to his game. I decide to just get into pajamas and sit up in bed awhile reading. I started reading a book on the plane. It's more welcoming to me right now than going back downstairs.

After a couple hours, I can hear Randy turning stuff off downstairs and coming up. When he walks into the room, I look up at him from my book.

The look on his face matches mine…one of indifference. Getting his night stuff done, he eventually crawls into bed next to me with not a word being said. As he props himself up and then checks things on his iPad, I continue to read until I just can't take it anymore. What's going on is eating me up inside. I have to say something! I can't just go to sleep and wake up in the morning to this…

"Randy, I want a divorce," I blurt out, surprising myself as much as him. That isn't what I expected to say. I don't even know why I let those harsh words slip out of my mouth. Couldn't I have said, "I need some space. Let's take a break." Something? Anything but the "D" word. But it's out now…

"A divorce," Randy says looking up from his iPad and staring at the wall in front of us filled with family pictures. It was in more of a statement than a question. But then he turns to me with his head tilted to one side and asks, "What am I supposed to say to that?"

"Okay?" Wow. I'm really being mean here. What's gotten into me? I'm not liking this side of myself at all. Maybe I'm tired from the trip? Maybe…I don't know what.

Randy responds, "That simple, huh?"

I don't want to look at him. I can feel some tears welling—but not the amount there should be after this many years of marriage. Have I really grown this callous toward my husband? The words then start to spill out in rapid fire. "I don't know what else to do. We don't communicate anymore. You're not happy. I'm not happy. We live here in this house, when we are home together, as two different entities, no emotion, no togetherness. When we do get around to talking, it's usually full of bitterness and resentment. I've had some time to think it through this week, and what I think is, I'm done. I guess my question is, are you?" Whew! How did all of that just come out? I turn to look at Randy, wondering how much of this matters to him at this point? He looks right back at me, not saying anything. I can't tell by the expression on his face what he's even thinking. After a minute or so he finally speaks.

"Done? No counseling, no time apart to reassess, no nothing?" he asks, almost too calmly.

My answer is more emotional than I would like it to be. I'm not even thinking about meeting with Trisha at this point. I just feel so angry, as I reply, "I think we're past that, Randy. Seriously. You're miserable. You're making me miserable. As much as I try to hold us up from my side, your side has gotten way too heavy for me to bear. It's dragging me under. It's affecting my job, and my focus, and I think even my health at this point. I'm too old for this…abuse." There I said it. Abuse. I'm shocked that I brought it to this level. Is it abuse? Really? Maybe I'm wrong about this…

"ABUSE? You don't know what abuse is!" he fires back. "I don't hit you. I don't harm you." Randy is worked up now. I think I've pushed this too far. "I'm working my job, helping to pay the bills. We live in a nice house. You drive a nice car. You wear nice clothes. You don't even know what you're talking about! You've got it good compared to some!" I can see him getting madder and madder.

My voice rises to meet his. I'm surprised I am battling this with him. This is not how I normally react except in some of the worst of our arguments—probably the ones that Rob and Hannah remember most vividly. But they're not here now to listen to this. So, I let it fly! "Compared to some? Interesting that you would say that. Who would you compare me to…us to? We don't have any friends! You are a loner, and when we are together, you aren't nice. You are mean! You show me no love. You won't even hardly talk to me when I'm out of town and try calling you. And when I get here, you're more interested in your ballgame than seeing your wife who's been gone for the week. You don't ask me how I am. And why? Because you don't care. I get that. Finally. And I've had enough. If you aren't unhappy enough to leave first, then I will! I can't live like this anymore!"

Getting out of the bed, I walk, no stomp, toward my suitcase that sits over by the door ready to be carried to the garage. Randy's words are flying fast now. He is venomous as he yells at my back across the room. I probably deserve some of it. I hit him pretty hard and quick with what I had to say. I could have handled this better. But it seems too late now. I need to get out of here, and fast! Finding some clothes to wear, I quickly pack what I think I will need. Rolling the suitcase out the bedroom door, I don't even look back. I carry the suitcase I just brought up the stairs back down, and to my car. Giving Venyce a call from the driveway, I don't have to say much. She can hear my tone, and she understands things have gotten bad fast. I'm sure glad I said something to her while I was in Chicago, so this didn't come out of the blue. This is not what I expected. I knew it wouldn't be good, but I never thought it would be this bad. Where is my life heading now? I hope God has a plan, because I surely don't. With that thought, I drive off into the night.

5

RANDY

I just left my wife in her hotel room in Chicago, holding a silenced phone. What's gotten into me? Did I really just do that again? Hang up on Linda? The words came out so fast, and I meant every one of them. Now I'm regretting, once again, what just happened. Oh, man, I could use some damage control here. It seems the longer we're married, the older I get, the less I'm able to control my anger even in the small stuff. A dirty shirt? Really? I have over 20 other shirts in my closet that I could wear, and I have to lambast her about the one I can't? Why am I like this? Where is that fun guy she met in college that would wear the same shirt four days in a row? What's gotten into me? Please, God, if You're out there, help me. This isn't who I want to be.

Heading off to work, I know it's going to be another busy day at the office. The trouble tickets are already coming in. I heard them on my phone, and sometimes long for the day when there were no cell phones. What used to go on at the office could stay at the office until I got there. Of course, there were no jobs like I have today…no computers to fix, no internet connections needing more speed…just the old rotary phone sitting on the desk, maybe connected to an answering machine. Those were the simpler days—right out of college, dreams as high as the sky seemed to go…marriage on the horizon, and kids…yeah, maybe 2.5 or whatever the national average was. We had the two. Who has the .5 child?

This darn traffic! It's always building up in the same areas. No wonder I have a short fuse, having to sit in this jam up every day. Why can't everyone just keep moving along so we can all get to where we're going? And where does that guy think he's gonna get to ahead of all of us?

Switching lanes like he's more important than the rest of us? Jerk! I think I'll just sit here where I am for now. Without the *two or more*, that lane on the left costs too much money every day to be in. They can just wait on me until I get there. And no, I'm not going to answer my phone…it's before eight, and I'm not on the clock yet. You can just wait!

"Hi, Emily." I say glumly, finally arriving at the office. Emily gets in at 7:30. She has the coffee made and the place warmed up by the time 8:00 rolls around.

"Hi, Randy," she responds with her usual smile.

It makes me think about Linda again, and how her day got started—with my anger about the shirt she forgot to wash now on her mind. Maybe life as a bachelor would have been better for me after all. Now stop thinking that! You know you thought Linda was the best thing on the market at the time. All your friends were jealous. You could feel their eyes on the two of you at the wedding. It puffed you up, so now just deal with it. This is your life. Live with it.

I'm glad to be off the freeway, in my office, and behind a closed door at last. Maybe no one will come looking for me for a while. I can watch a little sports update, make it look like I'm working—drink my coffee, and blow out some of the trash that got blown in this morning…mostly by me. I sent my old garbage truck down Linda's street there in Chicago. I pushed the button, lifting the tailgate, and out poured the words I can't take back once again. She's wearing that mess today. I know they're heavy on her. She doesn't take stuff lightly. I let it roll off my back. She piles it on and carries it. Maybe I can make it up to her when she gets back on Friday…take her to a nice dinner? Maybe a movie and buy her some popcorn. She likes that. I just feel so tired. Life is so heavy, and I don't really care anymore. But how do I get it all to stop? That's the question of the day. I wish I could put in a ticket with someone...maybe God. "Hey, God, are You listening to me right now? I need to put in a work order with You. Can You send down some of Your guys and have them fix my brain? And my mouth? I need to be rebooted. Do something. Anything!" Does it work like that? I don't know. Maybe there's someone who knows. My thoughts are interrupted by a knock on my door.

"Come in," I say, wondering what anyone could want so early. Breathe. Look happy.

Emily's head appears through the open door. "Randy, Denton wants to see you in his office at 8:30. Will that work for you?" she asks.

"Yeah. That's fine. Thanks." See, that wasn't so hard to treat Emily nice. Maybe I can start over with Linda when she gets home? Maybe I can start to talk nice to her again like in the early days. She's the one probably wondering why she ever married an old geezer like me. Well, I wasn't old then. Was I nice? I don't even know. Would she have married me if I hadn't been? Knowing Linda, she probably would have.

"Hey, Denton. How's your morning going?" I ask while taking a seat on his big soft leather couch. I wish I had an office like this...with this couch. Of course, I'd probably be napping on it a little too often. Denton's a good boss—not too demanding, an understanding sort of guy, really. He can act all tough, but I've seen him comforting employees when there's a death in the family, or other hard stuff going on. He and I get along well, for the most part. Although, I don't tell him much about my personal life.

"Going good, Randy. Long weekend. Sometimes work is more relaxing," he says.

"Oh really?" I don't really want to know, but I ask him anyway. "What was your weekend like?"

"Kids. Lots of kids. Basketball. Parties. The works—guess that's sort of a funny way of saying it. But it does feel exhausting sometimes."

"How about you? Anything big happening in your world?" Denton asks, typing some things into his laptop, but then stopping to look up and wait for my answer.

"Nothing much. Is there something you wanted to see me about this morning?" I really just want to get this meeting over with.

"Well, it's nothing huge. But I want to let you know that Anthony is going to be in town later this week. He's been in Texas, and now he'll be flying in here to check on some things. He wants to have a meeting with the two of us, go over some figures, see where we're at." Denton types a few more things. Then looking at me again continues with, "Just wanted to give you a heads up. I know it helps to not be surprised by the big boss."

"Yeah. I appreciate that. I'll make sure all my paperwork is up to date, and such. He's usually pretty calm," I reply, trying to be upbeat. It really just makes me more tired thinking about it.

"He is pretty low key, as long as we stay on task. Let's stay connected this week and make sure we're on the same page for when he gets here."

"Will do. See you later." Slowly rising from the couch, feeling like a slug not wanting to move, I make my way back to my office and shut the door again. I don't want to meet with Anthony or anyone, but I played it off okay, I think. Why can I pretend to be nice to everyone here? But then I dump on Linda like she deserves it? It's not making sense in my mind.

And it's getting worse. Maybe I need to see someone? A shrink? Would Linda think I'm crazy even considering that? Maybe I am crazy? Or would she be glad? Thankful? Probably so. It's been so tense for so many years. I don't know how much more either one of us can take. It's good she's out of town this week. I think she's about at her boiling point. Maybe I can find someone to talk with before she gets back, and it will give her a bit of hope in our relationship.

The rest of the day is so busy, I don't get a chance to check on any names of therapists until I get home. And by then, I just don't feel it. I want to sit on my own big leather couch and watch the ballgame. With Linda out of town and having picked up a burrito at my favorite Mexican food place, this is my preferred place to be. I can always check into a counselor or someone like that tomorrow. Linda doesn't even know I'm considering it, so she won't be riding me about it. I won't mention it to her until I need to. Maybe I can even go on my lunch hours, and she won't be aware of it. Then maybe she will just see a change in me? That would be a miracle. I'm so stubborn, and I know it. Nothing much moves me. Could a shrink break through whatever it is that's bugging me? I feel so frustrated all the time. I need some beer.

6

RANDY

The game is over, the food is gone, and the beer…well, there's only a few left in the fridge. I'll pick up more tomorrow on my way home.

Leaving the mess there on my TV tray, I head to bed. I don't like it when Linda's not here. But when she is, I don't seem to like that much either. It makes me wonder what it is I do like? I like burritos. I like baseball. I like beer. Those are easy. They don't stress me like the world does—like my wife seems to. Is she the stressor? Or am I?

Falling into bed, I turn the TV on again. Flipping through things, I see the channel I've been drawn to again lately—especially when Linda goes out of town. I sit on it a while…too long. It doesn't feel good. But it does. What other joy do I have in life? The kids raised and gone, barely seeing them. Hannah ended up near Boston with Blake, and Rob's in Florida. Could they have gotten any further away from the west coast? Maybe they moved that far for a reason? They said it was jobs and marriage. I'd move away, too, if I were them. I did from my own parents. I didn't want them messing in my life. Now that my parents are gone, do I miss them? I'm not so sure. I feel bad about that, too. Shouldn't I?

Drifting off to sleep, I wake up about 3:00. The TV is still lit up, and it's on the same channel. I watch it a while. It takes me places my mind and body want to be. I've heard talk about the sin of pornography. But they're talking about addiction. That's the sin. I'm not addicted to it this time. I can resist it when I want to. A little enticing TV from time to time won't hurt me at this point.

I must have gone back to sleep, because the next thing I know it's 6:38. The sun is coming up, and it's time for another *day in paradise*. The phone starts to ring. I see it's Linda. I'm a little surprised. But I shouldn't be—she always keeps on, it seems. No matter how mean I get. "Let me try this again," I tell myself out loud. Clearing my voice, I answer as best I can with a nice, "Good morning."

"Hi, Randy. How did you sleep?"

"Okay. Woke up a couple of times." I don't want to tell her what I did during those times. She doesn't need to know. She will think I've got a problem again, and I don't.

"I slept okay, too." Linda didn't wait for me to ask her. She probably knew I wouldn't as she continued on with, "I talked to Hannah last night. She's feeling good now that she's almost to the three-month mark, although still tired. They will find out the sex of their child soon. They're hoping for a boy. It doesn't matter to me."

"Mmm-hum." I answer while looking at things on my iPad.

"Randy?" Linda says in more a question than anything.

"Yeah?" I answer, not really even listening at this point. So much for doing better this time.

"Randy…I think we have some things to talk about when I get home," she says slowly.

"Sure. Um…yeah," I say, not really cluing into where she might be going with that. I know Linda likes to get to the heart of the matter. She's not a surface chit-chatter. I'm used to that. I'm just glad when it's over.

"Okay, well, I can hear that you're involved in other things, so I'll let you go," Linda says, probably hoping I'll ask her more.

"Okay. Yeah. I need to get to work," I respond. It's not what she wants to hear. But what she wants to hear I can't offer anyway.

"Bye, Randy."

"Bye, Linda."

Showering, I'm thinking about Linda, the woman I chose to spend life with over 40 years ago. Where have the years gone? I'm so bored. I'm so tired. I'm so frustrated by life. I can't even be nice to her on the phone. Suddenly, out of nowhere, I hear like a voice. But not a voice. It's saying, "Things are going to change." Where did that come from? What was that? Is it something I just thought?

Toweling off, I'm shaking my head. That seemed so real. What was it? I've never experienced that before. I normally have music playing while I'm in the shower. Why didn't I today? Would I have heard that if I had?

The drive to work was just as crazy as the day before. Same drivers, same bottleneck, and the same good morning from Emily as I walk through the door. But I'm not the same. As much as I wasn't listening to Linda earlier on the phone, I'm now really replaying in my head a voice I did or didn't hear in the shower. Am I losing my mind?

Entering my office, I shut the door again this morning. I really don't want to be disturbed. Thankfully no one even attempts to find me until ten-thirty other than the emails full of tickets that need tending to. But as long as I have my computer up and running, no one knows what I'm tending to or not.

I sit. I think. And I ponder. I get up and pace some back and forth, and then sit back down. I don't know what to do. Where do you go? Who do you ask, when something like that happens and you don't have a clue what it means? Should I call a pastor? Was it something spiritual? "God, was that You?" I just don't know.

Sitting back down, I google some things on hearing *voices*. It brings up a youth center, government agencies, entertainment. NO, this isn't what I'm looking for. Where do I even begin a search for a voice in the shower? What if I google that? I do. It talks about hearing voices when there is a lot of white noise. Maybe this is getting me closer to something. This is probably why I don't hear anything when I have the music on. What else is here? This one talks about whose voice it might be, conversations I might have had, how the brain works...

Suddenly, I remember what Linda said during our conversation when I really wasn't paying attention. Could that have something to do with it? She said, "I think we have some things to talk about when I get home." It's not like I've never heard that before. Was this time something different? I wish I had asked her more. But that's not normally my style. If I ask her, she'll tell me, and I don't really care. But what if the *change* means with Linda? Will I care then?

Before I know it, lunch is passed, I haven't eaten, and I haven't gotten much work done either. This is crazy making. I need to dismiss all this and get to the task at hand. I order in some lunch, and work at my desk with the door closed the rest of the day. By the time I pick up and head home, Emily is gone, and so is Denton and the rest of the crew. I'm glad. Once again, I don't feel like talking to anyone. I know I can be anti-social. But since I'm aware of that, it doesn't bother me either. People can just tough it.

Traffic seems unusually light tonight. That should make me happy. Instead, I'm angry. I'm tired. And I don't want to deal with anyone or anything. And what was it Linda was saying about our new grandchild this morning? That makes me exhausted just thinking about a baby crying again in our midst. I laugh to myself, what a grumpy old man I've become. I remember seeing that movie years ago about grumpy old men, wondering if that would be me? And here I am. Welcome to the late sixties. The era of new aches, more pains, and no patience for anyone or anything. I remember an uncle being this age. Did he feel like this? If he did, he didn't say much. Maybe I should just learn to keep my mouth shut. That might help everyone around me.

Pulling into the driveway, I see the neighbors have put up a *For Sale* sign. No skin off my nose. I never spent any time with them anyway. Linda would have long conversations with them. I never had the time…or made it. I wonder what Linda will think when she gets home? She probably already knows they're moving. She probably even told me so. But once again, I probably wasn't listening, and didn't care.

The house does seem quiet again coming through the door. Looking through the mail, I see there's an ad that's not normally in the stack of junk mail that comes. Tossing the used-articles' card away, and the envelope for a new credit card I've already been approved for, I notice the white card with simple lettering. It's from a church in town. It says, "Looking for a change in your life? Join us Thursday nights and get excited about the possibilities to come!" Hmmm…there's that word again, "Change." What's going on here?

Tossing the card back on the counter and wanting to ignore it, I flip on the TV, and settle in for another ballgame. I'm drawn to go back to the channel I was watching last night. I repeat a few times, "Think about baseball, think about baseball!" It works. See, I'm not addicted. While enjoying the rest of the game, the phone rings. I see it's Linda. I don't really want to talk. Maybe I can just send her a text and tell her I'm tired. She might be relieved, too. She's probably only calling out of obligation.

I text: "Linda, exhausting day. Let's talk tomorrow."

"Okay. Sleep well," she texts back.

Well, that was easy. I'm off the hook there. Back to the…BALLGAME!! When it's over, the other channel seems to be screaming at me again! What a pain, I sigh, flipping over to look at things that will only draw me in further. Is this problem really coming back? I thought I had kicked it. I should have never opened these floodgates. I had to stay away from TV way back then. It was the only way to stop it. Linda was supportive of me through it. It worked. Maybe the few beers I do have left will drown it out and put me to sleep. I surely hope so. I wish I'd remembered to stop at the store on my way home.

7

RANDY

It's best I didn't have more beer in the house last night. I would have had too many, and then be dealing with a headache today. Stepping into the shower, my ears are on full alert. I leave the music off, wondering if I'll hear that voice again. I don't. I'm disappointed. Or am I relieved? What was it anyway?

Toweling off, I see Linda's calling me again. Maybe I'll just tell her I was in the shower and missed her call. I really don't feel like talking to anyone yet. I need some coffee. I'll stop on the way to work and get some. I'm running late and don't have any time to make it here this morning.

Listening to Linda's voicemail, I can tell she's frustrated. She knows I'm avoiding her. I can't fool her. She knows me too well.

"Randy!" The barista calls out.

Stepping up to get my coffee, I grab it off the counter as the guy next to me bumps me and coffee goes everywhere! All over the floor, my shoes, and down my pant leg.

"HEY! Man! Look at the mess YOU made! GET OUT of my way! I DON'T have time for THIS!" My words come out fast and harsh.

"Sorry, sir. I didn't mean to…"

I see remorse on his face. But I don't care. "Well, YOU DID!" I yell at him.

"We will make you another one right now, sir. And don't worry about the mess," the barista says from behind the counter.

I step back, shaking the coffee off my hands, and getting some napkins to wipe it off my pants. It's good I didn't wear the tan pants from yesterday. Black hides the mess so much more.

"I'm really sorry. Can I pay for your dry-cleaning?" the young man says.

"NO! Just stay back. I don't want you to spill the next one on me, too," I growl at him.

It wasn't but a few minutes and I was on my way, but my whole day seemed out of whack now. Getting back in my car, I set my coffee in the center console, and speed out of the parking lot. Not that I'm late, I'm just frustrated. People are always standing too close, pushing their way in…why can't they wait?

"Hi, Randy," Emily says cheerfully, when I enter the office.

"Hey," I answer back, barely looking at her. Oh man, now I'm not even being nice to Emily.

"Denton wants me to let you know that Anthony is arriving today instead of tomorrow," she says to my back as I pass by her desk.

Flipping around, I give her a glaring look, nodding in disgust. It's not her fault. But I take it out on her.

"Great," is all I can say.

Practically throwing my chair toward the wall behind it, I slam my things down on the desk and stand there, fuming. This day is the pits already. And I'm going to need a steely face with Anthony. He doesn't put up with much. He can be nice and all, but he's a no-nonsense guy. I better cool my jets, and quick!

I notice an envelope on my desk that wasn't there from the day before. "What's this?" I say out loud, flopping into my chair and grabbing a letter opener. Slitting the envelope, I take out the letter, opening it to read,

Dear Mr. Barker:

You may not realize this, but your account is in default. A minimum payment of $358 is due now, with the balance of $4,296 to be paid out over a twelve-month period.

We must hear from you immediately regarding this debt and how you intend to pay it. You may call us at 676-565-4454.

Please, Mr. Barker, we do not wish to be forced to send this bill out for collection. I urge you to make at least your minimum payment today. A self-addressed envelope is enclosed for your convenience, or you may make your payment online.

Sincerely,

Steven Walker

"What the heck?! You gotta be kidding me!" I'm shouting out through a strong whispered tone. "I can't believe this! First the coffee, then Anthony coming early today, and now this?" I sit there shaking my head, trying to control what seems an uncontrollable rage in me. I need to get a grip, but I don't even know how. Getting up, I slam my door. My fist is pounding on my desk, and my heart is pounding in my chest. I want to get out, get away, and find some way to escape life. It's all too much of a jumbled mess. If everyone would just leave me alone and stay out of my way, maybe I could function like a real person. But NO, coffee guy, boss man, and now this? I've had it, and it's not even 8:30 yet.

"Randy," Emily says through the intercom, "Anthony called and said he will be here in 30 minutes. Just giving you a heads-up."

"Thanks." It's all I can manage to say, as the pressure increases in my brain. How am I supposed to be ready to meet with the boss in 30 minutes? My mind is spinning out of control. I need to calm down. Pacing back and forth, I try to breathe in and out. It doesn't seem to be helping. Maybe if I sit down and breathe, I can catch my breath. I see Linda's number on my phone as it rings. "NOT NOW" I silently scream to myself. "This bill is half your fault. We never should have taken that vacation to see those friends!" I don't answer it. Once again, Linda will know I'm avoiding her.

I see a sign on my wall. Linda put it there. "When you find a Bible that's falling apart, you'll usually find a person that's not." I laugh. My Bible looks brand new, and I've had it for eight years. What does that tell me? I don't care. I don't want to listen. That book can't hold the answers to how I'm feeling today. It's so old, and so outdated. I need something more modern that speaks to today's situation. I sit shaking my head.

Hearing a knock on the door, I know Anthony has arrived. Emily peaks her head in. "He's here."

"Okay. Hey, how did this letter end up on my desk this morning?" I ask Emily in an irritated voice.

"It got delivered to Susan's desk by accident, so I put it there this morning," she answers meekly.

"Got it." I shoo her away, and then wonder why I would do that? Emily means no harm. She's a hard worker, and I know I don't show her enough appreciation.

Walking toward Denton's office, I know if I don't pull it together, this will not go well. Emily looks down as I pass by her desk. I don't blame her. I've been a growling bear. She's probably heard my frustration through the closed door. I really do need to figure out my problem here.

"Hey, Anthony, good to see you," I say, offering him my out-stretched hand that, just a minute ago, was a balled-up fist. I fake a smile and try to look confident. This is going to be a long day.

8

RANDY

"It's good to see you, too, Randy. How's the wife? Kids?" Anthony asks warmly.

"Oh, Linda's out of town. But she's fine. Kids are busy. As usual." I don't really want to bring him up to date with my life that is seemingly cracking at the foundation.

"Life is hectic, isn't it," he says. "Let's get to it. I don't want to keep you guys away from what you're doing. But we have some latest figures to go over, and I want to make sure we're all moving in the same direction here."

For the next two and a half hours, there's lots of talk. Lots of figuring. Lots of readjusting. Then Anthony calls it quits, and I'm left to go back to my work. Why is my heart just not in it anymore?

By day's end, I'm feeling exhausted. The traffic is still there, the wife is still gone, and I'm still sitting in front of the TV, wondering how life got to this place, when the phone rings. I don't recognize the number but I answer anyway.

"Hello." I've got nothing better to do than talk down to some sales person. I'll enjoy letting them have it!

"Hello. My name is Eric Linton. I hope I'm not interrupting your evening. I was given your number by a friend of yours, and he...well, he said you might need some encouragement."

"What's your name again?" I ask, pondering such a strange intrusion in my evening.

"Eric. Eric Linton. Dennis Whitley gave me your number. He said he's known you for many years. I've spent a great deal of time with Dennis.

Now he thinks maybe you and I should get to know each other."

"And why would that be? Yes, I know Dennis, but I haven't seen him recently. He sort of dropped out of sight. I've been wondering where he went?"

"He actually 'went,' if I can say it that way, in a different direction in his life. And even though it's been helping him quite a bit, he's still hesitant to talk with you about it. That's why he had me call you, even though this isn't the way I normally do things. I just felt led this time to…"

"To what?" I am more stumped than ever.

"To go ahead and call you. See if maybe we could get together and talk," Eric says.

"What would we talk about?" I ask, still not understanding.

"Life. How tough it can be. How there are answers to questions you might have."

"Oh, really? And you have the answers to life's tough questions? You must be quite the man," I remark, now with an angry tone.

"I don't. But I know who does," Eric replies calmly.

"And who might that be?" I ask sarcastically.

"God." Eric stops there.

"God? Well, I have to tell you, Eric, I've known God quite a while and He's not giving me many answers. Although maybe you can answer a question for me. Does God talk to us in the shower?" I was half making fun of him, and half wondering if this was where I could get an answer.

"Why? Did you hear something?" he asks politely.

"I'm not saying I did, or I didn't. I'm just wondering."

"God speaks to us in many ways, in many places," he answers again in a respectful tone.

"So, you're saying it's possible?"

"Yes. Very. In fact, I've heard God's quiet whisper in the shower, and on walks, and even in my car. It's very distinctive when it's Him. Like no other."

"Are you saying you hear it out loud?" He's got me more curious than ever now.

"No. Not out loud. But it makes an impression on our hearts in a way that nothing else does. Does that help answer your question?"

"I guess it does. Thanks," I respond somewhat sincerely now. "What did you say you were calling about?"

"Dennis gave me your name. I'm wondering if you would like to meet up? Maybe talk some? He said you might be having a few difficulties, and a little encouragement might…"

Interrupting, I snap back, "I'm not your guy!" I'm suddenly realizing I'm talking to a stranger about personal stuff. I don't like it. He caught me off guard. "I don't know what Dennis told you, but in many ways, I think you've dialed the wrong number. Thanks anyway."

"Okay, that's fine. If you ever do need someone to listen though, you've got my number now in your phone. I'm not here to bug you. I hope you have a good evening."

"Yeah. You, too," I say flippantly, hanging up before he has a chance to say good-bye.

Who does this guy think he is? Calling me out of the blue like that. What nerve! Butting into my business. I need to give Dennis a call and see what's going on. Why would he do that? Why would he put this guy onto me?

Getting back to the ballgame one thing keeps bugging me now…and it's not Eric. It's that voice I heard, "Things are going to change." I wonder now if God had Eric call me, so I could ask him about that? Could that be possible? Strange timing there. Maybe Eric has some sort of connection with God? He didn't even think I was crazy asking him about that. I don't know what's going on. Hearing that, and then Dennis putting this guy onto me? I wish it would all just stop…everything—the world, the collection department, Anthony coming to town, and Linda coming back. I'm going to have to face her pretty soon. She gets back on Friday, and I can't deal with her wanting to "talk." Oh man, here we go again.

With the ballgame done, I'm headed to bed. I think I'm tired enough to resist those TV channels tonight. It will be good to have Linda back in town, if for nothing else, to keep me away from that. I know better, but it sure entices me. I've got two days before she returns. I really gotta give her a call in the morning. She didn't even try reaching me tonight. That's not good. Looks like the ball is in my court. I better serve it back soon, or else.

9

RANDY

Dialing Linda, I wait for her answer. It doesn't come. It goes to voicemail. Maybe she's in the shower. I'll try her back in a bit.

Grabbing a bowl of cereal, I sit down at the kitchen table. It's a nice view out back, lots of trees, and the hills behind. Life should be good, shouldn't it? Kids raised, nice home, long marriage, good job…what's my problem? Why am I so disgruntled? Is it me? Or is it life? Maybe I could ask Eric those questions. WHAT? Man, I didn't expect Eric to come back into my thinking so quickly. Maybe I do need some help? Is Eric some sort of shrink?

Picking up my phone, I see the number from his call last night. I enter him into my contacts. There, he's a real person in my phone now. I probably won't ever call him. But who knows how bad things are gonna get when Linda gets home? I feel like we're getting to the end of what the two of us can stand. There's no reason to stay together with the kids out of the house, is there? I don't know. I shouldn't even be thinking this way. Linda's got her stuff. But I feel like my stuff is piling up much higher these days. I can't seem to find any satisfaction in my job. I'm angry at everyone on the road, and everyone in the line at the grocery store. I can't get my bills paid on time. The kids never want to talk to me. And honestly, I don't want to talk to them. I'm not even excited about becoming a grandpa. Hannah is what? Three months pregnant? I'm not prepared for that. And I'm shooing Emily away when she's only trying to help. Even the friends that I do have, like Dennis, we've lost contact. Is it me or is it him? He seems to have moved onto bigger and better things. No time for me anymore. But maybe I'm not much fun to be around. I am a grumpy old man! I know that's what I am. At least I can admit it. But what do I do about it? Maybe life just gets to this, and we gotta hang in there until we die? Dennis seems to be making other choices. And Eric, he did seem like a nice guy. Would I want to talk to him? There I go, thinking about Eric. What's up with that?

Dialing Linda again, she answers this time.

"Hi," she says. No "good morning." No "How are you?"

"Hi," I answer back. "Sorry. Been busy."

Silence on her end.

"How's work?" I ask, trying to make some sort of contact, not that I really care.

"It's okay. I'm looking forward to being done with this week," she says mostly in monotone.

"What time do you land?" I ask.

"6:45. Don't pick me up. I'll get a ride."

"You sure?" I say, actually glad I don't have to fight the traffic to the airport.

"Yeah. I'll see you between 7:30 and 8:00. Don't wait dinner." Her tone hasn't changed.

"Okay. I'll see you tomorrow then," I say, ready to be done.

"Okay. Bye."

"Bye." I'm glad to hang up.

Yes, it's official. My life sucks! And I'm probably to blame. Might as well get to the office and see what other good news awaits me there.

"Good morning, Randy," Emily says in her usual upbeat tone as I walk past her desk. She must drink lots of coffee before she gets here, I think to myself.

I turn, face her desk, and say, "Good morning." It's the best I can do. Her face shows a bit of surprise, and then a small smile. Sadly, I don't return the smile, so hers quickly fades away.

Another day in paradise I think, as I switch on my computer, and fiddle with a pencil between my fingers. Wow, these were once used so much more. I miss pencil and paper days. I miss when life had promise, and each day didn't hold anger, resentment, and things I should be doing that I'm not. It seems like I'm missing out on so much of life while I sit here in my dark bubble of disappointment. I wish I had a big pin and could just pop the bubble, opening up my eyes to a different world, a different place, and different circumstances. Maybe the confetti would rain down over me, and I'd feel like a winner! Everyone would be cheering, and I'd feel over the top with excitement…

"Randy?" I hear over the intercom.

"Yeah. What's up." My "Victor's parade" vanishing from my mind at the interruption.

"We're ordering lunch in today from Amigo's. I need to know what you would like?" Emily inquires.

"I'll get back to you in a bit. Let me look at their menu," I answer curtly.
"Okay."

I've got a menu in my drawer. I figure out what I want and send her a text with my order. It's easier than talking with her. Lunch seems a bright spot to look forward to. But it quickly fades as I am deep into the work needing my attention. When the day ends, I've got heartburn from the burrito, and frustration from the trouble tickets left that I couldn't get to. I ask myself if I really care, though. Probably not.

Driving home, I'm stopped at the red light and notice the church on the corner that sent me the card in the mail. I see a sign out front, "Looking for a change in your life? Come on in!" I sigh and shake my head. Do they really think that sign does them any good? Who doesn't want a change? But in there? I doubt they have what I'm looking for. What I need is home, alone, with me, myself, and I.

Pulling into the driveway I see the neighbors out front. I push the garage door opener and pull inside. I don't want to interact with them and hear all about how they are selling their home and where they're moving to. Just not interested. The house is quiet, and I throw my stuff on the kitchen table. I don't want to go out and get the mail until they're gone. Probably nothing much there anyway…unless that church sent out another card. I pick up the one from the other day and look it over. It says on the back that "We all have things in our life that need to be changed, and God is the One who can help us." I don't think they can help me. I'm stubborn, grumpy, tired, and not interested. And, I've got heartburn!

Looking for an antacid, I knock a bottle out of the cabinet that I haven't seen in a while. It reminds me how I couldn't handle life at one time. It got to be too much. When my brother, Bennet, died, I was so angry at the drunk driver that hit him. My parents' accident was bad, but at least they were older. And drinking wasn't involved. I was so glad to see Bennet's guy locked up in that jail cell. He got what he deserved. I eventually got off the pills. But look at me now. Am I any better? I still hate the guy. He took my big brother away from me. Yes, we were grown men, but a brother is a brother. That criminal can just rot in jail for all I care. My brother is rotting in the grave because of him. Oh yeah, they say Bennet went to heaven. I believe he will be there. But is he there yet? I saw him in the casket, all made up, not really even looking like himself. What a horrible day that was, and so many that followed. So hard. I hate the whole thought of it.

Opening the fridge, I grab one of the last beers. Oh man, I forgot to stop again tonight. And since I just took the last antacid, I think I better make a run to the store. I don't want the burning to keep me up all night. That burrito just won't go away.

Getting back in the car, I hit the garage door button...nothing happens. I push it again. Nothing. Getting out, I check to see what the problem might be. It just won't open. I'm gonna have to take Linda's car that's sitting out front. I sure hope the neighbors have gone in by now.

"Hi, Randy," I hear as I come out the door onto the front walk. Looking up, I see the coast is not clear.

"Hi," I say, only wanting to make a beeline for Linda's car.

"How are you doing?" the wife says.

"Fine. Fine. And you?" I try to be polite.

"We're doing great. Gonna be selling the house. We'll miss being neighbors. But the mountains are calling us, and we eventually want to retire there," he says.

"That's nice," I say, almost to the car now.

"Has Linda been gone? Haven't seen her lately?" she asks.

"Yes. She went away on business," I answer, wishing I could just get in and drive away. But it seems too rude.

"Bet you miss her. She's such a sweet person," the wife says. What was her name anyway? I can never remember. I remember his name is Gil.

"Oh, yeah. She'll be home soon," I respond.

"Tell her hello from us," they both say, waving as they start to go back into their own house.

"Okay," I say, ducking into the car, relieved that exchange is over. A simple trip to the store was all I wanted. That darn garage door. It's done that before. I hope it fixes itself again this time. I don't have the money to pay for repairs.

10

RANDY

The grocery store is busy because everyone's off work. After getting what I need and going to the quick-check aisle, I see even it's lined up. I stand there, shaking my head, wondering why they don't hire more checkers?

Glad to be back in the car now and trying to avoid the busier streets on the way home, it takes me past the church once again. I notice the cars are starting to file into the parking lot. It must be starting soon. When the light turns green, something urges me to pull in, but parking far out so no one really sees me. I watch for a while as families seem happy to be meeting friends and going inside. There must be some program for the kids tonight, too. I wonder what they will be talking about? I've been to church enough to know Jesus is the Savior. I figured that was all it took, and then bing, bang, boom, life would be all perfect. Didn't much work out that way. I just felt guilty about some of the things I used to do before. Is that what it's all about? Guilt? I didn't need that. So why am I sitting here in the parking lot then? That darn card they sent me…is it drawing me here? Who would have thought that campaign would actually work?

Jesus, let me think about You for a minute. Who are You? Why are You so important? Pastors talk about You dying on the Cross, about Your blood and forgiveness. You rose from the dead. They say You have made a way to Heaven for people. It seems I have those facts clear in my head. So why haven't they made any difference in my life? In my marriage? At my job? With my kids? Is there something more? Have I missed something all these years? Does this Christianity thing work for everyone but me? I just don't know. But here I sit.

I can't help it, I slowly get out of my car and walk toward the church.

Thankfully, this isn't the church Linda and I have been going to on Easter and Christmas, so I don't know anyone here; like I would anyway. I need to feel anonymous. I'm way too angry and frustrated to play nice. Maybe no one will even talk to me. That will be better.

I take a seat way in the back, on the right. There aren't too many people here yet. The program I picked up said it starts in about 20 minutes, so I'm way early. I don't like that. But I don't want to drive home and come back. That wouldn't make sense. Does it even make sense that I'm here? I must be crazy to think I'll find some sort of *change* in here. I haven't in the other ways I've tried through the years. Is that because I never really wanted to? Maybe I was just going through the motions, wanting God or other people to do it all for me with no effort on my part? But isn't that what the pastor told us? Jesus paid it all. Jesus did it all. All we have to do is come to Him?

Lost in my own thoughts, I barely notice that the lights have now gone down and the band is beginning to play on stage. I'm used to at least a little choir up behind the pulpit. There is no choir here, only guitars, a drum set, and a keyboardist in the back. They sound good. Oh boy, these people are really getting into this. They are all actually singing with enthusiasm, and their hands are all over the place. Some have them in the air, some out in front, some clapping. I don't know what I think about this. I'm really wanting to just leave, but something keeps me here. I take a seat with everyone at the end of the music, and the pastor walks to the pulpit. He's a young man, probably 45, balding but using what hair he has left. He welcomes us all, and asks everyone, "Are you ready for a change?" They all respond with a resounding, "Yes!" I wonder how long this has been going on? Do they do this every week?

After prayer, and an offering, we are all instructed to turn to Luke 13:34-35. It's up on the big screen:

"O Jerusalem, Jerusalem, the city that kills the prophets and stones God's messengers! How often I have wanted to gather your children together as a hen protects her chicks beneath her wings, but you wouldn't let me. And now, look, your house is abandoned. And you will never see me again until you say, 'Blessings on the one who comes in the name of the LORD!'"

"What do we have to say about that tonight?" the pastor asks. "Are we looking for a change? Are we willing to have those changes made in us? Will we let our Savior, Jesus Christ, heal and deliver us from the things that are plaguing us each and every day?"

The crowd gives a resounding "Yes" to his questions, and then he continues on.

"You all came in here tonight looking for something—something that the world cannot offer you. You came here because this is where God wanted you to be tonight. Oh yes, there are many other things you could be doing. But no. You chose to be here. To dig into the Word together, and to grow together. And I'm one of you. I'm here to be in the Word and to grow, too. Just because I'm the one up here speaking doesn't mean that I have all the answers. But I know the One who does. And as we search the Scriptures together, we will find those answers. We will all be changed, for the better. We are here because we are willing to let Jesus change us, from the inside out."

I was listening as best I could, and it was a good sermon. But I left pretty much the way I came in. I didn't want to participate in all that they were doing. It seemed too farfetched. People talking about how God is working in someone's life? Being prayed for about healing? Being freed of the evil things that he said were affecting their lives? That all sounds a little too weird for me. I don't mind the good words he had to say, just like most pastors. But then he seemed to take it too far. I mean, I believe in God and all. And I'm glad to be reminded of the changes Jesus can make in my life. I do need that. But this other stuff? I don't think so. That's for the over-the-top Christians that I see on TV sometimes. They seem so fake. I don't want to get caught up in any of that. What would my family think? What would Linda think? Yeah, that guy that went forward did seem to have a real experience with the person praying for him. He seems to be relieved of something that had a hold on him. But still…nah, that's too much. And that other person who said they were once in great pain, but the pain is now gone? I think I just need to get home now. If Linda knew what I witnessed there tonight, she would think I had gone over the edge to even attend that church service. I don't think I'll tell her. No one needs to know.

Getting home, the beer is warm from being in the car. I stick it in the fridge and notice that my heartburn is gone. When did that stop? Thinking back, it was about the time the pastor started praying for healing. I hadn't put the two together. Interesting. That was quite the coincidence. It does feel better though. I'm glad for that.

The ballgame is just about over. They are into the bottom of the eighth, so I watch what's left of it, and then turn in. Linda will be home tomorrow. I better get some of this junk picked up around here in the morning. She doesn't like to come home to a messy house. It puts her in a bad mood. I'm sort of looking forward to her getting back. We'll see how it goes. We didn't talk again tonight. She would have been shocked if I texted her, "Sorry, can't talk. I'm in church." That makes me laugh. I never thought of going to any service except on Sundays, and mostly just at the holidays. Who needs it? Well, that's a strange question, since I just went. I wonder what got *into me*? From the look of things there, that was part of their question, and they seemed to have an answer to it. They told whatever it was *in* them—the pain, arthritis, anxiety—to GO in Jesus' name. I never heard of such a thing. Is that even in the Bible? Maybe I just missed it? But then again, I barely open it, so who am I to say what's in it? Maybe I should look those things up sometime?

I don't turn on the TV to that channel I've been drawn to. It seems disrespectful right now, having just been in church. Maybe that's why we only go once in a while? It's been easier to leave it there and spend our lives living how we want. With going tonight, it's just a reminder of all the things I'm doing that I shouldn't be. Who needs to be nagged in that way? I'm done thinking about it all. Falling asleep, I'm looking forward to the week being over.

11

RANDY

I need to get up a little earlier this morning to clean up the last of the mess I've made around here. It's kind of fun to just leave the junk and live like a slob for a few days. But I do like it nice, too. Food boxes and wrappers…I ate out way too much this week. It will be good to have more home cooking once Linda gets back.

I left my phone upstairs and I hear it ringing. I don't want to be bothered right now. I need to get this done. Cleaning the kitchen and putting what little dishes I have used into the dishwasher, I start to clean off the counter from all the junk mail. There's that card again. Well, at least I know more what goes on there now. I don't think I'll go back. But I can't say I'm uninformed. Did I understand it all? I didn't. But when I drive by now, I'll know what's up. If Linda ever mentions it, I wonder what I will say? Will I play dumb? Or will I confess that I've gone inside? I really don't know. I toss the card in the garbage.

When I get to my phone, I see it was Linda. I give her a call back. It's better to face her now rather than wait for tonight. It will be way too uncomfortable to have her walk through the door not having talked again.

Dialing her, she answers.

"Hi."

"Hi. How did you sleep?" I ask.

"Okay. Ready to get home," she responds.

"Yeah," was all I knew to say. She always said I'm a man of few words.

"Are you glad it's Friday?" she asks.

"Always. It's been a different sort of weird week," I respond, wondering why I even went that far.

"Oh, really?" she says.

"Yeah. Just stuff. I'm…well, we can talk when you get home. You wanted to anyway."

"Yes. I do. Okay, well I gotta go finish up here so I can catch my flight. See you tonight." She's trying to have a lift in her voice, but I hear the strain.

"Yeah. See you later. Have a good flight. Bye."

"Bye," she says and nothing more before hanging up.

I'm glad I got that little bit of an ice breaker done. It's not going to be easy when she gets back. Something is on her mind, and she's going to want to talk about it. I hate those talks. It makes me sigh forcefully. "Marriage," I say out loud. "It's not for wimps."

Arriving at the office, coffee in hand, not spilling any today, I try to be nice to Emily.

"Good morning," I say, but still passing by her desk without stopping.

"Good morning, Randy," she responds, but adding nothing more. I think she's had about all she can take of me.

The collection letter is still on my desk. I never took it home. I never did anything with it. I don't want it to get worse than it already is, so I better take care of it. Writing out a check, I put it in the outgoing mail. I don't know if I'll talk to Linda about it at all. I'm not feeling up for an argument. That was strange when they prayed for that one woman on stage last night. She said she has a lot of anger toward her sister. But when they got done praying for her, she was smiling and thanking God. I wouldn't want to go up there and talk about my problems in front of everyone. Not that they made the person say too much. Some just volunteered to be an example for everyone there. It was really sort of a teaching type of evening after the sermon. I kind of liked that. They showed how they did things. I'm not really sure what it all meant. But it was interesting to watch what was happening. Funny thing, I sort of felt better after it all, now that I think about it. Not just the heartburn was gone, but I felt lighter in a way. Could what they were talking about really be true? It sort of makes me want to go back and check it out again. But I better not. Linda will think I'm crazy. Better leave well enough alone.

Glad when the day is over, I drive home, picking up some chicken on the way. Linda said she wouldn't be here for dinner, so I'm not waiting.

I'm exhausted. It's not that the week was that hard, it's that I don't want to even try anymore.

When Linda comes through the door, I'm sitting watching baseball, again. She's not surprised. I get up to greet her as best I can. The hug between us is cold at best. Maybe she's just tired, too.

"Hey," I say, looking quickly back at the TV to see a great play happening.

"Hey," she says back. "I'm tired. I'm going upstairs to unpack."

I see her go, knowing I should offer to carry her bag for her. But I don't. That would entail some effort on my part. I sit back down to see a replay of what just happened. Another check on my "bad list." Let's put that one all in caps. SELFISH.

Linda hasn't come back down, and the game is over. I turn off the lights and go on up, hoping she's asleep. She's not. She is propped up in bed, reading. She looks up at me as I come in. The look on her face is not one I'm prepared to deal with. I'm not sure what it is, but it's certainly not happy. After taking care of a few things, I get in next to her. Well, really on the far side of our king-sized bed. I get out my iPad, looking through some things. It's not long, and Linda lays her book down and sits looking straight forward. I know something is coming.

"Randy, I want a divorce," she says, leaving it hanging there with nothing following. Simple. Straight to the point. Lacking emotion.

I can't say that I am shocked. I wonder to myself, "Do I?" Looking up from my iPad and staring at the wall in front of me, I let out a small grunt. Barely audible. But she knows I've heard her. I say nothing at first.

"A divorce," I finally say. She's still staring forward. I turn her way and all I can utter is, "What am I supposed to say to that?"

"Okay?" She answers, looking briefly in my direction. I can see that there is pain in her eyes, but I wonder how deep it goes.

"That simple, huh?" I respond.

Not even looking at me now, Linda lets me have it with, "I don't know what else to do. We don't communicate anymore. You're not happy. I'm not happy. We live here in this house, when we are home together, as two different entities, no emotion, no togetherness. When we do get around to talking, it's usually full of bitterness and resentment. I've had some time to think it through this week, and what I think is, I'm done. I guess my question is, are you?" She finally turns to look at me.

I look at her now, not saying anything. Is this what I've been waiting for? Is this what I've been wanting? Will this make me happy at last? Part of me thinks so. Part of me is scared out of my wits. Life without Linda would be so different. Would it be better or worse? I almost laugh to myself thinking, I'd still be me. I just wouldn't have her to pick on anymore. Would I then pick on myself more? That could be an even sadder state of affairs. I finally am able to say something.

"Done? No counseling, no time apart to reassess, no nothing?" I'm relatively calm at this point. Linda is getting more upset by the minute.

"I think we are past that, Randy. Seriously. You're miserable. You're making me miserable. As much as I try to hold us up from my side, your side has gotten way too heavy for me to bear. It's dragging me under. It's affecting my job, and my focus, and I think even my health at this point. I'm too old for this...abuse. There I said it. Abuse."

At that, I am shocked, and suddenly angry. And she knows it. "ABUSE?" I start in, "You don't know what abuse is! I don't hit you. I don't harm you. I'm working my job, helping to pay the bills. We live in a nice house. You drive a nice car. You wear nice clothes. You don't even know what you're talking about! You've got it good compared to some!" I'm mad now. I can feel it rising, and the pitch of my voice is going with it.

Linda matches me with her own tirade. "Compared to some? Interesting that you would say that. Who would you compare me to...us to? We don't have any friends, you are a loner, and when we are together, you aren't nice. You are mean. You show me no love. You won't even hardly talk to me when I'm out of town and try calling you. And when I get here, you're more interested in your ballgame than seeing your wife who's been gone for the week. You don't ask me how I am. And why? Because you don't care. I get that. Finally. And I've had enough. If you aren't unhappy enough to leave first, then I will. I can't live like this anymore."

If steam coming out of my head was visible, the room would be full of it by now. Instead, it shows itself in an angry barrage of words that fly back toward Linda's direction. And what frustrates me even more is she doesn't stick around to hear all of what I have to say. She is up, getting dressed, and packing the suitcase she just emptied. She says nothing after that, and when she walks out of the bedroom, I have a sinking feeling she is serious. I hear her close the front door with a bang. When did I lose control here? When did she get so strong? How did I miss this? To say I got any sleep that night would be a lie. But to say I was sorry would be a lie, too.

12

LINDA

The tears are coming now as I drive over to Venyce's. I'm going to be a mess when I arrive at her door. She will understand. But I hate what just happened. That wasn't the way I would have planned it at all. I think I just hit the breaking point, and it all spilled out at once. I don't really want a divorce. Why did I say that? What I want is a happy marriage. Now I've left Randy seriously ticked, and I don't know how or when we will talk again.

Pulling into the driveway, Venyce's porch light goes on, and she opens the door. She looks worried. I'm worried, too. This is many years of marriage maybe going down the drain. Venyce and Earl had such a good relationship. I don't know exactly how she's going to react to how I handled it.

"Oh, Linda. Come here," she says, holding out her arms to me. I pretty much collapse into them on the porch, sobbing. After a bit, she brings me into the house. "Sit down. Let me get you some tissues and water. Let's start there."

I take a familiar seat on the couch, trying to stop the eruption of emotions. I'm so glad my sister lives alone or I'd have woken up the whole house.

"Here you go," she says, handing me the tissue and water. Taking a seat on the couch next to me, she's just quiet for a time, rubbing my back and soothing me. Eventually, I can speak.

"Thank you, Venyce. I don't know what I would do without you. Where would I have gone?" The sobbing starts again.

"It's okay. Really. It's going to be okay," Venyce says.

"I don't know how," I'm able to eventually get out. "I can't believe my life has come to this. Maybe I should have just stayed quiet and put up with it until the 'death do us part' vow came true." I sort of laugh at that between the tears.

"Well, many do. But let's not go into all that tonight. There is a lot we can talk and pray about. But you've already had a long day, just flying in from Chicago. You must be exhausted. Why don't we get you settled in, let you sleep, and we can talk in the morning?"

"That sounds good. Thank you. That's probably best. I don't know that I can make any sense of all this tonight."

Venyce helps me with my bag to the guest room. It's a large room with a queen bed, a desk under the window, a large closet, and a comfy chair. The colors are light and airy, and even though my mood is anything but, there is a calmness in the room.

"Don't even try to unpack tonight. Just get out what you need, crawl in under the covers, and try to rest. I have to go out in the morning for just a bit, but I'll be back by about nine. Then we can talk. The coffee will be made for you when you get up. You know your way around. Just make yourself at home. This will all work out."

"I don't know how," I say, starting to cry again.

"God has a way through all things. He will be with you as we walk this out together. If you can't sleep, put a little worship music on. There's a radio there on the nightstand. It's easy to use."

"Okay, I'll try. See you in the morning," I say, giving Venyce another long hug. "You're the best sis ever."

Holding my hands for a moment, Venyce says a simple prayer, "Father in Heaven, bring Linda Your peace tonight. Help her to get some sleep. Let the healing begin, as we watch You work out the details in all of this. Thank You, Lord Jesus. Amen"

"Amen," I add.

Venyce closes the door gently as she leaves. Getting into bed, I'm shocked at how I thought I'd be sleeping in my own bed tonight and how quickly life changes. Even though I'd thought about divorce off and on, I guess I never really thought it would come to this. But here I am…

When morning comes, I glance at the clock. It's only 5:22. I know I'm still on Chicago time. It feels like I only got a couple hours of sleep during the night. I tossed and turned so much. The worship music helped a little, so I kept it on low most of the night. The house is quiet. My eyes are swollen from crying. Not a pretty sight, so I'll be glad to be alone for a bit.

While lying in bed, I hear the front door open and close. Venyce has left and I need to get up. Finding a mug in the cupboard, I pour myself some coffee, adding a bit of cream from the fridge, and make my way out to the back porch. It's a bit cool, but still nice enough to sit out. I can hear the birds and I watch as a squirrel scurries across the back fence. I wish my life was simple like that squirrel. Just find some food, and carry it back home. I don't know where they live or what they do, but I do know they are not in the mess I am in. Why has this happened?

Sitting here, I remember back to our wedding day. We were so in love. Venyce was my matron of honor, and Randy had his brother, Bennet, as his best man—I know he misses Bennet so much. We had just graduated, gotten our degrees in business, and everything seemed to be in place. We dated through most of our college years. We did break up twice for short periods of time. But it seemed we were meant to be together. Randy was a fun guy. He teased me a lot. But I always laughed along with him. Sometimes he would get moody. But I hung in there through those times, too. I figured we all get down at times. He worked hard on his studies, as I did mine. We were both good students and getting jobs right after college didn't pose much of a problem. I mainly focused on finances, and Randy tried that, but later became more interested in technology as it developed. He was good at it. The money was never an issue with two good incomes, and when the kids came along, our life seemed on track. I remember thinking, "What else is there?" We had our education, our careers, and our children. We bought some nice homes through the years, and we got along okay, especially early on. The arguments increased as the kids got older. But so did the tension with teens, decisions, and a few health problems. God was never huge in our lives, but never totally disregarded either. It felt right to take the kids to church when Christmas rolled around. And for Easter it was always fun to get dressed up in new spring outfits and take the kids to church. God was there. But we lived how we wanted. I wouldn't say I was happy, but I wouldn't say I was totally unhappy either. It all just seemed to be moving along as it should.

It was hard when Randy's parents died so young. They were in a car accident coming home from a trip to Las Vegas. A semi crossed over into their lane. It was a shock when we received that phone call. Randy was 42 at the time, and they were in their sixties. But then with his brother Bennet... It wasn't too long after that that Randy went forward at church one Easter. I was happy to see him do it. He needed something as the grief and anger was weighing heavy on him. He was so mad at the drunk driver that killed his brother. Of course, that was understandable. I had great hopes when I saw him make that decision at church that he would feel better. But nothing seemed to really change. In fact, in the years since then, we have grown further and further apart. I went forward a couple of years before Randy. Not out of great need, like Randy did, but because I was hoping for something more in life, I guess. I never really found it either. I always wondered if the smiles others wore at church were real? The pastor preached like there should be joy. I don't think either one of us ever really felt it. Maybe it's just for other people, and not us? Maybe if we had gotten more involved, we wouldn't have ended up here?

Rob and Hannah were good kids. They had their typical teenage struggles, and there were quite a few battles between Rob and Randy. But Rob seemed to handle them okay. Randy got angrier as the years went on. His words became harsher, he was less patient. It wasn't just with me, he was pretty hard on Rob, too. But Rob would just do his own thing and spend more time with his friends than at home. I figured that was normal for a teenage boy. Hannah and I got along well, and she did okay with Randy. He was a proud dad the day he walked her down the aisle. Although, I know he wasn't happy to hand his daughter off to another man, Blake seemed like a good guy. But I've seen some strain in their marriage. Not that I'm surprised. What marriage doesn't have that?

Life—it seems like it's been pretty normal, just not all that happy. My career has been rewarding, and now I'm looking forward to being a grandma. That seems like what most people aspire to be…and I'm right there with them. I just wish the kids didn't live so far away. Boston—could you get any further from California? It's not going to be easy to see the baby grow up. Thankfully, with technology we will make it work.

"Linda. Where are you?" I hear Venyce calling to me through the open window.

"I'm out here! On the porch!" I can't believe I've been sitting out here for almost two hours already.

Sticking her head out the back door she says, "I'm going to grab a cup of coffee and I'll join you, if that's okay?"

"Sure. I think I'll get a refill," I respond. Coming into the house, I meet Venyce in the kitchen. She gives me a hug and asks me how I'm doing. "Okay," I say with a shaky voice.

Taking a seat again out back, Venyce can see it was a rough night.

"I'm sorry for what you're going through, Linda. Did you get any sleep?"

"A little," I answer. "I did a lot of rolling over. Not only in the bed, but in my mind."

"I bet. This is a biggie in life. But I want you to hang onto something right off the bat," she says.

"What is it?" I ask.

"That this is the first day of something new. And although the enemy would have it look all dismal and dark and scary, God's light is so much brighter. And more powerful. This isn't the end of anything, but the beginning of everything. We just don't know for sure what it is yet. If, IF you are willing to work with God on this, there is great hope. And I'm not saying your marriage will be saved…but you will be."

"What do you mean by that?" I ask.

"God doesn't waste anything. Not even the bad stuff…or should I say, especially the bad stuff. He takes it and turns it into something beautiful even when it doesn't look like we would like it to when it's finished. Jesus said, *'Blessed are those who have not seen and yet have believed.'* Some things we won't see the reason for until we enter into eternity. But we can trust that God knows what He is doing in all things."

"I'm listening."

"I brought my Bible out with me, and here in Isaiah 12:2, it says, *'See, God has come to save me. I will trust in him and not be afraid. The Lord God is my strength and my song; he has given me victory.'* I have been living this out. Take my Earl, for instance…I miss him every day. It broke my heart to see him leave here without me. We always talked about going together one day, sort of like that movie. We lie down in a bed and wake up in Heaven together. But we knew it was a pipe-dream, as they say. When Earl was dying, we were upfront about it all. Nothing was taboo to talk about. We both knew that where Earl was going was going to be awesome. And we both also knew that me living on here without him was going to be difficult. But what sustained us as a couple was the hope we have in Jesus, and that this world and all its trials isn't all there is. We couldn't know why God would have Earl leave first. But we could know it wouldn't be wasted. And although I've had some very sad times these last few years, I've also found a new joy in the mourning—an intimacy with God that I never had before. I'm experiencing more victory each day. Why? Because of my need for it. In the need, there is a gift."

"What kind of gift?" I ask.

"The gift Jesus left us with when He ascended back into Heaven. Peace, not as the world gives. The world's peace fades quickly depending on our circumstances. Heaven's peace remains the anchor for our soul *in* the circumstances. Earl and I knew that before. But I have a much deeper understanding of it now, living without him. You will find, if you are willing, the same gift can be yours. Whether God mends your marriage, or simply mends your heart, you can know Him more and find His peace. There is no greater gift, other than His Son, Jesus."

"Thank you, Venyce. Peace is really my goal. God is speaking through you this morning. I will hold onto these words. And I might need you to repeat them to me along the way. I also think I should text Trisha back now. She sent me a text in Chicago, and I wanted to think on it a bit before responding to her. Now I know I NEED to. I don't want to lean too heavily on you through this."

"Trisha will be a great resource and encouragement for you. Yes. Get ahold of her," Venyce encourages.

"I think I'll go in and shower and do just that. Thanks for the coffee," I say, heading indoors.

"You're very welcome."

13

LINDA

The hot shower felt so good. As I curl up here in this chair, it's time to give Trisha a call. She said in her text I could call anytime.

"Hello?"

"Trisha?"

"Yes."

"This is Linda, Venyce's sister."

"Oh, yes. Hi, Linda. How are you today?"

"I'm doing okay. Thank you for your text."

"It's good to hear from you. I was wondering if you got home from Chicago okay? I didn't want to wait to contact you after Venyce gave me your number. I want you to know I'm available."

"That's very nice of you. Yes. I got home from Chicago last night. And I might as well tell you, I left my husband last night. The return home wasn't good, and I'm staying with my sister now, not knowing really what's in store for my future."

"Oh. Wow. That was a difficult return home for sure. I'm really sorry to hear it," Trisha says, comfortingly.

"Thanks." After a few moments of silence, I can tell Trisha is not wanting to rush me. I know I need to say something. "That's why I wanted to call you instead of text. I think…I know, I need some help. I'm not sure what that will look like, but…I don't really know what to say. Just that, I guess. I need help."

"That's a very good place to start, Linda. Admitting that this is bigger than what we can handle allows God to work in a mighty way in our lives. May I ask you a few questions, so I can get a feel for where we might go with this together?"

"Sure. Whatever you need to know. I'll try to answer as best I can."

"If it's okay, I'll pray first. That helps me know what I should ask."

"Yes. That's fine."

"Father in Heaven," Trisha begins, "You are a loving and all-knowing God. Nothing is a surprise to You. And although what Linda is going through now is a very upsetting situation, we can trust that You will have healing in this process for both Linda and her husband...what is your husband's name?"

"Randy."

"...for both Linda and Randy. They have found themselves where so many have, in a marriage that is broken. They need You in the midst of this, not only individually, but for their relationship to be what You created marriage to be. As Linda walks through this, if I can be of help, use me, direct me through Your Holy Spirit to love, guide, comfort, and pray for Linda in this trial. Apart from You, we can do nothing. But with You, all things are possible. We will cling to You, search for You, and find You to be the Helper that Linda so needs. It's in the name of Your Son, Jesus, we pray. Amen."

"Amen. Thank you, Trisha."

"Prayer is the only way to get to the heart of what God is doing. Thank you for letting me start there. How long have you and Randy been married? Tell me a little bit of what is going on?"

I began to tell Trisha how we met, married, our kids, our jobs, and some of the difficulties in our relationship. She was good to listen for a long while as I poured out my heart to her. When I finished, she thanked me for sharing it with her.

"Thank you for listening, Trisha. I hope I didn't go on too long?"

"Not at all. It is important to have a starting place, and now I do. I don't know how much Venyce has told you about me, but I'm not a professional counselor. What I do is listen and pray with people who need it. There are many ways to healing, and many tools that God gives us to use. Mainly, I try to use them all."

"Tools?" I ask.

"Yes. Would you like me to tell you a bit about them?"

"I would."

"You told me that you and your husband have accepted Jesus as your Savior. A few years apart, if I heard you correctly?"

"Yes. That's right."

"That is so very important, because the tools that God gives us to use in healing begin with surrendering our lives to Him. Submission comes before restoration. Think of submission as the tool box that holds all the necessities of a Christian life lived in victory."

"That sounds interesting. Okay. Where do we go from there?"

"When we believe Jesus died on the Cross, and rose again from the grave, that's a big step of faith. The very Good News is that He not only ascended back to Heaven after that, but He is also coming back to get us again one day."

"I certainly like the sounds of that."

"For sure! I can't wait. Now, in all of that, when we get to know who Jesus is, and all He wants to give us, we can begin right where He began."

"Which is where?"

"In the book of Luke. Although what Jesus is saying in Luke was first written about Him in Isaiah 61. Let me turn there, I want to read it to you. It says, *'The Spirit of the Lord is upon me, for he has anointed me to bring Good News to the poor. He has sent me to proclaim that captives will be released, that the blind will see, that the oppressed will be set free.'* That's in Luke 4:18. As we move through this season together, the things Jesus is saying here will start to make more and more sense to you. There will come a day when you will look at this verse and understand it because you are living it."

"Really? I hope you're right."

"Really, Linda. If you are willing, we will work together and watch the Lord do these very things in your life. It is a process, and it takes some time and effort, but it is well worth it. Jesus spoke these words in the Temple when He first began His earthly ministry. He was in Nazareth, in the synagogue, and He stood up to read the Scriptures. The scroll of Isaiah was handed to Him. He found the place where this was written. He read it. Then He rolled it up and handed it back to the attendant before sitting down. Everyone was staring at Him. Then He said, *'The Scripture you've just heard has been fulfilled this very day.'* Sadly, many aren't understanding what He was reading, and therefore aren't living it out. We can be so blind. And then, our enemy, Satan, capitalizes on our ignorance of these things. He has three goals—steal, kill, and destroy our lives. Satan cannot be fought and won without Jesus—without walking in the authority we have been given. Because you and Randy have both given your heart to Jesus, you have taken the first step toward this freedom. Now we need to keep on in that direction as you learn to walk in it fully. Jesus said from the Cross, *'It is finished.'* But too many Christians are still walking around in unfinished bondage, and not understanding what is happening in their lives. Mainly what I do is walk with you into the freedom you already have. Does that make sense? Is that something you're looking for?"

"It does make sense. And yes, I was looking for something when I went forward that Sunday. But it seems like I never found it."

"You found it, there at the altar. But when you went back home, you were a baby who needed some guidance. There is a verse in James 2:19 that reads, *'You say you have faith for you believe that there is one God. Good for you! Even the demons believe this, and they tremble in terror.'* We have to do something with the faith we have been given. Put it into action! It helps to have someone teach you how to do that along the way— just like your parents taught you to eat with a fork and ride your bike. Being in the Word, joining Bible studies, and fellowshipping with other believers helps you grow up in your faith. Those who are further along in their relationship with Jesus have a responsibility to teach those being born into the family after them. You can also think of it like an older sibling helping a younger sibling. It sounds like you have spent your years as a Christian in the baby stages, never learning and growing up. I'm not saying that to put you down, in any way. I'm only saying it to make you aware of what has happened. It's not that God is less than what you hoped He would be. It's just that you opened the gift of salvation, but never learned how to use it and the tools that it comes with. Most days, your gift just sits there, unused. You've never really experienced the joy it brings to each child of God."

"I sure haven't. And I'm ready to. From what you're saying, this seems possible."

"It is," Trisha responds. "It's all right there in our Instruction Manual."

"Instruction Manual? For what?"

"For Life. Think of the Bible as our Basic Instructions Before Leaving Earth: BIBLE."

"Oh, that's funny," I say laughing.

"It is," Trisha says with a bit of laughter also. "I sometimes think of this like I do my cell phone. I don't know all that my phone is capable of, like my husband does. He reads all about it and uses every function it has. I mainly make calls and send texts. I'm missing out on a lot of what it can do, and I know it. But I also know I'm not willing to put in the effort to learn. It doesn't interest me that much. That's sort of sad. But I can live with it. On the other hand, Calvin, my husband, gets so much more out of his phone because he puts the time into learning about it. Being a Christian is the same thing, sort of, but so much more. If we really look into all the things God has gifted us with, all that's talked about in His Word, it will blow us away! He has provided so much! And yet, too many of us are only using the texting and calling functions of our lives, and not using every app available to us as Christians."

"Wow. I can't really imagine what you're talking about. But I want it. Where do I start?"

"We have already started!" Trisha says.

"What?" I respond, surprised.

"Yes. By knowing there *is* more available now, it's like Calvin telling me what my phone can do. You now can make the choice to learn and grow. Or not. It sounds like you would like to."

"Oh, yes!" I respond with enthusiasm. "I can't imagine what I've been missing. But it seems, Trisha, you're a good person to teach me what I need to know."

"Well, what comes next is the step-by-step process of learning to walk with Jesus into the freedom He died to give us. The Word of God accepts us right where we are, having us drink milk at first, until we grow up in our relationship with our Savior and begin to chew on the meat of the Gospel. The first step, you have already taken, saying 'yes' to Jesus. Now I want to ask you, have you been baptized?"

"I was, as a baby. That's one thing my parents thought was important, even though they never really went to church a whole lot."

"I see. Umm, the church you go to, where you accepted Christ...do they talk about baptism?"

"Yes. I guess. We haven't gone very much, so I really don't know much about it."

"Well, Linda, maybe that's where we will start. We'll talk about it, and teach you what it means to be baptized as an adult believer, okay? This is not to pressure you, it's just to teach you what's available on your 'cell phone,' so to speak." Trisha laughs at that. "Would you like to meet tomorrow afternoon, and talk some more? I can come by Venyce's after church. I have a meeting after second service. But I can be there about 1:00, if that works for you?"

"That works for me. I really want to thank you for taking this time with me. I hope it's not too much trouble?"

"This is no trouble at all. This is exciting for me, to get to spend time with you and show you all the 'functions' that come with Christianity!"

"Great. I'll see you about one tomorrow then. Bye for now."

"Bye, Linda."

14

LINDA

Sitting around with Venyce on Saturday night, my heart is aching. Although it's peaceful in her home, being sort of officially separated from Randy is not a peaceful place to be. I don't know what will happen with Trisha tomorrow. But I'm ready for whatever it is. I don't want to live like this anymore, in this unhappiness.

"Thanks for helping with the dishes, Linda, you didn't have to do that," Venyce says, bringing me out of the dark thoughts I was wandering through.

"Oh, of course I do. You made us such a nice dinner. And you don't have to do that either. I don't want to be a burden to you while I stay here."

"I love to cook, so it's not a burden at all. It's nice to make dinner for two again. Earl loved my cooking."

"I bet he did. Can I ask you something?"

"Sure. What is it?" Venyce says with a sweet smile on her face.

"I think it's time that I make Sunday a priority. What I mean is, give church a better try. Would you mind if I go with you in the morning?"

"You would like to go to my church? We can go to yours if you'd like. I don't mind," she says.

"No. I would like to try yours. Get a fresh new start, and hopefully make it a weekly routine."

"That's just fine with me. The first service starts at 9:30. Is that okay for you?"

"That's perfect. I'll be ready."

Venyce and I continue watching the movie, although I'm not paying much attention. My mind keeps going back to what Trisha and I talked about earlier. I'm a bit nervous, but also excited to see her tomorrow. When the movie ends, and Venyce and I chat a bit more, I find out that Venyce met Trisha at church. So, I may see her in the morning, too. I wonder about Trisha's story? Who is she? What has brought her to where she is today? I want to ask Venyce, but I don't know if I should pry.

I decide to start in slowly with, "How long have you known Trisha?"

"Oh, a good many years. We met in a Bible study there at the church. She was a very different person back then."

"What do you mean?"

"Well...how should I say this? She came from a very religious background," Venyce explains.

"Religious? Isn't she religious now?" I'm a bit puzzled.

"Of course, she is very focused on her faith and all that God has for her to do in serving His Kingdom. But in her early years, it was different."

"In what way?" I ask, not understanding the difference. I'm glad it seems Venyce is so willing to talk about this.

"I know that Trisha will share this with you as you get to know one another better, but I can tell you a little. The church she grew up in was very legalistic. There were certain ways to do things, and ways not to do them. It wasn't so much about following Jesus, as it was following the instructions of the pastor and the elders of the church. What they said was law. Of course, we are to respect those in authority. But we are also to be reading the Word for ourselves, being like the Bereans talked about in Acts 17:11, examining the Scriptures every day to see if what is being preached is true to the Word of God. Trisha lived with a hard heart, as she will tell you. She was judgmental and critical about many things. When her marriage was about to go under, she grew desperate, as many do."

"Uh, yes. I get that," I remark. "I can't believe such a godly woman would ever be having marital problems."

"Marital problems are very wide-spread, even among the Christian community. Sadly, the divorce rate among Christians is equally as high as non-Christians. Earl and I had our own struggles. Thankfully, we made it through and ended up having an even more solid marriage. It became a marriage built on the foundation of Jesus Christ. Focusing on Jesus instead of your spouse's short-comings, helps a lot!" Venyce looked at me as she said that...her face growing concerned.

"Please, don't worry about what you're saying. I know Randy and I haven't done that, and it's probably why we are where we are today. This is what I need to learn."

Venyce smiles, and continues on. "Trisha and I are very close friends, and I don't want to overstep a confidentiality here. But she is very open about her past. You will either hear it from me, from her, or others who know her and have learned through her experience. That's where testimonies really encourage others in the church—we find out that we aren't so alone in our struggles when we hear what others have gone through. Trisha will be very open about her marriage being on the rocks, not the ROCK, and how it was a lot her fault. She was very controlling, manipulative, and critical of Calvin. And she will tell you how kind and understanding he was, almost to a fault. They both had to learn how to balance their relationship. And some of the things she will be working with you on, will be the very same things that set her free to be who she is today. She was held in a lot of bondage, and when she realized that, it was the beginning of her finding her own freedom in Christ. The Trisha I know today has been set free and continues to be set free daily. I only wish Randy would seek this out and find the same kind of help you will be getting. We need to be praying for him to find his own healing. Let's do that right now."

"Okay. Yes," I say, bowing my head.

Venyce begins, "Father in Heaven, there is so much we don't know. But we know You, and we know that You can help in any and all situations. Linda is wanting Your healing in her life, and in her marriage. We pray the same for Randy. We pray that he gets to a place in life where he has had enough of himself, and he looks to You for what is missing. Bring people into his life who will lead him in a godly way. Bring a man to him who knows You well, and can pray with him and free him from the evil one who works to destroy the lives of the children of God. Soften Randy's heart. Open his heart to healing and bring Your healing touch to him very soon. We thank You Lord Jesus. Amen."

"Amen. Thank you for that, Sis. I don't know if our marriage can be repaired. But I do want Randy to find his own healing, as I find mine. Please help me remember to pray for him when it's the last thing I want to do. I know I will have waves of frustration and anger as I go through this. And I won't know what to do at times. Thank you for letting me be here with you."

"You're welcome. Like I said, Earl and I had a good marriage, but not a perfect one. Jesus is the only Perfect Bridegroom, and He will make a way when we can't see the way clear of the mess we find ourselves in."

"I'm looking forward to all that is coming. I feel a small surge of hope inside—that life could hold more than what I've experienced so far."

"I understand. Even with Earl gone, I find great joy in all that God continues to do. Maybe by you being here, I will find even further healing watching you in this process," Venyce says with a comforting smile.

"If you gain from this, that would be awesome. I think we better turn in for the night. We have church in the morning!"

"Yes, we do," Venyce says, getting up and giving me a hug. "Sleep well little Sis."

"You, too."

15

LINDA

"Oh, Venyce, church was amazing! I can't believe how many questions were answered for me this morning. Why have I not been going weekly and learning about all these things?"

"It seems it's time, Linda. I'm happy to have you here with me. And it was nice that you got to meet Trisha after service. It seems like the two of you hit it off just fine."

"I believe so. I can't wait to see her later. Where would you like to go and get some breakfast, my treat?!"

"That's sweet. How about that new pancake place over by the park? Is that okay with you?" Venyce asks.

"Yes! Perfect."

It's a beautiful morning. The sun is shining, and my heart is feeling a bit lighter today as we drive to breakfast. Yesterday was so hard. It was such a struggle to think that my marriage may be over. I don't want to be single heading into my retirement years. I always thought Randy and I would grow old together. I really do need to remember to pray for him. He needs more of Jesus in his life, as do I—the loving God I learned more about this morning. Taking a seat in a booth, coffee is poured, and I want to discuss what the pastor had to say!

"Venyce, I made some notes this morning. Can we talk about them?"

"Oh, for sure. What did you write down?" she asks.

"A lot! The pastor, what's his name again?"

"Mark," Venyce responds.

"Yes, Pastor Mark, there was so much…let's start here. He talked about why Adam and Eve were kicked out of the Garden of Eden. He said it wasn't because God was mad at them, but because He loved them. If they had eaten from the other tree. . What is it called?"

"The Tree of Life," Venyce answers.

"Yes. Of course, because if they had eaten from it, they would have lived forever. And he said that would have been a terrible thing for us. We would have lived forever in what he called a 'fallen state.' Meaning, that things would have remained hard forever, right?"

"Right," Venyce confirms.

"And so now that tree, the Tree of Life, is in Heaven, and we can eat all we want from it because life is perfect there. Redeemed, he called it. God sent them out of the Garden because He loved them. He wanted so much more for us."

"Very good. You really absorbed it," Venyce says.

"Well, I have my notes here. Another thing that was so cool; he said that God didn't make Hell for us, and God isn't the one who sends us there. God made Hell for the devil and the fallen angels, originally. But even the size of Hell was expanded it says in Isaiah 5:14. *'Sheol has enlarged itself.'* How sad is that? It was big enough for Satan and his third of the angels in the beginning. But now so many people are headed that way, too, because of rejecting Jesus. He said God doesn't send people to Hell, that it's the people's rebellion against a very loving God that sends them there. They choose Hell over Heaven. He emphasized also that Jesus never did anything other than good, but He was totally rejected and tortured to death. What is wrong with us?"

"I wonder about that myself," says Venyce. "God is made visible in creation. Think of the stars in the sky. How can anyone look up at night and not see the wonder of God? Two things collided and made all this? Really? That takes a lot more faith to believe, than that there is a Creator of all things."

"Yeah. I don't know why I've ignored the importance of this for so long. My heart is so drawn to God right now. I want to go to church every Sunday and learn more!"

"And, there are Bible studies you can join that help the learning and growing process, too," Venyce adds.

"I want to find out more about that…"

"The waffle with bacon?" the waitress offers. "And pancakes with eggs?"

"Here, and here."

"I'll pray, okay?" Venyce volunteers. "Father in Heaven, You are a good and glorious God. You are love. You are Truth. We have so much to be thankful for today, even when things can be hard. Bless this time we have together as sisters, and this food, and all those who helped to prepare it. In Jesus' name. Amen."

"Amen. Thank you, Venyce. Another thing I put in my notes here…let me find it. Oh yeah, Pastor Mark answered another question for me about those who have never had the chance to hear about all this. He asked all of us who had thought about God as a child to raise our hands. And did you see how many did, me included? He said in Romans 1, it says that God Himself showed us He is real by all the things He has made. Like you said about the stars. And that we are without excuse because we really do know God exists, but we are the ones who reject Him. We know in our conscience that He is real. I remember wondering about God as a child. I remember asking Dad if he believed in God. He flat out told me 'No.' So I didn't believe after that until I was about 12. Then I began to wonder again, and I slowly found my way to Him. I'm so glad I did. It at least got me to church a couple times a year as an adult."

"Yeah. God wasn't a big deal in our home growing up, that's for sure. I think Mom believed a little. I saw she had a Bible. But I don't know how much she ever read it," Venyce ponders.

"I don't know either. That was funny when the pastor said he had met God personally! I was like, WHAT? And then he laughed and said all believers have. We can talk to Him every day. I know I want to make more of an effort to do that. I don't know if I'll ever be able to pray as easily as you do, Venyce. But I'd like to."

"Oh, you will over time. It is hard at first. If feels awkward. But you will grow through and out of that."

"I surely hope so. Maybe you can help me?"

"Whatever you need. Right now, do you need more butter? I do!" Venyce laughs.

"Yes, I do."

After asking the waitress for more fattening stuff to put on top of our already calorie-ridden breakfast that we were greatly enjoying, we continued on with our conversation.

"I think the title of his message was something like, 'Eternity is Your Choice.' Is that right?"

"Yes, I believe so," Venyce responds.

"And that makes sense," I add, "because he talked about our free will. Now that's a big question. Why would God give us free will when He could have just demanded that we love Him? It would have been so much easier to just have Heaven as our only choice."

"It sure would have. But God is too loving to do that, and He wants us to love Him in return, doesn't He! Think about it, everyone who ends up in Heaven, when all this is said and done, will be there because they have chosen to be. No one can say they were forced into it. It makes me think about something, Linda. People wonder why God would create Satan. He did, and He didn't. He created Lucifer, and he was amazingly beautiful. The Bible says that, *'God is Light, and there is no darkness in him at all.'* It was only when Lucifer wanted to rise above God, when pride got the better of him, that he became dark and ugly, so to speak."

"Wow," I say, shaking my head. "God wants us to choose to love Him. I can't force Randy to love me, although I'd like him to. I want him to choose to love me, and to want to be with me. That makes it so much sweeter, doesn't it? I wish it didn't feel like we have fallen out of love."

"I know what you mean. But don't give up just yet. You are starting to see some things that you haven't before. It can be true of Randy, too. God is in the business of miracles. We can pray, and hope. And we will."

"Yes. We will. And now we better finish up here and get home. Trisha will be arriving soon. I'm really looking forward to seeing how that goes with her. I don't know what she has in mind. But from what you say about her, I know I can trust her."

"You can. And yes, let's head on home. I've really enjoyed this morning with you. I'm saddened about you and Randy right now. But maybe one of the good things is spending this time with you for a bit. Who knows what God has planned for that?"

Smiling, I pay the check and we head home. What a good morning it has been.

16

LINDA

Answering the door, I'm glad to be meeting with Trisha.

"Hello. Come on in," I say inviting her into the house.

"Thank you, Linda. Good to see you. Oh, hi, Venyce. Wasn't that a good sermon this morning?"

"Yes. Very. Linda and I had a great discussion over breakfast about it. Good to see you. I'm going to leave the two of you now. I have some errands to run, and then if I come back, I'll go to my room and get caught up on some reading. You both take all the time you need today."

"Thank you! I appreciate that we can meet in your home. The privacy is good," Trisha responds in such a genuine way.

Walking into the living room, I feel a bit awkward. "I don't know where you would rather sit…the kitchen or on the couches here?"

"Couches are just fine," Trisha answers, taking a seat. "This is a beautiful room…so peaceful. Let's get started by just talking some, getting acquainted a bit more with what's happening, and then we can move on from there. This is a process, and we won't hurry it."

"Okay. Would you like anything to drink?"

"Maybe just some water. Thank you," Trisha says. I think she knows I'm nervous.

Returning with the water, I sit across from Trisha. She's looking through some papers.

"Linda, I have some things I'd like to go over with you. But first, tell me a little more about yourself, and why you are interested in meeting with me. I want to make sure we are on the same page with all of this," Trisha says. "I don't want to force you into anything you're not ready for."

"Well, as I told you on the phone, I'm separated from my husband. We are both Christians, but not real strong in our faith. I was baptized as a baby. You said we might talk about that today. Uh, I don't really know what else to add to what I've already told you… I do want to move forward with you in all this, although I'm not sure what this is even supposed to look like?"

Trisha smiles again, and I notice that she is calm, which helps me be a bit more at ease.

"This doesn't have an absolute certain look to it, it's different with all people. Yes, there are steps to healing and being set free from the things in life that have bogged us down. But we always take it as the Holy Spirit leads us, and He always changes things up on us! God keeps things interesting," Trisha says, smiling. "So why don't we just start out with prayer, and go from there?"

"Sure." I'm relieved to close my eyes at this point.

Trisha begins, "Father in Heaven, You are all knowing and all loving. Thank You for bringing the two of together here today. There are things that You would like to do in Linda's life that the enemy has kept her from. Your Son, Jesus, came to set the captives free. Thank You for that, Jesus. We ask Your Holy Spirit to lead us through these times together. Show us what is needed. For apart from You, we can do nothing. All the power, all the wisdom, all the freedom, is found in the name of the Lord Jesus. We give You all the praise and glory in advance for what is to come in these sessions together, and in Linda's times alone with You. Bless this process, and help Randy to also find healing in Your mighty name, too. Amen."

"Amen." Letting out a long sigh, and looking at Trisha, she smiles and assures me this is not a scary thing. This is what Jesus has called us to.

"Jesus went out and healed the sick, Linda. He cast out demons, and He raised the dead. Is that the Jesus You think about on Sunday morning?" she asks.

"Well, not really. I guess I mostly think about Jesus in the manger as a baby, and then dying on the Cross. Probably because that's what I've heard most about when I've been in church." I'm hoping that's not the wrong answer.

"That's very good. Those two events are pivotal in our walk with Jesus. But after that, there is so much more that is very exciting and powerful. There's a lot contained in the Good News of Jesus Christ. I shared some of this with you on the phone."

"Yes. I remember."

"That little baby in the manger lived for 33 years upon this earth. We don't know a lot about Jesus in His growing up years. The Bible only mentions a few things. In Hebrews, as an adult, it says He broke the power of the devil. I'll turn there…yes, here in *2:14, 'Because God's children are human beings—made of flesh and blood—the Son also became flesh and blood. For only as a human being could he die, and only by dying could he break the power of the devil, who had the power of death.'* Most of what we know about Jesus happened during the three and a half years of His ministry. During that time, He chose 12 men to walk with Him. He taught them who He was, what He came for, and what their assignments would be when He ascended back into Heaven after His Resurrection. I hate to say it, but for the most part, His disciples didn't get it until after He died and then appeared to them for 40 days before His ascension. They seemed a little thick-headed. But we do have hindsight now, which is 20/20. And we have the Holy Spirit living in us, which they eventually did, too. They couldn't read the whole story from Genesis to Revelation like we can. They only had the books of the Torah…and Jesus. So, I wonder if any of us would have done any better? Probably not."

"I guess you're right about that. I probably would have missed it, too. And sadly, I don't read the Bible I do have."

"Many don't. But that will come. When you find out about the great love of your Savior, and how the Father cares for you, it will become more of a draw for you. I used to let my Bible sit and gather dust, too. Now, it is very worn."

"Funny. It makes me think about the sign in my husband's office about having a Bible that is falling apart," I add.

"Oh, yes. I've heard that quote," Trisha responds. "Can I tell you a little about myself, Linda? It might help you to understand more of where we will be heading in this process."

"Of course. Please. Go ahead."

"I'd like to start with what got me to today, to sitting with you. I don't want to go into all the details. But I was truly needing God's healing touch in my own life. I have a wonderful husband. He is very patient, and kind. He has loved God his whole life, and he has always been drawn to reading God's Word. He walks in a lot of freedom. When we married, I came out of a very religious background. I was a rule follower, more than a Jesus' follower. I was in bondage and didn't even know it. I would see Calvin, and how he was, and wonder why I wasn't able to do what he did, have his joy. I thought maybe it was because of the things I had been through in childhood. But one day I asked Calvin about that. I asked him if that would always hold me back? He could see I was growing hungry for more. He knew I had to want it, and he waited for that time to come. He began to encourage me to do what you're doing today…sit with someone—learn about the goodness of God—about the authority we walk in as disciples of Jesus Christ. Little by little, I learned and grew into the fullness, the abundant life that Jesus said would be ours. Oh, don't get me wrong, it wasn't overnight. I was a hard nut to crack. I thought I knew! And until I humbled myself and submitted myself to God, it was like moving thick sludge through my veins. When I was told forgiveness was huge in this, and repentance, I balked at that. I had people I knew I could never forgive. And I knew I was a good person. What would I need to repent of? Lovingly, and gently, my mentor taught me that without forgiveness, I was stuck. Without repentance, it would be nearly impossible to understand the true meaning of Jesus' death on the Cross for my sins. She taught me about the power in the blood of Jesus. We went through it all, including restitution I needed to attend to. Eventually I confessed so many things I never even realized were sins in my life. Something as simple as playing with a Ouija board as a child."

"What? A Ouija board is sinful? I got one as a Christmas present from my parents when I was ten," I interject.

Trisha smiles again, saying, "Yes. So many of us did. Our parents didn't know that things like that can open a door to our soul that we should keep shut. Proverbs 4:23 says, *'Guard your heart above all else, for it determines the course of your life.'* We shouldn't be looking to a Ouija board, or anything in that realm, for knowledge of our future. It goes against the Word of God and can open our heart to dark things that are better left outside our 'door.' As we pray and ask the Holy Spirit to reveal these things to us, He will, and we can begin to clean out our Temple by confessing and receiving God's forgiveness—just like Jesus did with the money changers and merchants. Our Temples, our bodies, should be a place of prayer, too. But many times, we have thieves that have come to steal, kill and destroy our lives. We will get into all of that. But for now, why I'm telling you this is to let you know I didn't start out where I am today. It took someone to show me what was going on in my life, and what is available in my walk with Jesus. Slowly, but surely, I found out what Paul did, to be content with little or with much. I understood why I did the things I didn't want to do and didn't do the things I wanted to. Paul's struggles are very real for all of us—even the thorn in his side. But Paul found the answer, and we can, too, if we want to. The Bible says in Matthew 7, those who ask, will be given. Those who seek, will find. Those who knock, the door is opened. When we go after the things of God, He will gladly be found by us! We can live in more freedom than we ever thought possible, and not just because we live in the land of the free. This is not about our external circumstances, this is about our internal transformation preparing us for all types of 'weather.' Inner healing is so important for all of us. For so long, even as a Christian, I thought something was wrong with me. I was so relieved to find out that some of my greatest struggles were due to demonic spirits, and that Jesus provided a way to escape the bondage I was living in."

"I am very interested in all that you're saying. And thank you for letting me know that I'm not alone in where I'm starting from. Seeing and hearing you today gives me great hope. What do we do now?"

"You are welcome. We will begin today giving God all the praise and glory ahead of time for what He has in store for you!"

17

LINDA

As the afternoon passes, Trisha explains some basic things to me that I have been missing. I didn't realize how important baptism is. She tells me there is something very powerful that happens in the spiritual realm when we go under the water in full immersion and rise up again alive in Christ. She says it's not what gets us to Heaven. But it is an outward expression of what we already believe about Jesus on the inside—and that baptism is God's idea, not man's. She reads out of Matthew 28:19, *"Therefore, go and make disciples of all the nations, baptizing them in the name of the Father and the Son and the Holy Spirit."* Trisha explains baptism as an act of practical obedience, identifying us with Christ. Even Jesus was baptized by John. She tells me she will help me get that set up when I'm ready to take that step and encourages me to be in prayer about it. When I confess to her it makes me nervous, being up in front of others, she assures me I am not alone in that. But it will bring a peace to my heart by being obedient. It symbolizes new life.

"I would like to read a portion of Scripture to you about this, okay?" Trisha asks respectfully.

"Sure. I'm open to hearing about it," I answer.

"Romans 6:3 says, *'Or have you forgotten that when we were joined with Christ Jesus in baptism, we joined him in his death? For we died and were buried with Christ by baptism. And just as Christ was raised from the dead by the glorious power of the Father, now we also may live new lives.'* Baptism is such a wonderful way to leave the past behind and get on with the abundant life God is calling us to. It's our resurrection to a new life until our heavenly life begins."

"I'm not sure that I'm ready, although it sounds very important. Don't I need to learn more about all this before taking the 'plunge' so to speak?"

"That's a good question. But let me just say, there will never come a day when you feel you know enough about all this. In fact, the more you know, the more you know you don't know. We will spend our whole lives growing and learning and changing. If we look at the Ethiopian Eunuch and Philip in Acts eight, we will see that the Eunuch didn't understand everything he was reading. The Holy Spirit sent Philip to explain some things to him, and especially about the Good News of Jesus. As they rode along, the Eunuch spotted some water and asked Philip if he could be baptized. Philip baptized him right there and then, and then Philip quickly disappeared out of his life. Was the Eunuch fully educated on the things of God? Of course not. But he was on his way, and if we were able to follow up with him later in his life, we would see that his faith continued to grow and mature from that day onward. The Bible says he went on his way rejoicing."

"So, I can do this baptism thing right away, and it will stick?"

"Oh, yes. God will see your act of obedience and honor it all the days of your life."

"I will give it a lot of thought."

"Linda, I want to talk with you about forgiveness a bit more before we finish up today. This is a step you will do a lot of on your own. There are probably people in your life that you know right off the bat could be on that list, and then there are people you have probably long forgotten about. Either way, it will be good to make a list, prayerfully, of all those you have harbored any bitterness or resentment against. Even the littlest things will matter in this cleansing process. Start with the big ones if you want, those that have hurt you deeply, and eventually you can move to the guy who cut you off in traffic yesterday. Write down the names, and the offenses. Then one by one, pray through them telling God you forgive them, by name, and what they have done. And let me stop here, because I can see the look on your face. I know, this is a hard step. But it is an important first one. This is not saying that what they did didn't hurt you or that it wasn't terrible. This isn't even about how you feel about it or them. This is about giving all of that to God to deal with and letting Him heal your memories and feelings over time, however long it takes. This is a decision you are making, a choice, one that will begin to set *you* free. This is for you, not them. They won't even know it is happening. But your heart, soul, mind, and spirit will. Forgiveness will be pivotal in setting you free."

"Uh...I don't know. This makes me so fidgety just thinking about it. I guess I can start with Randy, huh?"

"Randy would be a good place to start, of course. Remember, this doesn't mean you have to run right over there and repair your marriage. This is about repairing your damaged heart...putting your own oxygen mask on first. Let God take care of the rest," Trisha explains. "This doesn't have to be done by tomorrow. I want to give you some time to work through this list. You can let me know when you're ready for what follows. But I have to tell you, without forgiveness, there is no freedom."

"It's that big of a deal, huh?"

"That big!"

"Okay. Let me get a piece of paper. I want to make a note of what I'm supposed to do. But can I call you if I have some questions?" I ask.

"Of course you can. Anytime. Please do," Trisha responds warmly.

"Okay, forgive...anything else?"

"As you work through this, your side of these things is going to come up, so do the same for yourself. Ask God's forgiveness toward you for things that you have done that might be an offense to Him. There again, ask the Holy Spirit to reveal these things to you. He will. When it comes into your mind, write it down. Then pray over it. Sometimes this takes fasting for clarity in these things."

"What is that exactly?" I ask Trisha.

"Fasting and praying is a way to cause a hunger in our soul for the things of God—to submit to God in a deeper way. There are different types of fasting. Sometimes giving up a certain food for a length of time. Sometimes going half a day, or a full day, or however long God puts it on your heart, to be without food. It's very personal between you and God. Once I gave up chocolate for 40 days as I prayed for my nephew. There are many ways to do this. We can talk more about it as we move along."

"Okay. I hear what you're saying. This is all very new to me, Trisha."

"That's okay. We will take this at God's speed. There is no great hurry. Once you have accepted Jesus as Your Lord and Savior, the rest is a process of growing and learning through our life...and Linda..." Trisha stops there.

"Yes?" I say, looking at her.

"Remember after asking for forgiveness, receive it. This is very important. You don't have to confess the same thing over and over, 20 to 100 times. God hears you the first time, forgives you right away, and then He removes it as far as the east is from the west. Don't remind Him about it, because He's forgotten it after your confession and repentance. Repentance simply means you are in agreement with God about what His Word has to say about it. It is different than remorse. This is about agreeing with God. We can be sorry about something but still not want to make any changes in our lifestyle or even in the words we speak. After you do this, leave these things there at the foot of the Cross—turn and walk away. They have now been covered by the blood of Jesus, and you have been washed clean."

I shake my head, writing that down, too. I know I am going to forget all this and am starting to feel a little overwhelmed. Trisha picks up on it.

"Let's do something that will help you for today. How does that sound?" she asks.

"I'd like that."

"I want you to just sit back, relax. I have some anointing oil here, and if it's okay I will put a little on your forehead."

"Sure. That's fine."

"I anoint you today, Linda, in the name of the Father, the Son, and the Holy Spirit," Trisha says this gently as she applies the oil.

"That smells nice. What does it do?"

"Good question. We are God's sheep. In John 10:14, it says, *'I am the good shepherd. I know my own and my own know me.'* Sheep need anointing oil on their head to keep away the infestation of flies, ticks, and such—they can even get into its brain, eating it away."

"Oh, yuck!"

"I know, it's not a nice thing to think about. This eating away can cause the sheep so much pain that they will bang their skull on rocks to ease the suffering. The oil protects the sheep from infestation, and also helps heal any wounds they might have. It also helps when two sheep get into a scuffle. They will then more glance off each other rather than hurt one another. So, in anointing you today, as one of the Father's sheep, it is a protection and a healing step before praying many times. It can also help in revealing ways the enemy is attacking you, manifesting what is not of God going on in and around you."

"Thanks. I never knew any of this."

"Let's go ahead and pray now. Close your eyes again, and let's spend some time with God, okay?"

"Okay," I answer, taking in a deep breath.

"Yes. Breathe in and let it out slowly a few times…there you go. What I'm going to do now is ask the Holy Spirit to bring a memory to your mind—something He'd like to heal today. We all have wounds. Many of us have never taken the time, or known how to go about this inner healing process. What we are going to do may cause some emotional pain in the process. But the end result will be worth it."

"Okay," I say, wondering how much pain she might be talking about.

"Holy Spirit, help Linda to think back, and recall something that has caused her, maybe, to be troubled in her life. Bring to her something that needs Your healing touch today. Show her if it was a person, a trauma, maybe there was some verbal or physical abuse, an incident with Randy?

Is it something that she's not proud of that she did? Whatever it is, bring that darkness into the light, Lord Jesus. I'm going to give you some time now Linda, no rush."

As I sit here, I feel a peace about what Trisha is doing. It isn't long, and a thought comes to me. It causes me to almost suck in a deep breath quickly, and Trisha can tell I'm remembering something.

"Linda, if a memory has come to you, just know that it's because God wants to heal you there. It may be painful. But the pain will only be for a short time. You will remember this incident after today, but it will no longer have the same hurt associated with it."

"It's a sad memory. The day my grandma died, and I got the call..."

"Okay. That's a good place to start. Grief is hard. We're going to pray together about that now. Holy Spirit, thank You for revealing this painful time in Linda's life. There is still hurt that hasn't been resolved it seems, but You would like to heal this wound in Linda. Thank You for that. And if any darkness pierced Linda's soul that day, causing her to be in bondage, then we will be seeking Your removal of that, also. It has no place in your life, Linda. Please say this after me, Father, I give this memory to You, and ask You to heal my heart from the lingering sadness..."

I repeat each of these things as Trisha continues to pray: "Holy Spirit help me to release this memory to You. I choose to be healed in Jesus' name, and to grieve as one who does have Hope in the eternal life You provide. Thank you that You are healing this memory."

Trisha then asks me to be still as she starts in with a firm voice saying, "I command all the shock, loneliness and whatever else pierced Linda's soul on that day to go right now in Jesus' name. I command any dark spirit that was associated with this, to this memory, and any memory of family dysfunction during that time to be healed also. We thank You, Lord Jesus, for healing Linda in this area. Jesus, You bind up the brokenhearted. I declare that the enemy can never cause Linda anguish over this memory again. She is healed in Your powerful name, Lord Jesus. Now say this after me, Linda... I thank You that I can remember the life my grandma lived now, being healed from the pain of her passing, and walking in the freedom Your death and resurrection provide. Amen."

Praying that after Trisha, I'm sensing some freedom from the hurt that has weighed on me for so many years. Trisha sits for a bit after this, giving me time to absorb it as I wipe away some tears. Eventually looking at Trisha, I smile with a new peace for the first time, I think, since she arrived. After praying all this, I'm thinking about my grandma again—but now it's a day when she was making cookies and she let me eat the dough off the spoon, chocolate chips and all.

"Wow. Something has changed in me, Trisha. I feel lighter, and a good thought came to me. I haven't been able to think about my grandma all these years without having a heaviness in the way she passed away. It was sudden, so unexpected, that I never got to say good-bye. After what we just did, it seems to not matter as much now—she's okay, and I'm okay. She's happy in Heaven, because she really loved Jesus and I can be glad for her. How does this work so quickly? It's like I see things differently all of a sudden."

Trisha smiles and nods at me. "God is so very good. We often don't realize there is a spiritual battle going on—many times it appears as a deceptive fog around our thinking. I don't want to over complicate it for you today, but let's just say, any time the enemy, Satan, can get his claws in us, he will. When a great shock comes, sometimes he will use that as an entrance into our house...our soul and/or body. The soul is our mind, will, and emotions..."

"Uh, wait! Are you saying he comes into me? I don't know much about this, but I have heard that Christians can't be possessed. Is that what you're talking about? Isn't that like the old movie with the girl whose head was spinning around?" I am starting to freak out a bit.

"Let me explain," Trisha says compassionately. "No, it's not like that movie. That is Hollywood. This is the Holy Spirit. Two totally different things. That movie has scared so many people. What a scheme of the enemy to get us to run away, or ignore, what is going on. With the battle between God and Satan, we need not fear, not one bit. God is so much more powerful. And we can't be possessed. You have heard absolutely right—that would mean ownership. The word in the Bible is more correctly translated as *demonized*. Think of it this way. If a thief breaks into your house, he doesn't own your house. But he can be there stealing, killing and destroying it until he's gotten out. So many don't acknowledge the break in, and don't understand the weapons we've been given to deal with this enemy that's warring against our souls."

"Well, that makes sense. And I'd want him out as quickly as possible. I'd be calling the cops!"

"Exactly, Linda! But instead of calling the cops, we call on the name of the Lord Jesus Christ! And we, then, soon realize anything that's come against us, like with your grandma's passing, can be *overcome* by the blood and power of Jesus. He's the best Cop ever!! Remember Hebrews 2:14, Jesus broke the power of the devil. All we have to do is what you and I just did—call on His name, tell the thief to get out, and we can be set free. What came into your life, the sadness of your grandma's passing, is very real. Grief is real, and the Bible doesn't tell us not to grieve. It tells us we are not to grieve as one who has no Hope, because we have the Hope of Jesus. Satan would like us to get stuck in our grief, and he will even send his army our way, tying us up and holding us in the bondage of sadness and hopelessness—sometimes for the rest of our lives depending on the loss. Jesus came to set the captives free from hopelessness, and so much more. Hollywood has made this into a spooky thing. It's not. In Luke 9, Jesus called His disciples together and gave them power and authority to cure diseases. He wanted them to tell people the Kingdom of God was among them, and they were to drive out demons with this power and authority. The reason they had to drive them *out,* is because they had gotten *in!* Just like that thief. And I speak firmly when telling them to go, because I want them to know we mean business. Jesus even raises the dead in Scripture. Honestly, once I'm in Heaven, I'd like to stay there."

"That's pretty powerful talk. I do feel better since we prayed. That's for sure. I don't know about all this other stuff. I guess I will learn in time."

"You will, Linda. This has been a lot today. You have some things to work on when I leave, but what we just did was so that you could experience a taste of the freedom that is available in all areas of your life. We all have wounds that need to be healed. We all have garbage that has come upon us that we carry through each day. All this is, is calling the garbage truck to come by and pick up the cans we set out for it. If we keep the garbage cans in the backyard, behind the closed fence, it will stay there and fill up to overflowing. As it piles higher and higher, it will become overwhelming and we'll probably just want to run away from it! But God is saying don't run away, face it, get it out there where you can see it and let Me set you free from the mess that's been created by the enemy. Linda, the garbage truck comes by once a week. So, what do you say we do this once a week for a while and see how it goes…if that works for you? Each week, we will discover new things to get rid of. And after a while, there will come more of the aroma of Christ instead of the stench of this world."

"It sounds interesting. I think I'm ready for this. I know I have things I need to do, and I will do my best. I really appreciate the time you are taking with me. I do feel better, even now, about my grandma, and the hope of what this whole process will bring. Like I said, I may need to call you…"

"That is just fine. I welcome your calls," Trisha says kindly.

"Okay. I will work on this forgiveness stuff. Do Sundays work for you? I don't want to take time away from your husband," I ask a bit nervously.

"Calvin is actually gone right now. He travels for business sometimes and he is on a long assignment in Idaho. I fly out there and spend time with him when he is gone for like six months at a time. So, Sundays are fine for me, right now, if that works for you?"

"It does."

"Okay then. Why don't we finish with a prayer of thanks and then see how Venyce is doing. I heard her come in a while ago." Trisha begins to pray, "Father, You are so good. Thank You, Holy Spirit, for leading us through this time. You are the amazing Counselor, and we can't do this without You. It wouldn't even be authorized without You. Please help Linda during the week, give her the strength she needs to work through forgiveness, finding the freedom You have offered to all of us. We give You all the praise and glory in this process. In the name of our Lord Jesus. Amen."

"Amen."

Getting up and giving Trisha a hug, I feel relief that we have begun, although I know there is so much yet to come. I wonder if any of this would work for Randy? I need to really keep praying for him, that's for sure!

18

RANDY

It's Saturday morning and Linda is really gone. After the *storm* of her return last night from Chicago, something *has* changed, just like that voice I heard. I'm just not sure how, when, or what I'm supposed to do about this now. Divorce? Is this really happening? Walking into the kitchen, I don't exactly feel single. It seems more like Linda is still out of town. But as I sit down at the kitchen table, I wonder…is this my life now? Am I to be a single man? Kids grown? On my own? Maybe I will like this? I don't have to think about what Linda wants, wonder where she is, if she will call, and will I answer? Maybe it's time to be a true loner? Do my job. Come home. Watch sports. Go to bed. Repeat the next day. If she had been more understanding of my needs, maybe this could have worked. She never understood me anyway. I was never appreciated by her, or the kids. They never even call now to say, "Hey, thanks Dad for all the years you supported me." They act like those years never existed. I've had it with all of them! Done! Being on my own might be the best thing that's happened to me. I'm just going to live my life and let them all live theirs.

Even though I eventually walk back upstairs seemingly settled on all this, satisfied that my responsibilities toward all of them could be over, I'm not totally satisfied either. It seems lonely, while also freeing. I'm angry, while also happy. Bored, yet occupied. Which is it? Is this what I want? Will this be the life I've been searching for? Is this really the "change" God was talking about?

———◆◆◆◆◆———

As the weeks pass by, I barely see Linda. She went to Venyce's and only comes by to pick up things from time to time. I'm not normally home when she does. I don't know if she's filing divorce papers or not. I don't ask her. It's easier to just ignore it all and go on with my life. Even though I don't like my job, I bury myself in it more and more, hoping it will be enough. But sadly, my heart's not in it. My heart's not in anything. Even baseball is losing its appeal. Who cares about batting averages and homeruns? It all seems to make little sense in the grand scheme of things.

One night while flipping through my phone, I see Eric's name. I haven't given him a second thought. I've really had no interest. Do I now? I fiddle with my phone a while, stalling. I don't really want to call him. It's too weird. And I don't really want to talk to anyone about my life. But for some strange reason, I push his number. He answers…

"Eric here. What's up?" he says.

"Hi. It's Randy. You called me a few weeks back."

"Hi, Randy. How ya doin?"

"Uh, I don't know. I don't even know why I'm calling you. I really didn't mean to," I stammer out the words.

"Oh. Well, now that you did, want to talk?" he asks without a hint of hesitation.

"I don't know." I'm not knowing what to say.

"Want me to start?" Eric asks.

"Sure. I guess."

"I could tell you a little about how I met Dennis. Is that cool with you?"

"I guess." I don't know that I'm interested, but it's easier than me having to talk.

"Dennis and I were hanging out quite a bit a couple years back. Want to know why?"

"I guess." I wonder how many times I'm going to say the same thing over and over. I sound like a dimwit.

"Dennis had come to the end of himself. His life was a mess, and he wouldn't mind me telling you this. He had withdrawn from most everyone he knew, and his wife and kids pretty much had disowned him. I met him at a soccer match for our kids. We got to talking on the sidelines. He wasn't really much interested talking that day either, but everyone can use a listening ear from time to time."

"Uh huh." That was an unintelligent response, I think to myself.

"What Dennis began to tell me reminded me of myself years ago. I was…well, I was a mean guy. I hated most everyone, and I didn't care that I did. I had someone come into my life that helped me figure out what was going on. When I told Dennis that, he got curious. We ended up meeting later for a pizza, and he told me more about his life. That's where we started, and he's come a long way since then. He's found there's more to life than unhappiness and loneliness. There's a whole big world out there that's waiting for what he has to offer."

"Which is what?" I finally ask, beyond *uh-huh* and *I guess*.

"The way he's been gifted. Dennis is a smart guy. He's talented in many ways. But he was buried under so much heaviness, he could barely see the light of day. And he didn't know how to get up and start to breathe again. He lost himself somewhere along the way, and he didn't even realize he was lost. He just thought that's how life is…we get older, life gets harder, and then we die."

"Oh. I can't say as I disagree with that," I respond.

"You're not alone…many think that way. I did. Dennis did, and now here we are. I don't think it's any accident that you called me today. Want to tell me a little about yourself, Randy?" Eric asks.

"Oh, I don't know…where would I start? Take Dennis' story, change the names and dates, and you pretty much have me. But here's the catch, I don't know that I care all that much. My wife has left me, and I don't even really miss her. I don't even know if I love her anymore…or if I have the capacity to love. I'm just empty of feeling….well, other than frustration, anger, and disappointment. Those are the emotions I seem to run on most days."

"Join the human race, Randy. If we took a poll, there are many who run on those emotions, and some even darker. Talk about an empty gas tank. Don't you wonder what we're all doing on this planet, anyway? What's the point? Why have we been put here? To do what? And why?" Eric asks.

"Those are good questions. Don't tell me you have the answers, because I'm pretty sure I won't believe you."

Eric laughs. He has a good hearty laugh. He seems sure of himself, and not put off by my grumpiness. Maybe this guy isn't such a bad dude after all. Just as I'm thinking that, Eric changes direction on me…

"I say we get together, Randy. Just like I did with Dennis. Talk over a pizza somewhere soon—see if there might be more to your story, just like there was to Dennis'? What do you think?"

"I don't know. Seems kinda crazy to meet a friend of a friend, to talk about life. Who does that? We're guys. We like to keep to ourselves. Not explore the things our women do. They're the talkers. I mean, try and shut them up! Makes me nuts. We're more the hang-backers. At least I am. Linda…that's my wife, she's the one who always wants to dive into this stuff. I always hated it. Talk about feelings…seriously? I don't think so." I can feel myself getting uptight and done with this conversation.

"I getcha. Well, I'm not here to push. I'm here to listen. If you ever do want to meet up, you have my number. Give me a call. And hey, maybe call Dennis someday. He said you have helped him."

"Me? How?"

"That's something you'll need to talk to him about. I gotta go now. But thanks for giving me a ring. Let me know if you ever want to hang out."

"Okay. Yeah. Thanks. Bye."

"Bye, Randy."

Hanging up the phone, I feel like I have this hole in me all of a sudden—that something is missing. Do I wish I'd said yes to Eric? Is that it? That's too strange. I don't even know the guy. But there was something very calming about him. And he didn't push me. In fact, he hung up before I might have been ready. That was a switch for me. I'm usually the guy who gets the other person off the phone as quickly as possible. I don't want to think about this anymore.

19

RANDY

The months are adding up and nothing is changing. In fact, it seems worse. Linda has basically moved most of her things in with her sister, Venyce. The house is getting messy, with a capital *M*! I think I need to hire a housekeeper. I thought maybe Linda would see it when she stops by and take care of some of it. That's not happening.

The neighbor's house sold, and some new people moved in. It's a family with two little kids. Not that I care, but I saw them running around when the moving truck got there. Now I get to hear their screaming and playing around in the backyard. Maybe I should move?—that thought overwhelms me.

Thinking back, this all really started to unravel when I didn't have the clean shirt I wanted. And now, I have to wash *all* my shirts. Did it start there though? That would be crazy to think it did. This is not about a shirt. It's about how unreasonable Linda is. She walked out, and for no good reason, really. Why? Because I'm not as talkative as she wants me to be? Because I get tired and just want to watch the ballgame when I get home from work? I didn't cause her any grief. She could do her own thing. In fact, I was glad when she did. She was out of my hair that way. Good riddance. I'm better off on my own.

Glancing through DuckDuckGo.com for cleaning services, I locate one that looks okay. I give them a call. They said they can come in a few days to give me an assessment. That's one thing taken care of. I think I'll go...

Now, who's that at the door? I haven't heard the doorbell ring except for packages in a long while.

Walking to answer it, I do remember that I ordered a new part for the computer. That must be it. But when I open the door, there stands my new neighbor. I don't know his name. I just recognize him from trying to avoid him when I get home from work.

"Hey, I'm Mike from next door. We haven't actually met, he says, holding out his hand. I shake it, begrudgingly.

"Hey."

"This package was delivered to our house by accident," Mike says.

"Oh. Okay, thanks," I say, taking it from him, hoping I can shut the door quickly. But Mike is in mid-sentence by now and I can't be that rude. My mom did teach me better than that.

"We're having a BBQ later, and my wife and I wondered if you'd like to come over. Got some good steaks to grill, and…"

I cut him off. "No. No thanks. Got some stuff to do."

"Oh, well, if you change your mind when you smell them cooking, you're still welcome. We've invited a few other friends, and there will be plenty to go around."

"Thanks. But no."

I can see the look on Mike's face, wondering what kind of a person would turn down a grilled steak? He doesn't ask though. He turns to go, giving me a small wave of his hand. Then he stops, looks me in the eye and says, "Nice meeting you. If you ever need anything, don't hesitate."

I shake my head, give him a nod, and shut the door.

I do smell the steaks grilling later. Part of me wants to go over and get one. But part of me wants to have nothing to do with the party of people that are laughing and joking over the fence. I can hear them.. and the splashes in the pool…kids yelling. What a racket! No, no steak is worth having to put up with the people I'd have to be nice to. Maybe I'll just go to the store and get my own steak.

With the phone ringing, and the kids screaming, I go into the house to answer it. I can see who it is, and not that I really want to talk to him, I answer it anyway.

"Hey, Eric."

"Hey, Randy. How ya doin'?"

"I'm okay. Hungry. The neighbors are grilling steaks, and I can smell them." I don't want to tell Eric I was invited.

"Oh, man. That's torture when we're hungry."

"Yeah."

"Listen. Irma is out of town, and I've been wondering what to do for dinner. I don't want to bug you, but it's been a few months since we talked. And maybe the timing is good. How about we go over to the Joe's Steak House and fill that hunger?"

The silence before I answer is extended. Eric doesn't interrupt it. It feels strange. But he waits… I eventually give him a weak answer.

"I guess."

Eric probably wonders if my vocabulary extends much past that.

"Great," he responds. "What do you say, around 5:30? Beat the dinner crowd?"

"Uh. Yeah. That's fine. I'll meet you there." I don't want Eric coming over to my place.

"Sounds good! See you at 5:30 at Joe's."

How did I get into this? Mentioning that steak, and now meeting with Eric! This is really not how I want to spend my evening. Why didn't I just say no. I'm busy. Another day. But I didn't, and now I'm stuck meeting with a friend of a friend who's not really even in my life much anymore. This is craziness.

Doing my laundry for the umpteenth time, I'm reminded that I'm alone. Really alone. I haven't talked to the kids in a long time, Linda barely speaks when she does come by, which is rarely. Is this the bulk of it? Life? Is this how it goes? My thoughts are dismal again… We grow old, people split up, kids go their way, and we die a lonely death. Where is God in that scenario? Not that I've thought of God much lately. I still see the cars at the church on the corner. But I haven't gone back there again. Those people are too strange for me. And now Eric…how strange will he be? I know he's a God lover. I can tell by how he talks. And he probably wants to tell me how good God is, what He can do for me, how I can be happy. Really? Happy? I don't think this world is a happy place. Just do your job, shut up, grin and bear it until your six feet under. I wonder who will turn up at my funeral? What will they say? I heard the other day that in an obituary it was said, "The pain in our neck feels better now." Is that what my family will say about me? Why not? I'm not much good to them or anyone it seems.

I guess I better finish that laundry so I can meet with Eric. What torture this is going to be! I hope the steak is good. Joe's usually has some pretty good food. Maybe it will be nice to not eat alone. I hope Eric doesn't talk too much.

20

RANDY

It looks like Eric is out front standing by the door when I pull into the parking lot of Joe's. If that's him, he's an on-time guy. It feels like my feet are dragging as I head across the parking lot toward this stranger. This really does seem more like torture than fun. I should have never agreed to this.

"Hey, are you Randy?" he says as I get close.

"Yeah. You Eric?"

"Sure am," he says, reaching out to shake my hand. "Nice to meet you."

"Yeah. You, too," I say, not really meaning it.

Getting seated in a booth, it feels more than strange. I don't like it at all. Eric is talking, but I'm not really listening. I'm looking around the restaurant only adding in an occasional "Uh-huh." Once we've put in our order, I notice that Eric isn't saying much now either. It couldn't be more awkward as we both spend more time looking at the game on TV than connecting with each other. I'd like to forget about the sirloin I just asked for, and head for the door. That's when something strange happens.

"Hi. I'm Willie, the manager here at Joe's." We both look up to see a very tall, very thin man of about 55 standing at our table. "I don't mean to interrupt, but I'm spending some time with all our patrons tonight to get a better feel for what's happening in our restaurant. I have a few questions for you, if you wouldn't mind before your dinner comes. I can offer you dessert on us for your time. Would you be interested?"

Eric looks at me, and I stare back at him. As if being with Eric isn't bad enough, now Willie wants to join in? But then, why not. Maybe it will be a good distraction.

"Uh, sure. I'm in," I say.

"Me, too," says Eric.

"Mind if I pull up a chair? This won't take too long," Willie asks.

"That's fine," Eric answers.

I'm thinking, this is really getting weirder by the moment. Now there's three of us?

Willie goes through some random questions about have we been here before? What we remember most from our last visit? How the service is, etc? And then this is where I see something happen that I can't say as I've ever experienced before. Looking at the two of us, Willie asks a question I'm not prepared for, although Eric seems to be.

"This is totally off the radar," he says. "But I've just gotta ask you guys what it is that brought you to Joe's tonight? And I don't mean the food, the ambiance, or the service. I mean this in another way. There's something different sitting here with you," Willie says.

Eric looks at me, and I look down at the table. I don't even know what I'm doing here, so I don't have a clue what to say to that. Eric takes in a deep breath, and lets it out slowly, as Willie waits for one of us to answer.

"Willie, let me ask you a question, if you don't mind," Eric eventually says.

"Hey, sure. What is it?" Willie answers.

"Do you know about those in Biblical days who would draw an arc in the dusty trail when coming upon a stranger?"

"Uh, yes, as a matter of fact I do," Willie responds, drawing an imaginary arc on the table cloth.

I'm watching now as Eric looks Willie in the eye, and then draws another imaginary arc underneath where Willie just placed his. Both men then smile at one another and reach out to shake hands. They give a hearty laugh, and I feel like I'm a fly on the wall...a wall of confusion.

"I thought so," Willie says, nodding his head. There was just a different vibe I was getting from you than the other tables I've been to so far tonight.

"Good to meet you, brother," Eric responds, smiling.

"Hey, do you guys know each other from another time and place?" I ask. "Did you go to school together?"

"No. Not exactly," Eric says. "What we're referring to here is something that happened thousands of years ago. You might come upon someone on the dusty trail, and you never knew who was friend or foe? Mainly, were they a follower of Jesus? When one would draw an arc in the dirt, and the other responded in finishing it to make what we know today as the fish you will see on the back of cars, the two travelers would then feel safe in sharing their faith in Jesus with each other. We don't deal with deathly persecution in the U.S. today, so we don't have to be quite so wary. Although, we are persecuted for what we believe many times. But in other countries, it can mean your life, as it could in Biblical days. I was just reading in Mark this morning about the disciples and how following Jesus was going to cost them their life. All of them were martyred except one, and in horrific ways—burned in oil, hung upside down on a cross, flogged, beaten. It was a dangerous time. But even in the last decade 900,000 Christians have been killed because of their faith in Jesus Christ."

"And people in the workplace have to be careful with where and when we share Jesus," Willie adds. "I can't just walk up to a table and start talking about the Good News of Jesus Christ to our patrons here. But there are times, like tonight, when I could sense the Holy Spirit was at this table—that God was working here, and I didn't want to miss the opportunity to tune into it. Yes, these questions about the restaurant are my job. But meeting with the people who come in here, and sometimes being able to go beyond that and hear about their love for Jesus, or share my love for Jesus with them, adds to the excitement of this job."

"Boy, I getcha. It's hard work to be a man of God sometimes—trying to share Jesus, and still keep it politically correct at the same time. How about you, Randy?" Eric asks, now looking at me.

"Uh, it's not...I don't...I don't know," is about all I can say.

"Hey, I don't mean to put you on the spot. Dennis told me you are a Christian," Eric says.

"Oh. I am. It's just that I don't make a big deal out of it. Work is work, and church is church," I say.

Willie seems to know it's time to move along as he says, "Well, I don't mean to keep you guys much longer. Your dinner will be here soon, and I don't want that getting cold. And remember, dessert is on me tonight. Just let your waiter know you talked with me, and he will know about it. Nice meeting you guys, and please come back soon. God Bless!"

"God bless you, Willie. Thanks. I hope our answers to your work questions have been a help, and it's always good to meet another brother," Eric says.

As Willie walks away, our waiter comes with dinner. Perfect timing, and I'm relieved. I don't know where our conversation will go from here, but I'm feeling hungrier than wanting to talk. Thankfully, Eric dives into his steak, too, and the conversation is kept to a minimum for a while. Oh, Eric talks about his wife and the kids a bit, but nothing much. Watching the TV from where we're sitting eases being here with someone I don't know. Thank God for baseball, I think to myself.

21

RANDY

"Great catch!" Eric says enthusiastically, as we watch an outfielder practically climb the wall like a super hero as he's going for the ball.

"Yeah! That was awesome!" I agree.

The food disappears from our plates. After taking a look at the dessert menu, we put in our order. We then get a chance to talk about the game some as it continues to play on the screen. It turns out Eric is a big baseball fan, so it's easy to talk with him about it. Maybe I can get out of here with just that and not have to go into anything that's uncomfortable. Although there's a part of me that would like to talk about the junk of life.

"This pie is awesome. I've never had dessert here before. I'm glad Willie came by our table," Eric says in his up-beat way. I wonder about this guy.

"Yeah. Pretty good stuff. I miss..." I stop there. Do I really want to tell him I miss Linda's cooking? And especially her desserts. I don't think so.

Eric looks at me but doesn't say anything. Now I feel like I have to say something. But I sure don't want to.

"Look, Eric, I have a pretty good idea what we're doing here, and I don't even know why I agreed to meet with you. I don't want to be a jerk...well, maybe I do. You have your agenda, and I don't really have an interest in it. Maybe I was just needing some company tonight. I'll tell you this, after my wife walked out a while back, I've...well, I don't know what. But she's still gone, and I don't expect this to turn out good. You probably want to help me get my life together. I can appreciate that. But you probably want me to devote myself to God, read my Bible, pray...all the things I hear about in church. I don't need to hear it again from you. I believe in God. I am who I am. If my wife doesn't like me, then so be it. She can go her way and I'll go mine." I stop there, wondering what Eric might say. He still just looks at me, waiting. Then speaks slowly, asking...

"Randy, what do you want?"

I look at Eric just shaking my head. "What do I want?" What is he getting at?

"Yeah," Eric says.

"That's it? *What do I want?* Aren't you going to tell me all the things I can do to change the mess I've made of my life? Aren't you going to tell me how good God is, and how much He can help me if I'll just go to church, get with other Christians, walk the narrow road to Jesus?" I am mad now. I don't want Eric probing where he has no right.

"Randy, it's not my job to tell you anything. It's my job to ask you, what is it that you want?"

"How can you say that? Aren't you a complicated guy who has all the answers? Didn't you give Dennis all the answers and fix him up? Aren't you wanting to do the same with me?"

"Uh, Dennis sought me out. He got curious so he asked for help. He knew what he wanted. His life was a mess, and he was tired. He'd had enough. We spent time together talking, and praying, and seeing how God could help him find a better way. When he asked himself the same question, 'What do I want?' and was able to give me an honest answer, that's when I knew change was possible for him. No one changes unless they want to. They have to realize their need, and then ask themselves if they're ready."

"Change? It's interesting that you use that word. I heard that word months ago...in the shower."

"The shower? Oh, I think you mentioned that. Hmmm," Eric says.

"Yeah. I heard that voice. I forgot I told you about that. It said, 'Things are going to change.' Well, they have, Linda is gone. I'm alone. That's what changed. Was that God's voice? It must have been since she's gone!"

"Could have been. Sometimes it's hard to know. What we do know, from what you've said, is that things changed. But here's the thing, Randy—if you want to work some things out, have someone to talk to, take it to God together for the help that might be needed, I'm your guy. I'm here for you. If you don't, then we'll finish our dinner, go on home, and get on with our lives. God doesn't force us to be in His will. But He knows when we really want healing...if we say, 'I want God's will for my life,' He helps us get on His path that leads to a better way of being. It doesn't make all our problems go away. But it helps us be at peace in the midst of what is going on around us."

Eric finished there and let that sit with me a bit. Taking the last bite of my chocolate brownie and ice cream, I lay my fork down and look at Eric.

"Here's the thing. I've been in church, Eric. I've seen how people are. I know those people go almost every week. They talk about reading their Bibles. But they don't have it all together. I know that. They can talk all they want. But I see things. I hear things. There are so many hypocrites in the church. I lose interest in a God like that. I don't really want to be a part of that club."

"I getcha. Neither do I. But I am, because we are all hypocrites. Even you. The Bible says in Romans 3:23, '...everyone has sinned; we all fall short of God's glorious standard.' People can be God's light in a dark world, but people aren't God. We, the people, make a ton of mistakes. We fall, and often. And God forgives, and often. If what you learn about God is only from watching His people, you may be looking in the wrong place. If you want to know who God is, who Jesus is, you might want to go right to the source."

"And what source is that, oh-so-wise, Eric?" I could feel my blood start to boil a bit.

"God's auto-biography. Look," Eric says confidently, equally matching the amount of testosterone coming from my side of the table, "if I want to know about someone, I don't look to other people and then make a judgement about them by what others are saying and doing. God went to great lengths to give us His story, to tell us who He is from His *own* pen. Shouldn't we at least read it? Some say God didn't write the Bible, men did. That's true. But not without the Holy Spirit's guidance over 1,600 years, in three different languages, with 40 different authors...containing one central theme of Jesus being the long promised Deliverer. How can that not be written by one Designer? It contains 300 fulfilled prophecies about the life of Christ before He was even born. If that's not a miraculous Book, what is? In there you will also find eye-witness reports of Jesus' life and death. You will see just what kind of Person Jesus is, and why He came. You will read about why He died for people like you and me. You will read about things that you see happening in the world today that seem to make no sense. It will change your perspective on the world around you. You will find, in red letters in many Bibles, the very words Jesus spoke. You'll find practical advice from the very God who made you and how best to live this life. There are instructions about how to heal through what is broken in our lives. It's all there, Randy, and it contains great power— power you can hide in your heart. No one can take that away from you once you've received it. But if you think you can get all this information by watching other people who are fallible, you will have a tarnished view of a very true, right, and holy God. That would make Satan very happy. If you really want to hear God's voice, and KNOW what's from Him and what's not, then you have a place to go for that, the Holy Bible."

"You know, Eric, I don't much like conversations like this. But I have to admit, you have some good things to say. I'm pretty much done here tonight, though. I don't know what to think about all this. So, let's call it good. I can tell that Dennis met his match when he met you. And maybe I've met mine. I just don't know. That's all I can say right now."

"I can appreciate that and will leave the ball in your court. I'm here, if you want to serve it back over the net…or hit it out of the ballpark! Give me a call. I'm available."

"Good to know." I realize I'm shutting Eric down. But he's handling it well. There is a part of me that wants to know more. But I'm afraid I'll get in too deep and there might not be a way out. I'd rather call it a night.

As we leave the restaurant and go our separate ways, I can see Eric across the parking lot getting into his car. I like the guy. He's straightforward, not too pushy, and very sure of himself. He rattled me a bit, I can feel it. It will be good to get home and be by myself again. Between the restaurant manager and Eric, it's been quite the night.

22

RANDY

It's been a couple of weeks since I met with Eric. For some reason, I keep thinking about that dinner. It seems more baseball was watched than anything, but he did leave me with stuff to mull over. Maybe that's why I can't let it go. I need something to change in my life, and maybe Eric could have gotten me started if I'd given him more of a chance. He probably thinks he blew it with me. But his words have had an impact, especially since my life keeps spiraling down. Linda's far out of the picture it seems. I feel heavy and depressed, like never before—a darkness has settled over me, and my house. Actually, sometimes, I just sit in the house at the end of a work day with the lights off—in silence, in the dark, alone. What a pitiful person I have become. Where's the change…is this it? This is a pretty dismal existence. I can't call Eric. It feels too strange. Maybe I can give Dennis a call. Picking up my phone, I dial his number. I know I'm desperate to be doing this.

"Hey, Randy, how's it going?"

"Hi. Fine. How are you, Dennis?" It seems like I should ask.

"Great. It's good to hear from you."

"Yeah…" I'm not sure what to say after that. This is probably a bad idea.

"What's up? Is everything okay?" Dennis asks. I can already hear the concern in his voice.

"Okay? Well, I hate that I'm even having to call you. I know we haven't talked in a long while. I don't want to bug you. I'm…well, I'm in a bad way Dennis." I can feel my voice start to crack, and that's the last thing I want to do with Dennis. What I want to do is hang up the phone, but for some reason I don't.

"I'm glad you called. Really. We can talk if you want to," he says in a quiet way.

"Honestly. I don't want to. But I think I need to." I know I said that a little too harshly.

"Yeah. I get it. Talking for guys isn't the easiest thing to do," Dennis replies.

"Nah. It's not. I did have dinner with your friend, Eric, a while back."

"Oh. Great! He's a good guy. He's really helped me."

"I may need some help, Dennis. I'm not sure what I need. Linda left me."

"I'm so sorry to hear that. You guys raised some great kids. How are they doing?"

"I guess fine. They're not talking to me much. I'm not talking to anyone much. I'm mad at the world, and it feels like the world is mad at me. I'm stuck, it seems. But I don't even know where or why, or if there's a way out of this Hell I'm in." My voice does break then, and I'm embarrassed. I push the button, so Dennis will just go away.

My phone rings...it's Dennis. I answer, even though I don't want to.

"Hey, buddy, did we get disconnected?" he asks.

I don't say anything. I can't. My emotions are starting to get the better of me. I hang up again. I sit in the dark, wondering...waiting...and there's nothing for about 15 minutes. Then my phone rings again. I have to answer it. It seems I need the lifeline at this point or I might drop through the floor into a bottomless pit of despair.

"Hey," I say.

"Randy, I don't mean to bug you. I know this is hard. I've been on your end of the phone before. I don't want to make it any harder on you than it is. But I don't want to give up on you either. Phone calls are harder than in person. Being face to face helps. I know that seems backwards, but it helps to be in the same room to get to the bottom of things. What do you say I come by tomorrow night after work, since today has been a long day for both of us? We could just sit and talk and see what's going on...see if there's anything I can help you with. Would that be okay?"

I'm silent for much too long. But Dennis is patient. He is waiting...

Finally I say, "Okay."

"Okay, good. I'll come about seven. And Randy?" he says, and then waits.

"Yeah," I answer.

"You're gonna wanna text me and cancel. I know. I did, too. But when I finally said 'yes' and Eric came to see me, it's really been a help. So please, hang in there. There is a way through this. Sometimes we just need someone to come along and show us how. I've needed people in my life. It's nothing to be ashamed of. We all need help sometimes. Let me come and see you. We'll do this."

"Okay. I'm hearing you. See you tomorrow."

"Sounds good. Tomorrow then," Dennis says with a calmness.

Hanging up the phone, I'm already wanting to text him right back and tell him to forget it. I resist that urge. I do turn the light on, and then the ballgame. I grab a sandwich, and sit, thinking, worrying, and really angry. Why has my life come to this? Why don't people understand me? Why am I alone when others are out enjoying life? Why? Why? Why? God, where are You? You're such a good God, so they say. And I gave my heart to You, and it hasn't made a whole lot of difference. Maybe I'm barking up the wrong tree? Maybe my answer is outside that door, with some other woman, in some other city, in some other job? I could get it together if I could change my surroundings. I pick up the phone to text Dennis. I have it written out, "Never mind. Maybe another time." I'm ready to push send, and after waiting a minute or so, I do. There's no response. Good. He's gonna let me be. That would have been nothing but a bunch of hogwash anyway. He would have come over, thought he could counsel me out of my funk, and left feeling so satisfied with himself—helping his poor lost buddy. No way. I don't want any part of that. I can do it on my own. I'm just fine.

23

LINDA

The week is going by quickly since talking with Trisha. I am very busy at work. But I'm making a determined effort to do the "homework" she gave me. Forgiveness doesn't come easy. I remember another thing that Trisha explained about forgiveness. She said it's like an antibiotic that keeps infection from setting in. I know I have a lot of infection going on. I sure hope this works. I keep adding people to the list that started with Randy. It's showing me I have a lot of bitterness toward my husband. Wow, maybe I haven't been all that wonderful to live with either? It has taken me a while to work through the Randy stuff, and I know more things will crop up. Trisha said to ask the Holy Spirit to reveal things to me…I'm glad God is doing it in little bits at a time. Even at that, it can seem overwhelming. I have held onto so many harsh words that Randy spewed at me, and the times he was too busy for me, or hurt me. But I've been too busy for him, too. And I know I've hurt him. Lord, please forgive me for the times when I haven't been loving and kind toward Randy. I bring these things to You. Wash me clean, make me new, help me to live in Your forgiveness. I need You.

I feel awful. I begin to cry. But the tears seem good. They are cleansing. I go on after that to think about other family members…my mom, my dad, a cousin who had been extremely mean to me. One by one, I'm cleaning out the garbage that's been accumulating. The list grows, and eventually I don't have to write them down. As the names and incidences come to me throughout the week, I choose to forgive each one immediately. Many times, God helps me to see my role in hard relationships, and I continue to ask for forgiveness for myself. As the days go on, my heart is feeling lighter. I didn't realize how burdened I have been with all this. I didn't understand there is a way to be rid of it. By the time I meet with Trisha again, I am ready to learn more. When she arrives on Sunday afternoon, I'm happy to welcome her in.

"Linda, so good to see you again. I saw you from afar at church this morning but wasn't able to get over and talk with you," Trisha says coming through the door.

"I saw you, too, but you looked busy. I knew I would be seeing you later. Come on in. Venyce has gone to a movie."

"Nice."

"Have a seat. I already got us some water. Can you tell I'm excited about what comes next?" I ask with a smile. Oh, how different I feel from the week before. "Trisha, this forgiveness thing really is freeing. I know I have more to do. But thank you for the assignment. It's been working. I feel the 'garbage' being taken away."

"That's great to hear. You're looking good. I see a difference in your eyes, on your face."

"Oh, wow! It's good to know the hard work is visible. I surely feel it on the inside," I say with an even larger smile.

"It's not easy, is it? But it's something we have to do practically daily. Just like our dishes. Even a glass of water puts a dish in the sink that needs to be washed. If we don't take care of our dishes daily, they will pile up."

"So true. What dish are we going to 'wash' today?" I ask jokingly.

"Sounds like you're ready to get right to it?" Trisha's eyebrows rise in amusement.

"I am. The more I experience this new freedom, the more I want of it."

"Well, today it might not be fun, but it's very needed," she begins. "There are two more points that need addressing before we can really move much further. It's the repentance and restitution. We talked about this a little last week. But we need to go into it a bit more today. Let's start with prayer, and see what the Holy Spirit has planned, okay?"

"Okay," I agree.

Trisha begins, "Father in Heaven, we meet together with You again today, seeking Your divine healing and deliverance from the darkness of this world. You told us in 1 John 5, that every child of Yours defeats this evil world by trusting Your Son, Jesus Christ, to give the victory. Thank You for the victory that is already ours. And thank You for all You have accomplished in Linda this week, and for the gift of Your forgiveness toward us. Your death and resurrection, Jesus, is the way into the Father's Throne Room. We are welcome, and can bring all things to You, laying them at Your feet, and be set free from what the enemy would like to keep us in bondage about. Thank You for taking the pile Linda has brought to

You and being so faithful to remove it from her as far as the east is from the west. We begin again today, seeking further freedom, wanting all that You died to give us, Lord Jesus. In Your name we pray. Amen."

"Amen."

"So...repentance. I would surmise that going through forgiveness, you have already been repenting for things along the way. It's almost just a natural part of seeking forgiveness, although remorse is different, too, as I said before. When we repent, we come into an agreement with God's Word and want to do things His way from now on. So just saying you're sorry, being remorseful, but continuing to choose that same action in life isn't repentance. It's not that we won't make future mistakes in that same area again from time to time, but that's different than continuing to *practice* that same sin over and over. As it says in the book of James, chapter one, I believe, we can't just listen to God's message. We need to obey it, or we are just fooling ourselves. Does that make sense?"

"Yes," I answered. "And I have found myself making some different choices this week. Even like when I want to be mad at Randy. Instead of dwelling on it, I stop myself as soon as I can, tell God I forgive him, and try to move on."

"That's good, Linda. James 1 goes on to say, let me turn there...yes, here it is. Verse 26, *'If you claim to be religious but don't control your tongue, you are just fooling yourself, and your religion is worthless.'* There's that *'fooling yourself'* again. I think we do that a lot. And we probably think we are fooling God, which is never happening." Trisha laughs at that.

"Probably not!" I agree.

"By realizing what's going on when you are getting mad at Randy, that is taking every thought captive to Christ. Why we need to do that is because our thoughts lead us into many dark and destructive places. Even making an 'Internal Vow' can cause problems, and we have no idea what happened."

"What do you mean by that?"

"By what part?" Trisha asks, looking at me.

"The 'Internal Vow' part. I don't know what that is?"

"Oh, right...let's see...say you make an internal promise to yourself. Like, 'I'm never going to get over this anger. It's just who I am.' Or something like, 'This marriage is never going to make it.' In saying that, you are coming into an agreement with the enemy, and he sees it as an opportunity to influence your life in just that way. There are also curses...no, really, there are. I can see by the look on your face that it sounds weird, but it's true. Some parents may put a curse of poverty on their child. They might say, 'You will never amount to anything.' Those words can be powerful in the spiritual realm. We have to be careful with the words that we speak. The enemy is tricky. He is always looking for a way to negatively impact our life. We want to give him as little ammunition to work with as possible in this battle. Remember, we have the Victory in Jesus. But there is a lot going on in the meantime of our lives. God is serious when He says in Psalm 19:14, '*May these words of my mouth and this meditation of my heart be pleasing in your sight, Lord, my Rock and my Redeemer.'* It's for our own good!"

"Okay. I get it—be careful with the words I use. Oh…but what if I have already done this, or said that? Am I doomed? Have I cursed someone else for all time?"

Trisha chuckles a bit at this. "No. No. It's okay, Linda. That's what we're learning here…how to reverse these things, get them out of our life, and find healing and wholeness in Jesus. We can be free of all of this. We perish for lack of knowledge. But when we know, we can LIVE! God's mercy is new every morning. When we forgive and repent, we get a new start. We can cancel any internal vow, and any curse, in the mighty name of Jesus!"

"Okay, good. I was worried there."

"No need. That is what we are doing here together. Learning about all of this, and being set free from everything and anything the enemy has been using to hold us in bondage. And to realize that when we notice an unhealthy thought, we should catch it on the way in. We need to toss it out as quickly as possible before it imbeds itself into our brain matter, and into the words we speak. If we let dark ways of thinking ruminate too long, they can actually change the physical structure of our brain. That's why God has to renew our minds. Rewiring is part of God's job description if we will 'hire' Him for the job. Sounds like you are doing that," Trisha adds.

"I guess I am. That's good to know. And what's the other word you said, restitution? What exactly am I supposed to do with that, Biblically?" I ask.

"This is if you have stolen from anyone, borrowed and not returned, etc., you are to pay back and return what is not rightly yours. This frees you also from the enemy trying to have control in that area of your life."

"Oh. Well, this isn't a big one for me, but I will give it some prayerful thought."

"Good. Without the Holy Spirit revealing these things to us, we can have very little concept of what it is that might be destroying us. Many times, we don't even recognize the thief in our own home—we get so used to him being there. Take anger for instance. Anger can be a thief. Something happens in life, even something simple like getting cut off in traffic, or landing in the long line at the grocery store. Although that might be more of a spirit of frustration in the grocery store. Have you ever walked out of the store afterwards and let out a long sigh? I have," Trisha says.

"I guess. Yeah," I respond.

"Well, when something happens that angers or frustrates us, the enemy can look at that as an open door into our 'home'. He's always looking for an opportunity to bug us, and then keep on bugging us. So, when we find ourselves in a situation like that, and anger comes upon us, we need to recognize what's happening, and then command that to leave in the name of the Lord Jesus. Same with frustration, or whatever. Say frustration, *Go*, in the name of the Lord Jesus. Sometimes even breathing out in the process, like when we let out that long sigh upon leaving the store. We can exhale darkness, and we can inhale light, as in the Holy Spirit. When we sing that song at church about the 'empty grave', I think of something like anger. When it leaves us, it is leaving behind an empty grave. Death resided there. And then I breathe in the Holy Spirit, asking Him to fill that empty grave with His life. Is this making sense?" Trisha asks.

"So far. Yes. It seems simple enough," I answer nodding my head.

"It's really not all that hard. But sadly, many don't know about these weapons God has given us for spiritual warfare. Too many are carrying heavy burdens that don't need to be carried. And they pile up. Quickly! This is all about recognizing and getting rid of these things before they get a foothold. I was just reading about that in Matthew 11 today, how Jesus' yoke is easy and His burden is light. If what we're carrying isn't God's will for our life, GET RID OF IT!! It's not of God, it's of Satan."

"Okay, then! I'm all for that!"

"Linda, all this healing is so that we can live this life more in the image of Christ. But what Satan wants is for us to look and act like him. This process of healing takes commitment. But it's well worth it. And forgiveness is what makes it all work. Just like Jesus' forgiveness from the Cross. Satan has no power anymore because of the Cross. That was taken away from Satan through Jesus' death and resurrection. Jesus took the keys back from Satan that were handed over to him in the Garden of Eden. Man handed over dominion to Satan by eating from the Tree of the Knowledge of Good and Evil. But Jesus got those keys back and returned them to man when He died and rose again, before He ascended back to Heaven. Jesus told Peter in Matthew 16:19, *'And I will give you the keys of the Kingdom of Heaven.'* And He did. We walk in Christ's full authority now. The only problem is, most of us don't realize it."

"I like the sound of that authority. I hope to learn…" my voice trails off because I know I have a long way to go.

"It's not as hard as it all sounds," Trisha says reassuringly. "Really. It's more a matter of being willing to listen and understand what the Spirit of God is saying just like it's talked about in Revelation. So many aren't even willing to listen in the first place. Jesus knew those who weren't. He prayed to the Father, thanking Him for hiding the Truth from those who think of themselves as being so wise and clever in Matthew 11:25. Healing is available to those who are willing—looking to the Father, reading and believing the Word for answers instead of trying to do this life in their own strength. Are there any questions you have, Linda?"

"Can you tell me a bit more about how forgiveness works?" I ask.

"Sure. Without forgiveness in this healing process, you will only have a temporary reprieve from the anger, frustration, bitterness, and so on. Unforgiveness is the root of the tree that all these branches of bitterness and so forth, will cling to. We can pray for things to be cleaned out of our 'house', cutting off the branches, but they will know they are welcome to come back if the root is still there. Sometimes we cling to that root like a comfy blanket…like it's our friend. It is a foe! We have to acknowledge the foe that it is, because God won't force us to get rid of something we want to hang onto. If we want to hold onto unforgiveness, which has limbs of anger and bitterness toward someone, we can surely do that. But when we have had enough and are ready to call them all enemies, then we can be freed from them. Jesus said in the Lord's prayer, *'Deliver us from evil.'* Obviously, He knows what He is talking about. When we start with forgiveness, digging out the root, many times a lot of the anger, rage, and so forth will leave right along with it. That's why starting with forgiveness is very productive in this whole process.

"The enemy seems very busy trying to destroy us with all of this," I add.

"Yes. He is truly evil. Anything that is not of God, is of the devil. Like the shooting that just happened in the church in Idaho. People try to figure out what the motive is. When I see the face of the man who did the shootings, I'm looking at his eyes. I know that an evil spirit, probably many, are what drove him to commit such a heinous crime. Things had probably been piling up in him for years. He probably knew nothing about getting the garbage out. In fact, he got so used to it being there, it felt normal for him. He so believed the lies that he carried around inside, he felt right about doing what he did. The enemy can really play with minds that are yielded to him. Say, would it be okay if we just took a little bathroom break? Then we'll talk a bit more before I go?"

"Of course, Trisha. I don't want to keep you too long today."

24

LINDA

"Ahh, that feels better," Trisha says, taking a seat again on the couch.

"Can I get you anything? Did you eat after church?" I ask.

"I did eat. But thanks," Trisha says, turning to greet Venyce as she comes through the door.

"Oh, Hi! How was the movie?"

"It was very good. I don't mean to interrupt…" Venyce says, putting down her purse.

"Not at all. We just took a break and I think your timing is perfect," says Trisha. "There's some things I'd like to talk with Linda about. But I think it might be helpful to let her know a little bit of what you and I went through together these past few years. Maybe give her some insight so it doesn't all seem too overwhelming for her. What do you think?"

"Sure. Do you mind, Linda? I don't want to take up your time with Trisha?" Venyce asks looking at me.

"It is perfectly fine with me. Come sit with us. I'd love to hear more about all of this from another person's experience. Trisha has been teaching me so much about forgiveness and all. Tell me a bit of what you experienced. We never got much of a chance to talk about that…or maybe I wasn't in a place to really hear about it?" I remark, looking at Venyce closely to see what she is thinking about that.

"Well, you're probably right. This isn't what most people are used to in the church. But Trisha has shown me that it really does work wonders when we are caught up in a lot of stuff from our past. Trisha knows this from experience, as we talked about, right Trisha?" Venyce asks.

"Yes," says Trisha looking at the both of us. "I had things bothering me for years and I didn't know their origin or what to do about them. I'm so thankful someone had the wherewithal to take me through these steps, setting me free from such bondage. I don't know if it saved my marriage, but it sure improved our relationship. Calvin is a very patient man and was sticking with me no matter what. But it has made his life, and mine, a whole lot better since. I was so angry and controlling. I let stuff pile up for years and did nothing about it other than trying to handle it all in my own strength...trying mostly to just push it aside. It's all I knew to do. But that only works for so long. Oh, I was reading the Bible. But I wasn't really understanding a lot of what it said. I was just trying to follow all the rules I seemed to find there, and I wasn't paying enough attention to all that Jesus died to give me. I was working so hard at the Christian life, yet getting very little benefit from it. When I finally got to the place where I was out of my own strength and my own ideas, Calvin was still there for me. And thankfully God brought someone into my life who was willing to take me on, pray with me, and help free me from the darkness I was held captive in for so many years. It takes boldness for that mentor, though. So many people are not on board with the idea that Christians can be demonized. They have heard for so many years that we can't be *possessed*, they end up rejecting all of this. And it's true, like I already explained to you, we can't be possessed, we can't be *owned* by Satan—he has no authority over us. But ask anyone in the church if they have tormenting thoughts? Are tempted? Lack peace? I bet every hand would go up! They would like to say it's only oppression, just coming from the outside—but then why was Jesus going around casting *out* demons all the time? One-quarter of the healings in Mark talk of deliverance. And these are the children of God, descendants of Abraham. Yes, they didn't have the Holy Spirit permanently indwelling them yet, but Paul did, and he had a tormenting spirit. He called it a thorn in his flesh in 2 Corinthians 12:7. If it's good enough for Paul, it's good enough for me! I'm not gonna stick my head in the sand and say it can't happen, when it's right there in Scripture. Sorry, I get a little worked up when Satan's lies keep Christians bound and tormented. I love to see people set free!"

"I'm with you, Trisha." Venyce joins in adding, "I've lived in this freedom for quite a few years now, and there's no going back for me. The more I walk in freedom, the more aware I am each time the enemy comes to try and steal it away from me. I tell him to move along, I won't have anything to do with him. From what I understand, we are sealed with the Holy Spirit, our spirit is safe, but our soul and body are not. We can be inflicted with all kinds of darkness and sickness from trauma and sin. These doors in our lives get opened to Satan and his craftiness."

"You ladies sound like you know what you're talking about. I'm so thankful this is where God would have me be while I spend this time sorting out my marriage. And it is probably so true, Venyce, if you had talked to me about this a couple years ago, before I got desperate enough to want it, I would have thought you were a bit far gone. But I need help now. I don't want to see my marriage fail. I don't want to live feeling so weighed down with the things of this world. I want to know if there is more out there than this, and it seems like there is." I say this with a smile and a nod of approval to the hope I'm feeling from all that I'm learning. It's making sense to me.

"We love sharing this with you, Linda. Where would you like us to go from here?" Trisha asks.

"I'd like to hear more about your experience, Venyce. If you don't mind." I request.

"Sure. Of course. Well, it was before Earl even got sick. You and Randy were busy with the kids, they were in college and all. Earl and I were empty nesters by then, and life seemed pretty good. Still, there was something that wasn't right in me. Maybe it was hormonal, I don't know. But I just wasn't myself. I came to church one day, and there was Trisha. When we met, it was like we were meant to be friends. What I didn't know then was God brought us together because He knew Trisha had what I was needing. More than friendship, she was learning about the peace Jesus left us with like no one else I had ever met. We started to spend time together, and little by little, she introduced me to the deliverance ministry that she was getting involved in. It was outside the church. Sometimes it's called a Cottage Ministry because not many churches have this on their campuses—probably because it isn't widely accepted. Trisha slowly taught me about forgiveness, like she is teaching you. It's so needed! And she taught me about the demonic realm. I've since learned that Jesus deals with demons 61 times...no one had authority over them until Jesus came. Let me get my Bible, I'll be right back."

When Venyce returns, she opens it to Matthew 8. "It talks about many people who had demons that were being brought to Jesus for healing. In verse 16 it says, *'All the spirits fled when he commanded them to leave, and he healed the sick.'* Even the man in Matthew 9 who couldn't speak, had a demon cast out of him. In verse 33, it says, *'Nothing like this has ever happened in Israel!'* Jesus also says in Matthew 9, *'The harvest is so great, but the workers are so few. So pray to the Lord who is in charge of the harvest; ask him to send out more workers for his fields.'* What is the work we are to do, Linda? I learned part of it is deliverance. But we're rarely taught that. In Matthew 10, Jesus gave His disciples authority to *'cast out evil spirits and to heal every kind of disease and illness.'* I didn't know these verses meant people like you and me! But then Trisha pointed out where it says in John 14:12-14, let me read it to you, *'I tell you the solemn truth, the person who believes in me will perform the miraculous deeds that I am doing, and will perform greater deeds than these, because I am going to the Father. And I will do whatever you ask in my name, so that the Father may be glorified in the Son. If you ask me anything in my name, I will do it.'* That must mean all of us? Right?"

"It makes sense so far," I answer. "So, then what happened?"

"Trisha showed me that what she could help me with was Biblical. She began to pray with me. Through a process, we asked the Holy Spirit to reveal what might need to be taken care of in me that was causing my distress. I mean, my life was good, the kids were healthy, and like I said, Earl was still well at that time. I was in church, reading my Bible, and praying on my own. What did I have to be anxious about? Or unhappy about? Nothing really. It made sense that it must have been something else. The Holy Spirit revealed there were wounds from the past that needed healing. I also had everyday concerns that I wasn't fully dealing with. I was just shoving them to the back of my mind because they weren't huge things. But when they weren't addressed biblically, the enemy gained some control in those areas. I found myself being anxious a lot of the time, and not really understanding why. The enemy was taking something like a small worry, and working it deep into my soul. When it got firmly planted there, it could begin to grow into a big worry. The enemy is clever…just when we want to have our wits about us, the spirit of worry comes and clouds our thinking, making us less effective in handling a situation. I didn't know when worry came upon me that I should bring it into the light immediately, and cast it away in Jesus' name. We feel like we need to worry. That is a lie! We need to trust God and cast *all* our burdens on Him! Trisha taught me how to battle the enemy this way. I have really learned to live in the freedom that comes with having this knowledge. Then when Earl got sick and died, that was a big blow. I don't know what I would have done had that happened earlier. I don't mean to say God wouldn't have gotten me through it…but knowing how to get rid of the things that came to torment me in my grief really helped. I didn't have to stay in the dark places as long. Even though my heart felt like it shattered into a million pieces, God is healing it."

"Where do you think I should go with this, Venyce? I mean, my situation is different than yours. I have a reason to be unhappy. My marriage is a mess. My job can be stressful. Things aren't good in many ways. Maybe it's just what it is, and I need to learn to live with it? Maybe I'm looking for a perfect life that doesn't exist?" I ask, really wondering if this is just a shot in the dark.

"You have captured right where most people are. We want to say 'Life is just life,' right?" Venyce responds.

"Yes. It seems so"

"Most people think, Christians included, that's as good as it gets…just hanging on by a thread, hoping to make it to the end with some sense of sanity left. But Jesus died to give us *so much more* than that. God wants us to know the joy He is offering us even when life is hard. Jesus wants us to live in the freedom He died to give us—not just on our good days, but to experience that freedom on our worst days. The Father wants us to know His peace. I'm not talking about happiness. I'm talking about a deep-seated peace that comes because we know Who is in control—our Father in Heaven. And nothing is happening out of God's control. Most times, a crisis is exactly what is needed to get us to His place of peace. Why? Because it causes us to be dissatisfied with this world, and go looking for more. Jesus is the 'More.' We can trust Him in all things—even when marriages fail, when jobs are stressful, when kids are sick, when spouses die. He wants to help us live this life with an eternal perspective and purpose. Most times that won't happen if we are too comfy here. That's sad but true. Our minds are so clouded over with the things of this world. We have to get to the place where we can say, I once was blinded by all of this, but now I see through it. The blind man on the side of the road was asked by Jesus, *'What do you want me to do for you?'* He answered, *'I want to see.'* His sight was restored in that moment. He felt his desperation, and he knew what he wanted. If we can say to Jesus, 'I'm not satisfied with the darkness I'm living in, I want to see.' He will gladly give us our sight. We will be able to see His glory, His goodness…here in the land of the living. We have to come out of our dark tomb, let Him unwrap the grave clothes Satan has us bound up in, and walk free into all He has for us. That's what this is about. Being set free! There is nothing to fear because God has not given us a spirit of fear, but of power, love, and a sound mind. There is everything to gain in this process." Venyce stops there, looking at me.

"I'm hearing you, Sis. And I like what I'm hearing. Thank you. Where do we go from here? I ask, turning toward Trisha this time.

"We will do another little exercise, continuing on from last time. This might seem intense in the beginning. But after a while, it will become more normal as we go through different areas in your life where it is needed. Little by little, the Holy Spirit will loose the 'grave clothes.' You will begin to feel lighter, and have more joy, no matter what is happening in life," Trisha explains.

"Let's do it. I don't want to fear it. I want all that Jesus died to give me."

During the next couple of hours, Trisha and Venyce began the careful process of ministering to me again. Trisha anointed me with oil, and then they prayed over me and with me. Feelings of regret and guilt were exposed, as well as many other things. I liked being instructed in how to really live the Christian life. When our day together ended, I knew things had taken place that can't be humanly explained. I trusted these two women of the faith and was so thankful for their boldness in ministering to me in this way.

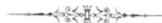

"Linda, it was a joy today, being with you and Venyce. We will continue on next Sunday with more of the same. You are a very willing participant in all that God is doing, and it is a pleasure to pray for you. I look forward to what God has in store for next time.

"As do I. Thank you so much for spending this time with me, Trisha. I have hope for the future through all of this. Bye for now." Closing the door, and turning toward Venyce, she smiles at me, and nods.

"Well done, Sis, she says. It's not easy. But you won't be sorry. It has been such a help to me. Let's get in our comfies and enjoy a good movie and some popcorn. That will be a perfect finish to a wonderful day."

"I'm with you on that, Venyce. Let's do it!"

25

LINDA

When the next Sunday comes around, I am more than ready to meet with Trisha again. I spent the week thinking and praying about all that took place during our last time together. She explained things so well. And knowing that Venyce trusts her, helps me to trust her, too. I don't know all that this Sunday will hold, but I welcome it.

Taking a seat in the living room, Trisha doesn't waste any time getting started. She asks me about the forgiveness process, my Bible reading and prayer, and if there was any restitution needed? I tell her I keep asking the Holy Spirit to reveal things to me, and each time He does, I am being obedient in taking care of it. I have been continuing to forgive people that I haven't thought about in years...and am also bringing my own sins before God. I let her know that sometimes it's so hard to even be honest with myself. I think I was one of those people fooling myself, and when I would admit it, I felt like I was telling God things He didn't know about me. Even though I knew that was crazy. I could get lost in that deception from time to time. During the week, I was learning to do a bit of my own deliverance by identifying a feeling of worry or frustration, and casting it all away, like we talked about. From what Trisha then explains to me, I was truly starting to walk this out. Things seem in a good place as she begins to teach me more about all of this. I am finding it very interesting and helpful.

"I'd just like to talk with you about a verse in Mark today," Trisha begins with. "From what you're sharing with me, I can see you have made tremendous progress already through the forgiveness process."

"Thanks. It feels like I have. It's been a better week in many ways," I say with a smile.

"The load is lightening, it seems," she says.

"Yes," I answer. "Even though nothing is changing with Randy. I am better able to trust God with it."

"Good for you! It pleases my heart to hear that. We will continue to pray for Randy," Trisha says with compassion. "The reason this process of deliverance is so powerful, is that before being freed of the multitude of things that have plagued us for years, we may feel weak—like we are carrying a heavy weight. We are not as able to handle many of the things that come against us in life in the way we would like to. We may have outbursts of anger, or feel resentment. Remember, anger doesn't usually hang out alone. There will be other things in that 'gang' of thieves. After we clear out this darkness, we can find a new strength in really knowing the power of Jesus, which is exactly what the enemy doesn't want. The Good News holds such power! Let me turn to Mark now. It's in chapter three…verse 27 where it says, *'Who is powerful enough to enter the house of a strong man and plunder his goods? Only someone even stronger— someone who could tie him up and then plunder his house.'"*

"What we have to realize is that there are different levels even in the spiritual realm. Ephesian 6 talks about this when it says there are evil rulers and authorities in an unseen world. This arrangement was not set up by Satan. It was set up in Heaven, and when a third of the angels followed Lucifer, they already knew their positions in his army. They know their assignments. But so many people on earth don't even understand what's going on because they can't see it. Sadly, too many try to pretend it's not even there."

"Wow," I say with a bit of a furrowed brow.

"I know, just stay with me here for a bit, and I think at the end you'll have a better picture of what I'm talking about," Trisha says gently.

"Okay. Go ahead. I'm listening."

"Darkness," Trisha continues, "to Satan, is a good thing. It's where he stays hidden. He doesn't want to be discovered. What we will be doing even more so today is bringing his schemes out into the light. The Light is where our enemy grows weak and is disarmed. Satan's name means resister—he will fight tooth and nail against us…against all this. 1 John 4:4 says, *'…the Spirit who lives in you is greater than the spirit who lives in the world.'* That's the NLT version. I like how it says it. I know we talked about that, and I'm going to be repeating it many times when we are together. It is SO important to remember, so we don't have to fear. The truth is, there is a huge battle going on, and we already have the victory. It's been won! We can walk in that freedom when we recognize there IS a battle, and Who won it! Jesus did. On the Cross. Jesus conquered sin and death. Lucifer has been had! And at the end of this story, he will be thrown into the bottomless pit. Our main responsibility now is to believe it and walk in that freedom more and more, as we've been talking about. We need to know what our weapons are and how to use them. Which takes us into better understanding the Armor of God. Please spend some time this week reading through Ephesians 6:10-18 about the Armor that is available. And when you get to the Sword of the Spirit, I want you to actually pretend you have a sword in your hand, and you're slaying the enemy with it. As you do this, quote a Scripture verse. Whichever one you want to use, they are all good. One good Psalm is 10:12, *'Arise, O Lord: Punish the wicked, O God!'* And when you get done, picture the enemy so wounded that he has lost all power in your life. He won't die…demons don't die. But the enemy will be weakened tremendously in your life. The dark spirits will know you are wise to them, and you have power over them whenever they try to come against you. Satan hates the Word of God, so when you say it out loud, it's torturous to him. Why not torture the torturer?! We have the weapons to do it. Satan spends so much time trying to torture us! We need to know how to battle back!

"I'm not much into war movies, but you're getting me excited with this battle you're talking about. I'm tired of being picked on by the enemy, Trisha!" I say, shaking my head.

"You should be! We have to learn how to fight like this, or we will be a casualty in these battles. What a sad thing that would be after all Jesus went through to set us free! The *war* has been won! Satan knows that! But there will still be many battles along the way. He's not going down without a fight."

"Okay. Good to be forewarned," I respond.

"And after going through the Armor of God, after putting on the six pieces and wielding your sword, move into the seventh piece of Armor which is prayer. It is SO powerful! I have heard it called 'God's intercontinental ballistic missile'. The guys would really like that!" Trisha says, smiling.

"Maybe that's a good one for Randy to know."

"Yes. Prayer is so powerful. Which brings me back to the strongman. Sorry, I may have wandered there some. I just get excited about all that God is doing for us in this life," Trisha says with a chuckle.

"I see your excitement, and it makes me want more of this. So, thank you."

Trisha smiles again at that before continuing with, "The strongman in that verse out of Mark that I was talking about earlier, is not one to be messed with if you don't have Jesus. Let me read that again, *'Who is powerful enough to enter the house of a strong man and plunder his goods? Only someone even stronger—someone who could tie him up and then plunder his house.'* Satan may think he is the strongman, but Jesus is so much stronger. The strongman can be bound up now, in the power of Jesus' name because Jesus has conquered the devil and taken back the souls of all those who believe in Him. Notice it says in that verse, 'the house of a strong man, and *his* goods.' Satan did have dominion after the fall in the Garden of Eden. He once had legal right because Adam and Eve invited him into their lives, and all the lives during Old Testament times. But no longer. Now, remember, a non-Christian, someone who hasn't invited Jesus into his/her house, are open to whatever comes their way. But for a Christian, the devil is actually an invader. Because of Jesus giving the keys of the Kingdom of Heaven back to us, as he told Peter He was going to do in Matthew 16:19, Satan has no legal right to us unless the door has been opened to him. That can happen in basically one of two ways that we've talked about: We either invite him in through some sort of sin in our lives, or he barges in through some sort of trauma in our lives. There are other aspects of this, but I'll leave it there for now. I don't want to complicate this. But say you do dabble in the occult like being involved in a card reading, or even that Ouija Board we talked about before. When you mess with darkness, you open a door to the enemy, making him think he is welcome in your house. Or say you were abused, and it's not your fault at all. Still, that trauma can intrude upon your life, unwillingly, and the enemy uses that wound as an open door to barge in and leave you with some sort of darkness. It can appear later in life as depression, lust, insecurity, or fear, just as examples. In all these things there is usually a 'boss' so to speak. Someone in charge of this team of evil. It is important to go to the Holy Spirit with this, once we realize there has been an invasion, asking Him who the strongman is? When the Holy Spirit identifies who is in charge of this gang of thieves, you can then bind them all together and cast them out of your soul, through prayer and the power we have in the name of Jesus Christ. ...I can see that this all may be a bit much for you to comprehend right now. But with a simple walk through of this, you will have a better idea of what I'm talking about. Should we do that now? Will you be okay with it?"

"Uh. Yeah. That would be helpful." I know I'm not going to remember all that Trisha is telling me. But when she actually does it, it seems to stick.

Trisha begins with saying, "Relax for a bit right now, Linda. Sit back, and let's pray. I'm going to ask God to reveal something to you again, sort of like we did before, and we will go from there into more areas that need to be healed. The Holy Spirit will walk us through this process. This is about the places in your life where the enemy has invaded your Temple...where he has found an entrance, a foothold. It's about getting the thief out of your house and off your property, so he can't steal, kill, and destroy your life anymore. Let me begin by praying:"

"Holy Spirit, help Linda to understand the freedom that is available to her in an area of darkness she may not even be aware of. Show her who a strongman is in her life, as we all have them. Then bring to her mind what this open door was that allowed this tormentor to hurt this precious child of God. Thank You, Lord Jesus. I anoint Linda today in the name of the Father, the Son, and the Holy Spirit. Amen."

"Amen."

"Now, let's give it some time, and you tell me what comes to you," Trisha says calmly.

Sitting and trying to hear something, I don't get anything at first. And then, a word comes to me, but I don't know if it's right. I don't want to say it. I could be wrong. But is there a wrong in this? I better just say it.

"Pride," I say, opening my eyes and looking at Trisha. "That's what I got. Is that something we're looking for?"

"Yes. Pride is a spirit," Trisha says. "Like fear is a spirit. And God has not given us a spirit of pride, or of fear. Remember how we talked about in 2 Timothy 1:7 it says, '*God has not given us a spirit of fear and timidity, but of power, love, and self-discipline.*' Some versions say a sound mind. Holy Spirit, please bring to Linda's memory when this spirit of pride first felt welcomed in."

I sit a while longer, trying to focus. And Trisha prays again, "Holy Spirit, reveal to Linda what she needs to know about the pride that has affected her life."

I begin by saying the only thing I can think of; "What's coming to me is a time when I came in first in a relay event in grammar school. I felt like I was really noticed. When I got home, my accomplishment was barely acknowledged. I remember thinking to myself, I'm going to hang onto this feeling of having done so well because it helps me feel like I'm somebody. Is that a problem, Trisha?"

"I wouldn't call it a problem. It's all in how we process these things. If we use them to bring glory to God, thanking Him for the ability that He gave you to run fast, then that can be a very good thing. If we use it to put ourselves above others, then it works to our detriment. Many think the Bible says that pride comes before the fall, when actually it says haughtiness comes before the fall and pride comes before destruction. Some haughtiness might have come in on that day, a bit of arrogance. Which is typical for a child, and even when we get older. This is how the enemy works. It's nothing to be ashamed of. It's just something to be dealt with. We try to hang onto things that make us not seem worthless when we don't yet understand our true worth in the Father's eyes. You may not have been getting the encouragement at home you needed, and this was your way of surviving that neglect. In all this, that was the 'fall' part; the haughtiness. But if we don't get up right after that 'fall,' so to speak, it can then become unhealthy pride, which becomes destructive. Pride has been known to destroy many marriages. I don't know the reason for your marital problems, but this could be one of them, on both sides. We all, pretty much without exception, struggle with a spirit of pride. Until it is identified and cleaned out of our lives, it can rule us, destroying many relationships along the way."

"I'm hearing you. I can see that with Randy and me."

"This is a very important spirit to identify here today, Linda. And here's how we deal with it. We will take authority over that spirit of pride, and clean your Temple of that strongman, that thief, telling any other spirits associated with it to go also. Remember, they usually hang out in gangs. Does that sound okay to you? This part can be a bit intense, but it's nothing to worry about. Jesus is all powerful."

"How do we do it?" I ask with a bit of trepidation.

"What I want to do now is have you face me, and I will be looking into your eyes. It's going to look like I'm talking to you, but I'm not. The eyes are the window to the soul, and I'm going to be speaking to that spot in your soul that would like to remain hidden, that spirit of pride. Remember I said Satan doesn't like to be discovered? But the Holy Spirit has shed His light into his darkness today—now we know he's there. He's gotta go. We always pray this in the name of the Lord Jesus, or Jesus Christ, or other titles associated with Jesus' name because there are false Jesus's in this world, and we need the power of the real deal, if you know what I mean." Trisha sort of laughs at that.

"I getcha. Okay, so I'm going to face you, and I'm supposed to look right into your eyes?"

"Yes. Let's begin, and remember, if my voice gets stern sounding, it's not at you. I'm talking to what's trying to hide within you that God wants to remove. I will take command over the strongman, with the authority Jesus has given us, and any spirit associated with him."

"Okay. Go ahead," I say turning and facing Trisha eye to eye, although it feels a bit uncomfortable.

Trisha begins, "Thank You, Father, that through Your Holy Spirit You have revealed in Linda today what needs cleansing and healing. In the name of the Lord Jesus, and by the power of Your precious blood, I bind up the spirit of pride and all those cooperating with it. Any unclean spirit associated with the spirit of pride, be bound together. Anything that has fragmented off of this spirit, be bound together. Now I order you all to GET OUT right now, in the name of Jesus Christ, the One and only Son of the Living God! Pride, and any spirits attached to you, identify yourself... Now Linda, if anything comes to you, just say it. What is causing the pride? What's further down toward the root of that?"

After a bit, I hear a very faint word, "Insecurity."

"In the name of the Lord Jesus, I command insecurity to leave now! Get out! Anything else under that?" Trisha asks.

After a few moments, "Insignificance," comes to me.

"In the name of the Lord Jesus, I command the spirit of insignificance to come out now. You are not welcome in Linda, she is a child of the living God, covered by the blood of Jesus Christ."

After about fifteen minutes or so of this process, digging deeper and deeper, saying what it seems comes to my mind, I feel relaxation start to flow through my body, and a lightness comes. Trisha must see the difference I feel because she begins to change what she's saying...

"Good. They have gone. Now breathe in the Holy Spirit, Linda. Go ahead, close your eyes. Relax. Fill in all the empty places with God's peace and love. Breathe out any remaining darkness...there...yes. Breathe that out. Yes, that yawn is also a manifestation of spirits leaving. Even the tear in your eye. They come out in many ways. Good. And now breathe in the Spirit of the Living God. Do that now...good...good. Again. And now repeat this after me, Linda..."

"Lord Jesus, I renounce any evil spirit that gained control over me. I claim this new freedom in the name of the Lord Jesus Christ. I break every generational curse, however far back they go!"

After repeating this, I look at Trisha again and feel such a peace. After a minute or so, I exclaim, "Wow, that was interesting. Words can't really describe what I'm experiencing."

Trisha smiles at me in a warm and caring way, saying, "That's how it works. It wasn't scary, was it? It's just a bit more freedom being brought into your life... Father, bless Linda on this day with Your many blessings. Pour Your peace and goodness into her life. Strengthen her with Your Holy Spirit filling every part of her being."

"Thank you. No. This wasn't scary at all. Sometimes it felt strange. But not a bad thing. I'm starting to understand more how this works."

Trisha explains, "Some will feel light afterward. Some will feel tired, but relaxed. There is no right or wrong way to feel. This is not about feelings, but about taking action against the enemy and his ways. He has to go when we command him to because we have been given that right by the Lord Jesus. Maintaining this freedom is actually more challenging than what we just did. After this, it is SO important, and I can't stress this enough, that you read the Bible, pray, and draw near to God. You will feel the enemy trying to worm his way back in. That is scriptural. You can read about it in Matthew 12:43-45. The unclean spirits go out, find some rest, and then try to return. We are told this so we recognize it's going to happen, and when it does, we can call on the name of the Lord Jesus to resist the devil once again. Command the intruders trying to regain entrance to leave. And use the Word of God as the Sword we talked about earlier, slicing and dicing those evil spirits until they don't want anything to do with you. Even Jesus fought Satan with Scripture, saying, *'It is written...'*"

"I'm hearing you. Thank you, Trisha. This has been very...well...eye-opening, amazing, and...I don't know what. I look forward to seeing how this week goes."

"You let me know if you have any questions or need help in any way. This is a process. There are many layers to all of this. We have to trust God and His timing...His ways through it all. Now, let's pray for Randy, and I'll leave you to the rest of your day. Father, thank You for today, and all that You revealed and freed Linda from. Please help Randy find his own healing. We pray for their marriage, and the plans You have for them in the future. We know that divorce is not what pleases You, so please heal their hurting hearts as they spend this time apart. In Jesus' mighty name, Amen."

"Amen. Thank you again."

Shutting the door behind Trisha, I want to just go sit on the couch for a bit and think about this. I feel better, but it is all so new to me. It is good to know I can trust Trisha.

26

LINDA

Working with Trisha through these past months has been so remarkable! She has been in Idaho for a few weeks, and I'm looking forward to time with her again today. Each week we meet there are changes happening, and healing from past wounds that I wasn't even really fully aware were there. It's interesting how the enemy is so good at hiding things inside of us, not wanting us to bring it into God's light. Getting baptized was also very good. Trisha never pushed me. But every time I had questions about it, or needed encouragement, she was there. The day I was baptized I would have loved to have had Randy there. But whenever I stop over at the house to get mail and such, it's not good when he is home. He seems angrier than ever, so I make my times there short, since they're not so sweet. As I grow closer to Jesus, it seems Randy is growing more resistant. I wonder if my prayers for him are being heard? Sometimes it bothers me a lot. I do my best to take even that to God and get rid of any lingering effects of those emotions. Trisha never tries to convince me that squelching emotions is what we are after. More, we are just learning together how to identify them, understand them, and ask God where those things started to take root—then dealing with them in a healthier way. She is showing me that Jesus provides in all these areas. Our job is to go to Him with our problems, and not try to handle them on our own.

Church was good again this morning, and Venyce just left with a friend to do some shopping. When the doorbell rings, my heart is happy to know that Trisha has returned. I can't wait to hear about her time with her husband and see what nuggets she has for me today to chew on during the week.

"Hi, Trisha!" Giving her a big hug as she comes in. "You're looking great! Was time with Calvin nice?"

"Why, thank you! And yes, it was good to be together. You look very beautiful yourself. How have you been?" she asks.

"Doing very well. Come on in. Take a seat and I'll get us something to drink. Just water again today?"

"Great! Yes. Water is fine. Thank you," Trisha says with her usual smile.

Once settled in, Trisha starts us with prayer. She is so good at always going to God before we begin. Then, looking at me, she says, "I have something I want to share with you. It's a common struggle, and God made it very clear to me once again how we can have the victory over it."

"Oh? I would love to hear it. Please, do tell!" I encourage her. Trisha doesn't waste anything. Whenever and wherever she sees God working in her life, she uses it in her ministry.

"Well, okay, then, here's what happened while I was gone. I was talking with a family member while in Idaho. They're someone I'm very close with, but something seemed to be off. I couldn't quite put my finger on it. He was hurting me with some of the things he was saying. He's not normally like that. I kept on, just hoping for the best. But it was wearing on me. Then a bad cold set in. I don't normally get sick, but I got what was going around. One night, when I was just worn out from the cold, I heard from him again and what he had to tell me was upsetting. I don't want to go into all his personal details, because that's not really what's important in this story anyway. I'll just leave it to say, I was not happy, probably because I was sick and very foggy-headed, I then didn't know how to respond to him. I wanted to handle it in a godly way, but I was stumped. What was coming to me never seemed quite right. Finally, I shared with Calvin what was going on. He knows this relative quite well, and they get along. They aren't as close as we are, but he understands the relationship. I asked him what I should do? And as I sat there looking at Calvin and praying that God would give him the words I needed, sure enough, within a few seconds what he said was perfect. But that wasn't the end of it...I'm still getting to the good part."

"Okay...wow, God really heard and answered through Calvin? And then something even better happened?"

"Yes. And yes! I went to bed still feeling angry about the whole thing. I was more confused than ever, even after Calvin's help and responding to this relative in a godly way. My spirit was so unsettled. And my cold was feeling worse, too. I was talking it over with God—probably complaining more than anything. And I didn't seem to be able to get any resolution until all of a sudden it came to me, *'Don't let the sun go down while you are still angry.'* Of course, I felt I had a right to be angry...don't we all at times? But I wanted to be obedient to this reminder, so I made the choice to cast out the anger I felt, in the mighty name of the Lord Jesus. I felt different almost immediately. I knew the anger had left me. Just like that. And then I knew forgiveness was in order, so I started to forgive all the ways that he had made me mad and upset. And suddenly, it was like the fog cleared, and I saw what was happening! There was a dark spirit that had been eating at me, wearing me down through many days. It was waiting, just waiting for when the cold had fully set in to let me have it with both barrels! Like a stick that has been whittled into a sharp point, and then it was plunged into my heart. It wanted me to erupt with vengeance toward this man! Thankfully, when we don't know all that is happening, the Fruit of the Spirit really helps us hold fast to what we know to be right. Even when joy, peace, patience, etc., gets eaten up by all the worms from Hell itself, the bookends, love and self-control, seem to hold tight. They did, and no damage from my end had been caused. And by the time I went to sleep, I was thanking the Father for what He was showing me—my perspective had totally changed, with no thanks to my flesh. It was completely a new spiritual awareness that came regarding this situation, reminding me how powerful deliverance can work in our lives. My relationship with this relative didn't change. What changed was how I was dealing with it from the inside. God brought His peace in the midst of it."

"This was something new to you? I'm not quite with you there," I question.

"Well, when I do this kind of ministry with people, sometimes I just need confirmation that what I am doing is right—that it is true to the Word of God. If I'm ministering to people and being used as an instrument for God's Kingdom to cast out demons in Jesus' name, I need a reminder that it really works, not only for others, but for myself as well...a refresher-course, so to speak. God showed me that once again through this situation. I couldn't get the fog to clear. And it wasn't the cold, although that didn't help. As soon as I was obedient to the Lord's commands, to not let the sun go down on my anger, casting it out because it wouldn't be 'crucified' in this instance...and then to *forgive* even when I didn't want to—that was it! Done deal! The Holy Spirit swooped in and said, 'ENOUGH' to the enemy. He had to leave! I was instantly relieved of my anger and resentment and was able to go to sleep in peace. And actually, there was more after that..."

"Which was what?" I asked curiously. What more could there be?

"The dark spirit that was in this man was shown to me, and I knew that it had been working through him to weaken me. Then with the cold I had gotten, the devil did what he does best, hits us while we are down! One last blow when I was at the depth of being sick and tired, and he thought he had me! I know now, even more, that we truly are to be as harmless as a dove, but as wise as a serpent. We are out there as sheep among wolves, as it says in Matthew 10:16. I don't know why we think these things will never happen to us? Because they do! All the time! But we can miss them thinking we are fighting against flesh and blood, when it really is a spiritual battle. This man probably didn't even realize what the enemy was doing through him. But Satan is no dummy. He watches and waits, like any wolf would…he circles, and is ready to pounce when the time is right. But with the weapons we have been given to fight with, we are Victorious!! Always! We just need to know when and how to use them. I was being taught them again. I'm so grateful!"

"It sounds great. But why do we forget? Why don't we do it all the time? Why don't we live this way day to day? I have been learning and making progress. But even with you, Trisha, you've been doing this a long time, but you're saying you can still get caught up in the devil's snare from time to time?"

"Yes. You are right, Linda. And this keeps us humble and shows us our need to constantly be in the Word, praying, and daily focusing on the things of God. The snares are there, we have to watch for them and get out of them as quickly as possible. These times remind us we won't get this absolutely perfected until we are in Heaven where there are no snares. We can't delude ourselves—this is a fallen world we live in. Bad things happen here. That's why we also have to help and remind one another along the way. And, like I said, if we don't have the Fruit of the Spirit operating in our lives, things are going to get a lot messier than they already are."

"How do we have the Fruit that you are talking about? I don't really get that."

"The Fruit is a byproduct of being attached to the Vine, which is Jesus. When we are in the Word daily, and when we stay in close contact with our Father through prayer, we are adding Fruit to our bowl. When we worship, and listen to teachings, and fellowship with other believers, our Fruit is ripening. When we forgive, repent, and walk in obedience, the Fruit grows strong in us. The greater the Fruit bowl is, the more sustenance we will have to work with when tough times weaken us. Between that and the Armor of God…"

"Yes, I have been reading Ephesians six. I have been going through each piece and getting to know them."

"Good. Good for you, Linda. The Armor and the Fruit help us through so much. Then when it all starts to hit the fan in life, we are prepared. It doesn't mean it's easy and nice. It means we are more than able to be conquerors when the battle has ended. I heard once from a young man who plays baseball, and is excellent at it, that the 'Separation is in the Preparation.'"

"What does that mean, Trisha?"

"To me, in this instance with fighting the enemy, it means that we are set apart for Christ. We are to live differently. The young baseball player became excellent at his game because he didn't live like the rest of the team. He didn't party in his off time, and other things the rest of the team did. He ate, slept and lived baseball, on and off the field. His preparation for the game set him apart from the other players. The scouts and coaches took notice of him. We should do no less with our faith in Jesus. If we live differently, biblically, preparing for when the battles come, we will be different than the rest of the world. As it says in Philippians 2:14, *'Then you will shine among them like stars in the sky.'* For this young man, it was a game, and he was a star. For us, it is not a game, it is our life. But God calls us to shine for Him."

"Okay. Thanks for explaining that to me. What did you say it was again? 'Separation is...'?"

"'Separation is in the Preparation.' That dark spirit thought it had me! And it was a close one! But I was prepared. And in the end, not only was Jesus victorious in my life, but I learned once again how powerful He is when we call on His name in the battle. It's a win-win for team God!" Trisha was smiling with eyes twinkling at this point.

"Trisha, thanks for sharing all that with me. I want more and more of this in my life. These last months have been so helpful to me, and I have to tell you, I am thinking about talking to Randy. I know he's not where I'm at, but I would like him to maybe know I'm at least willing to give this another try. What do you think about that?" I ask timidly.

"I think it's very good! I know we will continue to pray about it and see what God would have you do there. It can be very difficult when one spouse is drawing nearer to God, and the other one is more resistant. But we don't really know where Randy is until you talk with him. Is there anything you would like to work on today as you move toward this?"

"Yes. There is something. Many months ago, we dealt with pride, and I have been processing that. I know now that pride has played a big part in dissolving our marriage. We both thought we were right, and weren't willing to give in at all. I want to be more flexible now, more loving, but I also don't want to be overrun by Randy. I can't just bow down and let him be mean, right?" I ask, hoping Trisha will agree with this.

"Of course not. That's not what God is asking you to do. In the Bible it says we are to keep the peace as far as it depends on us. I think that is in…yes. Here it is, Romans 12:18, *'If it is possible, as far as it depends on you, live at peace with everyone.'* From your side, you should do your very best to be obedient to God, humbling yourself before Him, and surrendering your marriage to Him. What Randy does with that is not your responsibility. It could be very heartbreaking, or very wonderful. You will need to be fully attached to the Vine, be prayerful, stay in the Word, and let God work out the details."

"I hear you. Thank you for getting me this far. If we can just work on a few things that I am struggling with, I don't want to keep you much longer today. You have been so faithful in helping me. You have shown me that it is good to touch all the bases when living this life out with Jesus. If we try to run around toward home plate without touching each base, our run won't count. Maybe I'm talking this way because of your story about the baseball player?" I laugh at that.

"So true, Linda. I like baseball, so that's a good way of thinking of this. We have to cover all the bases. First of all, we start with love—so important in God's Kingdom work. *'We love because He first loved us.'* Then, we need to be fully immersed in the Word of God, understanding the Gospel message which is the Good News of Jesus Christ. He came, He died, He rose again! And He is coming back for us! We also have to make sure our flesh isn't getting the better of us, which brings us to that pride issue. Galatians 2:20 says, *'I have been crucified with Christ and I no longer live, but Christ lives in me. The life I now live in the body, I live by faith in the Son of God, who loved me and gave himself for me.'* We have to watch ourselves, and bring our heart and mind into the obedience of Christ…taking *'every thought captive'*…*'praying at all times and on every occasion'*. And then, if things are still out of whack, we can check and see if there is anything that's invaded our soul that we need to get rid of! Once again, starting with forgiveness and repentance. Sometimes as hard as we work at it, some things seem to still get the better of us…like my anger was in the moment. I had to identify that it was a spirit of anger that needed to GO! When it went, I was freed! Thank You, Jesus!"

"I love this process, Trisha. Thank you so much for sharing all this with me."

After more prayers, and discussion, Trisha left for home and Venyce and I enjoyed a Sunday dinner together. I knew I needed to talk with her about Randy, but I wasn't sure how deep into this I wanted to get. I already felt like I'd committed to doing this by mentioning it to Trisha. Do I really want to talk with Randy? What if it ends up being a huge mess that I have to climb out of again? Argh…I don't know what to do.

27

LINDA

I feel scared. When the movie ends, I know I need to say something to Venyce about talking to Randy. I can feel the urge within to do it. But it's so hard...what if I'm then committed to follow through?

I start in timidly, "Venyce, can I talk to you?"

The look on her face says she knows something is up. "Of course, what is it? Did everything go okay with Trisha today?" she asks.

"Oh. Yes. She is amazing. She's helped me so much...in fact, so much that I might be considering talking to Randy about our marriage." There, it's out.

Venyce looks at me with compassion in her eyes. I know she wants the best for me, and that she would like to see my marriage salvaged. I don't know what she's gonna say. So I wait...

She begins slowly. "Lin, I see obedience being very important to you right now. I know this isn't easy. It would be easier to just call it quits, and not go back and face Randy with this. I want you to know that I support you, always. If you do talk with him, and it goes well, I will rejoice with you. If it doesn't, I will pray with you through that also. Be prepared, especially when you first talk with him, that he may not receive this well. He has no idea what you have been doing these past months, and it will come totally out of left field for him. We know...but he doesn't. So, what we need to do is pray for his heart to be receptive, and for the things that need further healing, to be healed. You need things to be put in place for this to happen, to be put in motion, in the power of Jesus' name."

"I hear you, Sis. This scares me a lot. I don't like confrontation, and I don't think Randy is really ready for this. But I believe I am strong enough to face whatever happens. Even now talking to you about it, I feel a surge of courage that I didn't before. Maybe it really is bringing it out into the light that weakens the enemy's forces in this, as Trisha has been teaching me. I really didn't want to say anything to you about this. But I can see now that I needed to. Breaking through that barrier of wanting to hide, I feel free to really do this, come what may."

"That's awesome. Let's pray, okay?" Venyce asks.

"Sure."

Venyce bows and says, "Father in Heaven, You have been with us always. You knew all this would culminate in this discussion tonight. You have a plan in all of this, and we can know it is a good one. It would be nice to know how Randy is going to receive this…and maybe we really already do. So that's what we need to really plead with You about right now. Please prepare Randy's heart for Linda reaching out to him. Help him to not feel threatened, and to be open to at least considering their marriage is worth working on before completely giving up. Help both Linda and Randy to have a forgiving heart, to lay aside their differences, and to look at their future together as being a possibility. I know You would like nothing more than to have their marriage succeed, and that You want to bless it. We trust You in that, and we will watch You work out the details. In Jesus' powerful name we hope and pray. Amen."

"Thank you, Sis. That helps. God is in control of Randy. I just need to do what I need to do and leave Randy to Him. I think now is the time…" I stop there.

Venyce looks at me but doesn't say anything. She is waiting...

I look at Venyce and utter words that I don't even know where I find the nerve to speak, "This is crazy. But I think I need to text Randy right now." I say it quickly, adding, "If I wait, I might lose my nerve."

Venyce just nods in agreement. With hands shaking, I pull out my phone to text him, writing, "I need to talk to you." Pushing send, I let out a long sigh, knowing it's too late to turn back now. I wish I hadn't been so direct once again. I could have started with, "Hi," Something simple. But noooo, "I need to talk to you!" Seriously?! All this is flashing through my mind as I sit and wait for a response. Maybe he's already shut off his phone for the night? Maybe I won't hear back until morning? Uh oh…three dots. Here it comes! His answer is on the way. My heart is racing.

"Okay. When?" Randy texts.

"Venyce, he answered right back! What does that mean? Does he really want to see me?"

"I don't know, Linda. I hope it's an openness from his end," she says.

"What should I say? When should I meet with him? Oh man…I don't know if I'm ready for this."

"Lord, help Linda know where to go from here," Venyce prays.

"How about tomorrow night? I can go by after work?" I say to Venyce, like suddenly I have a plan.

"If that's what you feel led to do," she responds.

"I don't know. But I might as well get this over with!" I say while shaking my head like I'm confused. But I'm not. It seems clear.

I text Randy back, "Tomorrow night. About 6:30?"

"Okay," is his response.

Looking over at Venyce I let her know he texted, "Okay." We both just sit there. I'm pretty much without words and still shaking. I can see that she's hoping the best for me. She reaches out her hand to take mine.

"Sis, I'm proud of you. No matter how this turns out, you are doing well," she says.

"Thank you," I sigh. "I think I should go to bed now. I'm exhausted!"

"I understand. See you in the morning. And I will be praying for you, you know that," Venyce says.

"I know you will. Good night."

Lying in bed, I can't get to sleep. The thought of talking to Randy about all this is overwhelming me. I would love to cancel out at this point. But then what? I'd just have to face it again. I do what Trisha has been teaching me to do, I open up the Bible on my iPad. She said the Psalms are great, and since I really don't know where else to go at this point, I go there, clicking randomly on Psalm 32. It speaks right to my heart in verse six when it talks about having a *"window of opportunity."* I look to see what version I am in. It's the NET. Trisha said she likes this one. I guess that's why it's set to that when I look at it tonight. We had been reading together before she left. Is this my window of opportunity, God? It seems so. If I had delayed, how long would it have been before I got back to being obedient in this? It does feel like obedience. You have healed my heart of so many things these last months. I only pray that Randy will find the same healing. If we both work together on this, it could be good...I just know it could. What else does it say here...ahhh, *"You are my hiding place."* Boy, I need that! Instead of me hiding, I should hide in God. *"You protect me from distress."* I so want Your protection tonight, Lord. Oh, this is interesting, it says in verse seven, *"You surround me with shouts of joy from those celebrating deliverance."* God, this so seems like You, after learning about deliverance from Trisha. Is this the same deliverance? It sure seems similar when I read verse eight. It sounds just like Trisha when it says, *"I will instruct and teach you about how you should live. I will advise you as I look you in the eye."* That direct eye contact is intense when she prays over me like that. But it sure seems to work when calling out that darkness from within. Verse ten says, *"the Lord's faithfulness overwhelms the one who trusts in him.*" I'm feeling better as I read this. Father, I think Your peace is overwhelming those other overwhelming feelings about this whole thing with Randy. You are so wonderful. I want to do what it says here at the end of the Psalm, *"Rejoice in the Lord and be happy!"*

I end my night with praying, Father in Heaven, thank You for bringing me here tonight, to this place in Your Word. You are so faithful. Whatever happens tomorrow night with Randy, I will rest in You and trust You for the outcome of our conversation. I do want to be obedient, even when it's hard. It would be easier to stay away, but You are calling me into the battle—facing it with Your strength. I will do this with Your help. Thank You, Holy Spirit, for Your guidance in this. Thank You, Jesus, for Your love. In Your name I pray. Amen

When I open my eyes the next morning, I know beyond a shadow of a doubt it's time. I'm so grateful to have not missed *"the window of opportunity"* God gave me. It would have made it so much harder to not walk through that open door God provided. I breathe a sigh of relief and say a prayer. I know this day is going to be interesting, that's for sure. It could change my future in so many ways.

28

RANDY

Oh man, Emily is out sick! Now I'm having to handle things she would have. Work is filled with frustrations, and I have Linda on my mind. I was shocked she texted me last night and wants to talk. But then again, it's probably time to get on with things.

The trouble tickets are piling up already, and each one seems to have its own unique problems. I drive over to the burger place at lunch and the line is a mile long. I know I don't have time for it, but I wait anyway. Then they get my order wrong, but I'm already driving back to work while eating it. Forget it! No one knows how to do their jobs right! I try to take in a few deep breaths to clear my head just as my phone dings. I look...Uh oh! It's Dennis.

I read, "You canceled. I understand."

I actually have a good reason now with Linda. Maybe subconsciously that's why I said yes to her so quickly? Now I wish I hadn't.

I look over the texts from her last night..."I need to talk to you." Almost immediately I texted back, "Okay." Maybe I felt caught between a rock and hard place. Dennis or Linda? I really don't want to see either one of them. But now they're both in my face. Oh, man. I'd like to run and hide away some place.

When Linda wrote back, "Tomorrow night. About 6:30?" I wanted to say, "Are you kidding me?" I remember shaking my head. I don't want this. But it really does give me a good out with Dennis. I don't want to burn my bridge with him...I may just need him in the future. Ahh, he'd probably be there no matter what. I think he's found God in a new way, and that makes people do dumb things.

When I texted Linda back, "Okay," my stomach was pretty much in knots. If I hadn't already cancelled out with Dennis, I could have told Linda I was busy. This is getting confusing.

Texting Dennis now, I give him my good excuse. "Hey, Dennis. I want to let you know that Linda is coming over tonight." I don't tell him this happened after I canceled with him. He doesn't need to know that.

"Okay, great!" he answers immediately.

He'll leave it alone now. The day seems so long and exhausting. Maybe because I'm bracing myself for Linda talking "divorce." That's probably what this is about. I don't really want to be married. But divorce never seems like a good thing either. I'm glad when I'm finally driving home from work. Let's get this over with, once and for all.

Linda rings the bell right on time. Going to the door, I open it and am immediately surprised—she's smiling at me.

"Hi, Randy," she says in a tone I haven't heard in a long while.

"Hi," I answer, with skepticism. "Come on in."

"Thanks."

Going into the living room, we both automatically sit in our "assigned" chairs. It's been months and months since we've been here together like this. It seems right, and yet wrong at the same time.

"What's up?" I ask, trying in some strange way to act a little happy to see her since she seems okay.

"Thank you for letting me come over and talk with you. This is something I need to do in person. I know that."

Uh oh, here it comes. Divorce. Maybe that's why she seems happy? Maybe she's relieved that this will finally be done? "Sure. What is it?" I ask, like I don't have a clue.

"Randy, I have some things to say, and I'm hoping you can listen until I'm finished. There are some things you're not going to like, and there are some things you're going to be surprised about. But I need you to hear me out."

"Okay. I'm listening," I say, but silently hoping this won't take all night. What I'm thinking is, just tell me the court date so we can get on with this. My happy facade is completely gone now.

"I'm not quite sure where to start, but I know I need to. Randy, things have been tough between us for years and years. We both know that. It got to a point where I knew I needed some space—for your sake as well as mine. Why continue on like that when it seemed there was no love left between us? We had some good years, and we have some good kids, but those years and the kids didn't seem to be enough to hold us together anymore."

Linda stops there and looks at me. I don't know if I'm supposed to say something at this point, or let her continue to talk, so I wait in silence. This seems like the perfect lead into our divorce.

"Randy, what I'm going to say now is the surprising part, and I really need you to hear me out before you answer."

"Okay," I say, thinking I'm not going to be surprised at all.

After what seems more than a few moments, Linda finally speaks again.

"I want to try again," she says, in almost a whisper.

"What did you say? I'm not sure I heard you right," I respond in quiet tones also.

A little louder this time, Linda says, "I want to try again. I want to start again, but in a different way. This is going to sound strange, but it's the God's honest truth, I believe we can make this work. I haven't just been hanging out with Venyce these past months. I've been talking to a woman. Her name is Trisha. She's a strong Christian, and I've been spending time with her almost once a week. She's helping me a great deal. What's been going on between you and me is not all your fault, and it's not all my fault. There are many things involved, and there are answers, if we're willing to look at them."

"I think…"

"Please, let me finish before you say what I think you're going to say, that there's no hope for us. Because there is, Randy. I know that now. I can't say as I'm fully prepared either for what needs to be done, but with what I have been experiencing so far, and the healing I've found for myself with God, I really believe you and I could make this work. But I also really believe there is only one way, and that is with the help of Jesus. I know…I know…I'm probably going to sound like a Jesus freak here in the next few moments. But I really do need you to listen, and then you can decide whatever you want. Please, at least give me a chance."

I grunt, shake my head, and then Linda continues.

"I've gotten more clarity on what our issues are by taking a look at my own. Neither one of us was putting into this relationship the things it needed. But the thing is, we didn't even realize it. As the kids grew, and moved out, and our jobs moved on, there became this great void between us. It wasn't just because life happens, it's because we have an enemy in this life who is out to steal, kill, and destroy all that is good, holy, and right. You and I have attended church. We have had somewhat of an understanding of who Jesus is. Haven't we?"

"Yeah. We have. I know who Jesus is, and I believe. But…"

"Randy, I'm sorry to interrupt you but I need to finish while I have the courage. There's so much more to Jesus than what we've known. There is so much good, important, powerful stuff about Jesus that we have missed through the years. Yeah, we took the kids to church, probably more for them than for us. And we made sure we were there on Christmas and Easter, and once in a while we would even go in between if we had nothing else going on. But from what I'm learning now, it's not even about that. Jesus has offered us things we're not taking advantage of. And since I've been praying with Trisha, I have started to heal. It's been amazing. What I'm here to tell you is not only do I think we could have a chance at our marriage, but I'd like to try it by moving back in here—not in the same bedroom, but at least in the same house. If we are to ever have a chance, it seems we need to be face to face most days." Whoa, I don't know quite where that came from. That wasn't what I thought this would include.

"Uh, yeah! I don't know about that. Come on, Linda, you started praying more and you suddenly think all our problems are going to be gone? I see this as a disaster waiting to happen. I don't..."

"Randy, please, hear me just a bit longer. Please! This isn't only about our marriage, it's about each of us individually finding a new way of living life. Maybe we can do that together—maybe not. But we might not know what's possible if we don't at least give it a try before we call it quits for good."

Linda is sounding so strong, I start to wonder if all this might have some merit to it?

"Randy, I know you haven't been happy for a long time. And I know it's not just me—it's just the way of this world that drags us down so much. I'd been barely holding on, too. But to what? I had to find out. When I learned what it is I *should* be holding onto, it started to make all the difference. I want you to have that, too. I want you to find the joy that is missing in your own life, really, with or without me. But if we try to do this together, I believe it could actually save our marriage. Maybe our perspective could be adjusted through God's help? All I ask today is that you give this some thought. I won't force this on you. But I knew that I had to come over here and at least talk to you about it. It seemed God was asking me to be obedient in this. I'm discovering how much God loves and cares about all of us. There may come a day, Randy, when you will see me again, and you will wonder why I have a smile on my face. Why I have relationships that are meaningful. Why I'm in church more than twice a year, and why you are...well, lonely. I don't want to see you miserable like this when you don't have to be, and neither does God. He wants to help you. There is an enemy that is fighting against us, and when we recognize that, and see his ways, it can be the beginning of finding a new freedom and joy in this life. The lady helping me, Trisha, told me that the reason some Christians are not being set free and finding true joy is because they don't even realize they are in bondage. I am realizing the bondage I have been in, more and more, and I want to help you realize it, too. There is hope, Randy, real hope! And it's offered to you as well as me. Just think about this, won't you please?"

I can't hardly look at Linda. I look to the floor, then the wall and then to the floor. I know I need to look her way, but it's difficult. She seems so expectant, and I'm feeling more confused than ever. It seems our marital fate is in my hands, and I can't say as I like it. I don't want to look like the bad guy here. I'm finally able to look at Linda when I find some words to say. I can tell they will be harsher than I want them to be the minute I begin; "Well, you've spoken your piece, and I guess…I mean, I appreciate that you care enough to tell me this stuff, whether I believe it or not. But I can't jump right on board with you. I know that. You know that. It all sounds pretty far out there. I mean, I believe in Jesus. But that He can do some sort of miracle and bring any kind of sanity into the nonsense of this life seems far-fetched. I don't see Christians really any happier than other people I know, so I'm hoping you haven't gotten yourself into some sort of psychedelic cult with this Trisha lady. We all have junk in life, and we just have to deal with it. That's the way I see it."

"I understand, Randy, I do."

Linda looks sad, but still holding her own. There's an uncomfortable silence between us now, and I think she's realizing our time here is done.

"Sometimes, Randy, we have to realize we are blind before we are able to see. I don't know all I could about this. But what I do know is that it has been working for me. So just give it some thought. I'm gonna go now. But I will be back in touch with you."

"Don't push me, Linda. I hear you. But if you try to force your new 'thinking' on me, I'll tell you right now, it's not going to work. You need to give me time, so I can do this in my own way."

"Okay. Well, I'm gonna go, and let you be. Thank you for listening."

I can tell Linda doesn't know whether to give me a hug or not. She decides not to. And I don't offer one either. Walking her to the door, I'm not sure what to think or say. I thought she was coming over here to ask me for a divorce. After closing the door behind her, I'm now wondering what the heck is going on? She seems to really be encouraged by what she's doing. She's different, less angry toward me—like she really cares about me. I can't say the same. I don't know how I feel about her in this moment. What I do know is that it's been a long day.

29

RANDY

I haven't heard from Linda, Dennis, or Eric for over a week now. I can't say as I mind. It's a relief, truth be told. Life is just happening, and I'm rolling with it. That talk with Linda was a doozy. She seems to think she found some answers. I think maybe she's found some cuckoo therapist who wants her to think she has all the answers. Now that I've had some time to think about it, I'm not buying it. If it really is that simple, why isn't everybody cashing in on it? I'm gonna start with a pastry and coffee this morning, and just try to make it through the last day of this week.

"Hey, Emily," I say coming through the door. Whatever bug she had last week seems to have passed.

"Hi, Randy. Happy Friday."

"Yeah. Really," I reply, heading toward my office. I *am* glad it's Friday. The weekends are long and boring, but at least I don't have to deal with anyone. Sitting down at my desk, I notice that my stomach isn't feeling so well. I hope I'm not getting Emily's bug now. That's the last thing I need. Trying to ignore it seems to work until about noon—I'm not hungry for lunch and I have to grab for the trash can, losing the pastry and coffee. I know it's time to head home when the shivers quickly follow. Giving Emily a wave of my hand, I head for my car.

The drive isn't good as I have to pull over and let out what little is left in my stomach. By the time I reach home, I know I must really be getting a fever. The chills start to rack my body. Flopping onto my bed, I kick off my shoes. It's about all I can manage as I pull the covers over me. It's a long afternoon and then on into the night as I keep on with the dry heaves and super bad chills...

———⋅✦✦✦⋅———

"Well, hello. It's good to see you back in the land of the living." I don't want to shock Randy that I'm at his bedside. I don't know if he remembers me being here.

Turning toward what sounds like Linda's voice, I'm having a bit of a hard time focusing. "Linda?"

"Yes." I'm not surprised at the look on Randy's face. I'm not who he would expect to see sitting here. I've sort of dreaded this moment, not knowing what our exchange would be like.

"What are you doing...where...where am I?" My voice sounds shaky, and I feel like I've been run over by a truck.

"You're in St. Pete's Hospital, Randy. You've been here since Saturday." Can he really not remember a thing?

"Saturday? What day is it now?" I notice my arm has an IV, and I'm more than a little confused.

"It's Monday, Randy." He looks so tired and pale.

Taking in a deep breath, I exhale with, "MONDAY! How did I get here?"

"You called me."

"I called you?" I can see that Linda is sitting forward in a chair, her iPad on her lap.

"Yes. You called me. You don't remember at all?" This is scaring me a bit. I didn't expect Randy to be this out of it.

"Uh, no. This is Monday...so what day...what day did I call you?" I don't want to sound mad. But I feel very vulnerable all of a sudden.

"On Saturday. Do you remember leaving the office sick on Friday?"

"Yeah. I do, vaguely. I remember the drive home. That was tough. I felt horrible. I puked at the office before I left, and several times on the way home."

"Yes, you did. When I called Emily this morning to let her know you wouldn't be in today, she said she did find the trash can sitting on your desk. She saw you leave quickly, which she said wasn't like you. And when she checked to see if everything in your office was turned off, she saw you had been sick. She said she had been sick the week before. She felt bad about maybe giving it to you."

"Oh. Man. That's a bugger for Emily to have to deal with. But she probably did give me this."

"She was very concerned about you when I told her you wouldn't be in today. I filled her in. She said what she had was bad. But she was surprised you ended up in the hospital with it."

"So, let me get this straight. I left work sick on Friday, and Saturday morning I called you? That doesn't make sense." I can't believe I called

Linda for help. But then again, she would have been easy since she's on my speed dial.

"Yes. I saw your name pop up, and honestly, I thought maybe you were giving some consideration to what we talked about. That's why I answered your call so quickly. Now looking back, that seems like a real God thing. I don't know…I don't know if you would be here today, Randy, if I'd just let it go to voicemail for later. When Venyce and I got to the house, you were sicker than I've ever seen you. You had a tremendously high fever. And we couldn't maneuver you. We called 911, and they brought you here by ambulance."

"Sorry, but I don't remember any of that." Knowing now that Venyce was involved, I feel even worse. I wish I would have called 911 myself. This puts me in a weird place. Both these women were there, taking care of me? I wonder what they walked in on?

"You weren't really talking when we got there—more hallucinating I would say." I can tell Randy's not liking what he's hearing, but I need to let him know. "They started you on IV's right away and got you in here for even more medical attention. Seriously, you were on the way out of this world, I believe, Randy. The doctor said this flu bug going around can damage the heart if not caught in time." I don't want to scare Randy, but it's the truth. Maybe he will understand why I did what I did and I won't have to deal with his anger.

"So, how's my heart? Am I gonna live?" Linda is making this all sound pretty serious. I hope she can't hear the fear I feel in asking that.

"You're gonna live. But you will have to take it easy for a while." Randy's face shows some relief in my answer. But I do wonder how long his recovery will take. I don't really want him to know how scared I have been sitting at his bedside.

Realizing my watch isn't on my arm, I ask Linda what time it is. When she tells me, I wonder how long she's been sitting here? "Do you have my watch?"

"I don't. But it is on your nightstand. I saw it on the charger when we were at the house."

"How long have you been here?"

How do I answer that without sounding overprotective? I know he's not liking me being a part of this whole thing. But I do need to answer his question. "Awhile," seems the safest answer. Changing the subject I tell him, "The doctor said you would probably start recovering by today or tomorrow as the flu runs its course."

"Runs its course. I think it's done a heck of a job already." I know I should be thanking Linda or something. But all I can say is, "I'm hungry."

"Well, that's a good sign. Hunger is good. Other than a few sips of soup, you haven't had much to eat. I got some of that down you yesterday. But it was slow going." Uh oh, I probably shouldn't have offered up that info. But I have felt such compassion for Randy. Maybe my heart really has softened toward him in the whole healing process I've been going through.

"You were feeding me soup? Man, I wish I could remember this stuff. Really?" I still have a hard time believing all this. Shaking my head, it feels heavy and clouded. "Do you know what kind of meds they have me on?"

"I'm not really sure. Mainly they needed to keep you hydrated and get your temp down. It was quite stubborn. You were shaking big time for a while! And sweating. Wow! You looked like I did when I delivered Rob. Remember how I had sweat all over my face from pushing so hard? You looked sort of like that, but without the pushing." I'm laughing at the comparison to having a baby.

It sounds strange to hear Linda laugh. Has it been that long since we had any moments of light-heartedness together? It seems okay to laugh a little now, too, since she started this; "I do remember," I say. "You were working so hard bringing Rob into this world. I don't know how a woman does that! Makes me glad to be a man!"

What a time for the doctor to walk into the room! He's gonna think we are a happily married couple...

"Hi, I'm Dr. Edwards. I've been tending to you, along with your faithful wife here. She's barely left your side," he says to Linda with a smile. "It's good to see you awake. You've had quite the go of it."

Looking at him, and then at Linda, I see her eyes quickly shift toward the floor. It all feels very awkward. I know she's embarrassed by the doctor's words. I feel uncomfortable, too. He's got this all wrong. But I don't think Linda's going to say anything now that I'm awake, so I feel like I need to.

"Thanks, Doc. Uh, Linda said I've been out of it for a couple days now. Is it a bad sign that I don't remember much? Have I lost part of my brain function? Just how bad off am I?"

"You're going to be fine," he answers. "But you were in bad shape. Your wife calling the ambulance was the right thing to do. There was no time to waste."

"Honestly, I don't remember any of that...being in an ambulance." Both of their stares feel so uncomfortable. I feel like a kid—like I'm not able to take care of myself.

Dr. Edwards quickly says, "Well, that's how you got here. Things were really going downhill fast. This flu has taken the lives of some normally very healthy people. It's a tough one."

Linda is still being quiet. She's letting me play out this scene.

"Well, now what, Doc? How long will I be laid up like this?" I know I sound gruff, but I want to gain back my adult status in the room.

"We can probably get you out of here by Wednesday," he says, looking at me and then Linda. "We'll give you one more day to rest up—see that you're able to eat and drink. And then we'll send you on home. You will be quite weak at first. So I'm sorry to say, Mrs. Barker, you'll have to be tending to your husband even after you get him back home. I'll be back tomorrow to check on you again. Are there any other questions you have for me today?"

"No. I guess you covered it. Thanks, Doc." Looking over at Linda, she looks right at me. When our eyes meet, we don't say anything. I know she doesn't want to air our dirty laundry in front of the doctor any more than I do. But what am I going to do? I can't ask Linda to do this. After the door shuts, I ramble out, "Linda, I don't want you taking care of me. That's not your job. You got me in here, and I'm grateful for that. But you don't have to come to the house and play nursemaid. That would be wrong of me to even ask that of you."

"Who else will you have, Randy?"

"Uh, well, nobody. But maybe I can just lay in bed and have a pitcher of water next to me with some peanut butter and jelly sandwiches. I can probably get through this on my own." I'm picturing this scenario, and it seems to have promise.

"Do you want to do that, Randy? Maybe it could work…but then again, that's kind of crazy thinking. You will be very weak."

"Do I want to? I don't want to do this at all! You know how I hate hospitals and being sick." I can feel this has really knocked me for a loop. I don't think I've been in the hospital since I was a kid and had my tonsils out.

"Randy, happily married or not. I can help you, and I'm willing to. So, if you're open to it, I will come and stay at the house, in the other room, until you're feeling stronger. Really, Randy, don't shake your head at this until you've given it some consideration. I want to do this for you."

Looking at Linda, I see she means it. But I have so many reservations.

"Why would you want to, Linda? I don't deserve your help." I'm surprised to hear myself say that.

"Deserve isn't what I'm thinking about here. I've been learning some things, Randy, about what it is to serve, not deserve. Jesus died for us when we didn't deserve it, but He did it out of love for us. And He demonstrated for all of us how to serve one another. I want to be more like that. And I may sound different to you, but that's because I am, Randy."

Linda does seem different. She's never talked to me in this way before. There is strength in her words. Maybe it just seems that way because I feel so weak?

"The healing that I've been experiencing is helping my heart to be more loving. To forgive, even when I don't feel like forgiving. I'm learning that it's not about feelings, Randy. God will help the feelings catch up with the decision after some time has passed. So, I forgive you. Let me say that, right here, right now. And I seek your forgiveness, too. Not so we can be back together, that may never happen. But so that we can live free of the burdens that life has laid on us, no matter where we go or who we are with."

Wow, she really poured that out there. It's making me a little blurry-eyed. I'm feeling overwhelmed, and not ready for this. All this stuff she's been learning. But then again, I feel too weak to fight her on this. Maybe she can just help me get through the next few days. And then she can go on her way, and I'll try to get myself sorted out.

"I…I don't know what I think about all that, Linda. But I do know that I feel completely exhausted right now, and really, honestly, I think I'm scared to be totally on my own when I get home. I don't want to end up back in here. So, if you're really okay with helping me for a few days, then I'm going to say 'yes.' And, Linda…"

"What, Randy?"

"I'll try to be a good patient." I actually smile a bit at that.

"Thanks, Randy. I think we can do this. And who knows…"

"Oh, now don't start…" I don't want Linda to go running off with this, thinking we're moving back in together. I hope she can see my hesitation to even agreeing to this.

"No, Randy. That's not what I mean. What I mean is, who knows how long it will take for you to rebuild your strength. But I don't want you to worry about it. I have plenty of vacation time, and I will lose it if I don't use it up soon. God has provided for just such a time as this."

Good. Linda isn't thinking of this as being back together again. I let out a sigh of relief—vacation time was her concern. "Okay. I'm sorry to use your vacation days for this. But I'm glad you have plenty. Now, if you don't mind, I'm really tired and I can barely keep my eyes open. Would you maybe ask the nurse about me getting something to eat soon, and then I can sleep?"

"They usually bring lunch around now, but I'll check on that. If you need anything from home, let me know. I can bring it in next time I come."

"Thanks. Really, Linda. Thank you." I think I hear Linda say

something more as I close my eyes.
    "You're welcome."

30

LINDA

"Yes, it was crazy, Hannah. Now that your dad is better, I will fill you in on the details. I didn't want you to worry too much until I knew he was going to be fine. I got the call from your dad on Saturday morning, and I can remember yelling for Venyce. She came running to see what was wrong. I told her it was your dad on the phone, and he sounded terrible. She agreed to go over to the house with me and see what was wrong. I was scared that I wouldn't be able to handle him alone when I got there. It was good I did. We found him on the floor in the bathroom, burning up with fever. His shirt was soaked with sweat, and the cold medicine he was trying to take had spilled down the front of him and all over the floor. It was quite the scene."

"What happened then, Mom?" Hannah asked with grave concern in her voice.

"When I called out his name, he sort of mumbled, 'Wha..aa..tt?' I told him he had a high fever. I had Venyce look for the thermometer, but there was no way we could take his temperature. It just wasn't going to work...trying to hold that under his tongue. I wish we'd bought one of those newer kinds."

"Yes. I have that for the baby. No more of the old way, like when we were kids." Hannah laughed at that.

"Yeah, the things we did back in those days." She got me to laughing.

"So, then what did you do?" Hannah asks.

"Well, your dad started to mumble, 'Lin..da...are you here?' I could tell he was so out of it. And we couldn't get him into the bed. Not the two of us. We had no choice but to call 911. Venyce did that. I was shaking pretty badly out of fear for him. It wasn't long before we heard the sirens. When they got there, they checked his vitals and all, and they knew he needed to go to the hospital. I wasn't going to argue with them. I was relieved he would be getting help."

"Did you ride in the ambulance with him, Mom?" Hannah asks.

"No, I had Venyce drive us, so we followed behind. This was all shocking. I saw your dad on Monday, and he was fine. I didn't know when this started. I found out when I called Emily at work that he left there on Friday sick."

"Did they check him right in at the hospital?" Hannah wants to know.

"Oh, yes. His fever was probably as high as 105 or more. That's crazy scary for an adult. Once they got him into his room, I stayed with him. He just slept. He didn't even know I was there. I texted my friend, Trisha, and had her praying. I know all our prayers have helped."

"I hope so, Mom. I'm not a big pray-er, but I did what I could do."

"I know you did, honey. I sort of waited to call you and Rob. I didn't want you to worry. But by Saturday night, you both needed to at least know he was sick. I did my fair share of praying. It's good to have most of this behind us now. Your dad will be getting out of the hospital by Wednesday if he continues getting better. It could have turned out very differently…" My voice trailed off at that.

"Oh, Mom. Dad's going to come through this right? He's going to be okay?" Hannah's voice was shaky now.

"It's okay. Really. He is going to be fine. But there were moments… Once when he was so out of it, and I heard him say, 'Emily.' Honestly, I hate to say this because he is your dad, but I wondered if there was something going on there. You know, with our separation and all."

"Oh, Mom. What do you think? I would hate to…"

"It's okay, Hannah. The things he said after that, I knew he thought he was at work. He started to ask about a folder on her desk."

"Wow. I can't imagine Dad in such a weakened state. He's never been that sick from what I remember."

"He rarely gets sick. But I guess when he does, he does it all the way."

"Yes. Mom, do you think Dad will be able to come out when Jordan is born?"

"We'll have to wait and see. But with our separation, I don't know if that would have worked anyway. It's not something we've talked about."

"Will you still be able to come, Mom? I don't want to take you away from what Dad needs. But I want you here with me, too."

"I know. I really believe your dad will be fine by the time Jordan arrives. Maybe I will talk with your Aunt Venyce and see if she'd like to come with me. Would that be okay?"

"That would be awesome! How long do you think you can stay?" Hannah's mood lifted at the change of subject.

"I'll have to wait and see. I'm so excited to see our new little guy! I'll wait to hear from you, and then we'll make our plans. I know it will cost more. But I don't want to get out there too early and have him born after we need to get back here."

"I know. Thank you, Mom. I'm so glad you will be here. And that Dad is getting better. I was really scared after you called me. I can rest easier now. Will the two of you be okay?" Hannah asks with a bit of sorrow in her voice again.

"We will be. I've been working on things in my own life, as I've told you about. God will take care of us. Really, He will."

"Okay. Mom. We'll talk soon then. I know you're tired, so get some rest."

"I will, honey. You rest, too. Soon enough you will have a little one to take care of. Bye for now."

"Bye."

Hanging up, it was good to think about baby Jordan coming soon, and not just Randy being sick. That really was scary. It's nice to have something exciting to look forward to coming out of this. I need to call Rob now, and then get some rest.

31

RANDY AND LINDA

"Thank you for driving us home, Linda. I am too weak to attempt this alone. I really appreciate that you will be with me while I recover. The doctor was right when he said I'd be out by Wednesday. I guess they do know how long this flu bug lasts. I really don't want to be there anymore. I'll be glad to be home."

"I guess they do. Do you want to stop and get anything on the way? Or I could run out later for whatever is needed."

"I'd really like to just get home in my own bed, Linda. I still feel so tired."

"That's fine. Let's go get you settled, and then I'll check on food supplies and such. I have plenty of time off, like I said. So, I don't want you worried about this. I even have enough left for when Hannah calls about our new little grandson! Every time the phone rings lately I wonder if it's her?" I smile at this.

Looking at Linda, I can tell she's excited to be a grandma. I wish I could say I have some excitement for this, and maybe I will. Maybe when I recover more…I'll change my mind and be a happy grandpa. Maybe…about a lot of things…right now I don't have the energy to think about any of it.

By Wednesday night, it feels comforting to be able to eat a bowl of soup Linda brought in to me. It's her own recipe, and I've never tasted anything so good. I loved it before, but now it tastes even better after dining on hospital food for a couple of days. And I smell her baking cookies in the kitchen. It's been a long time since I've enjoyed her desserts. When Linda comes in to get the empty bowl, I know I need to talk to her.

Something is burning in me, and it's not from the fever anymore. I'm starting to realize I might be ready…ready for change. There's that word again.

"Linda, can you sit with me for a minute? And, thanks…thanks for the soup. It was really good."

"You're welcome. Sure, I'll sit for a bit."

"What are you baking?"

"Snickerdoodles."

"Oh. Nice. I haven't had those in a long time." Swallowing a couple of times, it's hard to get started. But I know I need to. "Linda, I've had some time to think, although I'm still not clear-headed completely. But what's coming to me scares me, actually."

"Scares you? Are you feeling like you're relapsing?"

"No. No. That's not it. But what I'm realizing is that I'm tired. Sick and tired. But not in the way the flu made me sick and tired. It's the way being *me* does."

"Oh?"

"I really don't know where I'm going with this. I don't even know where to start, or if I really have it in me to do this right now. But I've been thinking about the things you said to me before I went into the hospital. And you seem to be making strides in life. And you seem happier. Even though we aren't together, you're still here taking care of me. And I don't feel any edge to what you're doing. I don't feel like you're going to say, 'Now you owe me.' Nothing like that. And maybe if you can be like that, I can change, too. It may not save our marriage. But selfishly, maybe it will save me from my depression, if you can call it that. I don't know if you know it or not, but I'm a miserable man. Even on my good days, I'd give them about a two."

"A two?" My heart hurts to hear Randy say that.

"Yeah. And I'm exhausted from it all. I didn't realize how much until this flu hit me. Maybe it knocked me upside the head in a good way? This seems to have taken what little strength I had left to battle through life. I just don't feel like I can do it anymore. I'm not sure I want to. And that scares me, too." I can feel the tears wanting to break through, and I do my best to hold them back. This isn't about getting Linda to feel sorry for me. When I regroup, I'm able to say, "I don't know if you know, but I've got a couple of guys…well, you remember Dennis, don't you?"

"Yes. Of course, I do. You haven't seen much of him for a long while."

"Well, I talked to him recently. Mostly because he has a friend named, Eric. And Eric called me. Dennis actually put him up to it. Kind of strange, I know. But we had dinner together a while back."

"You did? With this guy, Eric?" I'm very surprised at this.

"Yes. And Eric, well, he helped Dennis. Dennis was a miserable guy like me. That's probably why we got along. We could sit and complain for hours, rag on people, make fun of people, and spur each other on to more misery. It worked for us. But Dennis changed. And I wasn't much interested in Dennis after that, or Eric when I met him, for that matter. But maybe this is what you've found? I don't really know. I hate the thought of any kind of help or counseling. But honestly, I considered it even a while ago. Something's gotta give, or I might just give in. The dark cloud over my head seems to be raining more and more, drenching me in a funk. It feels horrible. I could deal with it before, just grin and bare it...or forget the grin, just bare it. But I don't know that I can anymore. I feel more like giving up than ever before. And where is that going to take me? I hate to think."

"Oh, Randy." I'm so concerned for him in this moment—but gaining some hope that he wants help.

"I'd like to say I wouldn't do anything stupid. But I can't even say that. Most of the time I wonder what difference it would make anyway? You've got your life. The kids have theirs. And none of my long-lost friends would miss me." I could feel myself whining some, and I knew I needed to stop.

"Randy, I don't really know what to say. Other than, thanks for talking with me. I'm sorry you're so miserable. But I'm not surprised. And as for change, it can be a scary thing. But not changing can be even scarier...considering what you're talking about. I know these last few days have really taken it out of you. I can see your face is drawn, and you're pale. But if this is what it takes for you to feel better, and I mean really feel and *be* better, then I'm going to be thanking God for it...for you to be open to some help."

"Linda, I could have died, I guess. And part of me would have been happy to have been done. But since it must not have been time for me to go, maybe I should figure out how to stay and start over. Even with you. Now, I don't want to rush you, or rush me, but you asked about maybe moving back in here, and working on some things. I want you to know, you're welcome to move your stuff back in, if you can stand being with me once I'm well. I'm not making any promises that it will be all sunshine and roses. But I...I will promise to get some help. I've already decided that when I'm stronger, I'm going to give Eric a call and meet with him. I'll start there and see where it goes. I don't know if he has what I'm looking for, but at least I have a place to begin. Eric asked me a good question when we were at dinner. He asked me what I want? I didn't have an answer for him then. I may have an answer now; I want to feel better, and of course, get over this flu...but I mean really feel better...about life, about me, maybe even about us...and possibly God. If God is the way through and out of this, then I will try to find that out. If I do have some options, I need to discover them. I thought being a Christian just meant saying 'Yes' to Jesus. But that's not working so well for me. Is there more to it than that?"

"I believe there is, Randy. Really, I do." It was good to be able to answer this sincerely for him in this moment.

"Have you found the 'more'?"

"I don't know that I have completely," I answer. "But I believe I'm moving further along in the process of discovering there's an abundant life that Trisha talks to me about."

"Abundant? I'm just hoping for sane. Maybe a little peace." I was able to chuckle a bit at that.

"Well, Randy, if that's not with God, then who? Maybe as we both find our respective people to show us some new things here, we can even talk about this together as time passes? That is, if you want to?"

"Maybe. I don't know yet, Linda. I don't want to crowd you, and I don't want you crowding or forcing me. I can feel the pressure…but maybe it's me putting it on myself."

"I will keep my distance until you want to talk, Randy. Seriously, I will. And if after some time has passed and we still decide to end all this in a divorce, I won't fight you on it. But for now, let's see what can be done. Agreed?"

"Agreed. I know I need you here right now. I'm weak, and I don't like it. I need your help. And that's hard for me to admit. But maybe I need Eric's help, too. You've been good to me. Being here for me. I don't want you to rush right off when I'm better. So, just hang out. And maybe…well, we'll just see. Okay?"

"Okay. Can I get you any more soup?"

"No. Thanks. But I could eat a cookie or two!" This makes both of us smile. "Linda, thanks for hearing me out. I can be a real jerk, and you didn't have to come back and help me. I do appreciate it."

"You're welcome. I'll be right back with your cookies, and then I'll let you get some rest."

"Perfect." As Linda gets up to leave, I feel a glimmer of hope. Taking in a deep breath, I know there is a lot of work ahead, and right now I'm too tired to think much more about it. But soon, I will give Eric a call. Won't he be surprised to hear from me! I hope he is up for the challenge! I hope I am.

32

RANDY AND LINDA

"Linda, I'm going over to see Eric tonight after dinner." After two weeks, I'm finally able to be back at work and have enough energy to get some other things started now.

"I'm so happy for you, Randy. It's good to see you get some of your strength back." Living here and taking care of Randy, we have been acting like friends. That seems like a good start.

"I'm nervous about how this will go, although I'm glad to get started. I did okay with Eric the first time we met, but it seemed more about baseball then. From what you tell me about your time with Trisha, this could be good stuff. If it's the same."

"If it is, then yes. It's good." I want to encourage Randy as much as possible in this. I don't know Eric, but I'm trusting that God has brought him the right guy to spend time with. Could this really be an answer to all the prayers that have been said while working with Trisha? I hope so.

Sitting with Eric later at his house, he seems so sure of it all when he tells me, "Randy, there's a verse in the Bible that talks about having a mustard seed of faith. God can move a mountain with it."

"Eric, I hope you know, this mountain you're talking about is like Mt. Everest. It's HUGE! Are you sure you want to tackle this with me?" For the first time in my life I feel I may be ready to let the bulldozer dig through the dirt contained in my life.

"For sure. This isn't about what I can tackle. This is all about what God can and will do when we ask, seek, and knock. He will answer us, be found by us, and open up His Kingdom to us. God gave me my instructions a while back. It was in a book I was reading on an airplane. It said to not resist what God is calling me to, but to yield humbly and lovingly to it. It comes out of 1 Thessalonians 5:24 where it says, *'He who calls you is faithful, who also will do it."* On the flight, I was praying about the direction God had me moving in—and not just during the flight." Eric laughs at that, and then goes on. "I understood then that God was bringing me into this ministry of helping people find their freedom in Christ. When I saw that written in the book, I knew it was for me. What I have learned is that apart from Him I can do nothing, but with God all things are possible. God isn't afraid of your mountain! So neither am I!"

"Good to know!"

"And right from the start, I want you to understand the reason I will use scripture when I talk to you is not so I sound super religious. The thing with scripture is, it weakens the enemy. He HATES it! Think about how Jesus battled Satan in the wilderness for forty days. Every time He was challenged, Jesus responded with a verse from the Old Testament like, *'Don't test the Lord your God,'* or *'You must worship the Lord your God and serve Him only.'* Satan left Jesus eventually. He'd probably had enough. Oh, he would come back again. But in the meantime, the angels came and cared for Jesus. We want Satan to have 'enough' in our lives, too. So, we will be using the same weapon Jesus used—The Word!"

"It does sound all a bit much. But I'm going to try and ride this out with you, Eric. I will listen, you can talk, and we will see what happens."

"I appreciate your willingness," Eric replies. "Can I tell you a few things to get us started?"

"Sure," I reply, trying to sound completely on board. I feel like I've got my toe in the ocean, and I don't know if I really want to walk out into surf.

"This is not a short one-time meeting, and all-is-well type of thing. You didn't get to this place in your life in a day, and even though God does work miracles, most times He will take us through a process of healing and moving us through it. Some do quit smoking in a day, or things like that. But what we are probably heading into with you is clearing out years of the enemy shooting fiery arrows into your soul. Think of your spirit as being the center of a circle, and then around that you have your soul, and then your body. Your spirit is sealed with the Holy Spirit because you have told me you have invited Jesus into that place in your heart. It cannot be touched by the devil. But your soul and body can. And Satan has been very busy attacking you. I know you feel it."

"Oh. I do," I reply. "I feel the weight, if that's what you're talking about."

"It is. It's a heavy burden you're carrying. And you are right when you say we will need a bulldozer to move this mountain. But don't let that discourage you. God has *thee* best equipment ever, and He can do what's needed if we will only come to Him with a humble heart."

"Sadly, Eric. I don't see myself as being all that humble, so maybe we should just quit this right here. If I had a humble heart, I probably wouldn't be in the mess I'm in," I reply, feeling guilty.

"I understand, more than you know, Randy. But let's start there then. Just being honest with God, saying 'I don't have a humble heart.' God can take that, and work with it, just by you admitting it. You see, when we bring any darkness in our soul out into the light of God, there again, it weakens the enemy. He's no dummy. If he can keep stuff hidden, he knows that's where his power is. By you admitting you're not humble, the enemy has already lost ground."

"Really?"

"Yes. Let's just say you agree with the enemy on that point," Eric went on, "that you're not humble. That's actually a very powerful thing to do. Instead of getting defensive, just accept that you have sin in your life. Tell the enemy he has just reminded you how much you need a Savior. And how thankful you are that Jesus' blood covers all your sins. No sin outweighs Christ's forgiveness on the Cross when we come to Him and accept His atoning blood. Isaiah 53:5 says, *'...with His stripes we are healed.'* Some take this to mean we won't ever have sickness again, or troubles, or temptations. We have to understand this is a fallen world we still live in. We are "healed" for all of eternity; that is about our salvation. But until then, we have to stay in the Word and remain close to our Savior to be able to deal with the enemy and all his ways. Many of us will have a predisposition to certain things...addictions, sexual issues, anger, anxiety, and so on. Some things will tempt us in a greater way than others because of inheriting things that have come down through the generations. Exodus 20:5 talks about sins through the third and fourth generations and how God deals with them. But it also says God lavishes His love on those who love Him for a thousand generations. I like that balance. We can put a stop to generational sin in the power of Jesus' name. We are never without hope! And leaving our children and grandchildren a legacy of hope and faith is so important.

"I guess so," I respond while thinking about what Eric is saying.

"Randy, some of us have dark areas in our lives because of the choices we are making, and even the people we are choosing to spend time with— that can be a huge influence. If we want to live a godly life, then hanging around godly people can surely help us! But wherever we find ourselves, we can find freedom through Jesus and the ways He shows us to battle against all of this. So, do you wanna begin there, Randy? With humility? With your heart problem?"

"Uh, yeah. Let's do this," I answer, not really knowing what that will entail, but Eric seems to know.

"I'm going to open my Bible, and I don't want you to feel overwhelmed. I know a lot of what we are going to do is going to be new to you, and probably make you feel uncomfortable at first. But hang with me. I'm not here to preach to you, I'm here to introduce you to the One who has all the answers, because I don't. And if I attempt to do any of this without God, without the leading of the Holy Spirit, this will fail. Guaranteed. So, me opening the Bible first off is as much for my sake as it is yours."

"Okay. I hear ya."

"I'm going to read just a little here in Matthew five. That's where the Beatitudes are. That's a big word that just means blessings. Jesus sat down with His main guys, called the disciples, and was teaching them some things. There are eight blessings in the Beatitudes. I'm going to start this whole process like you're not well versed in the Bible, would that be okay?"

"Yeah. Sure. I don't know a whole lot so that's fine with me. I probably need it."

"Okay. So, Jesus is with His guys, and the reason I want to read just the first blessing here is because of where we all find ourselves when we eventually drop to our knees and call out to God. Jesus said, *'God blesses those who realize their need for him, for the Kingdom of God is given to them.'* Now this is in the New Living Translation, and I'm using that today because it might be easier to understand."

"It seems clear enough. But I want to hear your take on this."

"Okay, let me pray, Randy, and then we'll talk further about this."

"Father in Heaven, we are here today to get to know You more, through Your Son, Jesus Christ, the One who came in the flesh. This world will tell us about many named Jesus. But we only want the One True Jesus, the Christ. And we know the only way to You, Father, is through Him, and through the power of Your Holy Spirit that lives inside all those who believe. We come to You today, confessing that we need Your Son. We believe He came from Heaven, walked this earth, died on the Cross for our sins, rose again on the third day, and ascended back into Heaven where He now sits at Your right hand, interceding for us. We are in complete agreement with this, Father... Aren't we Randy?"

"Uh. Yeah. That's the way I understand it, and have believed," I answer.

"Good, then let's continue."

"Father, it's through the shed blood of Your Son, Jesus, that our sins are washed clean, and that we are eventually welcomed through Your Heavenly gates into eternal life. Randy and I are going to be on an adventure of healing together in the coming months, and possibly longer. We don't know what Your plan will be in this, but our plan is to be obedient to You to the best of our ability. I ask that You help me as I walk alongside Randy through this season of his life. I ask that You fill me with Your wisdom and Your knowledge, stopping me if I venture off into my own way of doing things. I need Your help, as does Randy, and we are here together seeking You. We realize our need for You, and we pray that the Kingdom of God will be near each time we meet. It's in the mighty and holy name of Your Son, Jesus Christ, that we pray. Amen."

"Amen. Wow. Huh. Is that how this is gonna go?" I ask, already a bit blown away.

"Yes. That, and so much more. And I'll tell you why. What's important is that we lay a foundation on the solid Rock of Jesus Christ, so anything that's built on that as we go along will be sure, steady, and true. If healing of any kind is not built on the Solid Rock, but instead on shifting sand, then it's not going to hold up in future storms. We're going for healing and restoration here that comes from Heaven above, not from earth. This world does not contain what we need."

"Well, it seems to me that God has brought me the right guy for the job. But please, be patient with me because this is a load of stuff already, and I don't know if I'm up for it," I say with probably a dumb look on my face.

"Randy, foundations need to be strong, so a lot of 'cement' is poured in the beginning. But now, as we go through this, we will build, or should I say, rebuild, your life little by little. We may come back to check on the foundation as we go along. In fact, I should say we WILL come back to this foundational teaching along the way, always refocusing on Jesus. But that's not to question what we are building on, instead it's to reinforce that we are building on the one true Source of healing."

"Well, you sound like a guy who's been there before. I'm a techie, and I know the system needs a well-designed mother board to work. So, I'll look at it that way. A fault in the motherboard will cause the whole system to crash with a BSOD."

"BSOD?" Eric repeats, not really getting it.

"Yes, a Blue Screen Of Death," I tell him.

"Oh. Exactly, Randy. And we want your 'system' up and running and fully functional. The enemy has been trying to steal, kill, and destroy your 'motherboard' up to this point. We are going to make sure that it is set in place and working as it should. Otherwise you will continue to see 'error codes' and such. Is that what you would call them?"

"That's it. You do understand this terminology."

"Somewhat. So, this is rebooting your brain, so to speak. The Bible talks about a renewal of your mind. Let me turn to Romans 12:2. Here it is. It says, *'Don't copy the behavior and customs of this world, but let God transform you into a new person by changing the way you think. Then you will learn to know God's will for you, which is good and pleasing and perfect.'* The NIV version, and many others, talks about it being *'a renewing of your mind.'*"

"Hey, if you can reboot my brain, that would be awesome! Get out those bugs that have been eating me alive."

"Exactly. I can't, but God can. Some live their whole lives not knowing that God makes all things new in this way, even our minds, when we come to Him," Randy explains.

"I'm all for that."

"Then let's get started, Randy. We have poured a lot of the foundation. Not let's see where God will take us from here."

The next two hours, Eric and I went over a lot of stuff. When I discussed it later with Linda, we could tell Eric and Trisha were on the same page. It was good to bounce these things off of one another. Eric had explained to me all about forgiveness, and he sent me on a quest of repentance and forgiveness before our next time together, just like Trisha had done with Linda. He also recommended I remove from my "space" anything that tempts me, that is dark, or just isn't what God would have me focusing on. I'm not so sure how that will go, and I can't say as I look forward to it. But I will try. It seems to have been helpful for Linda, from what she tells me.

33

RANDY AND LINDA

When I got home after that first meeting with Eric, Linda understood I had a lot to think about and work through. Eric was very patient and told me some things that really hit on target during our initial time together. The first night in the restaurant I don't really count—I was more interested in the baseball game. I wasn't ready for any of this. I'm still not 100 percent sure that I am as I sit here waiting to meet with Eric again. A lot of what he had to say was difficult that last time we met. It's good Linda is going out, so we can have privacy. She's doing well in giving me space with this as she continues to meet with Trisha. She's so much further along than me.

When Eric arrives, he doesn't waste time getting right to the point after we sit down. He prays, and then we talk over the forgiveness that I've been working through. He and I both know I have a ways to go. Eric encourages me to keep on with that, and then begins to talk to me about some other things. Eric keeps me on my toes. He's a no-nonsense guy. I can tell he is really in his element.

"Randy, I'm going to ask you some questions, and make some notes about what you struggle with, if that's okay?"

"Yeah. That's fine," I reply.

"Let me know what part of this hits home with you? Do you deal with anger, inferiority, and lust, to start with a few things that are common to many people?"

"Yeah. Pretty much," I answer, but not really wanting to admit it.

"How about fear, hatred, frustration?"

"Yes. Yes. Yes." Each word he says seems to cause me more discomfort.

"Do you deal with loneliness, depression, maybe suicidal thoughts?"

"Sadly, yeah. I have more of late," I answer. I can feel myself fidgeting. Eric notices it.

"This isn't to make you uncomfortable, Randy. This is to let the enemy know we mean business. His days of hiding in you will come to an end. We are going to call things what they are, and get them out into the light."

"Okay. Although the forgiveness and repentance exercises have kept me occupied and I don't feel as depressed lately." Maybe it was good I could add something positive in here.

"That's really good to hear. It's loosening some of the bondage you've been in. I would suspect the enemy is not in as much control anymore. In Ephesians four, it talks about throwing off our old sinful nature—we all have a former way of life—it says that we have been corrupted by lust and deception. But we are to let the Spirit renew our thoughts and attitudes."

"Wow. I like that!" I say with some surprise. "Is that what I've been doing?"

"Yes. Forgiveness is the beginning of renewing a lot of things that have buried us in deception. Okay, Randy, let's talk about what's hidden behind the curtain in all of this. I want you to know, this is not you. Although it feels very much like you. What you may not have realized in life is that there is a battle going on. It's talked about in Ephesians six, and how we are not fighting against people made of flesh and blood, but against the evil rulers and authorities of an unseen world. What this basically means is that what we see with our eyes is not our problem. The people we fight with, and even our struggles with our flesh, is not the problem. The problem lies a lot deeper, and actually a lot higher than that, and we have to have a willingness to let these things go. The verse in Ephesians six goes on to talk about wicked spirits in the heavenly realms."

"Whoa, that's not sounding good," I say.

"Actually, this is very good news," Eric replies.

"How can you say that?" I ask.

"Because there is an answer for what plagues us. What's hard is when we have a question and we don't know the answer, right?"

"Right."

"Well, we do know the answer to the question of why we are like we are, and why others are like they are. It's a spiritual battle. You and Linda, you argued, right?" Eric asks boldly.

"Well, yeah. We are on the verge of divorce, so that's pretty much a given," I let him know.

"Those fights, that anger you felt, is not of God. That's the enemy trying to get in and divide you two. I know when you're angry you feel you have good cause to be. And sometimes, yes, there is a good reason.

But most times, we end up fighting with our words, with our actions, instead of with our prayers. If we took what's wrong to God, many times, He is able to give us a much different perspective on the problem, and the anger will leave us. I know it's sounds too good to be true. That's because it is good, but this time it's also true. God is amazing! We just don't give Him enough attention in the midst of the battles to show us just how amazing He is. And sadly, many times, we Christians walk around like white-washed tombs wanting to ignore that Satan and his demons are actively pursuing our demise. We are more concerned with looking like we have it all together than really getting it all together. We end up fighting things out in our own strength, which is exactly what the enemy wants us to do. We are no match for the devil. Only Jesus can defeat him. If we turned it over to God, oh, how different our battles could be."

"How so?" I exclaim.

Eric answers me confidently, "God's children are Satan's main target. Not the unbelievers. He's already got them in his camp. And the enemy has specific goals in mind for us. First, he wants to keep us from knowing Jesus. But then if we do come to know Jesus, he will do everything he can to keep us from having a close relationship with Jesus and sharing His Good News with others. Satan is very, very busy at his work. And he has to be, since only a third of the angels joined his forces, while two thirds of the angels remained with God. When the split came, Satan was outnumbered from the beginning. That's good news for us!"

"Sounds like it."

"It is. So, Satan can't be everywhere at once, like God can. He sends his armies out to work in our lives, in our marriages, in our families, in our friendships…even in our churches. He wreaks as much havoc as possible before his time is up on this earth. There will come a day when he and all the rest of his cronies will be thrown into the bottomless pit. Halleluiah for that!"

"Yes. Then all this junk will be done away with?"

"Exactly," Eric answers. "But until then, what are we supposed to do?"

"I don't know. You tell me," I ask.

"We are to follow Jesus and do what He told us to do."

"Which is what?"

"Let Jesus set us free, and then share that freedom with everyone we know with the time we have left. But too many don't walk in that freedom, so they have very little to share that is appealing to the world around them. If there is no power in our lives, there is no Good News in what Jesus is doing in our lives, wouldn't you say?"

"Sounds right," I answer. "I certainly haven't been experiencing any of this power you're talking about."

"Well, let's look at Luke 4:18, *'The Spirit of the LORD is upon me, for he has anointed me to bring Good News to the poor. He has sent me to proclaim that captives will be released, that the blind will see, that the oppressed will be set free.'* Because we have the Holy Spirit now living in us, we should be able to bring the Good News of Jesus and the power of Jesus to others. We should be able to tell those who are bound up by so much junk in this world that they can be released from it. But first we have to let Him save us! We have to breathe in the Holy Spirit, filling us to overflowing. Then that overflowing helps the next person do the same. Jesus commands us to go and make disciples when we are walking in that freedom. And He gives us the power to heal the sick, cast out demons, raise the dead. That's a tall order! But it's very exciting work, if we're willing to be a part of it."

"That sounds way out of my league, Eric."

"I know. And that's because you have been living as one of the oppressed—and the blind can't lead the blind or they will both fall into a ditch. The other day I demonstrated that for my grandson. He's eight. I told him to walk behind me, with his eyes closed, and that I would close my eyes also. Then we walked forward together, and both fell into the couch, and laughed. But I wanted to demonstrate for him how the blind cannot lead the blind, like the Bible says. That's why those that have 'sight' help others to regain theirs, or maybe get it for the first time. Then, when they can see, they can lead another. That's making a disciple. It's like a ripple effect, and it has been going on since Jesus commissioned the early believers over 2,000 years ago. We are part of that same team, just in a different era—not less effective for the Kingdom of God, but maybe even more needed as the time of Jesus' return gets closer. That's what I'm doing here with you today."

"Sounds like you have a plan. I like a man with a plan." I could see that Eric doesn't pull any punches. I like his approach, though it isn't all easy to swallow at first.

"Jesus laid out the plan, as He got it from His Father, and we will continue on with that. It is fail-safe!"

"Awesome!" I respond with a bit of genuine enthusiasm, even though I have no idea what all this entails.

"The thing is," Eric continues, "we can't get all this just by sitting in the pews on Sunday. We have to allow it to penetrate and change our lives, every day. Because many leave God in church on Sunday, even Jesus' followers are not aware, many times, of what spiritual warfare is all about and how to battle it. And those that are aware, and are fighting this battle head-on outside church walls, can seem...well, weird to even other believers. But let me just tell you now, before we even get too far along in this, I have seen people set free in amazing ways. I have seen people who were fearful, gain confidence in Jesus. I have seen people freed from addictions. I have seen peace come into a person's life who knew no peace. I have seen things healed in myself, personally, that could have only come from Jesus. And I know with a willing heart, all things are possible. It's time to put the enemy in his rightful place as the weak opponent that he is and put Jesus on the Throne of our lives. Otherwise, too many of us will live defeated, shut down, and miserable, separating ourselves from anything and anyone that's good in our lives."

"You're pretty much describing me, Eric."

"Well, you don't have to stay that way. Not anymore, brother. I'm telling you today, there is Good News that will set you free. And like I said, it won't be overnight. But it will happen, as we walk this out together seeking the face of our Savior, and all He died to give us. If you remain passive, life will continue on as it has always been. But if you're willing to step out and receive all that our Father in Heaven wants you to have, it can be yours. I'm not saying that He's going to make you a millionaire or get you that big fancy house. What I'm saying is that you're going to live with peace in your heart no matter what your circumstances—just like Paul who lived content with little or much. He could do that because he lived free in Jesus. We can have that, too."

"You're making sense. I'm listening."

"Well, there's a lot more! I know this is a lot to think about for one day. And I do thank you for allowing me the privilege of being involved in your life right now. When I see people healed in Jesus' name, and set free in Jesus' name, there is no greater joy! When people finally get to the point where they say 'enough is enough,' and want something different, then it's time to begin. When we unclench our fists and let go of the way it has always been, we are ready with open hands to receive all that our Father in Heaven would love to give us. We have to come to a point where we draw a line in the sand between our old life and the new life Jesus is offering us. Are you with me, Randy? Is this what you want?"

"I think so, Eric. It sounds good."

"It's something to continue to pray about. 'Sounds good,' and it becoming a reality in your life, can be worlds apart. Being set free from many things can happen fairly quickly. Living in that freedom is what takes the real commitment. This is a lifestyle choice. Colossians 2:6-7 says, '...*you must continue to live in obedience to him. Let your roots grow down into him and draw up nourishment from him so you will grow in faith, strong and vigorous in the truth you were taught.*' I love teaching you these things. Only time will tell your level of commitment to this new way of living. Let's finish up here today with a prayer. We'll set another time to meet and continue on."

Eric bows and prays, "Father in Heaven, we are two men wanting all Your Son died to give us. We will walk this road together toward true freedom in Jesus, following the guidance of the Holy Spirit each step of the way. It's not an easy journey. That I know. But it is a very possible one when our eyes are on You, and our heart's desire is to be obedient to You. Please help us in all of that. With Your Holy Spirit, and the strength You give to us, we will learn to walk in the victory that has already been won through Jesus Christ our Lord. It's in Your name we pray. Amen."

"Amen. Thanks Eric. Is there anything I should be doing before our next meeting?"

"I'm glad you asked that, Randy. Think about any debts you owe, anything that needs to be repaid. And also, blow the dust off your Bible. I know you told me you've got one, but it's in pretty good shape. Mess it up! Read it, write in it, pray through it, learn from it. Wear it out! The Bible was given to us to warn us, shape us, guide us, teach us, and instruct us in so many ways. When we ignore God's instruction manual, it's not good for our body, soul, or spirit. We need to know our Maker, and how we are made. The Bible will tell us that. Try memorizing a scripture before we meet again. It doesn't have to be long and complicated. But get God's Word buried deep in your heart. It will come in so handy when there are battles to be fought."

"Okay. I'll give all that a try. I know I need to develop new habits. It just feels so hard."

"I know. I know. I've walked in those shoes already. Plow through the hard and you will see amazing results. See you next time, buddy. Call me if you have any questions."

"I will."

As I walk Eric to the door, I know I have my work cut out for me. I can feel the resistance already to the things he's given me to do. Was I really being honest when I told him I want this? I know I'm tired of the same old life I've been living. Maybe Eric is really on to something here? Time, and some effort on my part, will hopefully tell.

As I watch Eric drive off, I see Linda pulling into the driveway. Perfect timing; she's been out shopping. I give her a wave, and walk to the car, asking if I can help her with anything? I'm surprised at myself. It wasn't so long ago that I couldn't have cared less about helping her carry her suitcase upstairs.

"Thanks, Randy. I think I bought a little much," she says, handing me some bags. "But with little Jordan coming soon, I want to make sure I'm ready. Baby clothes are just too cute!"

I smile and nod at Linda, even though I don't get it...they are just clothes. Trying to be congenial, I inquire, "What's your plan when the news comes? I haven't asked that yet."

"I know the trip would be too much for you right now, Randy, from what your doctor said. So, I hope you don't mind that I asked Venyce if she would like to go with me to Boston for a week. She was excited!"

"That sounds like a good plan," I answer, somewhat okay about it. "I don't know if I would have gone anyway. You can send me some pics."

Linda smiles at me saying, "I will. Thanks for your help with these, Randy."

Walking into the house, I think we both sense there is something different between us—how long it will last, only time will tell.

34

RANDY

Linda has left for Massachusetts to see our new grandson, and I'm left to meet here with Eric again. I'm not feeling good about this at all today. It's been three weeks since our last time together. We did talk on the phone twice. But I can tell I've pretty much given up on the forgiveness stuff. It's just too hard. I don't want to tell Eric that—I don't feel like those people deserve my forgiveness. I mean that guy who killed my brother! Seriously!! He needs to rot in that jail cell and feel bad about what he's done. When I see Eric pull up, I'm not in a good way. With Linda gone, I've gone back to my old ways, and I don't want to tell him any of it. I'll try to keep quiet today.

"Hey, Randy. Good to see you," Eric says as I let him into the house.

Taking a seat, Eric is talking about some things, but I can't say as I'm really listening. I'm wondering how much of a façade I can keep up until he leaves.

"...so I went to the auto-parts store, and there was this guy there. I could see that he was really suffering. He allowed me to pray for him, and said it was a help. That's where it's at, Randy, just being there for people and letting them know about the power in Jesus' name. I'm sorry, I've kinda gone on a bit here. How are you today? Did Linda get to Boston okay?"

"Uhh, yeah. She did. The baby, a boy, Jordan, was born, and she's happy to be there." I want to just keep talking about Linda and the baby, so I don't have to talk about me, but Eric quickly takes us back to why we are here.

"That's great to hear! Glad about your new grandson. How have you been doing? Any news to report?"

I sit there, just looking at Eric. I can tell he's waiting, and waiting, and will wait, until I say something.

"Ummm, no not really." I know that's not a good answer.

"I'm thinking from our phone calls, and your demeanor today, you're a bit stuck. Is my thinking on target?" Eric asks, looking at me directly in the eyes.

"I guess," is all I can say.

"You guess…hmmm." Eric nods and waits again.

"Yeah. I guess. I don't know about any of this."

"Of what, in particular? Is there something I can help you work through?" Eric asks, with a kindness that's hard to resist.

"Forgiveness is not my strong suit. Let's just say that. And I don't know that I want to deal with working through these things. I don't think it's gonna happen, Eric."

Eric waits, and suggests we pray. Of course, he would. That's how Eric rolls. I agree to the prayer.

"Father in Heaven, we come to You today with grateful hearts for little Jordan entering into this family. Thank You that Linda can be there… And her sister went with her, Randy?" Eric asks.

"Yes. Venyce is there."

"Thank You that Venyce can be there with Linda in Boston…"

"Actually, they are in a town called Sharon. Just outside of Boston." I don't know if it's important, but for some reason I interrupt Eric to let him know he's wrong."

"Okay. Sure. Thank You for the ladies being in Sharon, and having this time with the baby and the rest of the family. We have lots to be thankful for today. But also, we have some things to discuss with You, Father, and with each other. I'm sensing a resistance in Randy, and we ask for the covering of the blood of Jesus to cleanse out any distractions and infections that have set into Randy's soul; especially while Linda has been gone. Holy Spirit, join us here, reveal to us what's needed. Bring any darkness into the light to dispel the workings of the enemy. Thank You, Jesus, for the authority You have given us to enter into these areas with power and healing in Your name. Amen."

I sit and wait, not liking the prayer, not liking being with Eric again, and just wanting to get him out of the house. But I know better, so I sit quiet.

"Randy, I'm not here to push you. I'm here to help you be set free through the promises Jesus gave to us. But this cannot be forced, if it's not something you want to do."

"I guess we can try." It seems that's about all I can answer with Eric today.

"We can try to proceed, or what exactly? I want to know your heart today. Are you having any struggles that you'd like to talk about, pray about? How can I help you clear out the confusion that seems to be clouding your mind?"

I don't want to talk to Eric. I don't want to tell him that I prefer the porn on TV at night while Linda is out of town over anything that will do me good. I don't want to tell him that I'm more drawn to those stations than ever after opening that door again. I don't want to tell Eric that I haven't read my Bible, and I have no interest in reading it. I don't want to tell him that I've tried the forgiveness thing, and I've given up on that now, too. I just want him to leave. But I don't want to tell him that either. So I can only seem to answer with, "I don't know."

After a bit, Eric starts in slowly... "Randy, it seems we have come to a wall here today. And I want you to know that I understand. I hit that wall, too, in my own healing process. There were times when I just wanted to be left alone, to do my own thing, and not think about God or any of this. I get that. And I can leave you with that for a time, if that is what you're wanting. It's not what I want. I want to see you discover your freedom in Christ. I want to be here to help you. But that can only happen if it's what you want."

"Yeah." That's about all I can say. But I'm thinking so much more, and it's not good. I don't want to waste Eric's time either. I know he's here to help me. But I don't want help right now. I just want to be who I am, and not change. This change stuff takes too much work."

"Is there anything you would like to talk about today, Randy?"

"I'm not sure."

"Is it hard having Linda gone?" Eric asks.

I can see Eric's not one to give up easily. It feels like he can see right through me. I don't want to tell him what Linda being gone means. That's the last thing I want to talk about.

"Randy, if we don't get to the heart of what's going on during these times, then the progress will be slower. If we just dance around stuff and play games, then we satisfy the enemy's desire to keep things in the dark, and we don't utilize the help that Jesus wants to give in setting captives free. Guys like us like to take care of business. This is God's business. And He's here for you. I heard someone say, 'The only reason you're out is because you choose not to come in.' Healing is a choice. God wants you in His inner circle of healing. He uses people like me to help you along on that path. But He will not force you, and neither will I. I will always be available."

"There's stuff going on and I don't want to talk about it." At least I finally say something.

"Here's the thing, Randy, the enemy would like to make our sins seem as large as the Titanic, and that we are sure to sink and drown. Satan is also good at making them seem insignificant so we will ignore them. Those are lies. Jesus died for every single one of our sins, big and small. God already knows all our struggles, and that's why He sent His Son for us. I would like to battle this with prayer if you agree to it—my words won't break through this wall you are putting up. But God can, if you want to give Him the chance."

"I guess we can try."

"Is that a yes?"

"Yeah. For now."

"Okay. Repeat this after me…Because of Jesus' blood, I am forgiven of everything I have ever done."

"Because of Jesus' blood, I am forgiven of everything I have ever done." Ugh…I hate this, is what I'm really thinking.

"I am redeemed because of the blood of Jesus. The devil has no control over me."

"I am redeemed because of the blood of Jesus. The devil has no control over me." I'm the one who wants to control me, is more what I'm thinking.

Eric continues on, with me repeating after him, "Walking in Your Light, Jesus, Your blood cleanses me, and always will. Through You, I am justified. Just like I'd never sinned. You have made me holy, and I am Yours. The enemy cannot control me. He has no hold on me. Jesus, You have totally taken care of me by Your blood."

Eric finishes, and as I repeat this last line, I know I've resisted all the way through the prayer. I still want Eric to go. He's a good guy, just trying to do his best. But I know I'm just not having it.

"Thanks Eric. I appreciate what you're doing. But I'm tired now. Can we just end this here? I need to take care of some things." I'm lying. I have nothing to really do. I just don't want to be doing this.

"Of course, Randy. Thanks for letting me come over today. God won't give up on you, and neither will I. You let me know when you are ready to talk again."

"I will."

Walking Eric to the door, I'm glad we're done. Closing the door behind him, I feel relieved, frustrated, sad, and hopeless. Why can't I just be left alone? Why does God want to mess in my life? I like the darkness, and I want to stay in it. Especially while Linda is gone. It's just easier this way.

35

LINDA AND RANDY

"Hi. Did you get the latest pictures I sent?" I ask Randy over the phone.

"Yes. I can't believe they named him Jordan Blake, though. Why did they use Blake for his middle name? Blake irks me sometimes. And now our grandson carries his name. Great. Just great."

"Randy, it's a perfectly fine name. And Jordan is so sweet. You will see when you meet him. He has the darkest hair, and his eyes are already so open for being so little. I'm glad I got here as quickly as did. I don't want him to grow up without me."

"Well, he's going to. You can't stay out there forever."

"Randy, what is going on? You sound on edge. Have I done something?"

"No. I really don't have time to talk right now. I'll call you later. Tell Hannah I'm happy for her."

Randy has hung up, and I feel like we are back at square one. I need to find Venyce...

"Venyce?"

"Yes. I'm in the back room here," she calls out.

"Something's going on with Randy. He's totally on edge. He's even mad about Jordan's middle name."

"What?" Venyce says with an astonished look.

"Yes. Well, you know that Randy and Blake aren't the best of buddies. But the kids have a right to name their son whatever they want. I'm getting frustrated now." Hanging my head, I can feel the tears start to well up.

"Linda, let's take a moment. Sit down here with me," Venyce says, patting the bed. "I don't want what's going on, on the other side of the country, to ruin the joy you have being here with the kids. Let's pray."

"Okay."

Venyce begins, "Father, thank You that whatever happens, we can stop, and call out to You. This is a blessed time for the Barker family, and the enemy would love to get in there and wreck it. His only goal is to destroy all that is good and right. Please put a hedge of protection around this family, and especially Linda right now... Linda, look at me for a minute. Let's get rid of this frustration and anything associated with it, okay? Just like Trisha has been teaching you to do. Why don't you go ahead?"

"I'm not very good at this. It feels awkward."

"It does feel a bit strange at first, Linda. But you will get to the point where it is just a natural way of getting through the hard parts of each day. I'm here to help you if needed. Remember how to start?" Venyce asks.

"Uh. Yes. Let's see, Holy Spirit, reveal to me what it is that I'm dealing with here. I know there is frustration that I feel. I tell that to GO right now in the name of the Lord Jesus Christ. Now, I can just blow out a bit, right?"

"Yes. It's not absolutely necessary. But it can help. Sometimes giving a good cough will help to let things go, too. Sometimes there is nothing you need to do."

"Okay. Let me do this again...frustration, GO in Jesus' name. I'm gonna breathe out...whoooo. Now, I should see if there's anything underlying the frustration, right?"

"Yes. Ask the Holy Spirit to continue to reveal whatever is there," Venyce says.

"Holy Spirit, show me if anything else is bothering me today? Anger. That's what I just heard. Anger, GO in the name of the Lord Jesus! And a loss of hope about Randy. Hopelessness, go right now in Jesus' powerful name... I think that's it. I'll cough a couple of times. Yes, I feel some relief. Did I do okay?"

"You're doing fine. Now move into some forgiveness toward Randy. I know you don't feel like it. But choose to do it."

"Okay. Because yeah, I don't feel it. So, Lord, I *choose*, in the powerful name of Jesus Christ, to forgive Randy's rudeness. To forgive his judgmental words about baby Jordan and Blake. I choose to forgive his disinterest in even being here with me. Help me forgive and then heal any wound that has been caused because of this interaction with Randy. Thank you, Lord Jesus."

"Very good, Linda. Now breathe in a few times, breathing in the goodness of the Holy Spirit. He will fill all those places that were once dark. His light will come in and lift you up."

"I do feel better. The anger is pretty much gone—yeah, I don't feel it right now. And I feel some hope returning. I feel more interested now in little Jordan, than in being mad at Randy."

"Thatta girl! It's really not hard to do. It's just needed more often than we would ever think. It's good to catch it quick and be rid of it. I believe this is why so many Christians are walking around in bondage—because of simple conversations like you had with Randy. Those leave a wounded soul behind. Our Father in Heaven doesn't want us staying in that place. He has so much more for us than that."

"It does seem simple. I guess the hard part is remembering to do it each time," I say, smiling at Venyce now.

"Yes. You're right," she says returning my smile.

"And making the choice. I would rather have remained upset with Randy, honestly. But now I do feel better. Why would I want to stay angry when it can be gotten rid of so simply?"

"Exactly. That was a good practice session. We have to keep practicing. It says in James that anger can never make things right in God's sight. We give God all the glory and thanks for what He is doing here today!"

"Absolutely!"

"Linda, remember that lady we met when our plane got delayed in Denver?" Venyce asks.

"Yes. I do. You had quite the prayer time with her. I couldn't hear it all, so tell me exactly what happened."

"That was such a blessed time. I'm not as at ease with this as Trisha is. But I have been learning through practicing. And so, when we got delayed, remember me saying to you that God might have an assignment there in the airport?"

"Yes. I do. And you were looking around to see who it might be." I remember Venyce had quite the look on her face in the terminal, scouring the people and praying for direction from the Holy Spirit.

"Yes. I was looking for my assignment. I didn't want to miss what God might want to do. That's just like what you did here. You had an assignment in this, and you tended to it. We have to constantly be aware that God has something for us to do, maybe something to teach us, or a way that we are to grow in each situation. In the airport, we ended up sitting next to that lady, Sophia. She was upset because she had a doctor's appointment to get to, and with the plane being late, she didn't think she would make it."

"I remember her saying that, Venyce. And then it was like you knew just what to do."

"Well, when I heard her say 'doctor,' it led me to ask how she was. She told me she had cancer and was going back for her checkup. I could tell she was scared. And then she volunteered the information that her feet were numb. That really led me into asking her if I could pray for her. She gladly accepted."

"She did. And you were so gentle with her, Venyce. I could hear you asking her if you could just put your hand on her shoulder and pray. She didn't seem to have a problem with that at all."

"No, she didn't. And God just let me calmly pray for healing in her feet. Then when I asked her if she felt any feeling in them, she said she actually did. She was surprised she could feel her toes. They weren't completely healed, so I prayed for them again, and then I started to pray for her fear and other things. I could sense the fear. It didn't require making a big scene. I don't even know if anyone could hear me praying. I was just telling the fear to go, the sadness to go. Remember how she said she was missing her kids?"

"I couldn't hear her very well. Where were her kids?" I ask Venyce.

"They were living in another state."

"Oh. You prayed for her for quite a while. She started to cry some. But not bad. Then we had to move to another gate, and I think we both felt responsible for her at that point. Just like we didn't want her to walk alone."

"I know, Linda. I felt such an affinity for her. And wasn't it fun when we started walking and she said she had feeling back in both feet? God is so good!"

"He sure is. It was nice to then sit with her over by the new gate. Just to keep her company, wasn't it, Venyce?"

"Yes. It seemed right. And she turned to me shortly before boarding and said she felt 90 percent better. I couldn't resist praying for that last ten percent." Venyce laughed. She was enjoying this.

"When that plane took off, Venyce, I looked out the window and my only thought was how much God loves Sophia. That He would delay our flight, so you could pray for her like that. We got to see miracles just because you were faithful to look for what your assignment might be. I'm proud of you, Sis."

"Thank you. Trisha has been a good teacher. You will see. She will take you far into your own healing and you will be amazed."

"Well, I look forward to more times with her. And I hope Randy will keep on with Eric. At this point, I don't know what he's doing. I will keep praying for him. Thank you for being here for me. I don't know what's going on with Randy. But I can take care of what's going on with me."

"We both can. Let's help each other along the way."

36

LINDA AND RANDY

Making plans to walk the Freedom Trail with Venyce today, I want to give Randy a call first. Maybe he will be in a better mood today. I know I am.

"Hi."

"Hey there. I know it's early for you. But Venyce and I are heading out for the day. I wanted to get ahold of you before we go and tell you the latest on Jordan."

"Okay." Sadly, I really don't have any great interest in my new grandson.

"Well, he's doing great. I sent you more pictures. Did you get them?"

"Yes. I got them." I know my voice is stoic.

"Randy. What is going on? You sound disgusted that I've even called. I'm just wanting to share with you about our grandson."

"Linda, look. I'm glad you can be there. I'm not all that excited about babies. You know that. Why don't you just spend this time with Venyce, and the kids, and then you can fill me in when you get back. I've got a lot going on right now."

"So, you're saying you don't even want me to call again? That we will talk when I get home?" I can't believe how cold Randy is being about our new grandchild.

"Yeah. That's about it. I'm stressed with work and all. And you're all about baby. So, do baby. I will do work. And let's leave it at that."

"Wow. Okay, Randy. I'm hearing you loud and clear. Sorry to bother you. Bye."

"Bye." I know I'm not in a good place, and it's better if I don't talk to Linda right now,

The tears start immediately upon hanging up the phone with Randy. I left California with such high hopes with where he and I were going, and now it all seems dashed. I don't know if I can do today. I was feeling so good, and now it feels like I just got kicked in the stomach again. I know what I need to do, but I want to call Trisha this time for support. Maybe she can help me make some sense of this. How many times…?

"Hi, Linda. How's the new little grandson?...Linda? Are you okay?" Trisha asks.

"I'm sorry. I'm…I'm so upset. Give me a sec…let me get myself together here….I…I just talked to Randy, and I don't know what's going on."

"What do you mean? Is he okay? Are you?"

"Trisha, when I left for this trip, he was doing okay. Not great. But he had been meeting with Eric, and things were moving along. He has been getting grumpier as the days go on. I didn't read a lot into it. I knew it had been a couple of weeks since he'd seen Eric. I figured they would meet again soon, and he could sort things out that might have come up. I didn't want to push him…"

"I'm hearing you. So, what's happening now?" Trisha asks compassionately.

"That's just it. I don't know. He's angry. He's short with me. He has no interest in our grandson. He doesn't even want me to call him again while I'm here. He says we can talk when I get home."

"Sounds like he is struggling in the process of healing. I can't speak to what exactly is going on, sorry to say. I don't know Randy personally, but maybe I can just share something with you?"

"Sure, Trisha. Anything might help at this point. I'm about to head out for the day with Venyce, and I'm such a mess."

"Okay. Let me take a moment and pray…" Trisha says.

After Trisha prays, and helps me let out some of my own frustrations again, I'm ready for her to help me understand what's going on with Randy. I have no idea what she's going to say. But I'm grabbing for anything at this point to help this make sense.

"Linda," Trisha began, "healing can be sort of well…complicated. It doesn't have to be. But I'm going to tell you an experience I went through to illustrate this. I don't want to use real names or places, because that wouldn't be right. But you'll get the idea with the details I can share."

"Okay. I'm listening," I say wiping the tears that don't seem to want to stop.

"Well, years ago, there was a woman I know. I'll call her, Denica. She had a troubled life. Layers of dysfunction from a bad marriage, sibling rivalry, kids who were inheriting unhealthiness. You name it, she needed healing in so many ways. And when we met, she seemed most willing. She seemed ready to strive for something more in her life. As we prayed through many things, and saw great deliverance from darkness in her life, things seemed to be better. She was anxious to keep on as she began to enjoy the new freedom she was feeling. Even though her marriage had dissolved, and her kids were not wanting a lot to do with her, she still wanted to try to find some happiness in her own life. Even if she was alone."

"Sounds like a pretty sad life, Trisha."

"It was. But God is such a Redeemer, we never give up. The Bible says those who endure to the end will be saved. It seemed that Denica was enduring and finding great Hope through the prayers we prayed together, and what I was teaching her do to on her own. I was willing to work hard with her through this, and she was willing also. But what's happening now with Randy may be what happened with Denica."

"Which is what?" I ask Trisha.

"Well, deliverance is an interesting thing. God will never force it on anyone. But He will gladly give it to those who pursue it with their whole heart, soul, mind and spirit—sort of the same things as loving our God. But with deliverance we have to go after it aggressively and claim it. It is not a game—of any sort. Battling our foe, Satan, is serious business. We have to stay focused on Jesus and His mighty power, and never attempt this in our own strength."

"I'm hearing you. Go on."

"When working through this, the devil would like to shut this work down. He will try to keep the person from reading their Bible. The enemy will make them tired on Sunday and not wanting to go to church, or even desiring fellowship. He will also do whatever he can to separate the person needing deliverance from the person praying for it with them. Actually, I don't know if you realize this, but this type of ministry is one of the most controversial types—one of the most attacked, because it is the one that tells Satan he has to *GO*. The enemy will work through anyone and everyone to stop its progress. The goal in deliverance is moving into the fulfillment Jesus is offering us after the huge price He paid on the Cross for our freedom. Jesus came to destroy the works of the devil, and of course the devil hates it."

"Well, I'm thankful for Jesus. I don't care about the devil. So how do you see this tying into what's going on with Randy?" I reply, still struggling with my tears.

"Linda, the enemy is being threatened big-time when Randy meets with Eric. Satan is trying to divide Randy's allegiance. In 1 Corinthians 10:21, it says, *'You cannot drink from the cup of the Lord and from the cup of demons, too.'* And I'm sure Eric understands that, but Randy probably doesn't as yet. He is so new to this. He has to make a decision in this process of healing, as to which side he is on. Eric has experienced this in his own life, from what you have said, and now he is excited and most willing to introduce it to Randy. At first, Randy probably felt desperate enough to want it. Didn't he even get physically sick, and it made him so weak, it scared him?"

"Yes. He got that bad flu bug."

"But then, perhaps having gotten some freedom, it has caused him to back off and operate in his own strength again, like Denica did. Randy may feel more empowered, which he is, but it's not his power. What happens when we strike out on our own without Jesus is that many of the things we have been freed from then feel welcomed back in to steal, kill, and destroy our life again. Apart from Jesus, we can do nothing. We need the miracle-working power of Jesus Christ to not only set us free, but to *keep* us free every single day."

"I hear you! Please remind me of this as we continue, because what I'm hearing in Randy is not good."

"This is what happened with Denica, and it wasn't good either. She experienced some freedom, and then she tried to run with it on her own. She didn't realize there was still work to be done. As much as I wanted to continue on with her, she walked away...not just from me—that would have been okay. But what she walked away from was Jesus and all He wanted to continue to give her. She eventually went back to her old way of doing life. And in some ways, it got even worse. When we choose to walk with Jesus, He is right there with us each step of the way. When we turn off on our own path, wanting what we want instead of what God's Word says, He gives us the free will to do that—as much as it must grieve the Holy Spirit. I tried to call Denica back into the light of Jesus, but she didn't want to listen. She listened to the enemy calling her back into the darkness and confusion instead. For her, it didn't turn out well. Last I heard, she was in prison on drug charges. It broke my heart. But I had to realize we all have choices to make. Freedom in Christ is not forced on anyone. I knew this wasn't personal against me. This was a huge spiritual battle. What saddens me is that it could have been won, because with Jesus we already have the victory. We just need to learn to walk in it."

"Do you ever hear from her? My heart hurts for Denica, and I don't even know her."

"Oh, yes. We write from time to time. I let her know I love her and continue to pray for her. And I'm always hopeful that she will find an earthly emotional healing through more deliverance. I do have great hope that heavenly healing will come because she did receive Jesus as her

Savior and Lord. Everyone experiences different levels of freedom while we walk this earth, depending on how much we desire. Too many Christians settle for less than what Jesus died to give them. I don't want to be one of those. I want every day to bring me into a closer relationship with Him. Some seem content to walk around in a smoky, toxic haze—maybe they don't even see it. I want the fresh, clear blue skies of Heaven to surround me each day."

"Oh, that's what I want...at least it's what I hope to fully want. I don't know that I'm totally there yet, Trisha. Do you really think that this might be what's happening with Randy?"

"I surely hope it's not, Linda. I hope he's just in a bad mood, and he's busy, so it will pass, and he will continue to meet with Eric. But if it is what Randy's doing, he's not in a good place. It is a decision that he is making that will have disheartening results...for both of you, I'm sorry to say. Prayer is the weapon you have against the enemy for Randy. Use it often!"

"Oh, I will. I really appreciate all you have told me. Even though this makes me very concerned for Randy, I do feel like I understand it more. To know this is a spiritual battle, like we talked about, and not one of flesh and blood helps me have some perspective on this. It's interesting that Venyce and I will be walking the Freedom Trail in Boston today. That's appropriate, don't you think?"

"I do! Try to relax and have fun. God has a plan for Randy's life. Sometimes it takes longer for certain people. As you walk the trail, pray for him and send me a pic or two."

"I will. Bye for now."

"Bye."

37

LINDA

"Venyce! Are you ready to go?" I call out. I wonder where she has gone? Then I hear the back door open.

"Oh. There you are—sorry to keep you waiting on me. I had a great talk with Trisha. I needed to clear some things out of my head. I was so upset about Randy again. I'll tell you more later. Let's just go now. I can't wait to have some of those cannoli that are so famous in Boston."

Venyce responds, "I'm looking forward to that, too."

"Blake said he would drive us to the train station. It's about a half hour ride or so into Boston from downtown Sharon. Let me go and just love on little Jordan before we go."

"Okay. No hurry," Venyce says. "I was having fun holding him earlier while you were on the phone. I love the smell of new babies. There's nothing like it. They grow up so fast, and their little legs get all filled in. I'm so thankful I could be here with you on this trip, Linda."

"It's so nice to have you with me. I'll be right back."

Finding Hannah in the bedroom feeding Jordan, I wait until she's done. Then I hold him and burp him gently before giving him back.

"Thanks for being here, Mom," Hannah says with a beautiful smile on her face. She has weathered labor and delivery well and has taken to motherhood with barely a hiccup.

"It is a joy, Hannah. I will miss being with you and Jordan today. But I know it will be good for Venyce and me to get some girl time in the city. She hasn't done a whole lot since your Uncle Earl has been gone."

"I know. I miss Uncle Earl. He was such a nice man. Have a great time and enjoy your cannoli! There are two places to get them. One is very famous, and you will see people carrying those white and blue boxes all over the city. But I've actually heard the one across the street from that one may even be better. So, don't follow the long lines to the most popular spot, try the other one."

"Okay. Gotcha. We'll see you tonight." Giving Hannah a kiss on the forehead and touching the silky arm of Jordan, I pull myself away for a day with Venyce. As Blake drives us to the station, he's nice enough to point out some of the sites in their area. Blake seems to have mellowed with the arrival of Jordan. He's been so good to Hannah, and to us.

"The east coast is so historic. Thanks for the tour, Blake," I say giving him a hug on his arm before getting out of the car.

"Have a good day. There's a lot to see!" Blake responds, waving goodbye.

After Blake drops us off, we find out the train just left, and now we have another hour or so before the next one. It gives us a chance to walk into the town of Sharon. There are such pretty older homes lining the streets, and we find a cute little café to sit and have coffee and a pastry. Our day has already begun, just being out and together. It is a sweet time.

Finally boarding the train and paying onboard, we enjoy the scenic ride into Boston. Traveling is always such an adventure.

"This is a lovely train ride. I'm kind of glad Hannah and Blake live outside of Boston," Venyce says, looking out the window.

"I'm sure it's nice for them to be away from all the commotion. Although compared to California, most things here seem calm."

"They do, Linda. Sometimes I really think about moving out of the state. I don't know that I will though."

"I don't think Randy would move here, but I sure would like to."

After an enjoyable ride and conversation with Venyce, we arrive at our stop. "Let's find our way to the start of the Freedom Trail. I don't know how long it will take us. Are you sure you're up to walking all this, Sis?"

"I have always wanted to," Venyce answers with joy in her voice. "I will make it just fine. Even if we have to sit from time to time."

Finding the very start of the trail in Boston Commons, we begin our journey through the city. It feels like following the yellow brick road. The trail is easy to locate because of the narrow red brick laid out the entire way. Many people are doing the very same thing we are and enjoying all the sites along the way. To see the Old City Hall from 1865, and King's Chapel with all the separate pews is very interesting. It says the box pews like this were in English churches in the 1500's through 1800's. When the families purchased a private pew in King's Church here, it was what funded the maintenance and daily operations. The boxes also trapped in the warm air that helped to keep the churchgoers comfortable in the colder months. I think I would have brought a blanket, too. I wonder if they did?

"Venyce, here is the King's Chapel Burying Ground. These old graveyards are so interesting. Oh, Mary Chilton was buried here in 1679. She was a passenger on the Mayflower. That's amazing! I'm loving this walk. But what do you say we get some lunch?"

"Sounds good to me. Those people we just met recommended the oyster house. I wonder if it's really that good?" Venyce asks.

"Only one way to find out. Let's go!"

After getting seated, and ordering, we are not disappointed—not only in the history of the place, but in the food. It turns out Kennedy would often eat here. They even have a booth with his name on it. It was one of his favorite restaurants. Looks like we were sent in the right direction.

"As hungry as I was, Venyce, now I'm equally full. We are fortified to make the rest of this walk, I believe."

Winding our way through the city, we hear music from an outdoor band, and pass more historic sites, before eventually coming upon a difficult decision...which cannoli will we enjoy? We have seen the white and blue boxes in everyone's hands throughout the city. It looks like there is a definite favorite. But we decide to listen to Hannah and make our way across the street and into a wonderful bakery full of sights and smells that wet our appetites again. Trying to decide how we want our cannoli, dipped in chocolate, whipped cream or cream cheese?...A sweet young woman hears our ponderings, and helps us figure it out by telling us her favorite. We are pleased when we find a bench outside and are able to sit and enjoy our treats. I don't know how good the other place would have been, but this is awesome. The young woman was right! Dipped in chocolate is perfect!

"I wish I could eat more than one of these," Venyce says. "But they are so big!"

"I know what you mean. They are so good! When we finish up, let's keep on the trail. I'd really like to get to the Bunker Hill Monument. Hopefully we can climb to the top. I've never done that."

"Okay. I hope I can make it. I'm not in that good of shape," Venyce says laughing a bit nervously.

"We can take it slow," I respond with a nod and a smile. "You can do it!"

"Oh, look at that...the Old North Church. 'One if by land, two if by sea.' I remember learning that in school. Never thought I'd actually be here."

"Me either, Venyce. This is so much fun. It was great to go by Paul Revere's house, too. I'm starting to get a bit tired. The crowds must be too, as they are thinning out the closer we get to the Bunker Hill Monument."

"It's been an amazing walk, Linda. What an experience!"

"I think we go in that building over there and get our tickets for the monument," Venyce points out.

"That's nice, that the tickets don't even cost anything. Makes me wonder what we're getting ourselves into," I say jokingly.

Taking in a deep breath, Venyce says, "Let's go do that climb. Slow but sure. That's pretty tall!"

Up we go, one step at a time. It's a narrow winding staircase to the top. The stairs have numbers along the way. We make it up all 294 of them, and the view is wonderful. But when we get back down again, I can feel the weakness in my thighs from all those stairs! "How are you doing, Venyce?"

"We made it! Now we only have to get over to the U.S.S. Constitution."

"It's not too far from here," I say with enthusiasm, trying to encourage Venyce.

"My legs are kind of wobbly. How are yours doing, Linda?"

"Wobbly, too. It's okay. We'll hold on to each other until they regain some strength. I'm glad we did that. But I don't think I will do it again. Not at my age. Unless I start training for a marathon or something!" I say, laughing out loud.

"That I would like to see, Sis," Venyce responds in good humor.

After touring the ship, Venyce and I make our way back over to the north side of town, looking for some good Italian food to eat. Amazingly, we have worked up an appetite again. We aren't disappointed with the place we choose. We are brought huge platefuls of pasta that we can't possibly finish. We will take the leftovers back with us to Hannah and Blake. They love pasta. Upon leaving the restaurant the crowds are lining up outside. It must be a local favorite.

Making our way back across the city, we are happy to be seated on the train again. We have seen and enjoyed so much together today.

"This has been such a fun day, Linda. I want to thank you again for letting me join you on this trip. You have such a sweet family. And then, getting to hold little Jordan at such a young age. I will always remember walking on the Freedom Trail. We have been so busy looking at all the sites, we've barely had time to talk. I did want to ask you more about why the morning was so upsetting for you, if you want to talk about it? I know you mentioned it was something with Randy. But I could feel you wanted to just enjoy the day and not focus on that for a while. Now that we are headed back to Sharon, would you like to discuss it?"

"I would, Venyce. Thanks for letting it just sit until now. It really has been an enjoyable day with you. But it has been on my mind...a little too much. I kept praying for Randy along the way. Being on the Freedom

Trail, and finding a new freedom in Christ through what Trisha has been teaching me, I so want the same for him. But I don't know if it's to be. I guess I'll have to wait until we get home to really know what's going on.

For the rest of the train trip, I fill Venyce in on how Randy has been on the phone, and what Trisha had to say about it. Venyce just listens, not saying much. It seems she understands. It's good to be in her company— to be with my sister, and my friend. I know that God is good.

38

RANDY AND LINDA

"I'm sorry Randy isn't here to pick us up from the airport. He said he had a late business appointment."

"It's okay, Linda. Really. Splitting the cost for this ride home makes it affordable. It will be good to sleep in our own beds tonight, won't it?"

"Yes. It will. Let's have the driver take you home first, Venyce, and then he can drop me at my house."

"If that's what you want to do. Either way is fine with me."

"I want to make sure you get inside okay. Randy will be home shortly after I get there, so I won't be alone. I'm so tired. Are you?"

"I'm sleepy. And my legs are still feeling those stairs…" Venyce laughs, pointing at her thighs.

"Mine, too. But it was worth it."

"It sure was. How are you doing? I know it was tough leaving little Jordan behind, and Hannah."

"I'm okay. It is so hard saying good-bye to the kids, knowing Jordan will change so much by the time I see him again. Thankfully I can see him over the phone. Hannah will be good about keeping in touch."

"She will."

Sitting quietly pretty much the rest of the ride home, I know we are both feeling satisfied with our time on the east coast. I'm apprehensive as to what I'm going to walk in on with Randy. I didn't even try to call him again other than about picking us up. And he said he couldn't. Which is fine. But my stomach is churning a bit as to what I'll be dealing with when I get home. I had so hoped we were turning to a new chapter in our lives…one where we could grow old together. I just don't know now.

Pulling up in front of Venyce's, I get out to give her a hug good-bye as the driver helps her with her bag from the trunk.

"Hope you sleep well, Venyce."

"I believe I will. Let me know how things go with Randy. My home is always available for you. But I really will be praying that the two of you can work things out."

"Thanks. It's good to know you're here for me. Bye now."

"Bye."

The short drive back to my house is filled with more than one deep sigh. The lights are off when I get there, so Randy must still be out. In some ways it makes it easier. I carry my bag into the guest room where I've been sleeping and go through the mail that's been left on the counter for me. Sitting on the couch and reading a thank you note from an old college friend, I'm deep in thought of days gone by. Back then we were so young, and full of fun. Her card tells a different story now as she shares the final days of her husband's fight with ALS, and the sadness of living without him now. There is no talk of God helping her through all of this. That makes me hurt more deeply for her—to think of her doing this with no hope in Jesus. I really do need to do more than just send flowers. I need to give her a call and see if I can tell her of God's comfort that's available in times of deepest pain. I sure need that right now myself. My thoughts are soon interrupted with a key in the front door. Randy is arriving home. Getting up, I greet him in the front hallway, giving him a light hug.

"Hi, there. How was your day?" I can tell he isn't happy.

"It was what it was. Darn meeting seemed to take forever. That guy just won't shut up. We have to hear all about his troubles with his sister-in-law, the mess with her teenage son, and then, blah, blah, blah…on and on. I just wanted to get work taken care of and get out of there. I'm beat."

Standing there, listening, I don't know what to say. Randy is in a mood, and I don't offer any words of encouragement, or tell him anything about Jordan. I think silence is best.

"I'm going to get myself a late dinner. Just something quick, and then go watch a movie to relax," he says.

With Randy not even asking me how my trip went, or about the kids, all I can say is, "Okay," as I watch him walk off. I'm hoping some time with Trisha soon will help me. I want to ask Randy when he will be meeting with Eric again. But I dare not right now.

Going to my room to unpack, I can feel the tears so close to the surface. I know what I need to do, but I don't feel like doing it. The anger wants to seep back in and take control once again. No wonder God says to be slow to anger in James. There seems to be nothing slow about it. I open my Bible and turn to James, reading from the beginning…forcing myself to do this. What I really want to do is crawl into bed, pull the covers over my head, and be sad, angry, frustrated, and…leave first thing in the morning. It's so hard to make this choice and spend these first minutes at home with God. But as I begin reading, I know it's right. It's telling me when trouble comes of any kind, consider it an opportunity for joy. That my faith is being tested, that my endurance is having a chance to grow. And when my endurance is developed, and complete, I will be ready for anything. This is good stuff! Help me soak this in, Lord. Help me really get this. Your Word is so amazing. No wonder the enemy wants to keep us out of it.

Continuing to read in verse five about wisdom; Yes I need it! It says You are generous, Lord, and You will give it to us. I don't want to waver. I don't want to have divided loyalties. I don't want to be unsettled like a wave of the sea. I don't want to be tossed by the wind. I want to be stable in You, Lord Jesus. In verse twelve, it talks about patiently enduring testing. Oh, Lord, Your Word is a lamp for my feet. You understand our struggles. I'm so grateful to You. I can always open Your Word and find help. I give You my anger tonight. I tell it to get out of me in the name of Jesus Christ. And I forgive Randy for hurting me with his thoughtlessness, and his disinterest. I forgive him. I don't feel forgiving toward Him. But You are always forgiving toward us. This is why Jesus went to the Cross. This is what Jesus' blood can do. Take my hurting heart and heal it with Your love. I agree with Your Word. I turn away from my own way of thinking and accept Your Truth. Transform my heart and mind and make me more like You.

I remember reading in Matthew while in Massachusetts—You told the disciples how they would all desert You, and then You told them You would rise in three days. Without a blip, You then said You would go ahead to Galilee, and they were all to meet You there. There was no resentment in Your words…no bitterness…just an understanding of what was to be. Help me to have Your discerning spirit…to see past the hurts that others can inflict in my life and expose the evil spirit that is behind them. This is not flesh against flesh, but an enemy that is out to destroy us all. Only with You, Lord Jesus, can we come through these times with any sanity and hope. When confusion and chaos seem to surround me, I can know it's not of You. You are not a God of confusion, but of order. Bring order to my days. Help me to follow You more closely, even if that means my husband will not be with me. I need to cling to You, always. You will protect and guide me. I thank You for never leaving me or forsaking me. I can always count on You. Tomorrow will be a new day, and the next, and the next. I will need You to guide me through these treacherous waters. And I know You will. In Your mighty name, Jesus! Amen.

When I lay my head on my pillow, I have regained a sense of peace, no matter what is to come. Looking through pictures of sweet Jordan before closing my eyes, I am grateful. He is healthy. He is a blessing to Hannah and Blake. And I want to be the best grandma I can be to him, teaching him how much Jesus loves him as he grows up. I am learning that when it all hits the fan, I should let the wind of the Holy Spirit take control. I didn't want to read tonight. I didn't want to pray. But I did. And I feel strengthened.

39

RANDY

Getting up extra early, I'm glad to be out of the house before having to talk with Linda. She said she's not working today since she took a few more days off to recoup from her trip. I know she's going to want to talk about stuff, and I don't…not with her, and not with Eric. But Eric won't quit, and he's got me meeting with him again tonight. I just want to bury my head in my work, and not look up. Coming through the door, I see Emily at her desk.

"Hey there," I say, passing by quickly.

"Good morning," she responds in her usual upbeat tone.

Sitting at my desk, it feels like things are crashing in on me. The pressure to perform at work, and then having Linda home from Boston, I don't know if I can take it. I want to escape. But I don't know how. I think I need to tell Linda to go back to Venyce's. This isn't working. I don't want it to work, to be honest. This is who I am. I don't want to change, and I don't want anyone telling me how I can. All this stuff may be good for Linda, but it's not for me.

The day is sort of a blur, phone calls, and paper work, all of which I care little about. When evening comes, and Linda has gone out for a bit, I'm sitting across from Eric again. I feel shut down and fed up. I know he can tell. He's not a dumb guy. But for some reason, he cares. I really don't know what it is that makes him tick.

"Thanks for having me over again tonight, Randy."

"Yeah. I did want to talk to you," I respond. Because it's the truth, only he's not going to like what I'm going to say.

"Well, that's good. I kind of got the feeling during our last time together that maybe you had changed your mind about moving forward with this."

"Uh, well, uh..." I just pause there. I can't get the words out.

"Is there something you want to say?" Eric asks with a knowing look on his face.

"Ummm..."

"What is it?"

I sit, wondering why it is so hard to tell Eric where to get off. Maybe because he really doesn't deserve what I'm about to say? I can see he wants to help me. How crazy is it of me to not want his help? But I don't. I really don't.

"Randy, to do what we are doing you will need to be open to the healing God has made available through Jesus Christ. Can I take you through some thoughts on this before you say what it is I think you want to say?"

"Sure. Go ahead." I feel like I've got nothing to lose. I agreed to have Eric come over. I don't want him to think I'm a total jerk by just telling him to come over, and then telling him to get out. After he prays, he goes into his 'spiel'.

"There are forces at work in our lives that we can't see, Randy. For much of our lives we think what we see, what we think, how we react to things, is real. And it is. But it isn't. Our perception of things is greatly skewed by the filters we see things through. Those filters are from the childhood we had, the pain we have endured, the people we have met, the jobs we've worked, the illnesses we have fought, even the movies we watched. In short, everything adds up in our minds. Our minds become hardwired through life, and to change our thinking and our lives, we have to go deeper than just trying to reason things out. There's a whole spiritual realm that many people, even those in the Christian community, pay very little attention to. I was the same...just living my life, doing my thing, worshipping God on Sunday, and living like the rest of the world throughout the week. It talks about this in Ephesians two, how we were once dead and living in sin, just like the rest of the world. We were obeying the devil. It even calls Satan the commander of the powers in the unseen world. Let me turn there...yes. It says in 2:2, *'He is the spirit at work in the hearts of those who refuse to obey God. All of us used to live that way, following the passionate desires and inclinations of our sinful nature.'* All of us, Randy. Not one person is excluded. But Jesus came to eradicate all of this power that belonged to our enemy, Satan. The problem is many people don't understand that, or maybe they do but aren't all that interested in it."

"Are you saying that's me?" I don't really like what I'm hearing.

"I'm saying that's *all* of us. Me included. I didn't understand the power that was surrounding me and working in me that was sooo dark. And I didn't understand the power Jesus has to defeat it. I didn't know I could call on Jesus in all the ways I have now found out that I can…that you can…that we all can."

"I don't know…"

"That's just it. And my passion is to *let* you know. To let everyone know the authority that we walk in because of Jesus—and how blind we are to what's available to us."

"Which is what, exactly?" It seems I should at least ask.

"Freedom. Jesus came to set the captives free. Isaiah 49:25 says, *'The captives of warriors will be released, and the plunder of tyrants will be retrieved.'* Who are captives in this world? We are, without Jesus setting us free! It goes on to say, *'…I will fight those who fight you.'* And in verse 26, *'All the world will know that I, the Lord, am your Savior and Redeemer, the Mighty One of Israel.'"*

"What does all this Israel stuff have to do with me? I'm not getting it."

"Do you ever feel like life just doesn't make sense? That the burden you are carrying is so heavy you can barely stand it? Do you ever feel like running away from everything and everyone? That's because what you're experiencing is all true—this world is a mess, and it has been since the fall in the Garden of Eden. And Jesus came to right it. All throughout the Old Testament there are references about the Savior. He is coming to set His people free. In the New Testament, Jesus arrives, and does just that. This isn't about just those who live in Israel, or about the Jewish people. This is about all of us. Jesus made peace between Jews and Gentiles by *'creating in himself one new person from the two groups.'* All who call Him Savior belong to the same family now. We don't have to fight each other anymore, we have to fight the enemy, Satan, together, as one. Jesus came to make it so that we can see clearly, we can walk freely, and we can be released from the ways the enemy has of destroying us. In Colossians 2:15 it says *'…God disarmed the evil rulers and authorities. He shamed them publicly by his victory over them on the cross of Christ.'* But we have to know that freedom is really available for us, and then we have to learn how to go after it. If we just remain blind, or even after having been given a little insight into it, we just sit back and do nothing about it, we can unknowingly let the enemy back into our lives. He will gladly steal, kill and destroy all that we have been given."

"Most days I feel pretty darn blind," I say, shaking my head.

"When God's light shines in the darkness, it becomes clear the evil this world contains. Have you ever seen those videos of people who are color blind receiving a pair of glasses that will help them see color for the first time?"

"Yeah. I've watched those. They always choke me up, even as a guy."

"I know, Randy, me, too! What gets me is that they didn't realize what they had been missing. Like the Bible says in 1 Corinthians 13:12, *'For now we see through a glass, darkly.'* They had no idea what full living color looks like. When they see it for the first time, it's so overwhelming to most of them they take the glasses off. Then they put them back on, then take them off again. It's too much for them to absorb. When we truly open our eyes to the Truth God has for us in His Word, we will be astounded! Maybe we will take it off for a bit, and then put it back on, until we get used to seeing things with more of God's perspective. When we truly get acclimated to God's ways, we never want to go back. We never want to *'see through a glass, darkly'* again!"

"I'm hearing you. You have a lot to say about all this, and I'm trying to absorb it as best I can."

"Randy, God's Truth can be made simple by really believing the Words of Jesus, and then following them. Jesus came to save us, not just for all of eternity, but each day we are still here. He doesn't want us living defeated lives. But too many people are—just trying to make it through each day as best they can. There's more than that to be had! In Ephesians 3:19 it talks about experiencing the love of Christ. It does say *'...it is so great we will never fully understand it.'* But when we start to experience it, it says *'Then you will be filled with the fullness of life and power that comes from God.'* After the fall in the Garden, yes, things got tougher. We lost that fullness and power. But when Jesus came, died and rose again, He took our authority back out of the hands of Satan. We got the fullness and power back. The Holy Spirit now lives in us! And even though the dark, demonic spirits are still operating all around us, they are under our authority again, just like in the Garden *before* Adam and Eve fell for the lies of Satan. In Genesis 1:28, it not only says be fruitful and multiply, it says fill the earth and *subdue* it. Rule over it. We *had been* put in charge. And now that Jesus died and rose again, we have been put back in charge...those that receive Him as Lord and Savior. That empty tomb that we can still visit in Israel, the one that once held the dead body of Jesus? It shows us how we too were once dead and buried, but we have been given a new life. Because Jesus rose from the dead, we, too, can rise now. We don't have to stay in that darkness anymore. *'...God is so rich in mercy, and he loved us so very much, that even while we were dead because of our sins, he gave us life when he raised Christ from the dead.'* That's in Ephesians 2:4. And in verse six it talks about being seated with

Him in the heavenly realms—all because we are one with Christ Jesus. This is our new position, and it gives us our new mission…sort of like that old TV show that says something about your mission, should you decide to accept it…"

"Yeah. I used to like that show. And then the tape would start smoking and burn up so no one could know what it said."

"Right. But we have the Word of God that hasn't been burned up. We can read it, and read it, and we know what our mission is until Jesus returns or we go to be with Him."

"And what does that look like for you, Eric?"

"For me, it means getting the Word out—that we can walk free. That the Word of God, repentance, forgiveness, restitution, baptism, prayer, fasting, tongues, deliverance, healing, church, fellowship, evangelism, love, and everything else associated with living as the children of God is available to everyone who is interested. Seeing people set free through the obedience the Bible talks about, including the eviction of dark spirits that don't belong in our lives, is exciting! This is the Christian life we have been called to by our Savior. Without walking in obedience to all that's talked about in God's Word, we will think we see, but we are actually spiritually blind. The reason I know this is because after years of being a Christian, and thinking I was seeing things clearly, there was still more smoke in my eyes. I still needed a better understanding of the demonization going on in my life so I could get a better view of things. Many times we are so used to how we are, we don't even see a need for change. But each time I would allow this work of the Holy Spirit, and the power of Jesus Christ to set me free, I would be astounded with how skewed my vision had been—how skewed my thinking was…and all the time I thought I was seeing clearly. Just as, when on our best day, our righteousness is as filthy rags, we can't possibly know how tainted things are until we see them as God does. Of course, this won't be fully accomplished until we see God face to face. But we can make so many more strides in this direction than many of us have."

"I'm hearing what you're saying. There's more available than what I'm living in now. Sadly, I don't even know if this is for me or if I even want it to be. But I'm trying to listen to what you're saying and sort through it. Can you let me sit with this for a time, and maybe we can meet again to talk about it some more? I'm just not sure right now."

"Randy, God is not in a hurry. He does things in a way that fits each person's personality, background and timing in their healing process. Understanding that you have invited Jesus into your life, to be your Savior, we can leave this here for now. I will pray with you as we finish up, and then we'll meet again in the future to see where you want to go with this.

Thank you for allowing me this time with you today."

After prayer, and letting Eric out, I have some things to think about. I was ready to shut Eric down before he ever got started. He really poured his heart and soul into this…into me. I wish I could say I want what he's offering. I guess, what God's offering. I don't know that I have it in me to pursue this.

40

RANDY AND LINDA

"Linda, I need to talk to you."

Just coming through the door at the end of the work day, I'm surprised by this sudden interaction with Randy. He's been so distant and quiet since I've gotten home from Boston. Any time I try to talk with him, he seems distracted in whatever he is doing. I know he's met with Eric. But it's been impossible to even discuss it with him. I've just let him be.

"Okay. What would you like to talk about?" I respond with a bit of hope.

"This whole prayer thing. I'm just not getting it. And I don't know that I want to. I think it's all a farce. It's probably something made up."

My heart drops as I hear his words and see the look on his face. Taking a seat in the living room, Randy sits down also. I'm not even sure where to go from here, so I just sit quiet, waiting. Randy does, too. It sort of feels like a stand-off—who will crack first—when suddenly the phone rings.

"Do you mind if I get this? It's Hannah," I ask, not really wanting to be interrupted in the moment, but this isn't the normal time she would call.

"Sure."

"Hi there, hon. How are you? Is everything okay?"

"MOM!! We're at the hospital with Jordan. He was running a fever, and it got worse. I am so scared! He's so tiny. I…"

Hannah is sobbing into the phone now, and my heart is racing a mile a minute. How do I comfort my daughter when fear has taken a quick grip of me, too?

"Hannah, listen to me. Take a deep breath. And another. Is Blake there with you?"

"Yes. He's here. He's holding Jordan so I could call you. Oh, Mom…"

After more sobbing, and trying to calm Hannah down, I know there's only one thing I can do, and that's pray. I'm so far away. But I know God is there with them.

"Hannah, I wish I could run right over to the hospital. I'm so sorry I'm not able to. What has the doctor said?"

"Not much. Just that sometimes babies get sick like this, and they will be keeping him for the night, and however long it is needed. They are doing a good job, and they are very nice, but it doesn't help being so scared for my baby. What if…"

"Let's not think about the 'what-ifs' right now." My mind is going to all the places that Trisha has taught me about spiritual warfare. I know this is a physical fever, but I witnessed this with Venyce in the airport—the way she prayed for that lady. Maybe it's time I give it a try? And now I'm reminded of the story in the Bible of the little girl who is sick, and Jesus heals her. All this has run through my mind like lightning speed before I say, "Hannah, I'm learning how powerful God's Word is. And I'm thinking of a story in the Bible. Can I get it and read it to you, since I know I need to pray for Jordan? But I'm sort of at a loss for words right now?"

"Okay. That's fine," Hannah responds, sounding like she is willing for anything that will be of help in her panic.

"Let me get my Bible…here is it. Now I think the story is in Mark. I was just reading through it the other day. Yes…here it is, Mark five, starting about verse twenty-one, it talks about a leader in the local synagogue who has a sick daughter. He is pleading with Jesus to heal her. He says in verse 23, *'She is about to die…please come and place your hands on her; heal her so she can live.'* Hannah, this is powerful. Have you and Blake done this for Jordan?"

"No. I didn't think about it like that," Hannah says, the sobbing slowing some now. "I mean, of course I called out to God, but…"

"I know this sounds a bit far out there, but I have been reading through the book of Mark, and Jesus heals so many people, in so many ways. He heals their sickness, He casts out demons, and in this case, as amazing as it sounds, He raises the dead. In verse 39 he says, *'Why all this weeping and commotion?…The child isn't dead; she is only asleep.'* I know this sounds strange, and it did to the crowd there, too, from what I read. It says the crowd laughed at Him. But as we know, when our child is sick, it is no laughing matter. Jesus went in, only taking a couple of people with Him, probably wanting to leave the nay-sayers outside. It says He held her hand and said to her, *'Get up little girl.'* She then got up and walked around! Her parents were totally overwhelmed. Well, who wouldn't be?"

"I know, Mom. That's every parent's hope and prayer isn't it? That

God would fix what's going on with their child?"

"It is. You were sick a lot as a child. I wish I had been reading things like this then. Not only reading it but acting on it and believing it. Let's do this for little Jordan. What have we got to lose?"

"Well, nothing, I guess. I feel weird. But I'm desperate, Mom. He looks so pitiful."

"Then put me on speaker phone, and let Blake know what we're going to do, and I will pray."

"Okay… Blake, Mom wants us to pray for Jordan's fever. To do what Jesus did in the Bible. I know this seems over the top. But I'm willing to give it a try. Is that okay with you?"

"Yeah," I hear Blake say.

"Okay, Mom, you're on speaker. What should we do?" Hannah asks, with a new calmness coming through her voice now.

"Both of you, put your hands on Jordan, and especially one hand on his little head. And I will pray. This is new for me, so bear with me." I feel nervous stepping into this role, having really only seen it done for others, but this is my grandchild… "Okay, let's do this. Father in Heaven, this precious child is so sick, and this fever is consuming his body. The doctors are doing all they can. But we seek Your help right now, in the name of Your Son, Jesus Christ. Just as Jesus healed the little girl in the Bible, we claim that same healing power right now for little Jordan. We tell this fever to GO, in the name of the Lord Jesus, and for all sickness, all weakness, all efforts of the enemy trying to harm Jordan to be stopped immediately— just like the girl You healed who immediately stood up and walked around. Jordan won't be walking, but we know You can heal his little body and allow him to grow strong and walk one day. I pray that walk will include a strong faith in You as we tell him of this day when You healed him from this fever. We thank You and give You all the praise in advance for what You're doing. In Your mighty name we pray, Jesus. Amen."

When I finished, I just stayed quiet for a time, waiting to hear from Blake and Hannah on the other end as to what was happening. It seemed longer than the few moments it probably was before they spoke, but when they did, there was an awe in their tone.

"Look, Blake," I could hear Hannah exclaim, "look how peaceful Jordan is. His discomfort seems to have gone, and he…he…feel his head now! Feel it!! It's cooler! It's COOLER!! MOM! Did Jesus just heal our son? Seriously?!"

Tears were welling in my eyes from across the country, as I heard the amazement and joy in Hannah's voice. I could hear Blake saying, "I don't believe this. Is this real?"

"I so wish I could be there to see this, Hannah! How is he doing? Is he really better? Cooler to the touch?" I ask in my own amazement.

"Yes. He really is. He seems different than he did just before you started praying. He was so lethargic. Now he's not! And his fever seems better, if not completely gone. We really need the doctor to see him, and soon! We will call you back with what we find out. Thank you, Mom! Thank you for being bold in praying this way. I didn't know healing could happen like this, and even over the phone. God is amazing me in ways…well…it makes me rethink a lot of things about God."

"I'm with you there! I'm learning and growing in all these things. And I'm beginning to realize there is so much more to God than church on Sunday. I'm going to let you go now. But call me soon with an update."

"Oh, I will Mom. Thank you. I love you."

"I love all of you, too. Bye, hon."

"Bye."

I suddenly realize that I was so absorbed with all that just happened, I totally forgot Randy was even in the room—that he was listening to all of this. I felt so full, so encouraged, so hopeful for little Jordan, and for what just happened that thoughts of what was going on with Randy and me didn't even enter in. Turning to him now, I can see he is just looking at me with different eyes. I don't want to say anything to break the flow of what I feel inside. I am not in the mood to argue with Randy about anything and am hoping he won't go there…but he does.

"What was that all about? Are you seriously thinking you can pray for Jordan and see healing like you read about in the Bible? Those things, if they were even true then, certainly aren't true now. I think you have really lost it, Linda. Really. I don't even know who you are anymore. Talking to Blake and Hannah like this stuff is real. I didn't hear their end of the conversation, but…"

"Randy, I'm sorry I didn't put this on speaker phone. I wish you had heard their end of what was going on. They were panicked over our little grandson. He was in the hospital with a high fever. What would you have me do? Just join in on their panic? I can't do that at this point, not after what I've been learning about the power of God, and the authority that we have been given by Jesus. What I just did is what we are supposed to be doing as believers in Jesus Christ. It should be normal for a Christian to pray this way. This is what Trisha has been telling me, showing me, and it was my turn to step into it and do it. And what better time than for our grandson, who was so very sick. And now from what the kids tell me, he is looking and feeling better already."

"Oh, that's hogwash. They are probably just imagining all this, like you are. Those things don't actually work. How can you pray for someone that is all the way across the country?"

"Randy. Where is God? I'll answer that, He is EVERYWHERE. And I don't know exactly how all this works, but I'm willing to give it a try. And especially now that I've experienced this with Jordan. I can't wait to hear back from the kids on how the doctor says he is doing. I don't care if you believe this or not, or if you think I'm too much into this type of thing…if it works, and if it's what the Bible tells us to do, then I'm all in."

"All in? And where does that leave me?"

"It leaves you right where you want to be, in or out. I can't decide that for you. You have heard the Truth, and the Truth can set you free. If you don't want to walk free, then you can live like the rest of the world that doesn't, and walk around with heavy chains weighing you down. I'm tasting freedom, and it tastes so very good! In fact, that is in the Bible, it says something like taste and see that God is good."

"I'm getting a bitter taste in my mouth from all of this."

"RANDY!! How can you say that? Our grandson was sick, and he is feeling better now! Whether you want to be free yourself, you have to have some sort of love for our grandson?"

"I do. He's a cute little guy. I'll grant you that. But praying for him to be miraculously healed is way out of the question for me. That's what doctors and nurses are for."

"And prayer!!"

"Whatever. I think I'm done with this conversation tonight," Randy says, getting up and walking out of the room.

As I see him go, it feels like my hopes for our marriage are going with him.

41

RANDY AND LINDA

Alone in my room, I continue to pray for Jordan. I am excited for morning to come so I can hear how he's doing. I'm sad for Randy. How can he be so cold hearted? Then I remember what Trisha was telling me, how in the end times the love of many will grow cold. I turn to that Scripture in my Bible.

Yes, here it is in Matthew 24:12, *"Sin will be rampant everywhere, and the love of many will grow cold."* I'm trying to remember what Trisha told me about this…something to do with…here it is in my notes: It has to do with relationships and Satan dividing us. With bitterness, there will be a lack of love. But why is Randy so bitter? Maybe because of the death of his brother? That would wreck anyone—to have a drunk driver be involved in the death of a loved one. But it's not just that, from what Trisha told me. It's not the accident. There are things causing the bitterness. What would be underlying it? Maybe Randy wants some sort of revenge? She said things like that can hinder healing in a person's heart. It hardens a heart toward others, and most importantly toward God. Even though what happened to Bennet is tragic, and Randy has every right to feel all those emotions, getting stuck there is not what God would have for him. It is so harmful to him and everyone around him—all the way down to little Jordan. That's even sadder—an innocent baby gets affected by a grandpa who won't go after the healing that's available. We don't realize the ripple effect that happens when we don't find our own healing—we think it affects only us. But it's so much more than that. Trisha said these hurting times in life give us a chance to learn how to love our enemies. I don't think Randy is interested in hearing that at all. No way! If he can't love a little baby, how is he going to love the man who killed his brother? Oh, Lord, please help my husband!

Waking the next morning, I realize I went to sleep with my Bible on me as prayers and thoughts were filling my mind. The light is still on, too. It seems I barely moved in the night. I must have been exhausted…maybe more emotionally than physically. I'm sure glad it's the weekend. I reach for my phone, so wanting to know how the night went for Jordan. Hannah has left me a text.

"Hi, Mom. Jordan is resting well. I know you're still sleeping but call me when you wake up."

Being that Boston is three hours ahead I know I can call immediately, so I do.

"Hi, Mom! I knew you would call as soon as you woke."

"Of course. I actually slept last night. How is Jordan? You said it was a good night?"

"Yes. And he is wide awake today, and the doctors have checked him, and are releasing him. Oh, Mom, thank you so much for praying for him. Even Blake agrees the prayer healed him. He had such a fast turnaround."

"Praise, God!!" I say with a huge sigh of relief. "This is the best news any grandma can hear! What a relief!!"

"Seriously. I was so scared, Mom. He was so sick, and barely moving. Now his arms and legs are going a mile a minute. He is his normal happy self."

"So good to hear! And you're taking him home today?"

"Yes, this morning. As soon as we sign the paperwork, we can leave. We will talk soon, after we get him back home. I'm glad it's the weekend, so we will both be with him and keep a close eye on him."

"Yes. That's perfect. Okay, I'll let you go. Thank you for letting me know! Love you, sweetie. Bye."

"Love you, too, Mom. Bye."

Once again, tears are filling my eyes. Jordan has been healed, and even if I didn't think my prayers would hold that kind of power, I prayed anyway. Like Trisha says, it's God's power, not mine. I'm so glad God helped me be bold in that. Now I need to get up and be bold with Randy. I wonder how that will go?

Entering into the kitchen, I can hear the TV on in the other room. Peaking in, I can see that Randy fell asleep in his chair. He's fully dressed with just his shoes kicked off on the floor. The sports channel is still on, just giving updates. I honestly don't know what that man would do without baseball.

Getting the coffee going, I pour myself a cup and sit at the table, looking out to the backyard. This is a nice house, with a beautiful yard. I wish I could say the same for our marriage. I don't know what happened to Randy while I was gone…oh, it really started before I left if I'm being honest about it. His willingness to make a change had changed, and not for the good. I could tell things were tense again, and he talked less and less about things happening with Eric. At the start, we would share with one another. We would compare notes, and they were very similar—the way Eric and Trisha worked with each of us. I could tell, even though I was farther along with Trisha, that Eric believed in the same things. He focused Randy on the Gospel Truth, knowing who Jesus is and how important His shed blood is in our lives. They also talked about repentance and forgiveness, just like Trisha did with me. She kept stressing forgiveness with me, how important it is, telling me she thinks it makes up about 80 percent of our healing. She said forgiving is the thing that keeps the healing going—forgiveness helps to keep our soul cleaned out. Oh, those powerful spirits of darkness can sure wreak havoc with our emotions. Trisha read to me recently out of Mark six and how the thought life is what defiles us. If we could really focus on taking every thought captive to Christ, how different our lives would be. The people around us may never change, but we sure can. How we react to people can be so different when forgiveness is activated in our own thought life. Without Jesus, we know no other way of being other than how we want to think and feel. With Jesus, He can show us a whole new way to live this life.

Walking out onto the back porch, it's good to have this time before Randy wakes. He was probably awake into the early hours of the morning. I see a beautiful blue bird perched on the fence, and I'm reminded of how God takes care of the birds. Father, thank You for taking care of Jordan. Thank You for hearing our prayers and for healing him. Let me never forget Your goodness.

Taking a seat, my mind continues to think of things Trisha has been pouring into me. It seems they are starting to really take root, and it is good. She says the whole goal of what we are doing is to make us more like Jesus—to have His love flowing through us toward others, and to receive that love for ourselves. She says that Satan can't defeat us unless we open ourselves to him. Oh, how many times have I done that very thing, thinking it was no big deal. I want to be very careful now what I watch, what I say, what I do, to give no entrance to the devil and his schemes. She says the devil is threatened more and more as Christ becomes more and more alive in me. I like that. And the more we accept God's unconditional love, the more we will be able to unconditionally love others. It all starts with God; everything else flows out of there that is good. Being able to see people as Jesus sees them, we will not be easily offended, and we will not be judgmental and critical. That seems a lofty goal, but as the Bible says what seems humanly impossible, is possible with God. When we repent and forgive others, we will be able to see things much more clearly. Until then, we are walking around in a smoky haze of deception. Oh, how many times have I thought I knew, when I didn't. When my own preconceived ideas seemed absolutely right. And now, after times in prayer with Trisha, when things that have been deceiving me have been evicted out of my soul, I have such a different perspective. I wasn't all right. The other person wasn't all wrong. The enemy pitted us against each other, flesh against flesh, when it was actually a spiritual battle going on. There truly is a veil that gets removed when we are receptive to the healing powers of Jesus Christ. She said not being easily offended by others shows a spiritual maturity. As it says here in Philippians 3:13, *"Forgetting the past and looking forward to what lies ahead."* That is so important to keep...

"LINDA? LINDA?"

"I'm out here, Randy."

"How long have you been up?"

"Quite a while. I saw you slept in the chair last night."

"Yeah. I have a kink in my back. Is there any coffee left?"

"Yes. I made a full pot."

"Okay. I'm gonna get some, then I'll be back."

Back? I think to myself. But I guess now is as good a time as any to talk. Lord, help me be loving and kind to Randy, no matter what he says. Help me to hear what he has to say and really listen with a loving heart. Remind me how he hurts, and to have compassion for him. And if even what he has to say doesn't make sense, remind me that chaos and confusion are not of You...that evil doesn't make sense. And Randy may be trapped in the snares of the enemy right now. Oh, Lord, how I pray he will seek freedom! It is the only way our marriage will survive...

"This coffee looks too dark. Let me taste it. Yeah, it's too strong. Linda, what were you thinking? It doesn't have to be like tar. It's so bitter."

I just look at Randy. "Bitter?" I think to myself. Could it be because his heart feels that way that it even taints the coffee? I know there is no need to respond. He woke in a bad mood, probably from not resting well in that chair. As he takes a seat, I can see that his back is kinked up.

"Would you like me to pray for your back? It looks like it hurts."

"NO. Don't be pushing that on me," he responds in a gruff voice.

"Well, I won't then. But I do want you to know that Jordan is doing much better and leaving the hospital today. So, believe it or not, I'm going to keep praying like that. God can work miracles, you know."

"No, I don't know. I've been thinking a lot about all this, and it's just so much work. And for what? A little healing. A little peace from time to time? I don't know that it's worth the effort it takes."

"Randy, it is. I know I can't convince you of that. But what other choice do we have? Misery? Yes, life is hard. But God has made a way for us to rejoice no matter what. It doesn't change our circumstances, or the people around us, but it does give us peace in the midst of it all."

"Says who?" Randy barks back in an angry, sarcastic tone.

"Says God's Word. Jesus set people free from the bondage they were living in. The sick ones, the ones with physical limitations, the ones with mental disorders, He healed them. And He still does today if we will believe and allow Him to work in our lives."

"I'm not so sure."

"Well, I become more and more sure the longer I pursue Jesus, and then see things like I did with Jordan. The enemy is lying when he says none of this is real, that none of this works. His goal is deception, Jesus' goal is setting us free."

"You really buy into all this don't you, Linda?"

"Buy? The wonderful thing is, it costs me nothing. I only need to have faith in the One who provides it all for us. Jesus died to give us liberty, to cleanse us from our sins, to bless us with an eternal life with Him. He paid the price for our freedom. All we have to do is say 'Yes' to it. Randy, even subtle lies can keep us in bondage."

"You know, Linda, I think I'll take my coffee inside and add some cream to it. I don't think this is a good morning to sit out here with you. My back is hurting me, and I'm going to get comfortable."

"Okay." It's all I can say. Randy is tired, grumpy, hurting, and not in any mood to talk about God in any fashion or form. I will pray for the Holy Spirit to open up an opportunity later. Right now, I'm gonna finish my coffee and enjoy the blue bird of happiness that's still perched there on the fence. I laugh to myself at that thought—God can bring laughter in the midst of this turmoil.

42

LINDA

It feels so good to be in church again this morning. I invited Randy, but he refused. After picking up Venyce on the way, we take a seat down front. A word from God would be most welcome this morning. My heart is hurting from the little to no interaction I'm having with Randy. As the pastor begins to speak, I'm all ears.

"Good morning. It's so good to see all of you here this morning. I want to introduce you to a good friend of mine. Everett, come on up here!"

A man seemingly in his late 60's leaves the front row and walks up, shaking Pastor Mark's hand.

"This is my friend, Everett Olsen. He is a retired pastor from Southern California, and just moved into the area. He will be sharing God's Word with us today, and hopefully we will be able to hear more from him in the future. He has a wisdom we all can glean from. And even though retirement is nice, Everett knows we never retire from the call of God on our life. Please welcome Pastor Everett this morning. I know we will all be blessed with what he has to say. Take it away, good buddy."

"Thank you, I appreciate the invitation to speak this morning. Would you all please stand with me as we read the Word and pray:"

"In Luke 16:10, it says, *'Whoever can be trusted with very little can also be trusted with much, and whoever is dishonest with very little will also be dishonest with much.'*"

"Father in Heaven, we are here this morning to honor You, to listen to You, and to follow the leading of Your Holy Spirit each minute of our lives. Your Son came to show us the way to You. He is the way, the truth, and the life. No one comes to You without going through the door of Jesus.

It is a narrow road, that few will find. Many will take the wide road that leads to destruction. We pray, not only for ourselves, but for everyone, that we would find and stay on the narrow path that will lead us safely Home to You one day. Until then, we will focus on Your Word, love You, and love others as we are called to do. Guide us now, Holy Spirit, as we spend these next few moments together. In the name of Your Son, Jesus Christ, we pray. Amen."

Looking out at us, Everett pauses. "Please take a seat," he says. He seems in no hurry to begin. It is a little disconcerting at first…but then a peace settles in. He smiles and begins slowly. I feel drawn in from word one.

"Some of you may be wondering why there is such a hesitancy in the church to walk in the true freedom we have been given. I would have to say, it's because many don't understand it. Many think their faith isn't large enough to experience it. The Bible says people perish for lack of knowledge. My job, as a pastor, is to teach. I am going to be held accountable for what I say from up here. One of my jobs is to help you understand all that we have been given through Christ's death and resurrection, and just what we are to do with it in this world. Pastors can't do it all, and we aren't called to do it all. We are called to help prepare you to go out and do it when you leave here. There is no greater joy for a teacher than to see students, in whatever subject it is, learn and apply the teaching in their lives. How great a feeling it is for a football coach to see a young boy go from his team, at say age ten, to then make it to college and possibly the NFL. The coach has a part in that young man's success. He instructed him properly in how to take the next steps. Or how about a drama teacher in high school, seeing one of her students make it to the big screen? When I see those I have preached to, worked with, prayed with, discipled, and studied alongside, apply Biblical lessons in the everyday world, it is such a great joy. When I hear of someone I have been involved with going out and setting another free from Satan's grip, or relieving physical pain through commanding it to go in Jesus' name, or bringing someone into the saving knowledge of Jesus Christ, then I am truly blessed beyond measure. I get to experience what Jesus commanded us to do when He said go and make disciples. Heal the sick. Cast out demons. Raise the dead. It's not just some story in an old book; it is the Living Word of God being applied right here, right now, in miraculous and exciting ways. Can I tell you a story? What are you going to say? 'No?'" Pastor Everett gives a hardy laugh.

"I was out to lunch with a young man I have been walking beside for a few years. So, for today I'll just call him the disciple, because he is. When we meet, quite often we frequent the same restaurant. Because of that, we've gotten to know the server there. I'll call him Jason. On this day, the disciple and I stopped and bought Jason some of his favorite chocolates before arriving at the restaurant. It was near Christmastime. We asked to be seated at Jason's table, and were happy to hear that he was working. After being seated, Jason greeted us warmly, happy to welcome us back again. We enjoyed a nice lunch and conversation. At the end of lunch, when Jason brought the bill, the disciple handed the box of chocolates to him. Jason received them with a smile and thanks, and then this young disciple proceeded to ask Jason if he knew the greatest Gift of all? I immediately knew God was on the move—the coach was watching his athlete out there on the field! When Jason's answer was something about friends and family, the disciple looked and him and said, 'Jesus is the greatest Gift of all'. He began to tell Jason about Jesus and what He came to do. Upon asking Jason, at this point, if he would like to invite Jesus into his life, Jason said, 'Yes' without hesitation. The disciple had Jason pray with him to not only invite Jesus into his life, but to invite the Holy Spirit to live inside of him. All in all, it was about a five-minute conversation that will have eternal effects. The disciple told Jason that now, when asked if he is a Christian, he can confidently answer 'Yes' from this day on. He can always remember this as the day his name was written in the Lamb's Book of Life in Heaven."

Pastor Everett paused there. I think he knew we all needed to take a breath before he continued on. It was a convicting message, and he knew it.

"Now, you may be thinking, 'I could never do that'. This young disciple would have said that at one time also. But because he had a teachable spirit and is in tune with the Holy Spirit he has come to know, he listened, and obeyed. How do I know this? Because he told me afterward, that while I was talking to him during lunch, the Holy Spirit began to speak to him about leading Jason to the Lord. His initial internal response was, 'Uh, I don't know about that. He's working today. He won't have time...You're going to have to help me'. When he told me this, I asked him why he hadn't said anything to me when he heard this from God? He said it was because he knew if he did, I would have held him accountable to it. He and I laughed at that. He was right. You see, this young disciple is still on the journey, like all of us. But he is willing to listen and obey, even when it can be uncomfortable. Even though initially he was making excuses, very quickly his thoughts changed to, 'You're going to have to help me'. And the Holy Spirit took that as a 'Yes' and gave him the opportunity and the words needed to complete the calling on his life at that moment. The Holy Spirit knew Jason was ready. God was just looking for someone who would push past the *ability* or *inability* he had, and be *available* when it was time. The disciple said once the call went out, he didn't think about it again until handing Jason his chocolates at the end of lunch. Then it all started to flow naturally. Yes, he had to open his mouth and speak. He had to get those first words out and ask Jason if he knew the greatest Gift of all? That was the easy part...the hard part came after that. But that's when the wind of the Holy Spirit swooped in for takeoff. The disciple wasn't in the pilot's seat; he was merely the co-pilot at that point, watching God do His thing so that none would be lost. I challenge you to read Matthew 10:19 when you get home today...and believe it. It is very true!"

Pastor Everett pauses again. I like his delivery. He is very confident and in no rush. He thinks before he speaks, like he, too, is listening.

"I say all this to let you know, I'm here, teaching, so you can go out for the doing. If you walk away from here today unchanged, unmotivated, and unwilling to desire a life as a disciple of Jesus Christ, then I'm not doing my job. But when I see this young disciple do what he did, I know it is possible for all of us to walk out this life of faith. This young man didn't start there. And I know he won't end there. Like the verse we read today in Luke 16:10, he was faithful in the little things, so God has more things in store for him. And I will take great joy in seeing him grow and learn along the way."

Pastor Everett is looking out at all of us. He seems to be connecting with each one individually before he speaks further.

"You may be asking yourself, 'Is he talking about me? To me?' Well, ask yourself this, 'Have I truly been born again? Am I saved through the blood of Jesus and going to Heaven when I leave this earth?' If your answer is 'Yes,' then I *am* talking to you. Some may question whether they are truly a child of God after having accepted Jesus. If that's you, then I want to ask you this, has there been even the slightest amount of change in your life?—in your desires since that decision? Is there a hunger and thirst for the things God is offering you, even if you don't know how to go about receiving them? If any of this even concerns you, it could be evidence of your salvation. Do unbelievers even care about such things? As you grow in your faith, are you experiencing a new love, a new joy, a new peace?—there should eventually be some *Fruit* evidence through the years. This young disciple was bearing Fruit at that lunch. There was a sweet aroma on his tree that day. You may say, 'But I've got so much going on in my life. I don't have time for this.' The disciple thought that same thing about Jason. He was at work, after all. He had tables to take care of. But God knows our schedules. He knows how to orchestrate things just so. Remember, when we are dealing with disruptions in life, it's because the Holy Spirit is preparing us for greater things. He is asking us to be faithful in the things happening today, because He has so much more in store for our life than what we can see. Going through trials…things that upset our apple cart…helps us to see the evidence that God is all He tells us He is: Our Provider, Protector, Counselor, Helper, and Lover of our souls. Our enemy doesn't like this. He doesn't want us to experience God in this way. He wants us to see bad as bad, and good as good. But God says He uses all things for our good when we love Him and are called according to His purpose. Always remember, He who is in you is so much greater than he who is in the world. We can do nothing apart from Christ. If we have wandered away from God in any way, it's time to come back home. Take a lesson from this young disciple who was once very much the prodigal son. My young friend came to his senses and turned back to His Father in Heaven. He was welcomed with open arms. And he is being used mightily by the Lord. It doesn't matter who you are or what you have done, you are loved by the Father, always."

The pastor had so many good things to say, I was making many notes, and was anxious to talk them over with Venyce at breakfast. She, too, was jotting things down. When the service ended, Venyce wanted to meet Pastor Everett and thank him for the great message. After doing that, we said our good-byes to everyone on the way out, and then decided on the local pancake house for breakfast. We were glad to not have to wait long for a seat. Sundays can be busy.

"I'll have the blueberry pancakes with link sausage, please," I say to the beautiful young girl now taking our order.

"And for you ma'am?" she asks Venyce.

"You know, I'll have the same; that sounds good," Venyce replies.

By the time breakfast is set before us, we are deep into the discussion of this morning's sermon.

"He was so spot on, wasn't he, Venyce?"

"Oh, yes! It is vital that we know these things. If we trust in our own strength, we are so going to fail. He talked about what we need to walk this Christian life out fully. Let me look at my notes here…we have to see our need for help and depend on the Holy Spirit. That's so important. He read in Luke 15:17, about the prodigal son. *'When he finally came to his senses.'* How many of us need to do that? If we won't admit we have a problem, we will be stuck in those problems for a very long time. When the prodigal son had finally had enough, he came home. And the father welcomed him with open arms, as will our Father in Heaven. What a good feeling, to know we are so loved," Venyce says.

"It is. My heart is hurting so for Randy. He seems to be withdrawing further and further from the Father, and in turn from me again. I just don't know where we will go from here? Will he ever come to his senses?"

"It's a sad state when people turn away from God instead of toward Him. The prodigal son says here in verse 18, *'I will go home to my father.'* The blessings that follow that decision are huge. I'm sure it was hard for the prodigal, but he did it. He got hungry enough for all that he was missing—he was willing to put away his pride and return home. He repented…he changed his mind. Who would have thought that the word we can be so scared of, *Repentance,* is simply a matter of changing our mind?"

Venyce stopped there and was pouring syrup on her pancakes. But the food was secondary to spending this time with my sister. She was always so good to talk things through with.

"He was very specific," I add between bites, "how our enemy, Satan, is what makes it hard to understand spiritual truths. Only the Holy Spirit can open our eyes, and we have to yield to Him when He does. He said that word, 'Divination,' that I have heard but didn't really understand, is the power of demons working through a person. It seems like we all struggle with that in one form or another. We need to be listening to the Holy Spirit, the way the young disciple did, and not to the darkness. I mean, look at the list he shared in Mark seven about what defiles us. Let me read a few of those, just to lighten the mood this morning," I say, laughing.

"Yeah, right!" Venyce chimes in.

"It says here, pride, slander, envy, wickedness, and so on. I see myself in this list, and without the blood of Jesus, I would be doomed for all of eternity!"

"As would we all," Venyce says with gusto! "Thank You, Jesus!"

"Yes. Thank You! Even anger, which I can feel so often, can find plenty of room in me if I don't quickly get rid of it like Trisha has been teaching me. It wants to get a foothold in all of us. But we have the weapons to fight with through the power of Jesus and prayer. She always says we have to tell it to GO, and quickly, whenever we sense it attacking us."

"So many times, we want to hold onto these things which gives Satan that foothold in our hearts. We don't realize the bondage it will put us in if we do," Venyce adds. "We can choose what spirit we will operate in, the Holy Spirit and His Fruit, or the spirit of the enemy and his evil ways. Destructive things can build slowly, taking hold very deceptively, and if we don't recognize them for what they are, they can grow large in our lives. That tiny mustard seed of faith grows into the largest of trees. Look at how it grew in that young disciple. Those tiny seeds of darkness certainly want to try to do the same. Satan is always mimicking God. We have to dig those bad seeds out immediately, or they will grow, and then birds of prey will make their home among the branches of that evil tree. What a mess that would be if we stood under it!"

"Yes. Those bird droppings are most unwelcome!!" I laugh out loud. "I'm glad I'm meeting with Trisha again this afternoon. She has been such a help to me."

"She is a wonderful warrior of God, Linda. She knows the weapons God has made available to believers in Jesus, and she shows us how to use them." Venyce says this with such a respect for Trisha.

"Trisha knows that demons are squatters—that's what she told me, Venyce. They have no right to a child of God. But if we don't know that, we will just yield to them. I like how Pastor Everett asked us those questions. I felt good about them, because I do see changes in my life. Small but sure. I do have a hunger for the things of God. And the conflict part he talked about...wow! It's hard to understand just how merciless Satan can be. I mean, to not have one thing good about him, nothing nice, nothing kind...a total liar. When we are the most down, that's when he will most likely attack. That's just crazy! But Trisha says the world makes fun of Satan so we won't know how serious he is. Thankfully, Satan doesn't have the power to keep us from coming to Jesus! Look at how quickly Jason said 'Yes'. The Holy Spirit did know he was ready. Trisha always reminds me the door to Jesus is open, 24-7. We just have to decide that going through it is something we want. Jason wanted it that day."

"Yes. He sure did."

"Trisha said the church doesn't talk about demonization a lot, or not at all, because they don't want people to be scared. They would realize that a Christian can be tormented, even though it has been taught the opposite for so many years. It seems that Pastor Mark, and now Pastor Everett, are willing to teach us these things. I mean, find me a Christian, or anyone, who isn't tormented daily by a multitude of things and I would have to say they must already be living in heaven!"

Venyce laughs at this, and agrees, adding, "Seriously. Even with Paul and his tormenting spirit, whether it was in his flesh, or in his soul, he was asking God to remove it. I was thinking about this the other day. God said His grace was sufficient for Paul in that moment in time. And there are times in our own lives where God takes us through things to grow us, to teach us, to build our character and endurance. Pastor Everett talked about that. I was thinking, how do we know that a month later God didn't say, 'Enough, tormenter be gone!'? And then Paul maybe moved on from there healed? How many times have I prayed for things, looking for immediate results, and not getting them? But now, they are no longer tormenting me or making me sick. It was all in God's timing."

"That's an interesting way of looking at it. I would tend to think that story is complete as is, but maybe not? You give me food for thought. And it helps me think about being more patient when my own prayers aren't immediately answered the way I would want them to be. God knows what He is doing, in His own way and time."

"Yes, He does," Venyce responds. "Sadly, some people go on sinning after being prayed for, and then they wonder why they aren't walking in freedom? They want to have their cake and eat it, too. The way I understand that saying is, if you're going to eat your cake, you're not going to have a cake! If you're going to live in sin, you're not going to live in freedom."

"Right. I know changes are needed following Trisha's deliverance prayers for me. And those prayers are what give me the strength from the inside out to make those changes. When the tormentor has been given an eviction notice in my life, I see things differently. I react differently. She always tells me that apart from Jesus we can do nothing. Our own efforts will fail. That is so important to let new believers, especially, know. We need the strength and healing of God to become new inside and out. And so much of it happens over time, and through experiences in getting to know God more and more each day."

"So much of our growth and change depends on us being open, honest, and willing. Let me turn to this verse in Isaiah, 12:2. It's so powerful," Venyce says, pushing her finished plate to the side, and accepting a refill on her coffee. "Oh, this isn't the version I was thinking of, let me get to the NET Bible here on my phone. Yes, here it is, *'Look, God is my deliverer! I will trust in him and not fear. For the LORD gives me strength and protects me; he has become my deliverer.'* Linda, we cut out cancer, many times, with surgery. Why not realize that we need God as our 'Surgeon' to cut out spiritual cancer in our souls? It makes sense. If only we could understand the power of Jesus, and all He has given us! It won't make our lives here perfect, not in this world, in the fallen state it is in. But it will make it an exciting and miraculous life if we walk it out with Jesus as He intends for us to."

"For sure, Venyce. That's what I want more of!"

"I think some pastors have not been taught this in seminary. I could be wrong, since I've never been. This Pastor Everett really seemed to go there, to not be hesitant about teaching what needs to be conveyed to those in the congregation. I really liked him. I'm glad he had a bit of time to talk with us there at the end. He seems so genuine, doesn't he, Linda?"

"Yes. He does."

"I think some pastors who do know this are not quick to share it. Maybe they are thinking they won't be needed as much if we can operate in this fullness and freedom. When truth be told, those that are willing and able to teach this to others will never be out of work! People will be lined up outside their churches wanting the freedom that is being offered by those who know and share the power of the Good News of Jesus Christ!" Venyce says this with even more gusto.

"I hate to stop this discussion, Sis, but I think we need to get going. Trisha said she would be over after she finishes her breakfast. I don't want to keep her waiting out front of your house. Thank you for letting me continue to meet her at your place, Venyce. I like having the privacy, not knowing for sure what Randy is doing…if he will be home or not."

"It's not a problem at all, Linda. My place is your place, any time you need it."

"I hope I don't need it more than an occasional meeting with Trisha, and time spent with you. But I'm beginning to wonder."

"I know… Here, let me get the bill today, and we'll get going."

43

RANDY

Seeing Eric pull up out front, my heart is beating super hard. Calling him last night was probably a mistake, but what's done is done. I'm gonna have to face this now.

Answering the door, I let Eric in. "Hey, there. Come on in. Linda is over at her sister's."

"Thanks. Good to see you. I'm glad you gave me a call. I was wondering if you were still interested in getting together."

"Ummm, have a seat. Wanna a soda or something? I'd offer you a beer but…" I don't even know if Eric drinks beer.

"Coke is fine. Thanks," Eric replies.

Returning with the coke, I ask, "Can okay?" handing it to Eric. I'm not really wanting to go to the trouble of getting a glass and ice.

"Yeah. Sure. I prefer it this way most times. Ice just complicates things," Eric says with a laugh.

"I guess." I'm not really sure what he means by that. I take a seat across the room from him—distance feels safer. Last night was questionable, and I just felt like I needed something. Some help. Eric was the only one I could think of that would offer me advice without judging.

"What's up buddy? You sounded very serious when you called me."

"Yeah. I didn't really want to talk about it on the phone with you. I'm kinda torn right now, Eric. Like I've got two different things at work in my gut. Last night…well, I did something I'm not so sure about. And it's…" I know I'm stalling… "I don't really know how to approach this."

"Let's do this, Randy. Let's take a few deep breaths. Then, I'll pray a bit. The Holy Spirit can really help in times like this to get things flowing."

"Okay." I'm not sure I want to do this. But I feel I have little choice.

Eric begins, "Father, You know and see all. You love all people. It doesn't matter who we are, or what we've done—the blood of Your Son, Jesus, covers it all when we confess our sins. You are faithful and just to forgive. Holy Spirit, help Randy to be freed up to talk about what is needed. Help him to know You are with him and caring about what is going on. Thank you that You brought us to this time together to pray and talk. The enemy's tactics can bind us up and wreck our lives. Randy needs your help to sort through whatever it is that is going on inside of him. Be with us now. Let our discussion be what it needs to be. In Jesus' powerful name we pray. Amen."

"Amen," I say, but not so sure. Eric is a good guy. He doesn't deserve to have this dumped on him, but I don't know where else to take it.

"I'm here to listen, Randy. You go ahead whenever you're ready. There is no hurry," Eric says with kindness and strength.

"I don't even know where to begin. Although, well, I...I'm just gonna put this out there. I...last night, well, I crossed a line that I haven't before. Linda and I have had a troubled marriage for years. We don't really talk a lot, about much of anything. Mainly she will talk about the kids, and the new grandson, Jordan. I...well, I reached out last night in a different direction, and it's got me confused. Linda and I aren't sleeping in the same bedroom here. That leaves a lot of hours for...other things, shall we say." Looking at Eric, I'm trying to read his reaction. He's just nodding and listening.

"Okay," is all he says.

"Well, those other things have taken me in a direction I didn't expect. I got in contact with an old girlfriend last night, and well, it got...sexual." I have to stop here, I wish I hadn't said that.

"With what? A phone call?" he asks with calmness.

"No. I guess they have a name for it these days. I just didn't think I would ever be doing it. I mean, I've texted plenty. But I've heard this is called 'sexting.'" I grimace at having to say the word.

"I've heard of it. Yes. More than I ever thought possible. This new technology opens up lots of things that we never had in the past. What used to stay in our minds, now gets out there on social media and through our phones like never before."

"Eric, ummm, this isn't something I wanted to be doing. It started off with a 'hello' and quickly went where I never wanted it to. But truth be told, I thought about it most of the night afterward, and she is supposed to get ahold of me again tonight. I don't even know how to say 'No' to it. Because, honestly...I want to do it." I hated being so blunt with Eric. But I hated "cheating" on Linda, too. Once divorced, I would be all over this.

But we are still living in the same house, supposedly trying to get our marriage working again.

"Your honestly is refreshing," Eric replies.

"Well, at least something good is going on here," I answer back. "Eric, I...I have had...I have an addiction to porn, too. I'm just saying... I gave it up some time ago, but it's back." I look at Eric for his reaction, and he still remains calm and unmoved.

"So many guys, do, Randy...even pastors and women. Children are the saddest cases. Especially with this sexting thing. It's all so available now that there's hardly a way to stop it. Our laws are trying to catch up with the rapid rate of its progress. But it's like that wild fire in Paradise, it's moving so fast and destroying so much in its path. I saw a news show on the fire there entitled, 'Paradise Lost.' What an appropriate name for what's happening in our world today. Don't feel alone in this—that's what the enemy would want. He wants all this kept in the dark, hidden deep, so that the Light of God can't eradicate it. God is not surprised by any of this. The Word talks about this in the end times."

"About sexting?" I ask, astounded.

"Well, not spelled out exactly in those words. It says here in...let me find it...yes, in 2 Timothy 3:2-4 it talks about people being *'lovers of pleasure rather than lovers of God.'* All kinds of pleasure, Randy, and especially sexual pleasures. But here's the thing, there is temptation, and then there is following through with it. We're all tempted. But when you realize that it's wrong, you have to make the decision to stop there and repent, which means bringing your thoughts in line with what God's Word says about sin. Not arguing your point with God, but agreeing with Him. James 1:14-15 says, *'Temptation comes from our own desires, which entice us and drag us away. These desires give birth to sinful actions. And when sin is allowed to grow, it gives birth to death.'* It's important to understand these are choices we are making. When we say 'No' to these temptations, it is disciplining ourselves and changing the course of our lives—keeping us in the light, and bringing life instead of death."

"That sounds awful!! Too hard!" I exclaim, frustrated. "I thought there would be an easy way out of this. What about all this praying for getting junk out of me? Can't we just do that?"

"I don't mean to laugh," Eric says with a little chuckle. "It's not funny at all, and there is some truth to what you are saying. Sometimes these things come in the form of spirits that can be evicted out of your soul, your mind, will, and emotions. We can cast them out in Jesus' powerful name. But there is also something called crucifying the flesh. That means staying in the Word, praying for help, focusing on the things of God and not the things of this world, and pushing our flesh out of the way and letting the power of Jesus in! We have our part to do in this, too, Randy. We have to want it."

"Oh," was all I could say in that moment.

"We can't just cast out bad habits if it's something we want to continue doing in our lives. How long have you been involved in porn, this time around, since you said you had given it up before?" Eric asks.

"About six months, I'm not sure. It started in gradually, just a little once in a while. Now it's every night, and sometimes even at my desk at work."

"Yes. When the door is opened, even just a little bit, it can become more and more of an invitation for serious infestation as time goes on. And sadly, it can lead to what we are talking about now, 'sexting,' among other things. Sexual sin affects many areas of our lives. If a foothold is not dealt with, it becomes a stronghold. Tearing those strongholds down takes lots of prayer and cooperation with God. We have to want to be free of it."

"I'm not so sure I do. I mean, if you would just wave your magic wand over me and get this to stop, I'd go for it. But it sounds like I would really have to put some time and effort into this God-way of living, and I'm tired. It sounds exhausting."

"You will find, Randy, that at first sins like this seem easy, fun and not exhausting at all. Even when it keeps you up all night. But it will become more and more of a draw on your time, your emotions, and your relationships. It will start to sever you from the people you once loved. It doesn't matter what it is, drugs, alcohol, sexual perversion, workaholics, fantasy, you name it…if it isn't of God, it is of the devil and it is destructive. You may think you sit on the fence with stuff like this. But what you will find in the end is that the *fence* belongs to Satan. You become his property. It's not that he possesses you, but you possess him with these choices. You invite him into your life. You gotta get out of his territory, off his 'fence', and come into the Light of Jesus for true freedom."

"Oh, Eric, you make it sound so black and white. Can't there be some grey areas where we can still get what we want, and get God, too?"

"That's a very good question, one that most people would like to have answered in their favor. Me, included. I want what I want, and when I want it. And who has a right to tell me otherwise? But I had to come to a place of humbling myself before God and wanting His ways more than mine. When I did that, I found a whole new way of living. A whole new freedom and joy that many never get to experience. It wasn't an easy choice for me to make either. I had many of the same temptations that you are dealing with, and it almost cost me my marriage, and in the end my life. Depression started to set in bigtime. For me it wasn't a chemical imbalance, it was something I invited in by the choices I was making.

When I changed my choices, my life was changed. Was it perfect? No. It's still not perfect. But it is a life that excites me every single day. I see the working of Jesus in my life and the lives of others. When Jesus is real in your life, there is no higher high—no greater satisfaction. The enemy brings us things that seem satisfying in the beginning, like your sexting…but in the end, they destroy us. What Jesus brings us is not only satisfying, it is edifying…it builds up our lives and our relationships. His burden really is light, and His yoke really does fit perfectly. We just have to be willing to try it on to see how awesome it is! When you listen to Satan, he is the one controlling your life. Not you. Him. When you listen to the Holy Spirit, and allow Him to control your life, then your life is everything that our Father in Heaven planned for it to be."

Sitting here, listening to Eric, parts of what he is saying make sense. Other things just go in one ear and out the other. I don't want to hear it. All I can really think about is what the night holds, what my old girlfriend will be saying to me in her messages in the dark of the night. It felt so good to have her want me in that way, and I wanted her. My love for Linda seemed to pale in comparison to the thrill of what started last night and would hopefully continue on into something more in the future. Eric can't know how drawn to it I am, and how hard it is for me to sit here even listening to him now. I don't even know why I called him. I shouldn't have. Maybe I thought he would give me a go ahead since it was only on the phone, and not in person. What was I thinking? He is a man all about God, not about wanting me to get any pleasure from this.

"Eric, uhh, I hear ya, and I will need to think about this. I was hoping for a different resolution I guess."

"Randy, the Bible doesn't say to ignore the devil, it says to resist him, after submitting yourself to God. The devil's goal is to make us think he's not there. But you were recognizing him, even if just for a little bit. By calling me about this, you did the right thing. Now the choice is yours to make…it always was and will be. Understand that deception is a key tool of the enemy in this. He deceives us, and then when we are deceived, we don't even realize it because of the deception. He's coming at us from all angles. But with God's Armor fully activated, we will be able to stand against him. The helmet of salvation protects our mind, the breastplate of righteousness protects our heart, the belt of truth protects us from the lies, the shoes keep us in peace, the shield of faith deflects the arrows that come our way, and the sword of the Spirit, being in the Word of God and using it, is one of the mightiest weapons we have. When we open up the Word and read the Truth, and pray, it can dispel the deception. The enemy will keep us as far away from the Bible as possible. I heard it once said, 'The farther you go in God, the less you can take with you.' We have to be crucified with Christ so that we no longer live but Jesus lives in us. When there's too much of *us* in the picture, we won't be giving Jesus room to operate on our souls, cutting out the stuff that isn't of Him. That's what you were hoping for today…hoping that the little sins don't count. But they do, and they lead us into the darkness deeper and deeper. We can surely pray. But as long as this evil is a friend in your mind, it's not going anywhere."

"Eric, thanks. I get it. And I need to think about this. Linda will be home soon, so I think we should call it quits for now. I'll get in touch with you if I have any more questions."

"Okay. Would you like me to pray for you before I go?"

"No. I think I got it. I'll pray later," I say, knowing that I'm lying. I can feel the urge in my gut to just get back to my phone when night comes. Walking Eric to the door, I honestly don't know if I'll be seeing him again. I know where he's coming from, and it's just not where I want to go.

44

RANDY AND LINDA

Coming through the door, I call out to Randy, but get no response. He must be in his room. I want to talk with him after my session with Trisha. I wonder if he will be receptive to it? After doing some things around the house, and putting in a load of laundry, I still haven't seen Randy. I look again to see if his car is out front, and it's gone. Now, when did he leave? He had to know I was home because my car is there. I can't believe he didn't say anything. Hmmm… This makes my heart sick. I came home feeling so uplifted after being with Trisha, hoping we could discuss some things, and he's gone. Sighing, I take a seat in the living room, and pray.

"Father, I'm at a loss. I want my marriage to work. But won't it take two of us? Can I possibly hold it up from my end until Randy is ready to work on it? I'm so exhausted from this troubled relationship. I know marriage is supposed to last a lifetime. I know Your Word doesn't support divorce. But what am I supposed to do?" I start to remember a verse that Trisha told me about a while back. I wonder if I can find it? Maybe I can just text her and ask her?

"Trisha, Hi, I have a question. What was that verse about divorce you told me about? When it is allowed. I'm sorry to say things may not be good here at all."

She texts back, "So sad. Yes, there is a portion of Scripture that talks about divorce. It is in 1 Corinthians chapter seven."

"Okay. Thanks."

Turning there, I read about how if a believing woman has a husband who is not a believer and he insists on leaving, we can let them go. But Randy believes in Jesus. How does that work? What if he doesn't want this marriage, as a believer? Then what? I better text Trisha back.

"Another question, sorry to bother you."

"No bother, Linda. What is it?"

"This says if the person is not a believer, and they want to leave, the believing spouse can let them leave. They are no longer bound to them. But Randy is a believer."

"Yes. From what we know, he is. Is he asking to leave?"

"No. It's just that I came home wanting to talk to him, and he went out the door at some point and said nothing. I don't know where he's at right now, physically or mentally."

"Oh."

"Yeah. It's not a good feeling. It got me wondering what position this leaves me in?"

"We can't make someone do something they aren't willing to do. That includes staying in a marriage, or even being set free from what is tormenting them."

"Right. I understand that. I guess I'll just have to wait until he gets home. Thanks! I don't want to take up any more of your time today. Thanks for your help."

"No problem at all. I will be praying for you."

I don't know where this leaves me. I don't know what Randy is thinking. Stretching out on the couch, I grab the blanket off the back and cover up. It feels good to relax.

Before I know it, I hear the front door opening and Randy is returning. I don't know how long I've been asleep. Sitting up quickly, I try to catch him before he disappears down the hall.

"Hey, Randy! Are you okay?"

Turning, he looks at me with a sullen, downcast face, responding sharply.

"What do you mean?"

"I didn't hear you go out earlier. Is everything okay?" I want to keep this as light as possible.

"I had some things to do. Do I have to report my comings and goings to you, Linda?"

Again, the edge to his voice makes me not want to engage in this, but I know I need to.

"Of course not. It's just that I got home from being with Trisha and I thought…"

"You thought what?!" I already wish I hadn't come back home.

"That maybe we could talk?" I can feel the tears making their way to the surface.

"I don't have much to say."

"Maybe if we just start, Randy, we could…"

"I don't think so. I'm tired. Looks like you just woke from a nap. I think I'll see if I can take one now."

Disappearing down the hall, Randy is once again making me feel hopeless. After all I just went through with Trisha earlier, I was so encouraged and…who is calling me now?

"Hi, Hannah. How are you? How's Jordan?"

"We are all fine, Mom. You sound tired. Are you okay?"

Hannah is so good at reading me. It's rare I can get anything by her. "I'm fine. Just woke from a nap." I don't want to bring her down with my life situation right now.

"Oh. Okay. Well, the reason I'm calling is because I'm so excited! Blake has a business trip coming up to California, and Jordan and I are going to be able to travel with him! We get to come and see you and Dad! I can't wait for Dad to meet Jordan, too!"

"Oh, that's wonderful!" I respond, hoping in the back of my mind that Randy will accept this news in a good way. "When will you arrive?"

"We will be arriving two weeks from Monday, and get to stay through the following weekend!"

"That's a nice long visit. I wish we could get Rob out here at the same time, but I know he's busy with work."

"Yes. I talked to him recently. He is doing well, though, so that's good," Hannah says in her big sister tone.

"He is. Will you all be able to stay at the house here? It would be wonderful."

"I was hoping you would offer. It would be easier than being in a hotel with Jordan. I know it will be noisier now with a baby waking in the night…and Dad…"

"Don't you worry about anything," I respond with a fake confidence. I have no idea how Randy will take this news.

"Great, Mom! I gotta go now. But I couldn't wait to tell you the news!" Hannah sounds so happy.

"We'll talk soon. Love you!"

"Love you, too. Bye."

"Bye."

Hanging up, I wonder how I'm going to break this news to Randy. When he reappears a few hours later looking for something to eat in the kitchen, I try to size him up. Is it a good time? Or not?

"Whatcha wanna eat for dinner? I don't mind making us something," I offer as kindly as I can.

"I don't know. I'm hungry, but I don't know what for."

He's grumbling, so I try to think of something that would satisfy him. "I could make us some spaghetti and garlic bread." Looking at me, he nods, saying nothing. "Okay, then, why don't you turn on a ballgame, and we can eat in there?" I know I'm trying to butter him up because my stomach is churning at the thought of telling him the kids are coming. And Jordan. But I know I better not wait too long. I want to give him time to settle into the idea after hearing it.

Once we are seated in front of the game, and halfway through dinner, I pray for the right words as a commercial begins. Then they just seem to tumble out all at once, good or bad. "Hannah and Blake get to come out to California in a couple of weeks! You will get to meet Jordan!"

Randy stops eating and looks at me. I can't tell what he's thinking. It's like there's a whole movie playing out in his mind as he stares at me. I remain quiet, hoping for the best. Is he trying to decide how to call it off? Is he playing out scenes of having a baby in the house? Is he angry or happy? I wish he would say something.

I can't believe what Linda just said. The kids are coming? I don't know what to say. At least this spaghetti is good....and the ballgame. I feel uneasy not answering Linda. But she wouldn't be happy with what I would say anyway. I think she can tell it's better I not say anything right now. She's leaving me to the game.

Sitting in uncomfortable silence, I realize I'm living with a man I should know as well as the back of my hand, but I don't. He's become a stranger to me as he stares at the TV, not even willing to talk about his daughter. How did this happen? How did we get here? Eventually just clearing the empty plates from our TV trays, I walk into the kitchen with my heart in my shoes. This is Randy's grandson. He's never met him. This is his daughter, who he got up with at night, and who he took to the park and pushed on the swings. How has he grown so cold and distant? He hasn't said a word to me since I told him they were coming. I don't know if I want to go back in and sit down. I'd rather go to my room and close the door, so I do. Picking up my Bible, I don't even know where to turn. Eventually finding my way to Romans, I begin to read bits and pieces, hoping something will jump out at me. My mind seems fuzzy. It's true that evil doesn't make sense. Nothing is making sense right now. After about an hour, I can hear the TV being turned off and footsteps coming toward my door. My heart seems to skip a beat...my nerves are on edge. With a knock, I call out, "Come in." Randy is standing there looking at me. He waits a moment before he says anything. I think we both feel uncomfortable.

"I'm going to bed. But I've been thinking about the kids coming. We need to do this. It may be the last time we will all be here like this in the house together. I don't know that you and me living here is going to work, Linda. I'm sorry to say it. But it's just so tense around here. I don't want this anymore. I don't want to work on this, talk about it, or be sorry for all this junk. We will hold it together until after their visit. But then I think it's best if you go back to Venyce's. Sorry."

"Randy, you know what you *don't* want. Do you know what you *want*?"

"Uh…Linda. Really. Let's not do this…I'm tired."

Randy closes the door with barely a hint of emotion. My tears are full force now. I'm thankful they held off until he was finished. I don't want Randy to see how vulnerable I am to his coldness—his rejection. It's breaking my heart—but part of me also agrees. We can't go on living like this if we aren't going to be working on our relationship. I know this time there will be no coming back.

45

RANDY AND LINDA

After telling Linda that her time in the house is done, I didn't feel good about myself. I had to tell her it was okay for the kids to come. What was I supposed to say? At least I can feel good about that. As the days go by, we don't really talk. She's excited for their visit. I can tell. I'm ignoring thinking about it as much as I can. I will be glad when it is over.

The texting thing with Kimberly has turned into more than just a nightly affair. Now I'm texting with her from work, and any other chance I get. There's little time for anything else when Kimberly is always on the other end of the phone waiting for me. It's like she's a magnet and I'm solid iron. I can't stay away from her. At first it was so exciting. Now, I'm not sure what to think about it. It doesn't qualify as cheating, really—not to me. I'm not meeting with her in person. She lives in another state. Linda doesn't ever need to know about this. It's not a real relationship. It's just fantasy.

I see there's another message from Kimberly tonight, right when I get home from work. I'm not surprised. She seems to be getting as much out of this as I am. Her husband is boring, she says. He brings no happiness into her life. He has his own things going on, and she says he wouldn't even care if he found out about us. I'm pretty sure Linda would care. In fact, I know that she would feel hurt. That makes me stop for half a second before texting back with Kimberly. What am I doing to the woman I promised to be with until death do us part? I'm telling her to move out, once again, for a fantasy on the phone? Does that even make sense? My mind is cloudy, and I can't think straight about this right now. I think I'll just text with Kimberly for a bit. I won't be on long.

Looking at the clock, it's been over three hours since I got home and disappeared in my room. When I come out, Linda has gone to bed, and I haven't even eaten dinner yet. In the beginning this seemed to give me a reason to exist. Now it seems like I am just existing for it and nothing more. Finally saying "good-bye" to Kimberly, I'm able to eat. But I'm left alone in my thoughts. I know she will be back on later. Guaranteed.

With the kids coming, what am I going to do with them in the house? And with a baby? They will be up all hours of the night. I'd better keep the light off in my room when I'm texting. I don't want them knowing I'm awake all night, too. This is affecting my concentration at work. And it seems I really have nothing to say to Linda anymore. It feels like she can read my face, my expression...can she? Maybe she sees the guilt written all over me?

Turning on the TV, eating a sandwich in my room, I want to disengage for a while—but I can't seem to just watch movies anymore. It's like there is no channel other than the ones that make me think about Kimberly. She has sent me pictures. I didn't want them at first. They seemed to be wrong. I am married. But after the first few, the shock wore off and I look forward to them now. She wanted pics of me, too. I couldn't do it at first. I'm not that kind of guy. But after insisting, I relented. I worry what will happen to them now. I know that wasn't smart. I feel like I'm drowning in all this. Should I call Eric again? What will he think? He's going to be frustrated with me, I just know it. He told me I was headed in the wrong direction. And look how far I've strayed from where we began. If only I'd stayed meeting with him regularly. Maybe I could have resisted better. I don't know. I'm tired. I think I'll just go to sleep.

When morning comes, my head is still groggy. Kimberly had me up half the night again. My thoughts are no better than they were last night. Getting out of the house early for work, I can avoid Linda. I can hardly look her in the eye. How will I look at Hannah when she gets here? And Jordan? Wow, that will be tough. He's an innocent baby, and I'm a dark old man. How will I ever gel with him? I don't even want him around. But he's my grandson... I sure wish they weren't coming here. I feel stuck, alone, and afraid.

Getting to work doesn't help. I walk quickly by Emily's desk as she says her morning hello. I don't want to look at her either. Once I get to my desk, I feel some relief. No one knows what I do in here. I know my work has been slipping though. All those hours texting has taken my concentration level to a bad place. There she is. I can't help but answering, as I get up to close the door…

"Randy?" I hear from the intercom. It startles me out of reading what Kimberly has just written.

"Yeah."

It's Emily. "Denton wants you to come to his office this afternoon at three for a meeting."

"Okay. Thanks."

A meeting? Why so last minute? Shaking my head, I try to get some work done. Lunch comes and goes and by the time three o'clock rolls around, I've spent more than half my time texting with Kimberly. Denton has to see a decline in my production. I hope that's not what the meeting is about. I can feel the sweat start to break out on my brow. It seems like life is going downhill fast. I take a deep breath, hoping to feel some relief. It only shows me I can't breathe very deep. Too much stress has built up in my gut.

At 3:00, I walk into Denton's office. "Hey there," I say, trying to avoid his eyes, and noticing that it's just the two of us.

"Have a seat, Randy." His tone is even, not mad, but certainly not friendly.

"Thanks." Sitting once again on the big leather couch, it doesn't hold the comfort it once did. It seems stiff today, or is it just my body that is unable to relax? "Where's everyone else?"

"We have some things to talk about in private, and it's not an easy thing for me. So, I'll get right to the point. You seem distracted, Randy. I have been watching a steady decline in your numbers, and it concerns me. Is there something bothering you? Health issues? Marital? Emotional? I know this is an office. I know we are about production. But I don't want to be insensitive either. If there is a problem, let me know, and we can work with you."

Looking at Denton, I don't know what to say. I can only look at him for a short time, and then my eyes dart away before looking back. It seems his eyes are burrowing into me. I wish I could run, but I know I can't. I have to face this, whatever happens.

"I…" What am I supposed to say? Do I confess? Or do I cover? Do I make excuses? Do I lie?

"You, what? You can tell me, Randy. If there's something I can help you with, I will," he says actually offering a bit of comfort.

"I don't think this is the place to go into it. I will try to do better. Really. I've been distracted with some things, and I know it's slowed me down here. Sorry about that. I will work harder at it. You can count on me."

"I'm glad you are aware, and I do hope we can come to a meeting of the minds here. You've always done an excellent job. That's why I'm surprised at this turn in your performance. I'm willing to give it some time."

"I..uh, I appreciate that. Really. I will get on this," I say, hoping it's true. With the distractions coming almost constantly now through Kimberly, I feel panicked.

Heading home at the end of the day, I feel my gut in a knot, my head pounding, and my thoughts of Kimberly wanting to override it all. I tried not to answer back as her texts came through the rest of the day. I don't want her to go away. I just want it to slow down some. I tried to tell her that in one text, but she wouldn't have it. She thought I was being mean and not caring about her needs. I tried to explain that I needed to focus on work. She wasn't interested. She said she has problems at work, too, but she's not putting them in front of our relationship. Is this a relationship? I'm not so sure.

Pulling into the driveway, I see Linda isn't home yet. That's one good thing. I can't face her coming through the door. Another text comes through from Kimberly. She is relentless. I ignore it until I get into the house. Then I answer her back. Her messages are full of perverse things. So are mine...things that neither one of us should be writing. We are both married. Would I have done this with her if I'd known she was married right from the start? I was too deeply entrenched by the time she told me. And she said her marriage was practically over anyway. I told her mine was, too. Although at that time I still had some hope, I guess.

Hearing the front door open, I dart into my room. I don't want to talk to Linda right now. I can hear her in the kitchen on the phone.

"...yes. Yes, I had an okay day. Randy is around here somewhere.......I don't know. I'll tell him when I see him. Thanks for calling, Venyce. I'll talk with you soon."

It's quiet now. I can't hide in my room forever. I find Linda sitting at the kitchen table going through the mail.

"Hey," I say, as I walk in and sit down across from her.

"Hi," I respond looking up at Randy. I'm surprised he's engaging with me. "How was your day?"

"Fine. How was yours?" I'm trying to make light conversation even though I have no interest in Linda's day.

"Good. Busy. I'm looking forward to some time off when Hannah gets here." I offer that up to see how Randy is feeling about the visit now.

"Oh. You're taking some days off?"

"Yes. I want to spend as much time with little Jordan as possible. He's growing up so fast. I can still remember his sweet smell. I miss him so much."

"Okay. Well, I gotta work while they're here. The load is pretty heavy right now. How long will they be staying again?" I wasn't really listening the first time Linda told me.

"From Monday until Sunday. I'll put them in that front guest room so if the baby cries at night, you won't hear it in your room so much." I'm hoping to appease Randy with this. I don't want him grumpy the whole time they are here.

"Yeah. That would be good. I don't want to be up all night from the baby crying." I say this knowing I actually haven't been sleeping most nights anyway. Not with Kimberly keeping me entertained.

"You won't be. Don't worry about it. Can I talk to you about something else?" Looking at Randy full on now, I'm trying to read his reaction. It doesn't look good.

"Like what? I really don't want to get into it, Linda. I know you'd like our marriage to be saved through all this God stuff. But I don't think God is much interested in whether we spend the rest of our lives together or not. He's more interested in us being happy I think."

"You think? What do you *know*, Randy?" I can feel myself getting frustrated already. Dear Lord, take this spirit of frustration and get it away from me, right now! In Jesus' name! I'm glad God hears our silent prayers.

"What do you mean by that?" I snap back at Linda.

"I'm sorry. I shouldn't have said that to you. We are all making our way, and I just want to get away from what I think, and line my thoughts up with God's."

"Oh, you do. Well, how exactly are we supposed to do that, Linda?" Getting up from the table I quickly add, "I've got some things to do."

"Randy...RANDY..." I call out, but he's gone down the hall. I can hear the bedroom door shut, just as I can hear any communication between us being shut down. I probably handled that wrong. But I don't know what to do any more. I hope Hannah and the baby bring some sunshine back to this home for a bit before I leave once again. I feel like the clock is counting down to the end of our marriage.

46

LINDA

Arriving at Trisha's house after church, I'm really needing some encouragement and help. Randy has been impossible, and Hannah and Blake are arriving tomorrow with little Jordan. I don't want them walking in on the tension we've been living in. And I really don't want to tell them I'll be moving out again after they leave. I want it to be a peaceful, joy-filled visit. Trisha invited me to her place today since Venyce wasn't feeling well. She's just getting over the flu, and it's best that we let her rest.

Ringing the bell, I can hear worship music from inside. It sounds soothing already, and when Trisha opens the door with her always ready smile, I can feel a little hope returning.

"Hi, Trisha!"

"Hello! Come on in, Linda! So good to have you over today. I hope Venyce is feeling a bit better?"

"She is. She just wants to make sure she gets some rest before the kids arrive. She doesn't want to be sick and not get to see Jordan. We had such a nice time with them when we went out for his birth."

"I know you did," Trisha says, ushering me into a large, sun-lit living room.

"This is beautiful," I remark before taking a seat on a beautiful white couch that Trisha has pointed me to.

"Go ahead and have a seat. I'll get us something to drink. Be right back."

Sitting here, I'm already thinking about how I've been working hard at keeping my "Temple" cleared out of the "thieves," as Trisha calls them.

It's challenging when they seem to invade my "home" so quickly. Trisha told me it says in Ephesians we are God's house, built on the foundation of the apostles and prophets. What a powerful way to look at our lives in Christ! And Jesus is the Cornerstone, with all of us being carefully joined together. That's a tight-knit family! And in that house, it's like she said, we have to do our "dishes" daily to keep them from piling up.

Looking around while Trisha is gone, I can tell she keeps a wonderfully clean home. I notice many family pictures, and a beautiful one of her and her husband, Calvin, over the fireplace. It's in a park setting, and then on each side of it are more pictures of her kids and grandkids. In the corner there's a round table with a lace tablecloth on it. It looks like an old family Bible is there, opened up toward the middle. A small candle sits beside it, and it is lit. There isn't a TV in the room, but soft worship music is playing from another room. Coming back with our ice water, Trisha takes a seat on an adjacent love seat. It feels good to be in her home.

"How is Calvin, Trisha? Is he traveling home soon?"

"Yes. He will be back in two weeks, and gets to stay for about a month," she responds with a warm smile. "It will be good to have some time together. He is ready for retirement in the next couple of years. We hope to do a lot of traveling then."

"That sounds nice," I say, my head sort of falling slowly forward, and tears suddenly filling my eyes. "I'm sorry. I'm happy for you. It's just so sad for how my marriage is failing."

"No need to be sorry. It is heartbreaking. Let's work on some things today that will help you endure during this time, and possibly shed some new light on just what is happening. God knows, and He cares. He wants to give you the strength you need for all things."

"Thank you. I surely need His help right now. Randy is so recluse. He barely comes out of his room when we are home together."

Trisha shakes her head slowly, and offers to pray; "Father, hear our prayers today. Wrap Your comfort around Linda. This is a hurting, confusing time for her with Randy. You see behind that closed door, and behind his closed heart. Please, we come to You today asking for help. Randy needs You; their marriage needs You. Bring Your healing and restoration to them. Let there be joy in their home during the visit this week. Let little Jordan be a bright spot in their lives. This family needs Your healing touch. Bless them, and this time we have here together today. In Jesus' powerful name we pray. Amen."

"Amen," I can barely add, while wiping away the tears. Trisha is kind enough to give me a few moments to calm down before she begins.

"Linda, let's talk about some things that we may have covered before, and then some things that we haven't. There is always so much to learn in this life, and how God would have us walk through it. He has a plan, even when we can't see it. He loves us, even when we can't feel it. He's working, even when we're sure He's not. I say that not from just any book, but from the Bible, and also from my own life experiences. There was a time when my marriage was failing, too. There's probably a rare person who won't be able to tell you of a difficult time in their own marriage. Life is complicated, and these days, there is so much coming against us. I heard an interesting bit of information the other day. In the days of old, during Biblical times, there were only millions of people on this earth. Today there are billions. That's a huge jump! And how in the world does the enemy get to everyone? His numbers haven't increased."

"How does he? That's true!" I ask, more listening now than crying.

"Well, media is huge these days—the way we can communicate with one another. Remember when we were kids…there was no internet, no cell phones, no social media. I was just thinking the other day and wondering, actually, what do the young people call it when they 'hang up' a phone? So, I asked my granddaughter that question when I saw her. I told her we called it that because we actually took the receiver and hung it on the wall part of the phone or placed it back on the phone sitting on the table. She looked at me like I was a little crazy, and said, 'We call it hanging up.' So, I guess the terminology hasn't changed, even though the action has. I told her that 100 years from now, they will be wondering why they call it that? It will be so far removed from the original meaning of it."

Laughing along with Trisha, I had to agree with her.

"So, anyway, I got off track there, Linda. Sorry about that. But with the mass communication we have today, and the way the enemy can and will operate through people, think of the access available now that wasn't around in biblical days! Even the movies we watch. If some producer wants to make a movie to get a satanic message across to his audience, he can. One hundred years ago there was no such thing. Satan had to work harder then. Today he can operate on cruise control, so to speak. We do so much of the work for him just by how we use the devices we've been given. It's so easy for him to get his dark message into the minds of the people in this world. We have to guard our hearts and minds in Christ Jesus, for sure!"

"Absolutely! I get what you're saying."

"What is it you're struggling with the most today?" Trisha asks gently.

"Well, it's hard not to just focus on my marriage. So let me think…I guess, well, my thought life, too. As much as I try to read the Bible, and go to church, my thoughts still seem to get the better of me sometimes. My eyes wander to places, and want to even watch things on TV, that aren't the best. I'm trying to weed out the shows that don't bring God any glory.

But that pretty much cuts out everything, doesn't it?" I say, laughing.

"Yes. I get you there. The other day I was at the movies, and the new movie ads are so dark—even the ones for children. I can't believe what they are putting in the so-called cartoons these days. Many times, I just look down, and wait until they are over. They are filled with wizards, and spells, and darkness. I don't want the movie producers putting their thoughts and schemes into my mind," Trisha says with conviction.

"It seems to happen so quickly. What steps can we take to protect ourselves from the things that surround us?" I ask.

"Always be in the Word, first and foremost. And pray while we are there! It is so powerful to be reading God's Words written to us, and then talk with Him about what He's saying. And of course, things like being with people of like mind and beliefs. There is such deception in the world. There are huge spiritual battles going on as we get closer to Jesus' return. It is talked about in the Word, and we can't be surprised by it. The thoughts you are having, we all have them. As we spend more time focused on the things of God, we will catch them more quickly, and get them out of our thinking. We will know not to dwell on them like we have in the past. It takes practice, but over time, we get better at it."

"Everything seems to take time and practice," I say, a bit dejectedly.

"The good things do," Trisha answers back with enthusiasm. "But they are so worth it. The other day I realized I had a spirit of guilt that had been with me for a while. I hadn't noticed how powerful it was, and how it was affecting me. When I noticed it, and I practiced again commanding it to GO, it wasn't until the next day that I could tell what a change it made in my perspective on something that was bothering me. I had a different view on what was being said about me, and I was astounded. It was so freeing. So many times we really think we are seeing clearly, and we're not. The enemy is very clever. He can pull the wool over our eyes. Think about that. We are God's sheep. And the enemy takes who we are and uses it to blind us. There is a spirit called Leviathan. It's a twisting spirit, grabbing hold of Truth and changing it. He is very active today, as he was in me through the guilt I was dealing with. We have to keep on top of these things…walking in the authority we've been given!"

"It sure sounds like it. And no one is safe, not even you, Trisha. And you know all about this stuff."

"Well, not all about…but I keep learning. All that you have been practicing, Linda, the forgiveness, the repentance, taking every thought captive to Christ, works. It changes lives. I know this because it still changes mine. You, too, will start to see things without the haze of this world. You will really start to see that we aren't fighting against flesh and blood, but against dark spiritual forces in the heavenly realms. This will help with Randy, no matter what. When we start to recognize things from God's perspective, we will know what's behind the words and actions of people. It's not the person, it's the enemy operating through the person. When things get confusing and we can't make any sense out of it, we will know that's not of God. The enemy wants to catch us in his trap. We should be as innocent as a dove, but also as wise as a serpent to avoid his trap. But when there are those times when he snares us, like he did with guilt for a time in my life, we can learn how to escape his plans of destruction for us."

"I like the sounds of that. I feel like I'm learning, but it is a slow process. And sometimes the harshness of life starts to really get to me. I just want Randy to join in this with me. It seems like it would be easier if we could work as a team."

"You are right, it would be. But not everyone has that in their marriage. But that doesn't mean you can't do it on your own, in the marriage or out. We will all face God alone one day. It will be us standing before Him, or I should say kneeling!!" Trisha emphasized that. "And we will give an account for what we did in this life. Not to be kept out of Heaven, but to be rewarded for the ways that we blessed God with our lives—lives that were given to Him while we are here."

"There really are rewards in Heaven? I like the sounds of that!"

"There are! One reward is talked about in 2 Timothy 4:8. It talks about the Crown of Righteousness, which will be awarded, and it will be given to all those who are eagerly looking forward to Jesus' appearing. I know I've got at least one with that! I can't wait until He returns—what a glorious day that will be!" Trisha says joyfully.

"I'm in! Come, Lord Jesus!"

"Amen. Linda, please know that in your marriage, you are not fighting against Randy. You have an enemy that wants to destroy your life any way he can. And he is not to be feared, but he is to be known about and fought against. You are a warrior for Jesus. And you already have the victory. We are to love one another and have compassion for one another, but we are not to show the enemy any mercy. We are to recognize him and defeat him in the power of Jesus' name. We have to know Jesus, and cast out any doubts that enter in. Do you ever wonder why John the Baptist didn't know for sure who Jesus was when he was imprisoned? I mean, he had baptized Jesus, and he had seen the Holy Spirit descending like a dove upon Him. The voice of God had even spoken from Heaven saying, *'This is my beloved son.'* And yet in prison, John sent his disciples to find out if Jesus was really the Messiah."

"I hadn't thought about that, I guess."

"It's in Matthew 11:3, where it talks about this." Trisha gets up and walks to the Bible sitting on the table, turning there, she says, "Yes, here it is. They ask Jesus, *'Are you the Coming One, or do we look for another?'* John was a man, flesh and blood, just like us. He battled the same things we battle. He had the Holy Spirit living in him since before he was born. We have the Holy Spirit living in us as believers in Christ. And the same things we battle, doubts, fears, discouragement, and all the rest, he had the same battles. Think about him, a great man of God, operating in the spirit of Elijah, and yet he sat in prison. And then later was beheaded. The enemy worked on him, too. The enemy tormented him even to his last days. But he remained true to God, as can we."

"That's good to know we aren't alone in our struggle. We just have different situations in life. What do you mean when you talk about the spirit of Elijah?"

"Elijah was a prophet of old. Have you heard about him?" Trisha asks.

"I've heard his name in church, but I don't know much more than that about him."

"Elijah was the head of the school of the prophets. Hundreds of men learned from him. He operated in a spirit that was so godly that today he is still talked about. When God took him to Heaven, his successor, Elisha..."

"What? They had the same name?"

"No. No, they sound very similar, but they are pronounced and spelled slightly different. One is 'jah' and the other is 'sha.' It's things like this that make the Bible more real to me. I mean, if I was writing the story, and it was fiction, I would have given them completely opposite names!" Trisha laughs at this. "But God used these two men with such similar names. Elijah actually means, 'The Lord is my God.' Anyway, he was so godly that when John the Baptist came, he was said to be operating in the same spirit of godliness that Elijah did. This doesn't mean Elijah was reincarnated in John the Baptist, because reincarnation is not true. It means that the spirit that controlled Elijah was a very good one, and the same spirit of repentance was also with John the Baptist. I desire that spirit. I want to hear God and be obedient to God like Elijah was."

"So, do you have it? I mean, it seems to me that you do, from the times I spend with you. You hear God well and live a very godly life."

"Well, praise God for you seeing that in me. It is the desire of my heart to follow Jesus closely, to be Christlike. That is what deliverance is for. To make us more Christlike. To get the devil out, and more Jesus in!!" Trisha says in a deliberate tone.

"That's what you're teaching me."

"We only have a little more time today, because I have an appointment this afternoon. Would you like some prayer before we end today? Has anything been bothering you that we can pray deliverance for? I know you mentioned your thought life, and we will pray about that."

"Yes. And I would like prayer for forgiveness toward Randy. I'm always getting angry at the way he's acting, and his insensitivity toward me and even the kids. I don't want to have this eating away at me, especially with them visiting soon. Maybe if we pray together, or you pray for me, I can get it out more at the roots."

"We can do that, Linda. Go ahead and close your eyes, and we will start. I'm going to put some of the anointing oil on you. Is this okay?"

"Sure. Of course."

I listen as Trisha says, "In the name of the Father, the Son, and the Holy Spirit," while making a Cross with the oil on my forehead.

"Now look me in the eyes," she says. "I know this isn't easy sometimes, but it's important to be able to look past the flesh and into the soul. What we see in the flesh is so different than what's going on in our mind, will, and emotions where evil spirits can take hold and try to control us. So, right now, in the name of the Lord Jesus Christ, all spirits of unforgiveness and anger, spirits of frustration and bitterness, we bind you all together. Any dark or evil thoughts that are lurking, or attempting to control Linda, we bind you also, to anything that is of Satan. We cast you out of Linda, right now, in the name of Jesus Christ. GO! You have no legal right to this child of God. We cancel your assignment against her. She is forgiven by the blood of Jesus and washed clean of any sin you think is being held against her. GO now, in the name of Jesus Christ. And any other spirit of darkness that has gained access, we cast you out to the dry places, to never return. By the blood of Jesus, and in the power of Christ's name, GO!... Now just breathe out a bit, like we talked about...maybe give a cough, and picture them leaving you. That's it. You go ahead and cough more if you need to. Good. Let them go. Don't hold onto them. They are not your friends, they are foes. They are not wanted. You are all being evicted today through the power of the name of Jesus Christ! Okay, now breathe in the Holy Spirit, Linda. Breathe deep, fill up those empty places with God's holiness. That's it. Breathe Him in. I saw your shoulders relax, and I see the peace coming to your face. How do you feel?"

After a few moments, I feel good. "I was definitely holding onto some things, Trisha. Wow. They build up so fast."

"Yes, they do, Linda. This has been good that we could spend this time before your family arrives. Thank you for sharing what's going on, and for allowing me to pray with you."

"And Father, we pray for Randy, too. He needs You! Bring Randy freedom in Your name Jesus! Bring him to his knees in repentance. Set him free, Lord Jesus. Amen."

"Amen. Thank you, Trisha. I appreciate all you are doing. I know you have a life, and I'm so happy that Calvin will be here soon."

"Yes. Me, too. And I will be keeping you all in prayer during Hannah's visit! Enjoy!"

"We will. Thanks!"

Driving away, my heart feels refreshed. I know I still have the music to face at home, but now I seem to hear the heavenly choir a bit more.

47

RANDY AND LINDA

"Hannah, honey, would you like some breakfast?"

"I'm not hungry yet, Mom. Probably after I feed Jordan, I will be. So, I'll wait."

"Okay. You just let me know."

Hannah and Blake arrived yesterday, and so far, it's been okay. It's nice to have some time off to spend with them. Blake has gone to work, and so has Randy. Little Jordan is outnumbered by the women for a time. Although he has grown so much, he's not so little anymore.

Sitting on the back porch, I wait for Hannah to finish feeding him, and it gives me time to think and pray. I have been so stressed about this visit. I wanted it so badly, but I worried about Randy. He has been extremely quiet and moody. I wish he'd give Eric a call. There was one night when I almost voiced it to him, but I decided against it. It has to be his decision. I can't force it. That will never work. I wouldn't have wanted anyone to force these times with Trisha. But once I was ready for them, they have been a God-send.

Turning to 1 John, and reading through to chapter four about love, it's just what I need this morning. It's easy to love little Jordan. Such a precious child. There's still such innocence there. Why does this world beat us up so badly? I know, but I wish it wasn't so—I wish Adam and Eve had never eaten that fruit in the garden. I so wish they had left it alone. It affected their family right off the bat, Cain killing Abel. What sadness that brought to them! Talk about having regrets. Was the fruit worth it? I bet if they could have turned back time, they would have done it all so differently. This makes me think about my own life—my life with

Randy—would I have done it any differently? Oh, I guess there are things all of us would change. But we had some good years. We worked as a team earlier on. Randy was a good dad. He spent time with the kids. That's what's so surprising with how he's reacting to Jordan. He seems uninterested. I know Hannah felt it last night when he got home from work. She wanted her dad to take an interest in his grandson. Randy seemed cold. He wouldn't even touch him. He just looked at him from afar. I can only pray that it will be different tonight. Maybe he's just nervous with babies at this point, being that it's been so many years.

"Mom!"

"I'm out here, Hannah!"

"Is it okay if I bathe Jordan in the sink in the kitchen. I have a little thing to lay him in."

"Of course! Whatever you need to do. The house is yours! Do you need any help?"

"No. I'll get him all cleaned up and then bring him out to you so I can shower."

"That sounds wonderful! I'll be waiting," I reply with enthusiasm. I think part of me is trying to make up for Randy's lack.

Going back to reading in 1 John, *"…let us continue to love one another, for love comes from God. Anyone who loves is born of God and knows God. But anyone who does not love does not know God—for God is love."* That seems pretty clear. Father, please help Randy to know he is loved by You. Help him to know that his family loves him. Reading on, *"God showed how much he loved us by sending his only Son into the world so that we might have eternal life through him. This is real love. It is not that we loved God, but that he loved us and sent his Son as a sacrifice to take away our sins."* You sent Jesus, for us. You are offering us eternal life with You, Father. I'm so thankful for that. I am learning that to love Randy as You would have me do, I have to look past the darkness he wears on the outside and see who You made him to be on the inside. His exterior has grown very cold. Not like the man I married so many years ago. *"Dear friends, since God loves us that much, we surely ought to love each other."* I want to, Lord. I want to continue to love Randy. But when I leave here and move back in with Venyce, I know it's going to be so hard on my heart. Help me bear that. Help me continue to love Randy with Your love. I need…

"Hi! We're all done, Mom! I'll hand him over to you and then go get ready myself," Hannah says, giving me her tiny bundle of goodness.

"He's so sweet! Look at his little hair all combed over like a big boy! Did he like his bath?"

"Not really, but he put up with it. He likes to be wrapped up tight,"

Hannah says with a wave of her hand and disappearing back into the house with a smile.

"Okay. I'll keep an eye on him... Oh, you're so warm and fed and happy, Jordan. Now I get to snuggle with you little sweetie."

My heart is full as I sit and look into the face of my first grandchild. I feel God's love. I see God in Jordan...the amazing way God designs the eyes, nose, and mouth. I gaze at his hands, with such tiny fingernails...hands that will one day grow large and perhaps become calloused depending on the career he chooses. Wrapping his fingers around mine, I notice my hands have sure aged over the years. Jordan's skin is silky smooth and perfect. I will be the older lady he calls Grandma. He will never know the young me. I hope someday to know the older Jordan and see him graduate from high school and perhaps college, if I should live that long. It's hard to imagine that right now. We can barely see his personality at this age. What will he be like? Happy? Quiet? A talker? "Father, please watch over this child. Bless his life with good things. Give him a sound mind, and good health. Mostly, help him to know You at a very young age. Surround him with people and things that point him in Your direction. Help him to know early on that You are love, and that He is loved by You just as he is. Bring him into Your saving grace so we will one day live in Heaven together forevermore. Protect him from the ways of the enemy. Put a hedge of protection around his body, around his mind, around his spirit, and fill him early on with Your Holy Spirit sent from Heaven above. Thank You for giving Jordan to our family. We praise You, Lord Jesus. Amen."

After breakfast, Hannah and I spend the day running some errands, and then stopping at the grocery store for dinner supplies. I decide to make tacos. They usually make everyone happy. Maybe it will even put Randy in a good mood. We are busy cooking in the kitchen when Blake returns from work. He immediately picks up Jordan after giving Hannah a kiss hello. As I watch their family, they are doing well. They are good parents. I can see that they are doing the best they know how with Jordan. I try to stay out of the way even though I have so many words of "wisdom" on the tip of my tongue. I have to remember once being where they are, and not really wanting to be told what to do with my children. It's gone from a child being seen and not heard, to now me needing to be seen and not heard as the adult. The less I say the better.

"Dinner will be ready soon," I tell them, stirring the taco meat and preparing the lettuce and such. "I hope your dad will be here to eat. Sometimes he does work late."

"Mom, is Dad okay? I mean, he seems so quiet," Hannah asks with a tinge of sadness in her voice. "I know he couldn't come out when Jordan was born because of the flu he had. Is he okay health-wise?"

"Oh, yes, hon. He's fine. He just puts in lots of hours at the office. And I've been honest with you, we are struggling. It's nothing to do with you kids. It's just a time…well, your dad and I are trying to figure some things out in ourselves and our marriage. We got caught up in life, and our careers, and I think we forgot ourselves, and each other, along the way. I'm not sure…well, I don't know…maybe that's all I should say for now. I hope you understand."

Looking at me, I can see Hannah's eyes are glistening. She is trying to be grown up about this, but I know she doesn't want to see our marriage fail. She wants us to be the grandparents that Jordan will need. The two of us together, visiting them, and them visiting us. I hope for the same. I just can't promise her that right now.

Finishing up with the tacos, I tell the kids we might as well go ahead and eat. Randy can join us when he gets in. As we take our seats at the table, I hear his key in the front door. My heart jumps a beat—I don't know what will be walking through the door.

"We're in here, Randy! Just getting ready to eat," I call out, hoping he will come in and sit with us.

When Randy appears in the doorway, I can see on his face that he's already frustrated. He's used to going right to his room. He stands there, not really knowing what to do. When he moves toward his chair to sit down, I feel like I can breathe a bit. He is going to join us. I don't know how Hannah would have felt if he had walked away. But then, I do. She would have been so hurt!

Taking his seat, I offer to say a prayer before eating. It's not until about halfway through dinner that my heart begins to break completely. Jordan has started fussing and Hannah gets up to get him and bring him back to the table. She is in the middle of eating, and Randy is finished, so she asks her dad if he would like to hold Jordan until she's done. Randy looks at her, and then looks around the table. He seems to not know how to answer. His plate is the only empty one, and it appears to be the right thing to do in taking him from her. Randy looks at Jordan in Hannah's arm, and then hesitantly puts out his hands toward his grandson. Will he receive him into his arms for the very first time? He is visibly shaking. My heart goes out to him—to be so nervous about handling a baby after so many years. Hannah notices it, too, and she tries to reassure her dad that Jordan's easy to hold, telling him he doesn't move around much yet. Before she is even able to finish, Randy suddenly clenches his fists, withdrawing his hands. Hannah looks at him bewildered, with sadness written all over her face. I think I let out a small gasp, not knowing what to think. Hannah turns to look at me, then at Blake. Her face shows torment, and then she turns and looks at her dad again.

"Really, Dad. It's okay," she says to him in a soft and understanding way through her own despair. "He won't break."

Randy looks confused. With a furrowed brow, there almost seems to be a snarl on his face. He's really struggling more than should be necessary. I can see Hannah is perplexed, as am I, as Randy looks up at her, and then back at his hands that he's now holding under the table on his lap. A deep sigh escapes from Randy, followed by a difficult swallow—then a clearing of his throat a couple of times as if he's about to say something. But instead, he begins to lift his hands back up toward Hannah as his eyes follow them, almost in slow motion. We all watch as his clenched fists unfold into open palms outstretched toward his grandson. I see a tear escape Hannah's eye and run down her cheek. Randy's movements seem cautious and tender as Hannah lovingly places Jordan into his hands and steps back. Randy slowly pulls Jordan in close, cradling him, rocking him, staring at him. We are all quiet. It seems a powerful moment. But we don't realize how powerful until Randy starts to weep. The tension breaks into full blown emotions running through all of us as Randy's cries increase into actual sobbing. We don't know what is going on. Is he overjoyed at the thought of a grandchild?

"Randy, are you okay?" I try to gently ask. "Would you like me to take Jordan?" I want to help in some way, but I don't know what to do. It feels like he needs rescuing, but from what? I don't even know. Randy doesn't respond. He just sits there, tears falling from his eyes, looking into Jordan's face. "It's going to be okay, Randy," I offer as encouragement. But I don't even know what I'm saying. What's going to be okay?

"Dad. I can take him back," Hannah says. "I don't need to eat right now."

Randy finally looks up at Hannah. I know he can see her bottom lip quivering like when she was a little girl. He shakes his head to indicate no, and then nods to her in the direction of her chair. Hannah takes a seat, grabbing her napkin and blowing her nose. It seems like 15 minutes, but I'm sure it's more like two or three when Randy looks up again from Jordan's face toward all of us. He hasn't said a thing until now, and it seems we all know to remain quiet, too—there is something in this moment we can't yet grasp.

"I'm sorry…so very sorry. I don't know how to explain myself right now. But if you'll give me a few minutes to collect my thoughts, maybe I can."

Randy's tears are still falling, but he seems unashamed of them.

Hannah gently asks again, "Dad, do you want me to take Jordan?"

"No, Hannah. No. Please let me hold him. He's not the problem. In fact, I believe he's giving me the courage to say what I need to say."

"Okay. Sure. We love you, Dad." I can tell Hannah is wanting in the worst way to comfort her dad.

After some moments pass, Randy seems ready, as he looks at each one of us.

"How do I begin? My heart feels broken. But I say that, meaning it in a good way. I have been a recluse. I...well, as you could probably tell, I haven't been involved with Jordan...with any of you, really."

Randy looks at me. I try to give him a look that says I love you, but I know I shouldn't interrupt. He is processing things, and we need to just listen.

"Something was keeping me from Jordan, Hannah. I'm so sorry. It's actually more than just something...I could tell you I don't know what got into me. But I do. I haven't been the man I should be...the father I should be, the husband I should be. I've been living a lie."

Randy pauses there, and my mind wants to take off in a thousand different directions. Please don't leave me hanging here, Randy. Then I try to remember what I've been learning, *take every thought captive to Christ.* I know I need to stop my mind from being consumed with dark thoughts and just listen—not start making up terrible scenarios in my own head. I need to wait and see what he has to say.

"This isn't something I can totally go into right now. But I will in time," Randy says looking directly at me. Then he looks over at Hannah.

"I don't know how to explain this in a way that won't hurt you...but when you were getting ready to hand Jordan to me, I wanted to refuse him. I did refuse him. I'm so sorry. It's not Jordan. It's me. It's something I'm struggling with. But then when I forced myself to reach out for him—when I made the choice to take him from you anyway, even with the resistance I could feel inside, something started to break in me. I could feel it. It was so intense. It hurt, but in a good way—like it was needed. And I knew it. Holding Jordan close to me unleashed emotions that have been locked up for a very long time. I heard a voice inside that I've only heard once before. It said, 'I love you, as much as I love this child.' It was like an arrow piercing my heart in that moment. That's as best I can describe it. It felt as powerful as a lightning bolt, but gentle at the same time. It seemed like I could feel blood rushing out of that wound. I know that sounds strange. But there was a warmth that began surrounding my heart when I made the decision to receive your beautiful child in my arms. For the first time, when I opened up my hands to him, I saw Jordan as the precious gift from God that he is. It began to soften what had felt so cold and hard inside of me..."

"Wow, Dad," Hannah says very lovingly, with her face aglow.

"I know I'm not explaining myself well."

"Oh, no, no, Dad, you're doing fine," Hannah responds with earnest.

"You really are, Randy," I offer from the other end of the table, through my own tears. Randy is now looking at me with such sincerity.

"My heart has been closed to all of you, starting with you, Linda. I haven't been myself for a long time—but even worse recently. I've been making choices that pull me away from you, and I'm sorry. I've been living in a darkness that has been overtaking every part of my being. I hate admitting this to all of you, but there's something urging me to speak now when I would rather not."

"We're listening," I assure Randy. "Say whatever you need to."

"I couldn't hold Jordan, Hannah. Not because he had done anything wrong. But because I had—and have been. I've been making excuses and lying to myself. Deep inside I knew I was wrong, and I didn't want my dirty hands to invade the pureness of his new young soul. I think I felt like I would transfer my ugliness to him. Honestly, I didn't realize that until just now—until I broke through that barrier and chose to hold him. Sadly, I could ignore all this when you were so far away. I could even tell myself I wasn't interested in being a grandpa. That was a lie, too. I'm sorry. Your son *is* so very special. But I think he had to be near, right here, in my face, to soften my heart. This had to be done up close and personal. God must have known reaching out for Jordan would force me to look at my own sin, my own filth, in the light of his innocence. Maybe it was the only thing powerful enough to tear down the walls I was hiding behind and face the truth. I'm so sorry."

"Dad, we love you," Hannah says with such gentleness as she witnesses her dad's transparency. She turns now to look at me. Blake hasn't said a word. He's fighting his own emotions.

Randy continues, "I appreciate your love. I appreciate the gift of this grandchild you have blessed us with, Hannah, and you, too, Blake. God knows what we need, and even though I have been in full resistance mode in my relationship with God, He still pursued me. I know that now. I believe your visit here shows me that. God brought you here. He set me up. He probably even had me finish my dinner first so that I would be the only one available to hold Jordan. I needed to look straight into his face… at the purity of a child, to see my own depravity. There are things I need to do, to *change*, and repent of. I know that. And I can only hope that you will have patience with me now as I work through these things. I hope one day to be able to share with Jordan how he has impacted my life, saved my life, really. I know I have a long way to go, but I truly believe I have found the beginning of freedom through this precious child—your son, Blake and Hannah…our grandson, Linda. For now, I think I need to be alone for a bit. If you wouldn't mind taking Jordan, Hannah, I think I'll go to my room, but I'll be back later."

"Are you going to be okay, Randy?" I ask with great concern.

"Yeah, Dad, are you?" Hannah asks, too. I can tell she is touched, but nervous.

"Yes. I believe more than okay. Please don't worry about me. I just need to collect my thoughts, make a phone call, and shut some things off immediately. I'm going to be fine. Thank you."

Getting up, Hannah says, "Here, you can give him to me Dad. Go. Take your time. We will be right here if you should need us."

"Yes, we will, Randy," I add, amazed at all that just transpired. My heart is swelling with the love of God as Randy gets up from the table, gives me a kiss on the top of my head, and disappears down the hall in a whole new way.

48

RANDY AND LINDA

Shutting the door behind me, I know what I need to do. I feel overwhelmed with what just happened. It seemed to come up out of nowhere. But I'm thankful. I believe I'm ready now... Dialing Eric, I hear:

"Hello, you've reached Eric. I can't take your call right now, but please leave me a message. Beep."

"Umm, Eric. This is Randy. I need to talk with you. The sooner the better. I'm sorry about everything. Please call me when you can."

Finding Kimberly's number, I set it on block. I know once I send her this next message, it's not going to be good from her end. I never should have gotten this started. I knew, but I didn't really want to think about it. Now I have to. I've confessed before the family that I'm not right. I don't know how much I will tell them of my "escapades." I don't know how much I have to reveal to be clean of this. That's something I will need to talk with Eric about. Texting Kimberly, it's not hard to know what to say, it's just hard to say it:

"Kimberly, this will be my last text to you. I am blocking your number, so please don't even try to respond. I will be removing your number from my phone. I don't mean to hurt you. But what we're doing is hurting me and you, even if you can't understand it right now. I barely do. You will not be hearing from me again. Please don't try to reach me in any other way. I need to get my marriage back in order, and I will be telling my wife about what I have been doing. I hope you have a good life. Randy."

Breathing a sigh of relief, I push send. I can't say that it feels good— but then again, it does. I feel strong in this moment. I don't know how long that will last. I know the next thing I need to do before going back out to my family, and that's pray. I need to get myself right with God.

"God, here I am…a broken man. I'm sad…really sad. And as hard as this may be for me, I know what I need to do. I want to say I'm sorry for the things I have done. I know they are wrong, and I confess that I need Your forgiveness. Please forgive me. I want to move forward in a new way of life, especially in my relationships. I'm not good at this. I know that, too. You know that. But I'm hoping with Your help, with Eric's help, with the help of Linda, if she will still be with me once I confess to her what I have been doing, I can heal through this. I feel so bad. I've let what's important to me slip away, focusing on things that weren't good for me. I have to admit, they felt good for a while. Please forgive me for even saying that. I'm just trying to be honest with You here. I'm a little confused at the moment, and tense. I know when Kimberly gets that text, she is going to be so mad at me. Please give her some peace and healing, too. I would like to help her, but I'm not the person to do that. Bring her someone who can walk with her and help her find her way out of the darkness. That's what I want. I want out! I want to be free! I'm sorry to be wanting so much, but I can't live like this anymore. Jordan has opened my eyes. The love I feel for him, now, overwhelms me. I want to be the grandpa he needs. I want to be someone he can look up to and be proud of when I'm sitting at his football games, or chess matches. However you have designed him, I will love him. Thank You for bringing me to my knees before my whole life fell completely apart. I yield to You now, with all my heart, as much as I can. I know there's more, but this is what I have to give to You right now. Take me, all of me, and mold me into the man You desire me to be. I give You my pride, my selfishness, my harshness, and anything else in me that needs to go. The lust, the perversion, the unwillingness I've had for things being Your way. I need Your forgiveness, and I need to forgive. Eric has talked to me about that, but I need to ask him more about this. For now, I'm doing the best I can to get clean. I feel like an addict that needs to throw out all the drugs. I promise I will take those channels off my TV as best I can. I promise no more sexting, and no more texting to any woman, ever, in that way. Help me to love Linda with a pure love. Wash me clean, please, Lord. I feel so dirty. Eric said it's Your blood that cleanses us. I need a good scrubbing. I don't care if it hurts. I already hurt. I already ache. But I yearn for more in this life. I want to know You. Help me to follow You. Thank You, Jesus. Amen."

Lying on my bed, I stare at the ceiling. I never noticed how the light shines off the texture in that way before. I see places that look like valleys, and places that look like mountaintops. I've seen too many valleys, really willingly walked through them. I want to climb those mountains, now. I want to see what it looks like from up there. I remember some good years, but there have been far too many tough ones. I have made so many selfish choices. I can't even believe Linda is still here, fighting for our marriage like she has been. It has to be God in her. No woman alone could put up with me. I've been horrible...so uncaring. I need to see if she will come in here and talk with me. I need to get this done tonight. I wish it could wait until the kids are gone, but that won't work. If I don't get right to this, I may slip back. I don't want that. It will be good to have Jordan here for the week. He will be my reminder of purity. I will try to be as attentive to him as possible after work. I will hold him. "Oh, Lord, please make my hands clean again. Please don't let any of this wash off on Jordan. Keep him safe. Thank You, Jesus. Amen."

Texting Linda, I ask her to come in and see me. It's only but a few minutes and I hear her knock on the door.

"Please, come in," I say, surprised at my own politeness.

Opening the door, I see Randy sitting on the edge of his bed. "Hi. You wanted to see me?"

"Yes. Sorry I can't come out there yet. I need to talk to you. I need to be honest with you and see if you still even want to be here with me. If you want to take the kids over to Venyce's for the rest of their visit, I will understand."

"Oh, Randy. I don't see a need..."

"I think you better hear me out before you answer that," I say firmly but hoping she knows I only mean the best in my answer.

"Okay. I'm here to listen. Can I pray with you before you start?"

"Yes. Yes, please," I answer with gratitude. I know I'm going to need God's help to get through this, and so is Linda.

"Dear Father, thank You. Randy and I have some things to discuss. You have brought us to this time together. Help both of us be loving and strong through this. Help us to have forgiving hearts toward one another. You work all things together for good to those who love You. We will trust You in this, to work it for good. In Jesus' name we pray. Amen."

"Amen. Thank you. Please sit down there in my chair. I will sit here on the bed, so I can look right at you. This is going to be tough, but I know we can't move forward without this. My heart is beating out of my chest..."

"As is mine."

"Lord, help us. Linda. There are some things that I need to confess to you. First of all, I know I have been a bear to live with. I haven't wanted to try. I gave up. I started with Eric after my flu, and I thought I would be on my way to catching up with where you are with Trisha. It didn't happen. After a short bit, I backed off. Eric tried, but he never forced me. I stopped wanting to grow in all this. It seemed too hard. Honestly, I just wanted what I wanted. Eric told me from the beginning to ask myself, 'What Do I Want?' I don't think I was truthful with him, or myself, when I did that. I thought I was ready to be made new in Christ, as he calls it. But I probably knew I wasn't totally sold out to Jesus. I didn't see a need to be. I thought I could just be a fence sitter. I learned that's Satan's territory. I needed to pick a side, which I didn't do. I wanted to live partly in the world, and partly in what God wants. I quickly found out that just makes me susceptible to the enemy and his ways. And because of that, I'm really sorry to have to tell you this part…" I have to stop here. I know this is going to hurt Linda, and I just don't want to do it.

I can see that Randy is trying his best to be honest with me, but I have to admit to myself, I'm afraid of what he's going to tell me. Will I be able to forgive him? I'm asking myself this even before he says anything!

"Linda, I not only have gone back to the porn addiction that you found out about many years ago. And I'm sorry for that. But I connected with an old girlfriend and have been texting with her." I have to stop here again, although I know there's more I need to say. I have to gauge this and see how Linda is handling it. Her facial expression is slowly changing as it sinks in.

When Randy mentions the porn, I'm not so shocked. I figured it was something he would struggle with on and off through the years. It really doesn't bother me all that much. I guess it doesn't feel like cheating when it's just on TV. But when he tells me about the old girlfriend, I can feel my heart start to break. Who is she? Do I know her from school? Have they talked on the phone? Have they met up? Have they slept together? Where is this going?! I know I need to wait and listen. I keep my mouth shut, almost raising my hand to cover it as a help to not speak. Either that, or it's because of the shock that my body feels.

"Linda, I need to tell you the rest. I can see that you're taking this hard, and I'm sorry. But I have to get it out so you can know whether you still want to be with me anymore. I don't blame you if you want to leave. And I don't want you to feel responsible for me. I am going to make these changes in my life from this point on whether we're together or not. This is affecting everything, even my job, Linda. It's not going so well. I've been so distracted. The truth is, it's not just texting…"

Oh, no. Here it comes. They have been together. The tears are right close to the surface, I don't know if I can handle this.

"…today, there is something called sexting. Kimberly, that's her name, lives in another state. I have not met with her. I have not talked with her on the phone. I don't think you know her. I knew her a few years before I met you. What we have been doing is completely wrong. She is married also. It didn't start off like this. It seemed casual enough, but I have the feeling Kimberly has done this before. She is very good at it, very engaging. I'm sorry to have to say that. I got pulled in. And I'm not blaming her. I was the other half of it. But I seemed to have learned from a master. She has a way that's very seducing, and I didn't put up much of a fight, if any at all. Each new step she took, I willingly took one right behind her. She led me down a dark and dirty trail of deceit and perversion. Sadly, it included pictures from both sides. I'm deeply ashamed of that. Linda, I'm sorry."

The tears are many now, from my side, as Randy tells me all. I am relieved it was only through the phone, but that doesn't seem to make it any less hurtful. Sexting? I've heard of it, but I thought it was mainly younger people, unmarried people. How naive have I been? My husband? And pictures? Oh…this makes me sick to my stomach. Still, I need to listen. Through the tears, I will listen.

"Do you want me to continue?" I ask Linda, seeing that this has hurt her deeply.

"Yes. I do. I want to hear it all."

"This is why I haven't been talking with you, and why my work has been going downhill at the office. This started off only at night, a couple of hours. But then it progressed. I think Kimberly is able to sleep during the day. She works mostly from home. So, she would keep me up most of the night. I don't want to blame her. I could have said 'No', but I didn't. At work I was tired. But then it started there, too. By noon, we were back at it while I was at the office. It became so hard to look you in the eye. I couldn't meet with Eric anymore. Why should I? I wasn't being honest with him anyway. But I want you to know, starting this very night, I am finished. I have phoned Eric and left him a message. I will be meeting with him regularly from now on. I want to be set free from this. I have also texted Kimberly and told her there will be no more communication between us. I have blocked her number and asked her to never contact me again. If she does, I promise you, Linda, I will not respond, and I will be honest with you about any contact she tries to have with me. I plan on changing our TV programming, or whatever it takes, to keep those things out of my sight, and also off my computer. I will not hide in my room, so you don't have to wonder what I'm doing in here. I will be out in the open, physically, verbally, and as much as I can, emotionally. I want to share my life with you again. If you will have me. I am not asking you to decide right now. Take all the time you need."

Looking at Randy, I can see and hear that he means all that he is saying. It doesn't make it hurt any less, but the longer he talks, I believe him. I've known him long enough to know when he is trying to just get on my good side and when he means business. He is completely sincere about this.

Whether he is able to stick with it, only time will tell. I know it's best for me not to say too much to him right now. I want to encourage him, even through the pain it is causing me. Even if our marriage doesn't make it, I want him to make it. I want to make it. God wants us both to make it.

"Randy, you know this hurts bad! There's no getting around that. Whether it was on the phone, or in person, it was cheating. It is adultery in my book. But, thankfully, I start each day reading in God's Book. I have to believe He knew this was coming, because I was reading through 1 John this morning, all five chapters. It is so full of love, and also forgiveness. I know now He was preparing my heart for all that you're telling me. I…and this is just coming to me right now, I would suggest that even though you will be meeting with Eric, you and I need to read those chapters together. Soon. We need to focus on what God has to say, not what we have to say to one another right now. It is said that hurting people hurt people, and I don't want to hurt you."

"I don't want to hurt you anymore either, Linda."

"So, let's leave this where it is tonight. Come on out in a little while and see the kids. Let's let them know that we have talked, and we will be working on some things, even though we don't have all the answers yet. And then, starting very soon, let's read the Bible together. Starting with 1 John. Would you be willing to do that with me?"

"I will, Linda. I will. Thank you. If you will give me this chance, I will do my very best to hold true to everything I have said tonight. You can ask me anytime how I'm doing, and I will give you an honest answer. And like I said, if you would like to take some time and go to Venyce's, even, do that."

"I don't think that will be necessary. I think we can figure things out here, and then we will see."

"Okay. I'll be out in a few minutes, and we'll spend some time together as a family tonight. Thank you, Linda."

"Don't thank me, thank God. He is the One helping me to listen and to love right now. Without Him, I would be in my flesh and packing my bag. But I have learned a lot these last months about forgiveness, and I won't let the enemy destroy me with this. You have been honest with me tonight, and we will work on this and find a way through. See you in a bit."

"Okay."

Walking out of Randy's room, I don't know whether to feel relieved, betrayed, or somewhere in between. I decide to let it rest wherever it is, and cling to God in the midst of it all.

49

RANDY

Linda remained very patient with me for the rest of Hannah and Blake's visit. We spent the evenings together as a family, and slowly I grew comfortable in my times with Jordan. Purposefully, I would take his little hand in mine and feel the newness of life, not yet tarnished by this world. I could sometimes sense the eyes of Hannah or Linda on me, perhaps wondering how I was going to react. I was okay. What I needed to tell Linda had been taken care of. I felt relief in that, although I knew it wasn't over. I had work to do in getting the healing I needed. Hannah didn't know, and may not need to know, all that I was processing during and after that night at the dinner table. She was very sweet as the week progressed and also most willing to give me Jordan whenever I asked for him. Linda was doing her best to love me through the damage I caused, and even told me a few days later that she was able to forgive me. She said with the willingness she sees in me, she has great hopes for our marriage. I'm so relieved. Eric has returned from being out of town, and tonight is our first time together. I'm surprised he'll even meet with me again. I've been so wishy-washy about it all.

Answering the door, I am nervous. I know this could be intense, but I want to face it. No more fence sitting—it's all or nothing this time!

"Come on in, Eric." I say, half shaking his hand and giving him a hug. "Thanks for making time for me tonight."

"I'm glad you called. Sorry it's taken me this long to get with you," he responds warmly.

"You have nothing to be sorry about. I know it seems like I'm a flake, back and forth with you."

"I follow God through these things, and I've seen all different paths that people take toward healing. It can be a very scattered journey for some," Eric says with kindness in his voice.

"You're a patient man. I hope you had a good time in Yosemite. It's such a beautiful place."

"It is. We stayed at the lodge there. It's spectacular—the views out of the windows from the dining room are amazing."

"Yeah. I've walked through, but never stayed there. Can I get you something to drink, Eric?"

"Just some water, please. Is Linda home?"

"No, actually, she went to her sister's for the night so we would have privacy and wouldn't have to rush."

"Sounds good. And thanks for allowing Dennis to join us. He will be here in a few minutes."

"Oh, good," I reply.

"It's wise when we do an intense deliverance time to have two or more in support. Praying and taking note of what is happening. I don't want you to be nervous, although it's hard not to be, isn't it?" Eric asks, with a knowing look.

"Yes. Sort of hard. But I'm ready. It's time. I have been making needed changes in my life. Things I've talked with you about. You might wonder about my sincerity in this, since we've been here before. But please know I'm totally engaged this time. I'm not holding back. I have been honest with Linda, and I will be honest with you."

"You have been working through the repentance parts again, and forgiveness that I told you about, Randy?"

"Yes. A lot! Going over and over it...oh, there's Dennis. I'll get the door. Hey, Dennis. Good to see you. Come on in. I know I left you hanging last time, so thanks for coming."

"Good to see you, Randy. It's my pleasure. From what Eric has told me, you are at a place of really wanting some healing and being set free. I've been there, and I appreciated the guys who surrounded me during that time. It's only right to be here for you now. I get the not wanting to. I did the same for a long time. Avoidance. But that gets us nowhere. I've always admired your strength. It's good to see you using it now to choose Jesus and not the things of this world."

"Well, again, thanks. It's good to see you."

"Okay, guys, let's take a seat here at the table," Eric says leading us that way. "Randy, why don't you sit there on the end, and we'll sit on each side of the table. I'm going to do some praying, and then we'll pray some together, and see how the Holy Spirit will have us proceed from there. Some of this will be a repeat for you, but usually each time is tailored by the Holy Spirit for what is needed. This is not really a time of airing all the dirty laundry, although I thank you for what you've told me already—that gives me a good idea of what you're struggling with. While we are together tonight, God knows the direction we should go, and He will bring up just what is needed for healing. Again, this is a process, most times. We may see some complete healing and deliverance of pain and darkness that need to go, and we may need to follow-up several times working through other things. We take it all in God's timing and His way. He knows what you need, and when. Dennis will be supporting us in this, praying, right Dennis?"

"You got it!" Dennis replies with confidence.

"Take a deep breath, Randy, and relax. We are with you in this, and God's love and forgiveness covers it all when we come before His Throne in this way. If you don't mind, I'd like to anoint you with oil before we begin. This is an important part of this process, helping things to manifest."

"Sure, that's fine. Go ahead."

"Randy, I anoint you now in the name of the Father, the Son, and the Holy Spirit... Thank You, Lord Jesus. We seek Your healing here today. We seek Your guidance, Holy Spirit. Shine Your powerful Light into the darkness. Reveal what's been hidden in Randy's conscience mind, subconscious mind, and even unconscious mind. You know, Lord, when we don't. Surround us with Your holy angels of protection from the ways of the enemy. We plead Your blood, Lord Jesus, as the antidote for all that is against us in this world. There's power in Your blood like nothing else. There's power in Your name, Lord Jesus, like nothing else. Randy is desiring a lifestyle of obedience. He is choosing You. Isn't that right, Randy?"

"Yes. That's right. I want Jesus to rule my life," I say with as much confidence as I can.

"You have invited Jesus to be your Savior and Lord?"

"Yes. I have and do," I reply.

"You have asked and received His gift of eternal life, and forgiveness for all your sins, through the blood of Jesus?"

"Yes. Father, please forgive me. I want to do right by You," I respond.

"You have received His gift of grace, and invited the Holy Spirit to live in you?"

"Yes. I want the Holy Spirit to guide and govern my life all the rest of my days," I reply, feeling the tears coming to my eyes."

"Holy Spirit," Eric says, "Come and lead us through this time. Randy has repented of his many sins, he has sought Your forgiveness, and is willing to forgive those who have harmed him in any way. Is that right, Randy?"

"I need some help in this area, Eric. It's mainly with my brother, Bennet. I have such a hard time forgiving the man who killed him in that accident. I just can't seem to get past it."

"Good to know. Thank you for saying that. It is important that we forgive all, and some are harder than others. When you offer forgiveness to this man, God will take care of it. He will know your heart struggle, and He will bring you healing there by your willingness to give it to our Father in Heaven. Let me read this to you, 2 Corinthians 7:1 says, '...*let us cleanse ourselves from everything that can defile our body or spirit. And let us work toward complete purity because we fear God.*' Are you willing to let God deal with this man, while cleansing and healing your heart in this area? Are you willing to say out loud, I forgive."

"Yes. I'm going to say it, Eric, even though it's hard. Father, I forgive the man...the man who killed my brother. I don't like what happened, I'm so mad about it still. I miss him so much. But I want to be able to forgive and move on."

"Very good, Randy. Here in Colossians 2, verse...yes, verse 15 it says, *'In this way, God disarmed the evil rulers and authorities. He shamed them publicly by his victory over them on the cross of Christ.'* We're disarming the devil with your forgiveness. He has no power over you when you give this to God."

"That's good to know. I want to give it to Him. And I do."

"Okay, let's take some time right now, and deal with the anger that you have held onto for so long. Please look at me. I'm going to talk to the anger. Anger is a spirit that has gained a foothold in your life. By leaving it there, other things were invited in—things such as bitterness, hatred, and such. My sense is that there are very big strongholds involved also...lies you are believing. Are you willing to let them all go when we pray for them to be evicted from your soul?"

"I want to. I don't like being angry all the time. I think I take it out on other people."

"That is what can happen. Others get hurt because of the pain you feel. I'm going to look in your eyes now, and although it can be intense, it's nothing to fear. I *command* the Spirit of anger that is imbedded in you to GO NOW, in the mighty name of Jesus Christ. You have no right in Randy. Your assignment is finished. Anger, resentment, bitterness, and any other spirit that is attached to you, GO NOW in Jesus' powerful name. Go! Go! Go! Now! In the name of the Lord Jesus Christ! There it *goes*! Did you see it, Dennis?"

"I did, I saw Randy's shoulders go up, and then relax back down," Dennis replies.

"I felt something leave me. That was strange," I add, starting to cough some.

"Go ahead. Give some good hard coughs. That jerking, Dennis, that's more releasing. Do you feel it Randy?"

"I don't know. Something is happening."

Eric says strongly, "Get *out* spirit of anger! Spirit of hatred, GO! That's it! Let it go, all of it. That heavy exhaling shows more darkness leaving. That's good. Keep on… Dennis, this is like with you. The groaning."

"Yeah. I remember that. It felt so good afterwards. I remember also experiencing a bit of what's written about in Acts…speaking in tongues. That was something else. I'm still growing in that."

"Sometimes when deliverance is taking place, it frees us to speak in a new tongue. Not always, but it is one of the blessings that can follow," Eric explains.

"How are you doing now, Randy?" Dennis asks.

"Good. This is working up a sweat in me!"

"Take a moment, Randy," Eric says, "to inhale with some deep breaths. Fill those places now free of that darkness with the Holy Spirit. And then we'll move on."

"Wow, I feel relieved of something. Like it was buried in my chest and now it's gone. I can take a deeper breath."

"Great, Randy." Smiling, Eric continues, "I've heard it said we have to labor to enter into rest. What you feel now is the rest that God wants to give you. But you have to go after it. Sadly, too many don't know how to even labor *with* Jesus, so they labor *for* Him and are so exhausted. Jesus came to give us life, not to exhaust us. That is the work of the enemy. In Mark 16:17, it says, *'In my name you shall expel demons.'* Most of us just get used to living with them instead of getting rid of them. Joel 2:32 says, *'Whoever calls on the name of the Lord shall be saved.'* We think of that eternally, which is very true, but it's also calling on the name of the Lord right here, right now, to be set free. Jesus came to set the captives free. We are those captives until we come out of the darkness, which is the domain of the enemy, and walk into the light of Jesus."

"It makes sense, for the most part," I can say honestly this time.

"In Colossians 1:13, it says, *'For he has rescued us from the one who rules in the kingdom of darkness, and he has brought us into the Kingdom of his dear Son.'* Randy, let's do something here," Eric says. "Pray this with me, Lord Jesus, I confess all my sins, I'm sorry for them. I renounce everything that I've been involved in that is not of You. Forgive me. Cleanse me with Your blood. You are my Deliverer. Just as Your prayer says, deliver me from evil; I seek that today. Break every generational curse today. However far back they go. I want nothing to do with them. You know everything that is tormenting me. I renounce all the works of the devil. I'm giving myself totally to You today."

After repeating all that Eric prayed, one line at a time, I am starting to feel some hope in this. I have to ask Eric, "Do you really see good results from these times?"

"Well, Randy, you're looking at two people who have walked this journey ahead of you," he answers, pointing to himself and Dennis.

"I guess that's sort of a crazy question to ask, now that I think of it," I say laughing.

"It's important to have people who have gone ahead of you and are then willing to turn around and offer you a hand of help. That is what we are doing here today. Why don't we let you absorb what's happened so far and take a little break. I need to stretch for a bit, and then we'll come back, if that's okay?" Eric asks.

"Sure," I respond, actually happy to have a breather. I want to let things settle in a bit before we continue.

50

RANDY

Returning to the table, Dennis and Eric take their seats, and I sit at the end again. I feel sort of on display, but I'm starting to trust this process. These guys seem to really care about me. I don't know why they would, but they do.

"Okay. That break was good," Eric says. "We can begin again. I want to go into some other things right now. I know this is a lot for one day, but I think it's important we hit this hard. You have been making good choices—you have been honest with Linda and she's doing well with it, from what you have told us. We want to stay on that track—not giving the enemy any room to mess with what God is doing here. Randy, it's important after we finish here today that you are reading your Bible regularly. It is a great tool that you have access to every day. Satan needs to know that you are serious about this. Is he watching and waiting? Absolutely! But you have nothing to fear. God is so much greater than any power the enemy thinks he has. But we have to cooperate with the authority that we walk in. We have to use it as it's been prescribed by Jesus. Does that make sense?"

"Yes. It does. I do feel greater strength and a clearer mind when I have been reading. Linda and I have been reading through 1 John together. She has grown and healed so much through Trisha's help. I'm seeing that now. I'm so proud of her. I know that's one of the biggest reasons she is able to forgive me and continue to love me through my own struggles."

"Oh, 1 John is a powerful book," Dennis comments.

"Yes. Linda was reading it the day all this hit the fan, and she insisted that we read it together. I agreed to do that with her, and I'm glad. I think it really helped us get through that first very rough week, even while the kids were still here. It really talks about sin, in a very frank way, and the forgiveness that's available. And especially, God's love. I want that to soak in! Because most times, I don't think I really understand the love of God."

"It is hard to grasp how great it is, isn't it?" Eric asks, then suggests, "Let's turn there for a bit. Maybe the Holy Spirit is directing us there during this time. We always want to be listening to where HE will lead us next. Oh yes, here in 1 John 1:8, it really can hit us between the eyes, can't it? *'If we say we have no sin, we are only fooling ourselves and refusing to accept the truth. But if we confess our sins to him, he is faithful and just to forgive us and to cleanse us from every wrong.'* Oh, and this, *'If we claim we have not sinned, we are calling God a liar and showing that his word has no place in our hearts.'* Calling God a liar? Wow!"

"Yeah, that's what Linda and I continue to read together. We are camping there in 1 John until God has us move on to other things. It just keeps hitting us, or me I should say, right between the eyes. But I know it's what I need right now. I've been hiding in the dark for too long. If the Truth sets us free, and this surely seems like the Truth, then I'm going for it."

"Good," Eric says. "Very good."

"All this to say, it hasn't been easy, Eric. I do have to admit, I'm sometimes still feeling a pull back to my old ways of being. I know I told you on the phone about the experience I had with Jordan. It was really what got me to the heart of things, literally. Dennis, one day I will tell you the whole story, too. For today, I'll just say that what I was doing, really the harm it was causing, came to a head when my daughter was going to give me my grandson to hold. I didn't want to touch him. I felt so dirty. And yet I could see the hurt in my daughter's eyes when I wouldn't hold her son. I got caught between a rock and a hard place, and I had to make a choice. I truly believe God put me in that position to save me from myself—to make me face the reality that what I was doing was destroying my life and deeply affecting my family. Turn to the second chapter in 1 John, Eric. I don't remember the verse. Here, let me take a look at it...yeah, right here in verse 2:15, it says *'Stop loving this evil world and all that it offers you'*...and then it says down here in 16, *'For the world offers only lust for physical pleasure, the lust for everything we see, and pride in our possessions. These are not from the Father. They are from this evil world.'* God makes it so clear. He doesn't pull any punches."

"You are so right, Randy," Dennis agrees. "He knows us. We are not a shock to Him. And He wants to help us through and out of these things. He will, too, if we will bring them to Him, like you have been doing. I remember reading that part about, let me see the Bible…yes, here in 3:5, *'And you know that Jesus came to take away our sins, for there is no sin in him. So if we continue to live in him, we won't sin either. But those who keep on sinning have never known him or understood who he is.'* I had to get that into my thick skull. First that Jesus is willing to take the sin all away. And also, that if I do keep on sinning like I was, then I either don't really know Him, or I just don't understand who He is. I needed to get that figured out. And I did, and my life is really in a much healthier place. It truly has saved my own marriage. When we stop playing around in the dark with the devil, we can enjoy living in the light of Jesus and all He died to give us."

"I was involved with a woman over the phone, texting, Dennis. Honestly, it was sexting. I told Eric this already. And when Linda and I read together there, I think it's in two, yeah, right here in verse 26, *'I have written these things to you because you need to be aware of those who want to lead you astray.'* It hit me so hard. Now, don't get me wrong, I don't want to blame this woman. But she was a powerful force in leading me astray. She knew what she was doing. I was learning from her. It was so alluring."

"Randy, you bring up a very good point," Eric adds in. "I'm going to explain something to you, and right now it may be a bit more than you can grasp. But it's important for knowing what you're dealing with."

"Okay. Shoot," I say looking back at Eric, having no idea where we're going now.

"Let's start this way," Eric begins to explain. "Picture in your mind a beautiful woman. This is not to tempt you, but it is to show you something."

"Okay. Got it. I've pictured Linda."

"No," Eric says with a bit of amused laughter. "For this, picture a stranger."

"Oh. Okay. A stranger. A beautiful stranger. Got it."

"Now, to the right of her, picture a hideous, ugly, dark creature that would be shaped like a human and about the same size as the woman."

"WOW. A dark creature, like from the black lagoon?" I ask, really wondering now where this is going.

"Yeah. Only worse. Really horrific," Eric answers.

"Okay. I got it. Now what?" I ask.

"This is how the enemy works. He wants us attracted to the beauty we see with our eyes. What he doesn't want us to know is that within some people there are ugly, dark, and horrific spirits operating that are very harmful. We get attracted to the flesh we can see, and don't realize that there's a powerful force working in and through some people that can steal, kill, and destroy our lives."

"You mean like with the sexting? This woman was filled with that harmful darkness, and drawing me in?"

"Yes. And sadly, you probably have much of the same darkness in you. That's why you were drawn to her. Familiar spirits are attracted to each other. After healing and deliverance—dealing with the wounds and getting rid of what has been tormenting you and causing you to lust after the physical pleasures of this world, as talked about in that verse from 1 John—these temptations will lesson. Then as we read our Bibles, pray often, make good healthy choices, and surround ourselves with godly people, our mind will be renewed over time. There will come a day when we will wonder why we were even attracted to such sinful situations. Dennis can attest to that, too. Right, Dennis?"

"For sure. One day, Randy, we will sit down and I can tell you all that I've come out of. There was a lot of darkness operating in my life. And I'm sure you remember that you and I participated in some of it together in the past."

"Uh, yeah. Sure do," I say looking right at Dennis. Few words need to be spoken there.

Eric explains more, "This dark ugliness in the world, and the lust for its pleasures, is to be expected as we get nearer to the return of our Lord Jesus. Things are ramping up because there is a war going on between the spirit of Elijah, and the spirit of Jezebel."

"You've lost me there? What does that mean?" I ask.

"Let me put it simply," Eric says, taking a moment to think about it before continuing on. "Immorality is on the rise, and repentance is sorely needed. Jezebel was a wicked queen who had this hideous spirit operating in her. It is still operating in the world today, through men and women alike. It is not a feminine spirit. It is only called Jezebel because of this queen's terrible and evil reputation in the Old Testament. Now the spirit of Elijah is the same, only the exact opposite. Elijah was a great prophet, an obedient man of God. Very influential in the Bible. It is written about in the New Testament that John the Baptist even had the spirit of Elijah because he was a very obedient man of God, calling for repentance and preparing the people for the arrival of Jesus. John didn't have that ugly, hideous creature inside of him. This is not to say that he was completely without sin. Only Jesus was without sin. But John the Baptist was filled with the Holy Spirit, even before birth. The Holy Spirit fills us with the Fruit of love, joy, peace, patience, kindness, and such. When we come to a faith in Jesus, we are to be Spirit-filled people, preparing the way now for the return of Jesus. But the enemy is working extra hard to stop this movement among Christians. With your involvement with Kimberly, and other things, you have invited the spirit of Jezebel to enter your life. Jezebel, and other spirits that come along with it, are working on destroying your life. You can get counseling for many of these things, you can read your Bible and pray, you can attend church, and join a Bible study, which are all very good things. By the way, if you don't have a Bible study group, Dennis here has a great one going on."

Looking at Dennis, I give him a nod. "I'd like to hear more about that."

"I'll get you the information you need. It's a great group of guys. You will feel very comfortable with us," Dennis encourages.

"Great." Now turning back to Eric, I ask him, "Where do we go from here then? I've invited so much of this junk into my life that needs to be taken care of."

"We all have, Randy. But Jezebel is a big one, with many attachments. That's why even with all these other good things that can be done— crucifying our flesh in that way—many times deliverance is *still* needed. Spirits can't be crucified. Spirits don't die. They need to be *cast* out. A huge part of Jesus' ministry was casting out demons and healing the sick. He knew what was needed. When he came to the Temple that day and read the scroll as talked about in Luke 4:18, that was the Good News! Yes, He died for our sins and rose again, and is now seated with the Father in Heaven, preparing a place for us when we leave here. But what about what's happening while we're still here? He told us! He said He came to bring Good News to the poor. We are the poor—the poor in spirit, and we need the Holy Spirit filling us. Jesus said He was sent to heal the brokenhearted, and to proclaim freedom to the captives. We are the captives! We need that deliverance. He said the oppressed would be set free! Ever feel oppressed? I sure do! Jesus provided so much for us! All we need to do is walk in the authority that has been given back to us when Jesus took the keys from Satan and gave them to us again. What Adam and Eve gave away, is now ours again! Devil be gone, in Jesus' name!!"

"I like the sounds of that. It makes sense to me!" I chime in.

"Then I think it's important that we pray again, Randy, for your deliverance from the spirit of Jezebel, and all like spirits. Is that okay with you?" Eric asks boldly.

"Absolutely! For sure! I don't want anything to do with Jezebel or anything like it! If it looks that ugly on the inside of me, get it out!" I say with total agreement.

"It's always important to remember, Randy, you will only maintain this freedom by obedience and growth in your relationship with Jesus. This is not a fix all, go on your way, and never face temptation again. This is not a game. 1 John here in 3:7-8 says, *'Dear Children, don't let anyone deceive you about this: When people do what is right, it is because they are righteous, even as Christ is righteous. But when people keep on sinning, it shows they belong to the Devil, who has been sinning since the beginning. But the Son of God came to destroy these works of the Devil.'* The spirit of Jezebel means business. But so does the spirit of Elijah that was in John, calling people to repentance, preparing the way for the coming Savior. He baptized Jesus in the Jordan River."

"The Jordan? Are you kidding me? That's my grandson's name! How cool is that?! I wonder why Hannah and Blake chose that name? I think I can see God working in this even more by him having that name."

Eric just smiles, and then says, "God works in many ways to get our attention. Our Father wants us to know He is intimately involved in our lives. I believe we are all seeing that here. Are you ready to go through more prayers for deliverance now?"

"Yeah. Let's do this!"

"Look me in the eyes." Eric instructs again, and then asks, "Are you ready to be free of the demons that have been tormenting you?"

"Yes. I am."

"Randy, are you willing to humble yourself before God completely today?"

"Yes." I answer most assuredly, picturing that gross person that might still be hiding in certain places inside of me.

"Do you repent of all occult activity you have participated in?"

"You mean like maybe going to a fortune teller? I did that once when I was out of town on business."

"Yes. That's what I mean," Eric responds.

"Lord, forgive me for that. And if reading my horoscope every day is wrong, too. Lord, forgive me for that, and anything else I did that was not of You."

"Now, Randy, in the name of the Lord Jesus Christ, and walking in the authority He has given us, I command all evil spirits, including anything associated with the spirit of Jezebel to be bound together. What is bound on earth is bound in Heaven. I command the spirit of lust, immorality, perversion, witchcraft, adultery, masturbation, pornography, fantasy, exposure, unreality, pride, depression, insomnia, compromise, lying, and such to be bound together and totally evicted on this day. Spirits of grief, sorrow, heartbreak, crying, sadness, GO NOW, in Jesus' mighty name. Be loosed! Jezebel, you can no longer have hold of Randy's soul. Be gone now, never to return. We break any soul ties, any unhealthy connections that Randy has made with any individual either in person or through technology. All demonic activity must cease, and evil spirits must GO to the dry places talked about in the Word of God. In the power and mighty Name of the Lord Jesus Christ, you all must go NOW! You have no right to this child of God after his confession of sin and his coverage by the blood of the only Son of the Living God. He has been washed clean and made pure!"

As Eric is praying this, I can feel things rising up in me. I almost feel a bit of nausea, and I start to cough repeatedly. Then laughter comes, and Eric assures me there are many ways that evil spirits will manifest, show themselves, and leave, during this time. Eric keeps encouraging me, and I let these things go as he names them.

"These are your enemies, Randy, and after today, they will no longer be a part of your life. Be free, in the name of the Lord Jesus."

After a while, I start to calm, and then the tears come. I'm a bit ashamed of the sobbing, but Eric continues to tell me it's okay. This is all part of the healing process. He says that humility and peace are signs of Jezebel's spiritual destruction. From deep inside, there is another groan that rises up and continues for some time. It feels like I am being set free from things that are buried deep. Once that is done, I feel exhausted, but in a good way.

"Randy, relax, and breathe in now. I believe many things have been evicted today. Keep breathing in the Holy Spirit. We are about to finish here. This has been a productive time together. After today, it is very important that you don't give Satan any open doors. Your commitment to this is *very* important. Deliverance is a step in the right direction. It's up to you to keep walking in that direction. Even the spirit of pride is so destructive. It is the subtlest, but the one we fall into most often. Keep a humble mindset about all of this. There will be like a honeymoon period after this. But during this time, work together with Linda, support each other, build your spiritual muscles alongside each other, if you can. As this becomes a way of life for you, it will get easier. Keep on with forgiveness. I need to forgive practically every day. So, don't think it's strange when you have to keep getting rid of these things. Just identify what is going on, call it what it is, and tell it to GO in the name of Jesus Christ. You can take authority over all these things now that you know how it works. Are you okay with everything we've covered? I know it is a lot, but you can call me anytime."

"Can we practice what this will look like for me in my every day? Say I'm driving to work, and I'm frustrated with...well, the guy who spills coffee on me that morning. And then someone tries to cut me off in the parking lot. What would I do, exactly?"

"Good questions, Randy. Okay, identify how the spilled coffee made you feel," Eric responds.

"Well, I was mad. I was thinking he was super clumsy," I answer, remembering that day when it happened.

"Okay. And what about the person who cuts you off in the parking lot?"

Eric asks.

"Probably, more anger, and frustration at them being in my way."

"So, you have identified a spirit of anger, perhaps a critical spirit toward the clumsy guy? There was some judgment and frustration, right? See how we can break these episodes down and recognize how the enemy operates in our lives?" Eric asks.

"Yes."

"Okay, now that you stopped long enough to realize all that happened and what you are dealing with, you call them what they are. Doors got opened, and the thieves came in. We're going to kick them out, and shut the door behind them. I would say there is forgiveness needed, too."

"Oh, yeah. Probably so," I respond glumly.

"Start with the forgiveness. What would you think to say?"

"Maybe, Father, I forgive the guy who spilled coffee on me. I don't know what's going on in his life and I was mean to him. Please forgive me also, for my meanness toward him, and I forgive the driver in the parking lot."

"Good, Randy—giving and receiving forgiveness is key most times. I strongly believe it opens the exit door for the spirits to leave. Now what do you think you should do?" Eric asks.

"Deal with the things that came in?"

"Yes," Eric replies reassuringly.

"Okay, uh…spirit of anger, and frustration, get out of me NOW, in the name of the Lord Jesus! And any judgmental spirit, or critical spirit, you GO, too, in Jesus' mighty name. I am a child of God, you have no right to me. Get out, now!! Thank You, Lord Jesus. And now I breathe that stuff out, and breathe the Holy Spirit in?"

"Yes. Very good. And like we talked about before, sometimes it helps to picture them leaving. And if they don't feel completely gone, you can repeat this until they have. Some can be stubborn, especially if they have been there a while. Randy, this is something you can use in your everyday life. These things will always be happening. You now know the tools/weapons needed to fight this battle of invasion into your soul."

"Okay. That seems possible. Thanks, Eric."

"It's not hard, is it? And it's not scary. It is simple but very powerful. You may not even notice a big difference in the moment. But later you will see that it has not bothered you all day like the enemy meant for it to. This is spiritual warfare. When we learn how to do this with the smaller everyday stuff, we will be more prepared to handle the really big stuff when it comes along," Eric explains.

"I think I got it, and I will practice this. Eric, I would like to see you maybe once a week or so for a while, if that works for you, just to keep me on track." And looking at Dennis, I add, "I'd like to talk with you, too, about your group."

"You bet, buddy," Dennis replies.

"I was hoping you would suggest that, Randy," Eric adds. "This is all your call, and you're making good plans. After a while, you will be able to handle this on your own, with a once in a while check-up, so to speak. Let's finish with prayer today. Dennis, would you please do the honors?"

"I'd love to. And thanks again, Randy, for letting me be a part of this today... Father, You are all powerful. What we have witnessed here today is miraculous, as Randy is being set free from what the enemy has been trying to destroy him with. We give You all the praise and glory for Your healing powers, and for giving us the authority through Your Son, Jesus Christ, to evict the enemy anytime, and anywhere we see him working. He has no power over us! We desire to walk in Your power. Thank You for all You do for us. Put Your hedge of protection around us, and especially Randy and Linda as they work together on repairing their lives and their marriage. We have seen You do mighty things in our own lives, and we eagerly look forward to seeing the same things with the two of them. Holy Spirit, come! Fill us! Empower us to walk more closely with You each day. Pour Your blessings from Heaven onto Randy and Linda as You heal their hearts. In the name of the Lord Jesus Christ we pray. Amen."

After saying good-bye to Eric and Dennis, I take a seat in the living room. I am feeling so thankful. I know I have lots still to do, but I truly believe this time I'm ready, that this is what I really want. Jesus was baptized in the Jordan, and today I feel washed clean by the blood of Jesus, helped along by a little baby named Jordan—his innocence helped me know I was way off course and headed for total destruction. I want this renewal in my life. God, I want this change that You talked to me about in the shower—I believe now that *was* You. I want to be the grandpa that leaves a legacy of faith to Jordan and any other grandchildren that come along. It's because of Your Child born two thousand years ago that makes all this possible. My heart could not be more grateful. Thank You, Lord Jesus! From the bottom of my healing heart! Amen.

CONCLUSION

RANDY

Sitting on the plane, our flight is headed to Boston. I can't help but think back to the voice I heard in the shower saying, "Things are going to change." I've never forgotten those five words. As I glance over at Linda sitting here beside me, I know so much has changed. It could have only been God speaking to me that day. I certainly had no hope for change, although something deep inside of me cried out for it before I even knew I wanted it. God heard the cry of my heart. He answered me in ways I never could have imagined.

Jordan is having a little sister, and I am traveling with Linda to meet our new granddaughter. Two and a half years have made a huge difference in my life and in our marriage. As Linda continued on with Trisha, I spent many hours in prayer with Eric. He has been a godsend to me. I can't say that it was a piece of cake. I struggled along the way and had some hiccups. But I was able to correct my course and come back into the light when I did falter. Linda worked with me, as I remained honest and open with her in my struggles. I never did connect with Kimberly again, but the enemy sent other temptations my way. Eric let me know that the thoughts I was having weren't sin—it was in letting them take root or acting on them where the problems would begin. I knew if I kept things hidden and in the dark, they would grow like mushrooms. With Eric's encouragement, and Linda's love, I found out that God's forgiveness brings total freedom. I learned that the devil is out to cloud my thoughts. With inner healing and deliverance, the smoky haze is removed, and I can see clearly—it felt like a spiritual detox. I have a peace and contentment in my life now that I never thought was possible.

Linda and I read through 1 John together for a long time. It seemed that God had us there until we understood how great our sin is and how great His love is for us. The Bible tells it like it is, and I learned to accept it and agree with it more and more. I continue doing so to this day. God isn't just pointing out our faults, He is leading us to restoration. Whenever I yield to Jesus, His victory is mine!

The spirit of Jezebel is obvious to me now when I come across it. I see it on TV, in the theaters, and really everywhere. Darkness is on the rise, but along with other true believers in Jesus Christ, those filled with the Holy Spirit, we have a much greater Spirit living in us than the one living in the world. To think that it was the spirit of Jezebel that asked for John's head on a platter! What a vicious spirit it is! I'm thankful I was shown compassion by Eric, and by Linda, when this darkness was directing my life. But they were also strong enough in their faith to show it no mercy. Eric knew I needed to be set free, and he helped me find that freedom in Jesus.

Everything I have learned is spilling over into all the other areas of my life. The Fruit of the Spirit becomes more obvious now. It seems the more I learn to walk in the Light, the more I can love others around me, including my neighbors. It's not just Linda who says "Hi" with a smile when we see them out front. We have actually joined Mike and his family for BBQ's more than once. Dennis and I are hanging out again, too—in Bible study and other times. I asked him what Eric meant when he told me Dennis said he'd been helped by me? Dennis revealed it was the strength he saw in me. He watched me go through the death of my brother. His own brother died when they were kids and it helped him to not feel so alone in that. Knowing we had that common bond strengthened him. Our friendship has really changed from one of complaining and lamenting together, to one of talking about important things like that, and encouraging each other as good buddies should do. We both learned that if we keep a right attitude toward sin, we can keep the demons at bay. Even Emily, at work, noticed a change in me. I stop at her desk on the way in now, and ask her how she is doing? I've learned that she has her own problems in life, and I try to listen and even pray for her about those things. When I was in my own world and miserable, I thought I was the only one struggling. Now that I've stopped being so focused on myself, I know that this is a hurting world, and people need God's love, as did I. The meaner I was, the meaner I got. It was a vicious circle—probably because I was so guilt ridden over it all. But Eric clearly explained that Jesus not only makes us nicer through the power of the Holy Spirit, he takes that guilt away through Jesus' death on the Cross. Satan has been shackled, not us. Satan's weapon of guilt has been turned around by the Truth of Romans

8:1, *"...there is no condemnation for those who belong to Christ Jesus."*

Rob will be joining us in a few days in Boston with his new wife, Jane. They met at work, but Rob wasn't sure he wanted to get into a serious relationship in the beginning. They were married three months ago, and I was so privileged to be asked to be his best man. We have grown close, and he took me off to the side at the reception to tell me that his faith in marriage grew watching his mom and I repair our relationship. He said he can see that we truly enjoy each other now; something he never saw while growing up. I told him it was only the love of Jesus that could repair what was once so broken between us. I had shared with him my struggles after a few months of meeting with Eric. It seemed only right. Maybe I had passed some of those things onto him, and I wanted him to know if I had, there was a way to be healed. I didn't want him accepting any of my old practices. He thanked me for my honesty.

Venyce has remarried. Who would have ever thought that Pastor Everett would be my new brother-in-law? His wife had been gone about a year and a half when he moved here from Southern California to be closer to his children. God has healed Venyce through her grief, and Linda is so excited to see her sister in love again. Venyce never criticized me, and always supported Linda when she needed it. She displayed what a true Christian looks like. Venyce told me that evil is not *imagined*, it is very *real*, and it wasn't me. I realized she understood about that ugly being inside of me that Eric taught me about. She knew it wasn't a battle against flesh and blood, but against evil rulers talked about in Ephesians 6. She is such a wise woman.

As I sit here, looking out the window and thinking back on these past two and a half years, I have such gratitude in my heart. Linda could have given up on me. I believe she definitely had her moments, but God helped her to forgive me and love me when I least deserved it. Isn't that what Jesus did, and does? To be set free, we need the blood of Jesus. And to stay close to Him, we have to be reading the Word and following His path.

As for the man who killed my brother. I no longer feel the same anger toward him. I miss my brother every day. But I know now that the enemy wanted to not only kill my brother, he wanted to destroy me in that process. I won't give the devil that satisfaction. I will see my brother again one day on the streets of gold. We will laugh and enjoy eternity together. I don't know if the man who sits in prison knows Jesus, but I pray for him, that he does. He needs God's love and forgiveness, just as I did, and do. If I harbor a grudge about this, I will be stuck in my old self. Eric has shown me there is a better way to live by allowing healing through time and prayer.

Linda and I will be traveling to Israel next year with our church. While there, I want to be baptized in the Jordan River, just like Jesus was. To go back to where all this started with Jesus and remember how our little Jordan impacted my life, seems so right. When Jordan calls me Grandpa now, I can fully accept that role. He will know of my faults. I will share those with him one day when he is older. But I will also share with him how Jesus makes us new again. Maybe I will tell him the Word of God should be taken as regularly as you take your vitamins little guy. It will keep you well!

I particularly love the verse in 1 John 5:21 where it says, *"Dear children, keep away from anything that might take God's place in your hearts."* I know why now. Any part of my heart that is not given over freely to my Lord and Savior becomes a place for the enemy to steal, kill, and destroy me. Things can quickly become an idol in our life. When Eric first encouraged me to ask myself, "What Do I Want?" I didn't have the right answer. I do now. I want all that Jesus died to give me. I want to honor His death and resurrection every day of my life through obedience to His commandments until I meet Him face to face. I want to give Jesus my whole heart with nothing held back, being fully filled with the Holy Spirit. In return, my Father in Heaven blesses me so much more! I want to, now, give Him all the praise, and honor, and glory forevermore! I once was blind, but now I see!

LINDA

Having Randy sitting here with me on the flight to Boston to see our new granddaughter fills my heart with so much joy! I can scarcely believe we've come this far after all seemed lost in our marriage just a couple short years ago. All the prayers that were prayed are being answered, slowly but surely. I wanted to rush it. I wanted it to be how I would plan it. But God has a better plan all along. The verse in Psalm 55:22, *"Cast your burden upon the Lord and He will sustain you…"* means so much more to me now. Jesus cast out so many demons, and I see Him still working in the world here today. He has been working in my heart, and in Randy's, cleaning out our Temple and making us more like Him. We didn't know the bondage we were in, until we started to experience the freedom that Jesus died to give us.

Randy told me he had to face what was happening when Hannah wanted to hand Jordan to him that night at dinner. He came to a fork in the road. I'm so very thankful for the choices he has been making since then. Not that we haven't had our fair share of trying times. Randy had some difficulties along the way, and I've had my own struggles. But as far as I know, he has been honest with me each time. And Eric has been such a huge help to him, as Trisha has to me.

I am so happy that Rob will be joining us in a few days with Jane. He moved slowly in their relationship. I remember when he first told me about Jane, and I was afraid that our marital problems were a discouragement to him in making a commitment to her early on. When Rob asked Randy to be his best man, I knew so much had been made new in all our relationships.

I don't meet with Trisha now, like I used to. In fact, Venyce and I have started helping others be set free by praying for them when God gives us the opportunities to do so. Her new husband, Pastor Everett, works closely with Venyce, too, in this ministry. He is such a godsend in her life, and I believe she is in his, too. They both had good marriages and are now enjoying a new life with one another. Her smiles come easily now, and it so wonderful to see God bring her through her grief.

I have been able to share my testimony with women at church who are in very troubled marriages, and some have gained great hope in what God can do in their own lives. I let them know to keep praying and to wait on God. His timing is always different than ours. It's been amazing watching God work the good out of the bad, just as His Word says He will. Philippians 3:13 about *"...forgetting the past and looking forward to what lies ahead,"* is so important as God repairs relationships—we can't cling to the old and find the new.

Randy and I are going to make a trip to Israel, to walk where Jesus walked. We are both in separate Bible studies, and then do a twice a month couples' Bible study together. We are looking forward to seeing Scripture come to life in Israel, up close and personal.

I never tell anyone our lives are perfect, our marriage is perfect, or our family is perfect. Jesus was the only perfect One to ever walk on this earth. But I do tell people that with a perfect Jesus as your Savior, you can see miracles happen in your life, in your marriage, and in your family. Years ago, I knew what I wanted for my marriage and my family, I just didn't know how to get there. God's Word says that people perish for lack of knowledge. My life was perishing, in so many ways. Oh, I would have gone on. I would have clung to Jesus with everything I had, and made it to the end alone, if need be. But how much better is this? So much! Jesus came to set the captives free, not merely to just hold on for dear life until He returns for us. I realized along the way that I needed to give Jesus my all, or nothing was all I would get. And now look, I am flying to see a new grandchild with the man I chose to spend my life with, and we are...spending the rest of our lives together.

I know not every story will turn out with a happily ever after ending.

But why not give Jesus a chance and see what He will do? Trisha said many people will not be set free because they refuse to recognize the bondage they are in. I guess when your marriage blows up in your face, it starts to become pretty clear that changes are needed. Deliverance has now become a lifestyle for Randy and me. We hold each other accountable to what is bugging us, calling it what it is as quickly as possible. If we don't think about what we're thinking about, it can just get stronger and cause deeper wounding. But if we recognize our thoughts for what they are, confess any sin associated with them, and cast out anything that needs to go, including unforgiveness, we can walk in freedom daily. I realize, now, how important it is to take every thought captive to Christ, and then follow the advice given in Philippians 4:8... *"think about things that are excellent and worthy of praise."* It puts the enemy in his place and gives him no control in our lives.

Reaching over to take Randy's hand, he turns and looks at me from his window seat.

"How're you doing, Randy?"

"Very well. I'm so thankful to be making this trip with you. I know you and Venyce had a wonderful time together last time you flew out to see Jordan born. But knowing that Venyce is happy in her new marriage, and we are happy in ours, is such a blessing. How are you feeling about it all?"

"Amazing. This trip will give me even more fodder for encouraging others in their marriages, and in their relationship with Jesus. I read that peace overwhelms Satan. I hope he is totally and absolutely overwhelmed with us right now."

"Me, too, Linda. Me, too!"

ANSWERS TO QUESTIONS
ABOUT OUR BIBLICAL HOPE

Most of us understand that our enemy, Satan, is out to steal, kill and destroy our lives. How, where, and when he does that can be strongly debated. It is one of those things where we may not know the "bottom line" until we see Jesus face to face. Until then, what do we do about it? We know that demonic power is not comparable to the power and might of our Lord Jesus Christ. But even so, as Christians, filled with the Holy Spirit, our lives can still be hindered along the way.

Satan cannot separate us from the love of God, but he can wreak havoc with our freedom. How do we live the full, abundant, and healed life with the enemy in our midst? To not be devoured by our adversary, we need to use every weapon made available to us as described in the Bible. Satan is a clever one, but Jesus is so much Greater!

One question we may ask concerning this: Can our enemy be where the Holy Spirit is? Since the Holy Spirit is everywhere, it seems so. Satan had access to the presence of God as we read about in Job—being in the same space is different than a personal relationship. Another good thought is about demonic possession…some believe once we are filled with the Holy Spirit, demonic possession is not possible. That is true. We need to understand that the word "Daimonizomai" used in the Bible when translated correctly is not "possession," but instead "demonization." Two very different things. Demonization involves someone being under the influence or control of an indwelling spirit. Jesus taught the disciples to pray in Matthew 6:13, *"Deliver us from evil."* No believer can be owned by Satan. We belong to our Father in Heaven. But no text rules out the possibility of demonization. Jesus casts out demons, as do the disciples. When we are tempted, harassed, or oppressed it's not necessarily demonization. The Holy Spirit will help to reveal what is happening, and what prayers are needed for healing and freedom to be found. Demons are known to enslave, defile, deceive, compel, and even make people weak, sick, and tired.

Are we sealed with the Holy Spirit when we become a true believer in the Lord Jesus Christ? Yes. Are we immediately freed of everything we have ever struggled with up to that point? No. The Bible tells us to continue *"to work out your salvation with fear and trembling,"* as stated in Philippians 2:12. This includes crucifying the flesh, tearing down strongholds (lies), casting out demons, and giving no foothold to the devil in the future. No, we cannot *"drink the cup of the Lord and of demons,"* as is written in 1 Corinthians 10:21. But this verse is about moral things, not physical ones—things that don't go along with being a Christian.

Are demons *only* cast out of unbelievers? To cast a demon out of an unbeliever would leave the house "empty"—with no Holy Spirit filling. They could end up worse off than before as stated in Matthew 12:45. Inner healing and deliverance is needed in a *believer's* life. Salvation is what is most needed in the life of an *unbeliever.* With a heart then submitted to God, they will begin to *want* what Jesus is offering concerning the other aspects written about in the Bible—finding inner healing in the process. When Philip was in Samaria in Acts 8, preaching the Good News, the crowds listened intently to him. Impure spirits came out of many, and the sick were healed. We don't know if this was happening before or after conversion, with believers or unbelievers…but it was all working together to heal and set people free as they gave their heart to Jesus. Faith in Jesus' life, death, and resurrection is what sets people free.

There isn't a lot in the Epistles, after the filling of the Holy Spirit, that talks about all that Jesus did in healing, casting out demons, and raising the dead. But there is also no use of the word "mathetes" which means "disciple" in the Epistles either—we don't conclude from this that making disciples died out. Is the concept still there in the New Testament? Absolutely, like with Philip. Right after the filling of the Holy Spirit in Acts 3, we can read how Peter and John gave the lame man what they had…not money, but healing him by saying, *"In the name of Jesus Christ of Nazareth, get up and walk!"* This man was leaping and praising God after this, and went into the Temple with them. Peter used this opportunity to share the Gospel with all those there that day. He said, *"Faith in Jesus' name has caused this healing…"*

Let's take a look a little further on in Acts 5:12-16. The apostles were performing many miracles among the people, and *believers* were meeting regularly at the Temple—believers now filled with the Holy Spirit. *"More and more people were brought to the Lord."* (Make Disciples) *"Crowds came in from the villages around Jerusalem, bringing their sick and those possessed by evil spirits, and they were all healed."* (Heal and Cast out demons.) Notice it does say "all". Again, perhaps there are times we should pray in this way for unbelievers, too? Maybe it will prepare their heart to receive Jesus. We should always be prayerful and follow the guidance of the Holy Spirit. And in Acts 20, there was a young man who fell out of a window and died. Paul said, *"Don't worry, he's alive!"* (Raise the dead)

The Great Commission was given to us by Jesus, *"All authority in heaven and on earth has been given to me. Therefore go and make disciples of all nations, baptizing them in the name of the Father and the Son and of the Holy Spirit, and teaching them to obey everything I have commanded you. And surely I am with you always, to the very end of the age."* What are some of those things we are to obey? Jesus told His disciples in Matthew 10:7-8, *"Go announce to them that the Kingdom of Heaven is near. Heal the sick, raise the dead, cure those with leprosy, and cast out demons. Give as freely as you have received!"* Who? Us? Yes! Jesus said, *"I tell you the truth, anyone who believes in me will do the same works I have done, and even greater works, because I am going to be with the Father."* The apostles, Peter, John, Paul, and Philip, were doing these very things Jesus told them to do.

Satan was cast out of Heaven (Revelation 12:9). Adam and Eve were driven out of the Garden (Genesis 3:23-24). And our sins are removed from us as far as the east is from the west (Psalm 103:12). Hallelujah! It's the devil's turn to be cast out of us and away from us since Jesus took the power out of the enemy's hands and gave it back to us.

So what are we to do with all of this? As one person recently said, "Let's WAKE UP!" Let's give inner healing and being set free a try and see what happens! *"For he has rescued us from the one who rules in the kingdom of darkness, and he has brought us into the Kingdom of his dear Son. God has purchased our freedom with his blood and has forgiven all our sins."* (Colossians 1:13-14) Why do we fear what Jesus demonstrated for us in the Gospels? Does Satan have us duped and living in a smoky haze when amazing freedom and clear skies are waiting for us? *"For what will it profit a man if he gains the whole world and forfeits his soul?"* (Matthew 16:26) This is a bit out of context, but I'm using it as an example of how we can miss out when resisting what God wants to freely give to us through His Son, Jesus Christ. We have two promises: Our salvation in Jesus Christ for all of eternity, and many *resources* supplied by the Holy Spirit we can utilize right now.

In 1 Corinthians 1:14-22 Paul talks about not participating with demons. He used the word "Koinonia," meaning fellowship...opening up to the influence of the demonic. In Ephesians 4:26-27, we are told not to give a "foothold" (Opportunity) to the devil. The term used here is "topos," which when used in Luke 11:24, it is an inhabitable space. The Bible clearly warns us of these things. Demonization can bring disastrous results! It is written of Ananias and Sapphira in Acts 5 that Satan filled their hearts. It is the same term used in Ephesians 5:18 for being "filled." Were they demonized or oppressed? Either way, it was not good!

To be *in* Christ is about eternal salvation and belonging to the family of God. When dealing with demons, it is about influence and persuasion, not ownership—two different things. In whatever way we are attacked, through oppression or through demonization, the result is the same—we are being tormented by demons one way or another. We all deal with different types of wounds and bondages in this fallen world. But there is so much power in the Good News of Jesus Christ!

Let's clear away the toxic haze so many are living in, prayerfully, biblically, and powerfully, through the mighty name of Jesus Christ our Lord! Whether it's located *in* a believer or *outside* of a believer, we can all agree we want it **OUT** of our lives! We can employ powerful, intentional prayers that will set us free and give us a fresh new perspective on life!

"You will know the truth, and the truth will set you free."
John 8:32

ACKNOWLEDGMENTS
GIVING THANKS

Lord, You have taken me on quite the journey of writing these last two years—from not even being interested in reading fiction, to writing five novels, leaves me shaking my head. I don't know exactly what You are doing, but I'm enjoying the "ride". Thank You for giving me the thrill of writing, for taking me to locations that have added to these stories, for teaching me things I never realized were important, for helping me dive headfirst into research, and for continuing to stretch and grow me. I look forward to all that You have planned for the future. Life has been very challenging, and extremely rewarding. You are a great and awesome God! I thank You and Praise You, always!!

Jim, after more than 45 years together, there has been a lot accomplished. Three children, six grandchildren, and now birthing books together. This would not be happening so quickly without your computer expertise and amazing patience with me along the way. You are so quick to help me when my technical skills are severely lacking. All the ways that you have been gifted, I have not. That is why God said when we were sixteen years old, this will be a good match. Very good. He wanted the two of us together to accomplish all that He had planned. I know we will keep on until Jesus returns to take us Home! Thank you! I love you!

Son, Jimm, this book was finished in your office, the day you noticed there might be a bit too much commotion in the house for me to concentrate. It was God's perfect timing to complete what I didn't know would be the last chapters…but God surely did. Thank you!

Sons, Jimm and Chris, and daughter-in-law, Holly, we are so proud of the people you are and the parents you have become. We know it's not easy in today's world to raise confident, healthy children. But you are all doing an amazing job. I pray what is written in this book will bring freedom, not only to our family, but will radiate to all those we know and love…and beyond.

Denell, Jackson, Laila, Kylie, Maren, and Cooper…the six of you bring such joy to our lives! As I write about little Jordan in this book, I find inspiration from the love I feel in my heart for each one of you. I pray that the legacy I will leave to you as your Oma is one of faith and hope in our Lord Jesus.

Thank you, Wilma V. Shore, my wonderful mother-in-law, for allowing me to use your middle name. You faithfully read my books, and I appreciate it! I know it's hard when some characters die, unexpectedly—but it is fiction, after all. Don't worry, I'm pretty sure Venyce makes it to the last page!

Connie Fulmer Dixon, you patiently waited for this book to be completed—and then you welcomed it with open arms, making the edits needed. It's such a joy to know your heart is willing, even with all that you have going on in your own life. You touch many lives there in Ohio, and even though we don't see each other face to face, you touch mine here in California. We have surely gotten to know one another across the miles. Technology is a wonder! Thank you so very much! I pray God's very best for you and your family.

To my Beta readers, Lynn Tredway, Denise Croghan, Susan Silva, and my hubby, of course, I appreciate you all so much. I love to see your comments, corrections, and suggestions. It is good to have many eyes on so many words. This book is over 111,000 words. That's a lot of letters. Your excitement for what God gives me to write keeps me inspired. Susan, you said this book is, "A combination of true fiction and real life." You are so right—where does one stop and the other begin? God keeps it interesting. It's not always easy to experience what I must, to be able to write what I do. Yes, names are changed, places are changed, situations are changed, but many of the things I write have actually happened in one form or another. God makes it real for me, so that it can be "True Fiction" for all those who will read my books.

Rick Beyer, Micah Beyer, Lynn Tredway, Drue Little, Maria Franz, Katja Heinsch, Denise Croghan, René Biel, Jennifer Hatton, Lilia Knight, Karen Platt, Mercy Fancher, and so many others: When I spend time with you, read your comments, talk to you on the phone...I hear words of wisdom that I can't help but use in my writing. I usually give you a heads-up as I make note of what it is you have just said that needs to be recorded for others to read. I hope you will enjoy seeing some of our true conversations in the lives of these fictional characters. Thank you for being in my life!

Debbie LeBlanc, my BFF. I was just thinking this morning, we met in a bowling alley in Germany—and I don't even like bowling all that much! But God knew I needed to be there to meet you, and spend these last 25-plus years growing and learning together with you. When I share what it is God is teaching me and taking me through, you listen and encourage me, always. I love you, and appreciate your friendship every day.

Annet Hammond, your phone photos were just what was needed to complete the cover of this book. Thank you VERY MUCH for allowing me to use them! When I first saw them posted, I knew it was a great visual to show what God does through healing and deliverance. As you stated, those pictures were taken "only four days" apart. One shows the beauty that can be seen when the air is clear, so to speak. The other shows how dark and dense things can become when smoke fills the air. What a tragedy the Paradise Fire was for so many. I pray God uses what was bad for good, showing many that with His healing power, the blind can see!

Allie Bowman, we walked the Freedom Trail together. We ate cannoli together. We climbed Bunker Hill Monument together…and I held onto your arm until my shaky legs were stable once again. (More "True Fiction") Thank you for adding to my books. We make good travel buddies!

Richard, Maureen, and Kathy, thank you for your hospitality in Sharon— the wonderful conversations, and transportation to the train station. I didn't know what book the trip to Massachusetts would end up in. Here it is! It was a pleasure meeting all of you! (And your son!)

Thank you to those who have helped me on this journey into the deliverance and inner healing ministry. Your trust in Jesus, and the freedom He is offering, has been essential in this learning and growing process. Thank You, Holy Spirit, for clearing away the smoke in these precious lives. I have been encouraged by their testimonies!

To my Wednesday morning Bible study group, you gals are amazing!! Your morning smiles, your hugs, your prayers, and your encouragement inspire me! Thank you, one and all!

To my writers group, WOW! We are a conglomeration of different ages and styles of writing—but we share a common love for Jesus, and desire to follow Him in whatever way He would have us go with the gift of writing. It is a joy to meet with you and talk writing! Thank you for a place where we can be vulnerable, and accepted.

Pastor Rick Fry, thank you for following Jesus! You lead our church on that narrow path toward the gates of Heaven! I know you will see parts of your sermons in my writings. As I sit and listen to you, your words sink deep into my soul. When you mentioned Smith Wigglesworth some five years ago, I had never heard of him. I went home, found his book, and read it in two days. My life hasn't been the same since.

Pastor Cindy Fry, thank you for the opportunity to share with those at the Rock Church. When we met for lunch, I left excited, knowing that God was opening a door for even more people to find healing and freedom through all that Jesus died and rose again to give us! The keys to the Kingdom have been placed back in our hands. And your faithfulness and support in this helps to let so many know this is true!

To all the authors, pastors, speakers, teachers, You-Tubers, etc....who contributed to this learning process, thank you. I don't mean to plagiarize anyone, but you have spoken volumes into my life. I pray it will all be used for God's glory! They say nothing is new under the sun. I know all of you learned from those who went before you, and I have now learned from you. I pray these pages will be used to help even more people find how healing and freedom is not only possible, it is a God-given right to those who trust in Jesus! We are all one body, united in one purpose, here to serve
Jesus Christ our Lord!
Amen

ABOUT THE AUTHOR
dianecshore.com

Diane C. Shore lives in San Ramon, CA with her husband Jim of more than 40 years. They are enjoying these years together after raising three sons, and now being the grandparents of six. Writing and sharing stories about God is Diane's passion. God continues to lead her and show her new ways of how He expresses His love toward us each day. Whether it is sitting one-on-one with someone, or speaking to a group, Diane is excited to boldly proclaim the Good News of Jesus Christ and how He works in our daily lives.

FICTION BOOKS BY DIANE C. SHORE

When YOU Do
ISBN: 978-0-123456789

ROSIE I
ISBN: 978-0990523192

ROSIE II
ISBN: 978-0-990523185

ROSIE III
ISBN: 978-1732678507

NON-FICTION BOOKS BY DIANE C. SHORE

ISBN: 978-0990523161

ISBN: 978-0990523130

ISBN: 978-0990523109

ISBN: 978-0990523147

dianecshore.com

296

www.ingramcontent.com/pod-product-compliance
Lightning Source LLC
Chambersburg PA
CBHW020300200626
46814CB00006BA/2010